DEFIANCE RISING

ALSO BY AMY MILES

THE AROTAS SERIES
Forbidden

Reckoning

Redemption

Evermore

THE IMMORTAL ROSE TRILOGY
Desolate

THE RISING TRILOGY
Defiance Rising

Relinquish

Vengeance

THE WITHERED SERIES
Wither

Captivate

In Your Embrace

THE RISING TRILOGY

BOOK ONE

DEFIANCE RISING

AMY MILES

This book is a work of fiction. Any references to historical events, real people, or real locales are used fictitiously. Other names, characters, places, and incidents are products of the author's imagination, and any resemblance to actual events or locales or persons, living or dead, is entirely coincidental. Copyright ©2013 by Amy Miles Books, LLC.

All rights reserved, including the right of reproduction in whole or in part in any form.

Also available in ebook format.
First paperback edition 2013
ISBN 978-1466206564

ACKNOWLEDGEMENTS

To Rick and Landon~
You know you mean the world to me. I love you with all my heart.

To Sue Brown~
Without your love and encouragement, this novel may never have been given wings. Thanks for enduring all of the obsessive re-writes over the years.

ONE

I've been told that this world used to be a beautiful place, filled with twinkling electric lights and tables overflowing with food. A place where children played in parks and couples took leisurely strolls on Sunday. A time when humans weren't slaves to aliens or nature. Staring out over the concrete graveyard before me, I find that hard to imagine.

I have no idea what the name used to be for this place. It has been lost to the past, like so many things. Now, my friends and I call it what it is—the City.

All that remains of my parent's Earth are cracked sidewalks with grass and weeds growing up through the pavement. A maze of rusted cars and twisted lampposts scattered along each street create a web of devastation. Tarnished coins and glass shards form a glittering river winding through the City. In the distance, I spy broken skyscrapers rising from the ruins at jagged angles, symbols of a life long forgotten.

This is where the Caldonians live, where the Sky Ships land each night after scouring the woods for us. No one knows how many of them there are. I think my friends are too afraid to find out. If I were honest, I'd admit to being nervous as well.

My concern has swelled over the past couple weeks. That's when the tremors began. My friends say it's nothing, but I know whatever is causing the tremors is something important. I can feel it in my gut, and I'm hardly ever wrong.

After my mother died in a raid six months back, my friends and I were left in charge of the commune. There are a couple of the elders who remain but are too crippled to help maintain the rebellion. The children had to be protected, so we became the leaders.

Toren was the obvious choice as the head of our group and has risen as a natural leader. I can't say that I like taking orders from him, although I think he actually despises giving them more, knowing that I will disobey.

His girlfriend, Aminah, is my friend. Her sweet nature and mothering heart is a beacon of hope to the children of our group. She broke through my rough exterior when we were kids and, despite our many differences, still finds a way through my defenses.

Eamon is my closest friend and is notably the best hunter of our group, apart from me. Since the time I could hold a stick, we've been sparring. What once started as pretend stick sword fights led us to spear tossing, knife throwing and hand-to-hand combat. He is always at my side, watchful and quick to administer a reprimand if he sees fit. Eamon thinks I'm reckless, but I think adventurous suits me better.

Zahra is the last of our group and is as vain as she is obnoxious. We've been butting heads for as long as I can remember. It's not my fault Eamon is my best friend or that he hardly pays Zahra mind when I'm around.

Standing here, overlooking the City, I think of my friends, each one as dear to me as my own blood family. As a tremor ripples up through the soles of my boots, I know that I have to enter the City this time.

Clutching the strap of my canvas satchel against my chest, I rise from a crouch. "You can do this," I whisper, steeling myself.

I've been here several times over the past week, on this ledge, with fear wedged so tightly in my throat that I wonder if I'll be able to snatch my next breath. My fear is irrational but that never stops me from doubling over with crippling nausea.

It's not like I can't take care of myself. I'm stealthy enough to avoid Caldonian detection. I'm skilled enough to fight off any scavengers that might cross my path, but each time I come to this very spot, my pulse begins to thump out a cadence in my ears. My palms slicken with sweat and the pit of my stomach coils uncomfortably. The sense that I'm doing the right thing is evenly paralleled by trepidation.

"Don't chicken out this time." Pinpricks of pain shoot up my legs as I stretch up onto my toes, working out the kinks in my lower back. I've lingered too long on the ridge. Night will be upon me soon and I must seek shelter.

The Sky Ships come at dusk and dawn, like winged scavengers seeking yet another carcass to consume. Being caught out in the open is suicide.

When I was younger, the black ships would send me running for my mother's arms. I've never known a life without Caldonian oppression. My pathetic version of freedom has been paid for with gallons of spilled blood.

My parents chose to be part of the rebellion. I was born into it. Aminah and Zahra were never cut out for this life, so it was up to Toren, Eamon and I to learn how to hunt for food, set traps and scour the woods for salvageable ammo.

Eamon has an affinity for spears. He likes the feel of the smooth wood grain between his fingers just before he strikes. I'm the opposite. I prefer the rigidity of a blade—serrated and lethal.

I stomp my right foot and wait for feeling to fully return. I can't take any chances. I must be on top form when I enter these desolate streets.

The far horizon glows with beautiful shades of lavender and pale rose as I leap down the hill, riding the loose dirt like a surfer. A cloud of dust rises from the soil, clinging to my black shirt and pants. I dig the heels of my boots into the slope to slow my wild descent.

My arms pinwheel, compensating for the uneven terrain as I jump and land on a hard, unforgiving surface. Pain reverberates up through my legs and spine, but I ignore it as I stare wide-eyed around me. I can't believe I'm actually here.

I dip low and brush my fingertips across the rough ground and a word surfaces in my mind—sidewalk. I can't but wonder what the people here were like, when they didn't need to fear death or certain capture. Did someone fall in love in this spot?

Did a little boy chase after a runaway dog? Did a mother soothe her crying baby on the rusted wrought iron bench nearby?

I close my eyes and smile at the uneven texture of the path, storing this detail for later consideration. It's so unlike the smooth stone of the caves where my friends and I live. I prefer this rough surface.

Debris litters the street before me. Brick rubble tumbles over from a squat one-story building on the corner. Crumpled plastic chairs and disfigured metals tables spill forth from various storefronts. Brittle autumn leaves spiral down the deserted sidewalk, a reminder as bitter as the harsh winds that whip against my face, chafing my cheeks.

I try not to think about how angry Toren will be when he finds out I've come here, or how disappointed Aminah will be when she discovers that I'm going to miss my surprise birthday party tonight. She should have known better than to entrust Zahra with that secret.

Eamon will take my coming here the hardest. There have never been secrets between us so this betrayal will cut deep. I didn't really have a choice, though. He would never have approved such a rash decision, but the tremors are increasing and I must know what is causing them.

I crouch low and race across the street, dropping down behind a partially melted car. Its shape is odd, as if the metal were heated then dripped over the side. It reminds me of a picture of a melted clock painting from one of the few books salvaged during the Assault. My mother's passion for art was one of the few things she and I shared. It never failed to draw me into her long forgotten world.

Peering over the hood of the car, I search the path ahead for any sign of life. Rumors claim that scavengers still dare to enter the City. Considering that I'm one tonight, I find this rumor to be dangerously plausible, but it's not *them* that I fear. Scavengers fight out of desperation, but the Caldonians fight on a completely different level.

The aliens look just like humans——two arms and legs, intelligent minds and oxygen rich lungs. They are beautiful in the most raw, elemental way possible. Their eyes are not confined to the limitations of blues, greens and browns like human eyes. They dip into rainbows of purples, oranges, reds and even some colors I struggle to place.

I squint up into the fading light as my fingers grip tightly around my pistol. It's loaded with a round in the chamber, ready for whatever might lurk in the shadows. My right pocket holds the spare magazine I managed to scavenge after the last raid, not enough to hold off a group of aliens but enough to create a diversion and run like heck back into the woods.

A pair of knives clings to my back, tucked into the braided rope around my waist. I like to keep them near just in case things get personal.

It is eerily silent as I push off from the car and skirt along a partially crumbled building. Some of the brick wall still stands. In parts, it rises well above my head. I can imagine there must have been another level above the ground floor but one glance through the window frame reveals only remnants of an upper floor. The back of the building is gone, blasted out during the Assault, the first and only day of the invasion.

I hold my handgun out before me as my boots crunch over an endless sea of glass shards. As far as I can see, only vacant windowpanes remain. I pull away from the wall to stare at a small reflective sliver, wedged into a twisted metal frame of what appears to have been a bookstore.

Rising onto my tiptoes, I peek through. Leaves and dirt clutter the floor. Small corners of yellowed paper flutter in the wind, the corners trapped under broken mahogany bookcases. Much of the interior of the building is stripped away. A large, charred circle near the center gives evidence to a fire, mostly likely from a scavenger holed up for the night.

Craning my neck, I peer up through the roofless building. Whoever lit that fire must've been desperate. A fire would've been easily spotted from above. Sinking back onto my heels, I can't help but wonder what happened to the former resident, but a reflection of myself tugs my curiosity in a new direction.

One violet eye blinks back at me, its lashes long and full. I pull back further to note the fullness of my lower lip and the small smattering of freckles that cross the bridge of my straight nose. Hunching over, I catch a glimpse of the wild mane of blonde hair whipping about my shoulders.

It has been a long time since I've seen myself. Our commune used to have a small hand mirror to share among everyone, but it was broken during a spat between Zahra and a younger girl who suffered from a serious case of "Eamonitis." Their ongoing feud to capture my best friend's heart started several years ago when he hit puberty and quickly topped the "most eligible guy" list.

Staring at myself now, I can see the subtle changes that have come with age. The image before me reveals a young woman instead of the adolescent girl I last saw. My pistol grazes my cheek as I push my unruly hair behind my ear and turn to observe my profile.

"You gonna stare at yourself all night, Princess?"

I whip around and take aim at the dark figure half a block behind me, leaning against the back end of a silver car. Judging by his height and build, I'd say he's about my age, give or take a few months. Two arms rise toward the sky. "I'm unarmed!"

With him in my sights, I approach slowly, waiting for a sound of ambush. I don't want to fire off a shot for fear of drawing attention to myself, but surely this guy isn't alone. "Who are you?"

"The name's Bastien."

"You got a last name, Bastien?" I creep closer. My pulse tap-dances in my ears as I pause less than ten feet from him. I clench my fingers around the gun as I try to ignore the sweat gathering along my neck. Adrenaline pumps through my veins, making me alert.

I take several deep breaths as I plot out my next move, as if this is a hunt and I'm staring down my dinner. What does he want? Is he a scavenger or one of the human traitors who collects women to sell to the Caldonians?

"Adair. It's Scottish." He cocks his head to the side. "Guess that little tidbit doesn't really matter when you've got a gun aimed at your head."

"Your heart, actually." My finger hovers over the trigger as I scan the guy standing before me.

Shoulder length raven-black hair tosses about in the wind, thrashing against his angular face. His chest and shoulders are broad, tapering down to a well-defined abdomen, although the exact contour is hard to determine hidden beneath a woolen sweater.

His raised hands are encased in threadbare gloves. Some of the wool fingers are missing, with frayed bits of yarn poking out. His jeans are stained and faded, patched with poorly stitched bits of random cloth. Light stubble clings to his chin and jawline, enhancing his rugged good looks with annoying perfection.

I notice all of this with a simple glance before meeting his curious gaze. Vivid blue eyes with pupils ringed in gold betray intelligence and, if I'm not mistaken, a hint of humor too.

"Something funny?" I ask through gritted teeth.

"Well, that depends." A ghost of a smile stretches across his face.

"On?" I adjust the gun in my hand. Although he doesn't move or show any signs of hostility, I find myself deeply unsettled by him.

"On whether you think your little toy pistol can beat my shotgun." He slides his arm down from the trunk of the silver car, revealing a sawed off shotgun. I silently berate myself for letting him get the better of me, although his concealed weapon doesn't come as a huge surprise. More of an annoyance. I don't like losing the upper hand.

"A bit old school, don't you think?" I smirk, not letting my gun drop a millimeter. "Now what do we do?"

Bastien's gaze rises to the sky. The final wisps of pastel blue and lavender begin to fade into black. "I'm going to invite you back to my place. I know it's a bit forward, but I'd rather carry on this delightful chat inside."

I drop my gaze to his hands, noting the sure steadiness of them. My mind screams for me to take my chances but my gut tells me that he's more than willing to pull that trigger. This won't end well for me.

"Fine." I dip my head in agreement, knowing that time is running short. Already I can hear the whirl of the Sky Ship's engines as it takes off. "Drop yours first."

The rising winds whip Bastien's hair about his face, obscuring his features, but his eyes remain locked on me. "You're insane! You really want to do this now?"

I twist my head just enough to hear the hum of an engine approaching from down the street. I chew on my lip, knowing I have two choices: trust this complete stranger or take on a Sky Ship with just a handful of bullets. It's not a hard choice.

"Lead the way." I lower my weapon but my finger remains on the trigger as he cocks the shotgun over his shoulder. Without another word, he turns and dashes across the street, weaving in and out of the abandoned cars.

I try to keep up with his fast pace, reminding myself to breathe as the winds funnel harder down the street. The Sky Ship is nearly on top of us.

"How far?" I glance back over my shoulder to find the tip of a black wing appearing over the edge of a building two blocks away. A hand grasps my forearm and pulls me through a dark opening in the wall. I stumble forward out of Bastien's grasp, fighting to remain upright as I falter down a steep set of stairs.

Metal clanging overhead alerts me to his location. I wait, gasping for breath as the walls rumble around me. The Sky Ship must be directly above us now. I press back against the wall, clutching my gun to my chest as I lift prayers for safety heavenward.

I jerk my pistol up to eye level as a light flares in the dark. Bastien shields his eyes with his arm and rears back. "Don't go shooting that thing in here! It'll kill us both!"

I drop the gun, squinting up into the light. It doesn't flicker like a fire. Its core is pure white instead of vivid blue or orange. Metal encases the cylindrical object, scratched and worn but showing little sign of rust. "What is that thing?"

"A flashlight."

I roll the word around on my tongue. "Never heard of it."

He shoots me a scathing look. "I wouldn't expect a tree hugger like you would have."

My brow furrows and I'm sure he's just insulted me in some way. Bastien slowly steps down the narrow staircase. As the light broadens around me, I begin to notice the dingy cement walls, lined with posters and advertisements. "Where are we?"

"It used to be a subway." He pauses beside me, waiting for some sign of recognition. This time I nod in understanding.

"My mother told me about these. Long, winding tunnels underground that would shuttle people from one end of the City to the next."

"That's the basic idea of it, yeah." Bastien waits for me before descending the final steps. "This is the safest place to be during a raid. I found this entrance a couple months back and haven't been bothered once." His arm brushes against mine as he squeezes past through the narrow doorway. I follow his lead deeper underground, passing silently by aged wooden benches and an empty enclosed booth with the picture of the subway on the side. The further we go, the quieter the hum of the Sky Ship becomes.

I stay close as we leap down onto the track and wind through the deserted tunnel. The air is thick down here, different from the caves. It feels weighty, filthy.

"This way." He flashes his light onto the track ahead and I see a glint of white and red.

"What is that thing?" I ask, as we approach the large metal object filling the tunnel.

"It's an old subway car." Bastien reaches up and cranks the metal handle on the door. I hesitate as he offers me a hand up.

His smirk widens. "It's rude to refuse the aid of a gentleman, you know."

"Who said you were a gentleman?"

He stares pointedly at his hand, wiggling his fingers. "Don't leave me hanging here."

I swallow my trepidation and place my hand in his. The scratchy feel of his wool glove lingers long after he releases my hand.

TWO

He passes me the flashlight once I'm through and hoists himself inside, latching the door behind him.

"Afraid someone might break in?"

"Nah. Just force of habit." He moves between the rows of seats toward the back of the car. If I thought the air in the tunnel was thick, it's far worse within this small, confined space. With no windows to open and both doors sealed, the scent of sweat and stale air permeates everything.

As I approach the middle of the car, I notice obvious signs of long-term habitation. Small burlap sacks, lumpy with concealed supplies, line the space beneath the cracked plastic seats. Larger bags fill an open-air compartment near the ceiling. A blanket and stained pillow run parallel between the final rows of seats.

Bastien reaches down and lights a lantern to replace the flashlight before plopping down onto a bench. I stand awkwardly in the aisle, glancing all around. "The Hover Wings will be up there for a while." He leans into the bench, resting his arms along the seat back. "There's no rush."

"You call them Hover Wings?"

He shrugs. "Sure, that is what they do. Why?"

I slowly sink onto the bench opposite him. It feels hard, cold and unwelcoming against my backside. I lean into it, trying to think of what it might be like to jostle along the dark track. I don't think I would've liked it one bit.

"We call them Sky Ships."

"Makes sense, I suppose." He thinks it over. "I'm sure the only ships you've seen are the transports flying over the mountains, but the Caldonians have many metal contraptions."

"Are you ok?" Bastien leans toward me, concern pinching his brow. "You look really pale."

I blink, surprised by the question. "Why do you care?"

"Hey, I'm just trying to be nice, ok?" He raises his hands in mock surrender.

I sigh and slump down on the bench, my gun still held tight in my palm, but pointed down at the floor. "Sorry," I mutter, shoving my hair back out of my eyes. "I'm not real comfortable in tight spaces."

Bastien grins. "It's a heck of a lot cozier than in one of those Hover Wings!"

"Good point." I drop my gaze as I feel my lips curling into a hint of a smile. "So this is where you live?"

"Yep. Welcome to Chez Bastien." He spreads his arms wide to encompass the tight space.

"Huh?"

"It's French." He rolls his eyes when I stare blankly back. "I'm guessing you never learned that."

I look around the space for any signs of books. I'm surprised when I don't find a single one. "How do you know so much?"

Bastien takes a deep breath and looks past me, staring at the darkness beyond. "My mom was a teacher before the invasion, history mostly, but she loved all forms of learning. She used to tell me about this grand library near the center of town, with wall to ceiling bookshelves stuffed full of knowledge. When I was younger, she would sneak out and bring a couple books back for me, but then the Settlers moved in and she couldn't go any more."

"Settlers?"

"It's what I call the aliens who live here. Some are transient, coming and going from city to city, but the ones that stay behind are the Settlers."

"Do you have any other names for them?" I ask, intrigued by his insight into our enemy.

"Sure, you've got the Grounders, who work on the outskirts of town, the Squaddies, who patrol the streets on foot, the Droners, who man the spider machines and the Gentry, the snooty what's its who run this place."

"You seem to have a good lay of the land here," I muse, tucking my feet under my legs.

"Yeah, well I was born and raised here. You sort of get a feel for the place."

My brow furrows. "How did you and your family manage to survive so long?"

"They didn't." He rubs his hands on his thighs and falls into an uncomfortable silence.

"I lost my parents, too." I don't like to speak about them. A part of me worries that I might be treading on their memories if I do. My father took a red laser to the chest when I was fourteen. Mom went down after being shot in the back. I found her lying face down in the woods the next day, left to rot out in the open.

Bastien clears his throat and rises from his seat. He paces halfway down the subway car and then returns with determined steps. "It's been a while since I've seen anyone willingly come here."

"And?"

He stops pacing to stare at me. "It's not safe. You should go back to the forest and stay there."

"I'm not leaving." I cross my arms over my chest and glare back at him. Does he really think I don't know the risk?

I'm the first of my generation to step foot here. Part of me is proud of this fact, but it won't matter if I can't make it back in one piece.

"Are you always this stubborn?" Raising his arms overhead, he grasps the metal rack railing and slowly swings back and forth.

"My friends would say so."

"There are more of you?" His eyebrows arch so high I'm sure they'll disappear into his hair line.

I flinch as I realize my slip. "There are always more."

The skin around Bastien's eyes creases as he drops his gaze to focus on the floor. "Not always."

A faraway look slips over his face and I squirm. This guy may have saved me from the Sky Ship but he's too melancholy for my liking. I guess he has every right to be, but I'm not comfortable with emotions, or strangers, or bonding on any level.

He expels a weighted sigh and looks up at me. "You look thirsty. Want something to drink?"

"That depends," I hedge. What I really want is to wait for dark and get the heck out of here, but it's impossible to judge how much time has passed since I entered this underground prison.

"On what?"

"Why am I here?" I sit forward, resting my gun on my knee, present and unforgotten.

Bastien casts a hesitant glance down at it before he shrugs. "You're the first human I've seen in months. I thought we could chat."

"Chat?" I scoff, watching as he dips low to search through one of the burlap sacks under his seat. Although his back is angled away, he darts several cautious glances back at me.

"Yeah. You know, talk, shoot the breeze, cut loose. That sort of thing."

"I know what chat means," I grind out, watching his every movement carefully. If he pulls a gun on me, I'm aiming straight for his heart.

My finger flinches over the trigger as he rises. Two red metal cans rest in his hands. I squint to read the letters in the dim light, sounding them out slowly. "Coke?"

"Never had one of these before, huh? Oh, you're in for a real treat." Bastien holds out a can toward me. "Try it. Don't mind the expiration date. I've been ignoring those for a while now."

Hesitantly, I take it from him and watch as he tugs on a metal tab on top of the can. My eyes widen with surprise as a brown foam bubbles out over the top and onto his fingers. He quickly dips his head to slurp up the mess. "Delicious. Go on, give it a pull."

I stare down at the can in my hand. It is cool to the touch, smooth and completely foreign to me. Deciding it's obviously not poisoned, I tug on the tab and frown as the foam spills over my hand and onto the floor.

I guess that explains why my boots feel like they're permanently stuck to the floor, I muse.

Keeping Bastien in sight, I slowly raise the can to my lips and take a small sip. "Yuck!" I spit out a sugary spray all over the floor.

He laughs out loud as he sinks back onto his bench. His Adam's apple bobs as he drinks deeply from the can. A small stream of liquid spills around his lips and drips onto his sweater, but he swipes it away with little thought.

"This stuff is disgusting." I rub my tongue on my sleeve, trying to get the sugary aftertaste out of my mouth. "What is this?"

"It's soda, the most popular drink of all time. People used to drink it by the gallon."

"It's revolting." I pinch my nose with disgust as I hand the can back to him.

"Well sure, if your diet only consists of berries, rainwater and squirrel." He blasts me before chugging the rest of my can too.

"We eat more than just squirrel," I retort. I know I should hang my head in shame for that lame comeback, but the sting of his jab takes me by surprise. Why am I letting this guy get to me so easily?

"The point is that you tree huggers don't know how to appreciate real food."

I cross my arms over my chest, tucking my handgun into my side as I roll my eyes. "At least we don't hide in filthy subway cars."

"You got a problem with my house?"

His tone implies sarcasm, but I'm not sure if I've just insulted him. "I'm just saying you can't compare the two together. Living here, in the City, isn't like surviving in the woods."

He sets the soda cans aside as the skin around his eyes pinches ever so slightly, his gaze hardening. He leans forward, capturing my full attention. "You're right. It's not."

I stand up and tuck my gun into the back of my pants, right between my knives. The pressure of the cool steel against my skin is reassuring. "Look, I'm grateful for you letting me hide out here for a bit but I think I should be going."

"Wait!" He leaps to his feet and pulls me back as I head for the exit.

"Don't touch me," I growl, yanking my arm from his grasp. I reach back for my knife, knowing I can slice through his abdomen before he can even turn for his shotgun.

"Sorry." He holds his hands up in surrender, backing away. "I just can't let you go out there."

"Why not?"

"Although you may *think* you know what it's like here, you'd be wrong, Princess. Those Hover Wings don't just come for a fly by and go on their merry way like they do when they pass over the forest. They're dropping off soldiers."

"More of them?" The urge to kick him in the shin for calling me "princess" is nearly too hard to resist, but I reign myself in as I think over the implications of his words. More aliens means more search parties. How long can my friends and I remain hidden in the forest?

Like it or not, I need him.

"They're looking for something," he continues, biting on the side of his fingernail. His hands look grimy; no doubt it's been a while since he took a decent bath. "Don't ask me what, but I just know they are."

"How do you know?" I cross my arms over my chest, trying to get a read on him. His tone is even and his eyes are locked onto me instead of drifting off the side. There's no sign of sweat along his brow or even a twitch in his fingers. He's either a really good liar or he's saving my skin right now.

"Well…" he scratches the light stubble across his jawline. "Promise you won't do anything stupid?"

I puff up with indignation. "I *can* be careful when I want to be."

"Must not want that too often then, huh?" He chuckles to himself.

I reach back and grasp my knife. The temptation to lash out and knick the chin of his pretty little face curls my lips into a smile. He follows the curve of my arm around my waist and takes a step back. "Wise decision."

He smirks, crossing his arms over his chest. "You're feisty. I like that in a girl."

"And I'm going." I turn and stomp toward the door at the far end of the car.

I have no idea how he manages to get in front of me. One moment he's standing behind me and the next he's flipping off the wall and landing only a couple inches from my nose. I gasp and stumble backward but strong fingers clasp around my wrists and yank me upright. His hands are large and calloused against my tender skin.

"Do you mind?" I hiss, yanking free of his grasp

"Actually, I don't." His fingers uncurl from my arm and I step back from him, unnerved by his proximity.

"What's with the acrobatics?" I lower my hands to my sides, resisting the urge to rub my sore wrists.

"Do you want to see my proof about the Grounders or not?" He asks, evading my question

I purse my lips as I try to decide. A huge part of me wants to know, but that would mean spending more time with Bastien and right now I'm not so sure that's a good idea. He makes me feel annoyingly flustered and I can't quite figure out why.

"Look, I'll show you the way. Once we get there, you can decide. Fair enough?"

I look beyond him into the dark tunnel. I can't say that I fancy wandering around out there on my own trying to find the exit, but what if Bastien knows about the tremors? I have to know what is causing them before I leave.

"Fine," I sigh, shaking my head in disbelief. How did I get myself into this? "I'm in."

I try to ignore his triumphant grin as he leads me toward to rear of the car. He dips low to retrieve his flashlight and shotgun. I raise an eyebrow at the second item. "Rats," he shrugs in explanation.

"Must be some large rats."

"You have no idea," he laughs. The way he says it makes me wonder if Bastien might just have a hidden fear of furry little rodents or if he's hiding something.

He unlatches the metal handle and shoves the door open. I wince at the squeal of rusted metal echoing ahead of us into the tunnel. Bastien hands me the light and leaps out confidently onto the darkened track. When he holds up his hand to me, I peer over the edge.

The drop onto the tracks looks to be only to be about four feet, but leaping out into darkness makes me nervous. What if I land on one of the tracks and twist my ankle? Then I'd be stuck here, with him and mutant rats.

"You coming?"

"Yeah," I mutter, gripping the edge of the doorway. "Can you give me some light?"

Bastien sighs and sets the flashlight down on its end. The white beam of light pierces through the darkness, shining up to the ceiling above. I squint, trying to see the curve of the track.

"We don't have all night, Princess." He offers his hand to assist me.

I clamp my fingers tightly around his and leap to the ground, easily missing the wide tracks. When I let go, I'm pleased to see him shake out his bruised hand.

The light bounces before us as we walk, casting dancing shadows around the domed tunnel. Our footsteps echo as we follow the metal tracks leading away from the subway car. The hairs on my arms and neck rise as I struggle to peer through the oppressive darkness around us. "Don't you ever get claustrophobic down here?"

"Sometimes," he admits. "It's still the safest place in town."

The scampering of feet nearby sends me reeling into Bastien's side. He reaches out and steadies me, snickering as he lifts the light to reveal the mother of all rats. Its brown fur is matted and its beady eyes gleam in the light. "Let me guess, you don't like rats either."

"I don't like being startled by them. Big difference." I pull away from his grasp and run a hand through my disheveled hair.

"Uh-huh." I can tell by the way the light bounces that he's laughing at me. I grit my teeth and walk on without him. Thankfully, he rushes to catch up or my bravado would've come to a grinding halt without his light. We walk for several minutes in silence.

"So why *are* you in the City?" he asks.

"You're gonna go with mindless chatter now?"

"No," he says, turning to point his flashlight at a set of steps that rise up to another level. I start to mount the first step, but he pulls me back. "I really want to know."

I chew on my lip, thinking over the ramifications of my words. What if he's a spy for the Caldonians? He's certainly hot enough to fit the bill, but his eyes are true blue and his words hold the slightest hint of an accent. "I ran out of food a couple days back. I'm low on ammo and it's getting cold. Seemed like a good idea."

Bastien raises the light to peer at me. "Short, sweet and with as little emotion as possible. That seems to be your M.O."

"Like you would know," I scoff.

"Fine," he shrugs. The light sways, illuminating discolored ceiling tiles overhead. A large exit sign hangs down over the steps. "You don't have to tell me about your friends or how you learned to aim a gun like that. I'm sure you just read it in a book somewhere."

My hand drifts to the back of my pants where my gun is wedged. Memories of years' worth of training sessions with Eamon in the woods near our camp filter through my mind.

Bruised muscles, cracked knuckles, torn ligaments…good times. I still have the scars to go along with Eamon's spear fetish.

Life in the rebellion has never been easy. Food is always scarce and medicine is practically non-existent.

My days are consumed with either training or hunting, although I prefer hunting. The woods are my sanctuary, the only place I can escape the rigidity of stone and regulation.

I shake my head to clear out the memories and stare Bastien down, not giving him an ounce of information. "You said you have something to show me?"

He shoots me a pointed look, one that tells me he knows I'm holding something back, but he doesn't question me further. Instead, he raises his finger toward the stairs. "Follow this to the top and you will find a metal door that leads out onto the street. Open it slowly. It tends to stick so be careful with that. Once you're on the street, turn right and make your way to the building on the opposite corner. You'll find a set of stairs in the back. Go to the roof and take a peek, but keep your head down."

"You're not coming?" I ask as he holds out the flashlight to me. Now that I'm here, faced with who knows what on the street above, I have to admit I'm a little unnerved. I can handle anything that the forest throws at me but the City seems to play by completely different rules. Maybe having Bastien next to me wouldn't be a bad idea after all.

"I said I'd show you the way. That's it. Besides, you seem capable of handling yourself." His voice is tight as he shoves the light into my hand then turns and plops down on the bottom step. "I'll be here when you get back."

I raise the light to shoulder height and peer up the stairs. This section of the subway seems older, dingy and stained yellow by years of disuse.

Each step I take buries Bastien further into the darkness behind me. I'm nervous, but I refuse to show it. Maybe this is what he planned, for me to beg him come with me.

The stairs level out onto a wide platform. A patchwork of cracked, gray tiles leads to the outer door, where an old chain dangles from a broken latch. I shine the light on the door, surveying the hinges, and notice they are rusted and pulling away from the wall. I'm surprised the door has remained standing this long.

Taking a deep breath, I press the button on the back of the flashlight and fall into complete darkness. I consider calling out to Bastien to make sure he's still there but choose not to. I don't want him thinking I'm scared.

I curl my fingers around the cold metal knob, twist and pull. Nothing happens. I try again and again with the same result.

"Need help up there?" Bastien calls from the tunnel below. I can almost hear the smirk in his voice.

"No. I can do it on my own, thanks." I swear as I yank on the knob. The door only shifts slightly and I have to remind myself not to yell in frustration otherwise this entire stealth mission will go down in flames.

"You are more stubborn than an old mule!"

"You don't even know me," I grunt, straining against the door.

"Don't need to. It's pretty obvious."

Releasing the handle, I crouch down and search the floor for pieces of broken tile. Latching onto one the size of my palm, I hurl it down the stairs into the darkness. It smacks into the wall and shatters.

"Throw like a girl, too!" He howls with laughter.

"Urgh!" If I don't get this door open soon I swear I'm going to throttle him. I twist and turn the knob until I'm a sweaty, panting mess. "What is wrong with this door?"

"There's a trick to it." He pauses for what I assume to be dramatic effect. If he means to increase my frustration then it's working. "You have to say please, though."

"Seriously?"

"Um-hmm."

I roll my eyes, wishing I'd taken my chances with the Sky Ship earlier. This guy is pig-headed, obnoxious and combative, three things I can't stand in a guy. "Fine. Please."

"Nope. Gotta make me believe you."

I curl my lips into a sneer, annoyed that I can't even blast an evil eye at him in the dark. I take a deep breath, seeking a calm that I don't feel. I take three more just in case. "Bastien, will you please tell me the secret to opening this door."

"Hmm...needs some work but I guess it'll do. Lightly tap the lower right corner with your foot and it'll open right up."

"Anyone ever tell you that you're annoying?" I hiss over my shoulder at him.

"No." The silence rising up from the tunnel makes me pause with my foot pressed against the door. "There's no one left to talk to now."

THREE

I press my foot against the door like Bastien suggested and feel it give way. I suck in a breath, not because of the squeak of the rusted hinges, but because I find myself rooted in place. What if there is a group of Squaddies right on the other side waiting to pounce on me?

"Stop being such a baby," I mutter to myself.

"What was that?" Bastien calls from below.

"Nothing." I shove the door open and find myself on a completely deserted street, not at all unlike the one I came in on earlier. I poke out my head and look both ways to make sure the coast is clear before closing the door behind me. Creeping down the darkened street, I feel a bit like a ninja.

I learned about the stealthy men in black from one of my dad's small collection of books. He called them comics. As a kid, I used to spend hours poring over the colorful pictures, memorizing every detail.

I hug the rough textured brick wall as I slowly advance. A strange thumping, like the beat of a large drum, ripples up through my fingertips. I pause and listen. No matter which way I crane my neck, I can't tell where it comes from. *I wonder if this is the source of the tremors.*

This part of the City has less glass blanketing the streets. The buildings are higher here, with fewer windows and doors. Large signs hang at odd angles from the rooftops, the letters too faded to tell what they said. I step nimbly over the jagged cracks in the path where weeds have sprouted and thrived.

A large truck lies on its side, nearly sealing off the narrow street. The wheels have gone flat, the underside has corroded from weather and the back half is blackened.

Skirting along the back end of the truck, I notice the interior has been ransacked. There's no way to tell if it was done by scavengers or aliens. Resting my hand against what at one time was probably one of the back doors, I peek around the truck toward the street ahead. It comes to a T less than twenty feet ahead of me.

My fingers curl instinctively around the handle of one of my blades but I release it with a weighted sigh. It will do me little good against a Caldonian laser. Shifting my hand, I grasp my pistol and sink low as I leave the protection of the truck.

Moonlight temporarily brightens my path as the clouds shift overhead. The biting chill in the air makes me shiver as it pierces my shirt, making me long for the coat I outgrew last year. In our commune, everything is second hand. You outgrow a shirt and pass it down the line. Most of our clothes are more stitching than fabric now. I make a mental note to be on the lookout for a replacement as I make my way through the City. Perhaps scavengers haven't pilfered everything of worth yet.

"Easy," Bastien growls as he catches my arm to deflect my gun as I whip around at the sound of his footfall right behind me.

"How did you do that?" I hiss, relaxing my grip on the pistol. I point it at the ground and reset the safety.

"I've survived living here all my life. I know a few things about being sneaky." He presses back against the wall beside me.

I glare back at him, annoyed but deeply impressed at the same time. I pride myself in never letting anyone sneak up on me. It used to drive Eamon crazy when we were sparring. Bastien has just moved one notch above contemptible in my books.

"What are you doing here?" I ask, staring back the way he came to make sure he wasn't followed.

"I thought you might need me."

"Hardly." I roll my eyes and shift away so his arm no longer presses against mine. I might be slightly impressed, but that's no reason to allow touching. When I study his profile in the dark, I notice a faint tick under his left eye. "You got scared all by yourself, didn't you?"

"Please," he snorts. "I live down there, remember?"

I smirk at the slight waver in his voice. Maybe he's not so tough after all. "Well, now that you're here, why don't you lead the way?"

Bastien snatches my free hand and yanks me toward the corner. I grit my teeth as his fingers wrap around mine. The strange thumping sound swells as we reach the end of the block and veer straight through a large dark opening in the brick wall. Shattered glass and wooden shards decorate the doorframe where double front doors once resided.

The interior of the building is vast and mostly empty. An overturned metal table greets us at the front of the building. Yellowed paper and other supplies lie scattered about. Our shoes leave prints in the dust as we pass through the small room and into a vast space beyond. I pull back to cover our tracks, but Bastien tugs me forward. "No one ever comes to this factory. We're safe."

His voice echoes about the room as we pass by large hulking machines, silent and powerless since the day of the Assault. Nearly fifteen different varieties of these rusted relics dot the wide expanse. "What is this place?" I ask, staring all around.

I feel small in this cavernous room. The ceiling rises high overhead. Our passing echoes through the hollowness.

Bastien points to a long, low table with wheels on top. "This was a fabricating plant. These rollers were used to shuffle parts back and forth."

"What did they make here?" I ask, running my fingers along the rollers. I pull back my hand as several feet of rollers begin to spin as a result of my touch.

"Not really sure. It was picked clean several years ago. Come on," he tugs on my arm and leads me toward a set of metal stairs near the middle of the building.

Moonlight fragments through bits of glass protruding from window frames along the steps as we climb to the floor above. I pause to lean over the railing, wondering what it must have looked like when electricity gave life to this machine mausoleum.

We round the second floor banister, passing by a row of offices with glassless windows that look out over the factory floor, and proceed up two more flights of stairs. I had no idea the building was so large from the outside, but by the time I hit the landing for the roof I'm panting. Bastien releases my hand, wiping sweat from his palm. "We can't go out there with you panting like a grizzly bear."

I scowl up at him, clutching my chest. My side burns as I lean back against the wall. "Follow me back to the forest and we'll see who can get to the top of the mountain first."

He rears back with an air of mock disbelief. "Are you inviting me to follow you home? That's a bit forward don't you think, Princess?"

I grind my back teeth. "My name is Illyria, not Princess."

"Really?" He laughs. "I would've pegged you for a Sarah or Jill."

I shove him out of my way and open the door to the roof. He follows close on my heels, his laughter trailing off as he eases the metal door shut behind us. A layer of black gravel-like pebbles blankets the roof. Our shoes crunch with each step we take, but I realize I don't have to worry about being heard over the rhythmic thumping that rises from the city below.

Bastien motions for me to duck down and I crouch, careful to keep my head low. We scurry across the wide expanse and huddle against the waist-high ledge that lines the roof. I peek over the side and gasp.

The City is laid out before me, sparkling like sunlight on a rippling pond. A sea of windows are illuminated from within by white lights a thousand times brighter than Bastien's flashlight. Never before have I seen such vibrant evidence of life. Everywhere I look, men are working, laughing and arguing.

Is this what the world used to look like? I wonder.

I can see people moving on each floor of the building closest to us, men dressed from head to foot in black uniforms. Beds, dark wooden furniture and open doors within the walls that overflow with clothing, adorn the rooms of a building that stands five windows high. Each room has a similar décor, worn and smothered with a hideous floral design, from the blankets to the material hanging at the windows. I can see images surrounded by golden rectangles on the walls and small tables with books stacked high.

"They have electricity?"

Bastien nods, placing a finger of his lips for me to be quiet. He jerks his head back toward the City and I fall silent.

"See those cranes?" He points to the left at tall metal machines shifting large chunks of rubble. "The Settlers began cleaning the streets a while back. They use the cranes to do the heavy lifting. Then those large flat-bed trucks roll in to take the debris away."

I stare down at a huge vehicle with metal belt-like wheels as it rolls up and over abandoned cars. "What is that?"

"Military tanks. I like to call them the Sweepers since all they do is clean up their own mess. The Sweepers work in a grid each night. They've already cleared away most of the north end. Now they are working their way toward me."

I glance over at him. His jaw clenches and his fingers clamp down on the metal ledge. "Do you think they will find you?"

He nods, not turning to look at me. "It's bound to happen someday, right?"

Everywhere I look, there is movement, like a bee hive abuzz with life. My stomach begins to twist at the thought of just how many Caldonians live here. I was a fool to think my parents could ever make a dent in something this big.

A part of me wishes I could run back to the forest and hide from the truth, to forget this confusing place with all its foreign objects that all look like they want to kill or maim me. Before I came here, I felt like I could make a difference, now…I know better.

I look to Bastien beside me and wonder how he has managed to survive on his own for so long. He is all alone here. If he were attacked, no one would be there to cover his back. No one would come to help if he gets hurt.

I can't imagine what my life would be like without my friends, without someone to talk to or get angry with. Someone to share life with.

A few streets over, I watch a Squaddie patrol march down the street. There are twenty aliens total, each marching in sync with the next. A patch of red adorns their upper right chest but I can't make out what the symbol is from this distance. I grit my teeth in anger as I see that they clutch large, cannon-like guns.

The night my dad fell to a Caldonian laser, I learned that red means dead. My mother told me that when the Caldonians first arrived, the streets were flooded with red——blood illuminated by laser fire.

The Squaddies disappear around a corner and my gaze is drawn to the right, deeper into the City. Three brilliant white lights shine up into the sky, bouncing off the wispy clouds as they pass. Each circular light has been placed in a triangle around the last remaining skyscraper, apparently to illuminate all sides. I squint, peering through the light at the webs of metal that encase the building.

"What is that around that tower?"

"The Shard?" Bastien turns away and sinks down onto his backside, leaning against the roof railing. I follow suit. "It's called scaffolding, used for constructing tall buildings."

"Build? But that place is a ruin. Why would they-" I cut off as realization hits me like a slap in the face. Electricity, street cleaning crews, building teams…"Why are they rebuilding the City?"

He shrugs and shakes his head. "Beats me. I thought they would've built their own cities by now, but apparently they want to take ours."

I rub my forehead, trying to process the possibilities. "It doesn't make sense. Why go to all the trouble when they tore it down in the first place?"

He grabs a handful of black pebbles and sifts them through his fingers. I watch him, curious at how little this discovery seems to affect him. Surely, he has to be worried about capture.

How could he not? He's practically living underneath hundreds, if not thousands, of aliens. "Did you figure out what that thumping is?"

"No."

"Take another look. This time look behind us."

I rise up onto my knees and peer across the rooftop and over the ledge. Bright lights glow in the distance, but instead of building up, it looks like the machines are going underground. I watch a large crane with a claw on the end gouge into the earth and pull out a scoop full of dirt.

I sink back down next to Bastien. "They're digging?"

He nods, his gaze hardening as he stares back at me. His eyes look almost sapphire in the dim glow of the lights nearby. The light stubble on his face is a carpet of shadow in the faint light. "I told you they're looking for something."

"So that's it? The thing causing the tremors?"

His eyes narrow. "So that's why you're here? To find the Grounders?"

I clam up, wishing he'd stayed behind so I could deal with this revelation on my own. "They can't just be using cranes. I've felt the tremors in the forest."

"They're using Diggers, long tube like machines with a giant drill on the front. It's about the length of my subway car and I'd say it could hold at least twenty Squaddies, maybe more."

"But why? There's nothing out that way…" My breath catches as I realize the aliens' intent. "They're searching for us."

Bastien nods, dropping the stones through his fingers. They plink against the other rocks, settling back into place. He brushes his fingers over them and then dusts off his hands on his jeans. "That's what I'm thinking. Any idea why?"

I chew on my lip, wondering how much I can tell him. He didn't have to save me from the Sky Ship, but he did. He didn't have to give me this revelation tonight, but he did. I sigh and lean my head back against the ledge, staring up into the sky. I can just glimpse a wide expanse of glittering stars beyond the shifting clouds.

"My parents were part of the rebellion. A few years ago, they managed to do a lot of damage to the Caldonians in this area. They attacked supply lines and drove the aliens into the City. Once they realized we must be located nearby, they started hunting us down. At first, it was only one death here or there, then a couple per month. The war waged throughout my childhood and our numbers dwindled. Some people fled in search of help but they never returned."

My throat constricts. "Six months ago, my mother was among a scouting group that was wiped out. They were the last adults among us strong enough to lead, to fight back. All that is left to keep the children safe are my friends, a few elderly people and me. The rebellion has crumbled."

Bastien's head dips so low his chin meets his chest. His arms rest across his raised knees, fingers twiddling with a bit of plastic he has ripped off one of the pipes. "So you're on your own now?"

I nod. "We're it."

He scowls and tosses the plastic away. "We're never going to win this war."

"War?" I scoff. "There is no more war. We don't have the supplies to fight back any more. They have more manpower, more guns, more everything. How can we fight that?"

"I don't know!" He slams his fist down into the roof, his knuckles burying into the gravel. "We can't just give up."

I hesitate before laying my hand on his arm. The contact feels…awkward. "We're not. We just have to regroup. I'm sure there are other survivors out there."

"Like me?" He snorts. Bitterness drips from his words. "I'm all alone here on the front lines. A lot of good I'm doing, hiding out with the rats."

I scrunch up my nose and squint my eyes, torn by his pain and my loyalty to the commune. I let out a deep breath and decide to take a chance. "Come with me."

The words escape my lips before I can steal them back. It's insane. There's no way my friends would let him step foot into our cave. Our loss has been great this year and too many wounds still fester to allow for trusting a complete stranger.

I can feel Bastien watching me. He doesn't speak or move. From the corner of my eye, it looks like he's holding his breath. "You don't mean that."

I groan, burying my head into my arms. "I don't know what I mean. I can't stand the thought of you being all alone down in that subway. I don't know if I can trust you or if I should toss you over the side of this building."

Bastien chuckles softly, swiping a lock of hair from his forehead. It flaps around his face before he tucks it behind his ear. "I'd prefer you trust me."

A smile tugs at my lips as I raise my head to look at him. "I want to, but it's hard. You've been a pain in my butt all night."

"Look who's talking."

I shove my hair back from my face as the wind picks up and curls over the ledge, sending it into a tangled frenzy. "Do you hear that?"

I strain to hear a faint sound over the thumping of the Grounders. Bastien's brow furrows as he glances up at the clouds overhead. They move swiftly in fine feather-like bands. His hair blows back off his face as he turns to look at me, his grip tightening on his shotgun. "Hear what?"

The sound grows louder and I stiffen as I realize what's causing the hum. "It's a Sky Ship! Run!"

FOUR

I only make it three steps before the roof explodes in front of me. Gravel turns into flying missiles, pelting me and leaving what are sure to be wicked bruises. Sweltering heat blazes around me, an inferno sparking high into the air. The smoke is so thick I can hardly catch my breath let alone see where the black ship is located against the night sky.

Bastien cries out as his shotgun flies out of his grasp and falls through the hole in the roof as he slams to the ground. He groans and rolls to his side. "We gotta move!"

His strong hands grip my waist and pull me to my feet as hurricane force winds whip the smoke into a gray cyclone.

As he pushes me around the gaping hole, I feel heat radiating through the soles of my shoes. Charred roof tiles fall through the gap and clatter to the concrete floor three stories below. My hair thrashes against my face, stinging my eyes as I stumble blindly ahead, hands outstretched to find the door.

We dive through the opening and into darkness, our panting echoing in the stairwell beyond as Bastien kicks the door closed.

"How did they find us?" I choke out, my lungs burning in my chest.

"Doesn't matter." He yanks me to my feet, pausing only a brief moment to wipe a stream of blood from my hairline. I wince at his touch, noticing the stinging pain for the first time.

Crimson light explodes through the lower level, illuminating the stairs. The machines below groan as the laser melts right through them. Bastien's feet barely touch the steps as he leaps to the landing below. To see the laser's destructive powers in action is both terrifying and awe-inspiring.

"Keep up!" Bastien shouts, as he turns to find me staring at the boiling devastation below.

My heavy breathing sounds hollow in my ears as I land on the second floor. I peek through the metal slats of the stairs and see streaks of flames crisscrossing the concrete floor below, like a trail of oil set alight.

I can hear the Sky Ship's engines rotate as it hovers mere feet above the street. It's swirling crimson glow illuminates the wide expanse of glassless windows running the length of the building. My thoughts slow, horror choking me, as the ship's cannon rotates, recharging for a second shot.

"Run!" Bastien's fingers dig into my arm as a deafening hum echoes throughout the vast room. The mechanic whirring of the charging laser frees my limbs and I let him drag me away from the stairs. There is no partition, no extra floor between us to save us from the blast. My feet slap the concrete floor as we race across the open walkway toward the closest office.

"Get down!" Shoving us through a doorway, Bastien slams me to the floor as a cloud of heat bursts through the glassless window overhead. I cover my head with my arms and scream as the world turns red. My skin blackens and the scent of burnt hair fills my nose as Bastien throws himself over me as a human shield.

His weight is suffocating as I struggle to get air into my lungs. What little I manage to snatch burns as it passes my lips, drying out my mouth.

The roar of the laser below is deafening, drowning out my screams. Bastien's hand fumbles down my arm until it reaches my hand. I squeeze back, praying for relief from the scorching heat.

And then it all stops. I lift my head and listen as the Sky Ship's engines whir to life and the crimson glow vanishes. "Is it gone?"

Bastien groans as he rolls off me. Tendrils of smoke rise from his sweater and the ends of his raven hair appear to be singed. He struggles to suck in gulps of air into his lungs as wracking coughs double him over.

"Are you ok?" I push to my knees.

"I'll be fine." His soot blackened arm quivers as he reaches for the door handle. He cries out, tucking his hand in close to his chest. He swears under his breath as I catch a scent of burnt flesh. "Don't touch anything metal."

I crawl forward, one hand outstretched, as I work my way toward the door. I can feel the heat on the other side, as flames lick the wooden doorframe. "We're trapped!"

"No." He shakes his head, coughing. I reach out for him and pull him next to me, holding him against my side until his fit subsides. He looks to the jagged glass protruding from the window at the back of the office, partially tucked behind a row of melting file cabinets. "We can go through there."

I rise unsteadily to my feet and peer out the window. There is only a small ledge, about five inches wide, to shimmy along. Beyond that is a sheer drop to the lower floor. "There has to be another way."

Bastien clutches his side as he rises. "It's our only shot."

Staring down at the narrow shelf, I try to envision the rock ledge over the waterfall back home, my favorite place to escape. "You can do this, Illyria," I chant as Bastien smashes a desk chair against the jagged glass, clearing our path.

He tosses the chair aside. "Get going."

I don't normally like having commands barked at me, but as I turn I notice movement near the front of the building. Three shadows inch close to the front entrance, their hands raised to shield their faces from the blistering heat. With any luck, they'll be held back by the same force that traps us, but how long will the heat last? I can already feel the air beginning to cool slightly.

I tear my gaze away from the front office window as Bastien lifts me through the back opening. "Be careful but haul tail."

Balancing on my toes, I shuffle along the lip. My calves begin to burn as I press my cheek against the wall, straining to keep my weight shifted forward. Bastien quickly follows, right on my heels. I can hear his grunts of pain as his injured hand cups the wall but I don't stop to look back.

I dig the tips of my fingers into the cracks of the concrete block wall, pulling myself along. My heart thunders in my ears, covering the sounds of Squaddies approaching from the street.

It's only a matter of time before we'll have to fight our way through an entire army.

Bastien's hip presses against mine, urging me on. I shuffle faster, inching past three more open window frames toward a waist high concrete banister that wraps around the side of the offices. I breathe a sigh of relief as my fingers grip the ledge and I hoist myself over.

He quickly follows, pulling me low as three black soldiers slip through the front door, their guns trained before them as they search for us. "Head for the stairs," he whispers into my ear.

The heat is less intense now, escaping through a gaping hole that's been blown out the back of the building. I can almost see the rippling waves in the moonlight as heat escapes through the windows above me.

I shake my head, frantically motioning to the men below us. The glowing red cores of their guns illuminate their path with a dim light, allowing them to see into the deep shadows of the factory. If we're quiet we might be able to sneak out of here, but our chances of that happening are dismal. The stairs to my left are only fifteen feet away, but their descent will lead us straight into alien territory.

"We can make it," Bastien insists.

I pull his face toward mine. "They'll see us!"

Trust me, he mouths and rushes toward the stairs. I curse silently as I crouch low and follow. Bastien waits for me at the top step, his eyes narrowed with fear. "What's wrong?" I whisper, surprised that he's suddenly developed a healthy dose of concern.

He points to the metal stairs. They descend half a flight and then end in a landing before jutting in a sharp right, back toward the front of the building. Now all that remains is first half of the flight. I peer over the edge and find the lower portion crumpled on the ground below.

Now what? I mouth to him. He jerks his finger over the ledge and mimes climbing down the stairs. *No!* I shake my head with a silent scream. *There's no way I'm going down that.*

He grips my arm and pulls me close, so near I can feel the heat of his breath wash over my face. "Trust me," he whispers.

I stare at the drop-off, judging it to be about eight-foot high. Not deadly by any means but certainly high enough to twist an ankle or knee.

"Don't drop me," I warn as I grab his hand and ease down into a crisscross position on the top step.

He holds up his hand and I pause. Poking his finger through one of the slits in his shirt, he slowly tears the fabric into a long strip. I can hear muttering from below but no rush of footsteps toward our location. He rips another cloth and we hold our breath.

The Squaddies form a small group just inside the lobby. Why aren't they searching for us anymore? What are they waiting for?

Bastien carefully wraps the strips of cloth around my hands to protect them from the heat. I wish I had something to cover my mouth so I don't feel like I'm breathing acid.

You can do this, he mouths, placing a hand on my shoulder. I nod and shrug off his touch as I uncurl my legs and lower myself down to the first step. I pause, listening before I climb down three more steps.

The metal is hot but not unbearable against my palms. I keep my fingers aloft, trying to keep them from blistering. The stairs shudder beneath me with each movement. A loud groan echoes through the factory as the stairs suddenly shift and I duck low to look at the aliens.

"Go!" Bastien waves at me to hurry as the aliens break out into a sprint.

I clamber down the final steps with no regard to noise. My stomach lurches as the top of the stairs begins to peel away from the second floor, the metal groaning as it tosses me off balance. Bastien's eyes are wide with fright as the first hint of red light comes into view.

He leans over the edge. "Jump!"

"No!" I readjust my grip on the bottom rung. "I'm not leaving you."

"Just go. I'll be fine!" He disappears from the top step, leaving me to dangle eight feet over the floor. Over the shouting below, I hear a crash as Bastien kicks in one of the office doors.

"Up there!" a Squaddie shouts as he slides to a halt just below the walkway. The walls glow scarlet as the aliens aim high, their lasers charged and ready.

I hiss as my thumb rests a bit too long on the metal step. I can feel the burn sinking into my flesh, but I hold back my tears. For now, I'm concealed by one of the machines, but one cry will send them racing in my direction.

With a loud bellow, Bastien rushes from the office and hurls something down at the Caldonians. The three Squaddies leap out of the way as metal drawers from a desk crash to the ground.

"We've got one trapped in the old fabrication warehouse. Send backup." A small black device on the alien's shoulder crackles as a response arrives a second later. My heart sinks as moments later I hear boots, pounding up the street at a dead run, over the groaning of metal machines slowly disintegrating.

Bastien heaves an armful of drawers over the ledge and I close my eyes. *One. Two. Three.*

As the aliens take cover from Bastien's newest office supply assault, I tuck my head and drop. A chair crashing to the floor masks my grunt of pain when I land. The roller wheels pop off and spin in all directions.

I stagger to my feet in the shadows and back up against the outer wall. The air on the second floor looks thicker, laden with smoke, but the first floor offers a hazy mix of moonlight sifting through thick clouds of smoke. I cup my hand over my mouth, filtering my breaths through the wool cloth.

Black clad soldiers pour through the front door opening, fanning out in a line. I sink low, crouching behind the remains of a machine as the Squaddies fire random shots to the second floor walkway. Bastien times their fire, waiting until the Caldonians are forced to recharge before attacking again.

Office supplies rain down from above, pelting the aliens as their reinforcements arrive. A tall alien marches forward to stand beside the three soldiers. His eyes are deep-set and flicker like the flames all around. "What do we have?"

"One teenage boy on the walkway directly above, sir."

The alien nods and steps back as a gray, two-drawer cabinet is flung over the solid railing. "Is he alone?"

"Yes, sir. As far as we can tell."

I breathe a sigh of relief that I've gone unnoticed but that relief quickly fades as the tall alien speaks into a black device, identical to the one used only a moment ago. It is clipped to his chest, directly over three vivid red moon emblems. "Land a squadron on the roof. Let's flush him out."

He must be a Gentry, I think as a rhythmic beating of a Sky Ship's engine approaches. We are running out of time.

I could escape through the back wall, and I might even make it if I cling to the shadows, but I can't leave Bastien. Not after he risked his life for me.

Even if I manage to get off a couple good shots, I know I'll be taken by the reinforcements at the back of the factory. I've only got two blades but maybe I can do enough damage to take that Gentry alive and use him as a bargaining chip.

No matter how I look at this, I know this isn't going to end well for me, but I still can't bring myself to leave Bastien behind. I bend over and crawl on my hands and knees, inching my way past the fallen stairs to get a better view.

"Get him down, now!" The Gentry growls as he dodges a disfigured metal trashcan. It clatters past and rolls to a stop against one of the machines. I peek out from my hiding place and watch him plant his feet, rigid and motionless apart from a tic under his right eye. His gaunt cheeks pull taut as he leers up at the floor above, a crazed fervor gleaming in his eye. I shudder as he fingers a long curved blade at his hip.

The way the Gentry caresses the black hilt reminds me of Eamon's affection for his spear. I reach back and run my finger along my own blades and feel a jolt of realization. He's a hunter.

I have no doubt this man will take pleasure in personally gutting Bastien when they catch him.

Suddenly, a strange burning sensation in my fingers grabs my attention. The burn climbs through my fingers and reaches my wrists. I gasp as tears sting my eyes.

Something is wrong.

I sink back against the wall and clutch my hands to my stomach. Like dipping frozen fingers in water, the burn is nearly unbearable. I fight back a moan, knowing I need to move, to get in a better position, but I'm paralyzed by the pain.

My pulse quickens as I tug at my arms. An irrational desire to remove the pain from my flesh with my knife makes me bite my lip. I open my mouth in a silent scream as I claw at my forearms.

Pressing back against the wall, I hardly flinch when the second floor erupts with fire, bubbling the paint off the concrete block wall. I can feel the residual heat but it can't compete with the internal agony crawling up toward my chest.

"Cease fire!" The commanding alien holds up his hand. The device at his shoulder comes alive. "Roof structure compromised. Unsafe to land."

I lean my head back against the wall to peer through a second floor window. The moon disappears directly overhead as the Sky Ship moves away.

The Squaddies inch forward, obviously anxious for a fight. I can see it on their faces. There is a wild gleam in their eyes, lit by the crackling fires all around.

"Commander Drakon? What are your orders, sir?" I bite down on my lip as the pain vines up my arms, twisting around my elbows. I strain to listen to the Gentry's answer but his words sound jumbled in my mind.

I watch as Drakon tilts his head to the side and contemplates the walkway. His gaze darts across the wide, silent expanse. It has been nearly a minute since Bastien launched anything over the side. "He's out of ammo. Attack!"

Drakon turns on his heel and marches toward the front of the factory as his men rush forward, clumping in two small groups as they hurl some sort of rope and metal claw up over the ledge. I know I should do something to help Bastien but I can't think past the agony winding its way up toward my shoulders.

As the first two men begin to climb, I lurch to my feet. I have to do something. Anything. Commander Drakon turns to watch when he reaches the overturned reception desk as his men scramble up black ropes. More Squaddies arrive at the door, but he holds up his hand and they fall back.

A tall alien with a wide mustache calls back over his shoulder from the base of the rope, "Shoot to kill?"

I lean around the machine, desperate to see his commander's response but I don't need to. Judging by maniacal grin that stretches across the soldier's face, he got the answer he was hoping for.

Anger tears through me, rippling through muscle and bone. I can physically feel it, boiling and visceral in my belly. As the first two aliens slip over the ledge, disappearing from sight, I hear a guttural scream from above.

I lose control.

When I step out into the light, I'm shaking from head to foot. The scalding energy bubbling within me is excruciating. Sweat streams down my brow, stinging my eyes but I barely notice it. "Get away from him!"

An alien plummets head first from the backside of the second floor. I hear his neck snap and he slumps over, unmoving. The sound of fighting on the second floor escalates.

The cluster of aliens at the bottom of the ropes turns and centers their targets on my heart. "There's another one!"

Drakon comes at me in a sprint, but I perceive everything in slow motion. The staircase overhead rattles. Nuts and bolts spring in all directions as it peels away from the second floor. The aliens cast terrified glances over my head but I don't focus on them. All I can feel is the pain mingling with my rage, seeping from my very pores. I have to save Bastien.

Another alien falls from the second floor but I hardly take notice this time; I'm blinded by six laser guns as they hum to life, charged and lethal. The screeching of metal muffles my scream as the staircase rips away from the wall. My fingers curl inward like claws as I raise my arms over my head. I feel the weight of the stairs hovering overhead but I don't stop to consider how this is even possible. I just react.

My vision darkens as I thrust my arms out toward the aliens. The metal staircase slams into the first group, while the second barely has time to turn before they're broadsided. Sparks fly as the stairs hurtle across the floor, pinning Squaddies as it goes until it slams into the far wall in a twisted heap and a sickening crunch.

The heat vanishes from my fingers, suddenly and completely. I slump to the floor, gasping for breath as pain carves into my chest. Sweat clings to my body like a second skin, sticky and oppressive. My anger fades with each labored pant. Weakened, I rise slowly to my feet to face off with Drakon.

"Who are you?" he asks, eyes wide.

I can feel the weighted stares of the soldiers as they appear at his back, resigned to follow their commander's barked order to remain back. I wipe my brow, feeling the sting of sweat in my eyes.

"Who are you?" he demands again, taking a step closer.

I raise my hand and he pauses. I know the pain is gone and the anger has fled but he doesn't. "Stay back."

He moves backward three steps, eyeing me with a mixture of awe and something else. Something shrewd and calculating. "I won't hurt you."

"Like I'm going to believe you." I struggle to keep my voice strong.

"You have my word."

I shift my stance slightly and dart a glance over my shoulder. I find Bastien peering down at me from over the ledge. A wide bloody gash has opened over his right eye and the other looks like it's going to be swollen shut by morning.

I glance back at Drakon, noting that he has inched closer. I glare at him. "Will you let my friend and me leave?"

It's easy to read the bloodlust in the eyes of the aliens behind him, but the commander has a far more potent expression. The color of his eyes shifts, taking on the appearance of dark molasses. I know I have to be careful. "I'm afraid I can't allow that. There are…rules against letting humans run free."

"Figured you'd say that," I mutter and take a step back. A Squaddie breaks out of rank behind Drakon and aims his laser directly at my chest. I stare into the core of his gun, at the core that swirls beautiful green instead of crimson. It is mesmerizingly beautiful.

"Duck!" Bastien screams from overhead.

Brilliant emerald light slices through the air toward me. I drop to the ground, landing with enough force to bruise my ribs. I clutch my side as I roll and notice the burn mark on the wall where my head had been only seconds before.

I throw out my hands and shove the nearest machine right at the squadron of soldiers. Drakon grunts and dives to the side just before it hits. The sound of screams and breaking bones fills the room as I scramble to my feet. "Run, Bastien!"

I spin and sprint for the back of the warehouse, straight for the gaping hole in the back of the factory. I can hear Bastien's feet pounding on the second floor and catch a brief glimpse of him as he rounds the far stairwell and thunders up to the third floor.

I pause to search for Drakon. Blood drips down from his temple and his nose is bent at a crooked angle. His hands clench into fists at his side. I've never seen such evil before, such unrepentant fury.

I turn and run for my life.

FIVE

I clutch my arms around my knees as a trembling reverberates through me. I begin to rock, thinking of how close I came to enslavement…or worse.

What happened back there?

I hold up my hands before my eyes but they remain unseen in the dark. Traces of heat linger in my fingertips, as if the fires might spark to life again. I clasp my chest as pain continues to radiate around my heart.

Something is wrong. I can feel this truth buried deep within my core. I've never lost my cool before. Never come so close to unbridled rage. I shake my hands and clench them into fists. *What is happening to me?*

What about Bastien? Did he make it out ok?

I can hear the aliens in the distance, coordinating a search for us. I don't have long to linger, but I can't seem to make my legs work properly. My mind refuses to think on anything but the way I tore a staircase off its hinges and hurled it across the room, or the way I shoved that machine with my mind.

I killed those aliens.

I can't find it in me to regret my actions. I only wish I could understand them.

The pounding of my heart is nearly loud enough to drown out the sound of the aliens approaching. I push back on the wall to rise, stomping the blood back into my legs before I sprint through the alley and burst through the other side.

Shouts rise behind me and I know they're on my trail. I don't know how many are coming after me, but all that matters is that I get out of there quickly.

Block after block blurs past. I scour the streets, searching for an entrance to the subway. If I can get down there I might stand a chance, but luck is obviously not on my side. I don't see any way of getting underground.

I glance back over my shoulder and see emerald light glowing a couple blocks back, dancing onto the walls as the aliens run. They are faster than I am. Whatever power it was that I tapped into back at that factory has left me weak and vulnerable. I have to hide.

I grab a metal street sign and sling myself around the corner of a building. It's hard to maintain a full out sprint with a cramp forming in my side. My pace slows to a lurching run and then a fast walk. I clutch my chest as my lungs constrict, making it nearly impossible to draw a full breath.

Spying an alley halfway down the street, I hook right and race to the end.

"This can't be happening!" I slam my open palms against a chain link fence that blocks the exit. It rises high overhead, and a spiral of spiked wire runs the length of the top. I turn and press back against the rusted fence, curling my fingers around the wire as I peer behind a large green container with a large, faded sigh that says GARBAGE on its side. No signs of rats or any other foul vermin so far.

The scent of trash has long since faded. A large hole gapes open on the lower right side of the container and a fine dirt mixture pours out from within. I grasp a handful of soil and breathe in deep. It is compost, something I'm very familiar with from growing up in the forest.

I peer around the edge of the container and listen. Boots slap the sidewalk as they approach. There's no time to run.

Glancing back at the rusted hole, I decide to take my chances with the dirt. I wiggle inside headfirst, scratching my hip as I pass. I tuck my lower lip behind my teeth as I grip the floor and pull myself through. The edges of the metal hole scrape layers of skin from my sides and I bite down hard on my lip to still my cry.

Shouts rise from the end of the alley, and I rush to bury myself in the garbage remains. The soil is cold and the metal floor frigid against the narrow swatch of skin at my waist where my shirt has risen up. Goosebumps rise along my body as I wiggle down as low as I can go.

I manage to get my lower half completely covered but my top half will be difficult. There isn't enough soil left to completely hide in.

"Any sign of her?" My head whips up as I struggle to hear through the thick metal box. The voice is loud but muffled by the walls.

"I could have sworn she came this way." The alien's tone is raspy, hardened with age. If he were human, I would've said that he'd smoked one too many dogwood bark cigarettes.

"Maybe she doubled back? I heard Commander Drakon was close to getting his hands on the boy. Maybe she went back for him?"

The second voice is higher in pitch, not all that unlike a girl's voice. I've always wondered how young the Caldonians start out their soldiers. By the sounds of it, the boy can't be a day over fifteen.

Suddenly, a tickle begins in my nose as the dirt shifts. My pulse shoots up as I plug my nostrils and pray that I can hold off my sneeze until the aliens leave.

"Think we should head back?"

I can hear their boots shifting on a mixture of glass and rubble out on the street. I close my eyes and hope that they'll just leave.

"The Commander will have our heads if we're wrong." The older soldier's gruff response sends my hopes plummeting into cold oblivion. I suck in a deep breath and wait.

The sneeze escapes before I can stifle it. I cup my mouth and clamp my eyes closed, straining to hear.

"What was that?" Footsteps shift on the street and I'm sure that they know exactly where I am. "Came from down there. Let's check it out."

I rip my shirt over my head and rub dirt into the material, tearing at the frayed ends of the shirt to create long, wide ravels. I scrub the dark compost all over my face, chest and abdomen to hide my pale skin. I rub my head along the floor, matting my sweaty hair with refuse.

Their approach is slow and cautious. I can see the bouncing light of their lasers as they draw near. Draping my torn shirt over my chest and head, I sprinkle compost over it. I bury my arms into the soil and focus on taking tiny breaths. I wish I could see myself from above to know if any part of me is visible.

The scrape of a boot beside the dumpster and the rattle of the chain steal away my breath. Terror roots me to the metal floor as I suck in my stomach and pray that my concealment looks natural.

"I don't see anything." The man's voice is loud enough to sift through the hole at my feet.

My lungs burn but I continue to suck in only partial breaths. I can't risk another sneeze now that I'm buried in this shallow grave.

I clamp my eyes tightly closed as a bright light pierces through the hole. "See anything?"

Shifting just enough to get my arm behind my back, I pull out my gun. My finger hovers over the trigger, ready to take out these aliens the instant I'm discovered.

Seconds seem to drag by with agonizing indifference to my predicament. "Nah. Just some dirt and crap. She's not here."

I allow a tiny breath of relief as the light vanishes. The chain link fence rattles as someone kicks it. "Darn cats are a nuisance."

"Now what, Tuz?"

The older alien, Tuz I presume, spits. The glob splatters against the dumpster and I scrunch up my nose with disgust. "We keep looking. She can't have gone too far."

I wait to take my first deep breath until the sounds of their retreat have completely vanished. My fingers uncurl from my palms, leaving stinging half-moon cuts. I tear my shirt away from my face and sit up, gasping for breath as my lungs expand to full capacity.

Compost shifts down my body as I rise to a crouch. My pants are filthy, my hair is clumped with compost, and my skin itches in more places than I care to count. I pull my shirt down over my head and take in the damage.

The jagged hem of my black shirt is now about two inches shorter in places. Large rips lead up my sides and one up the center of my stomach, stopping scant inches from my chest. "Good thing no one's going to see me like this," I mutter as I wiggle back through the hole.

Fresh blood and dirt mingle in the wounds as I rise. I cup my hand over my right side, knowing I pulled a bit too far to the right. The wound is deeper than before.

I take the alley at a run, keeping to the deeper shadows until I reach the end of the street. I poke my head out and survey both ways. No signs of my pursuers, but I'm sure they're not too far away.

I sweep the roofline in search of which direction to head. The moonlight breaks through small openings in the cloud cover, lending just enough light so I won't face plant into a wall. I can see the glow of the City above, gaining brightness behind me. A rumbling rises from the ground, intermittent but increasing in intensity. I peer down the street and see a towering shadow gaining purchase on the buildings several blocks away. I don't know what it is but I'm not sticking around to find out. I sprint straight across the street and flee to the darkness.

Wooden boards creak underfoot as I climb a set of rickety stairs. The banister rocks under my grasp, threatening to collapse onto the floor below. I cling to it, unsure if it is holding me upright or vice versa.

The wallpaper on the stairway wall is faded, concealing its original design. It peels away from the weathered molding near the ceiling. The plaster behind is cracked from evidence of water damage. Everything feels dingy and almost sticky to the touch.

My steps are labored, echoing through the abandoned housing building. Exhaustion shrouds me as I round the second floor and struggle up the next flight of stairs. The landing is blanketed with tile shards that poke up into my shoes as I pass. A large, glassless window at the end of the hall allows in shifting beams of moonlight. What was probably once a white cushioned window seat just below has deteriorated to a moldy lump. I scrunch up my nose at the obvious evidence of rodent habitation.

I have no idea where I am, or how far I've run; all I know is I can't go any further.

It has been an hour since I heard the aliens. Not long after I darted out of the alley, I heard a laser fight a couple blocks over and I can't help wondering if Bastien made it out alive.

I should have gone back for him and fought beside him. I try to reason that I shouldn't care, that we're only two strangers whose paths crossed at the wrong time, but it doesn't feel right. He is human and, by default, my kin.

Shuffling my feet along the threadbare carpet, I head toward a door at the end of the hall. As I get closer, I realize the off-white door has a smattering of holes marring the surface. I run my finger along the splintered wood.

"A shotgun did this." I push the door and stumble inside. A black metal number 15 rattles and drops to the floor outside as I close the door behind me. I feed the lock through the slot but it slips through the tarnished metal plate and rolls out the end. I sigh and move on. It's not like the Squaddies can't get through if the lock did work.

A shattered doll greets me with vacant, staring eyes, half its porcelain face ground into the carpet. I wince as my weight crunches what remains as I survey the room in front of me.

Black scorch marks and splattered blood intensifies the eerie feeling that hangs over the room. I spy eight more bullet holes throughout the room, as if the shooter was aiming at a jumping jackrabbit instead of an alien.

Dust blankets everything, layering the room in dismal shades of gray. A tan fabric couch fills the center of the room, pointed toward a wooden wall unit, its shelves stocked full of books. I stumble forward despite my exhaustion and run my fingers along their cracked bindings: a forgotten library at my fingertips.

I dip quietly down a hallway, peeking into each of the rooms to make sure they are vacant. I have to squint to see in the dim moonlight. It wouldn't be good to assume the coast is clear and later find a group of raiders nestled in the back bedroom.

Each of the rooms are exactly how I assume they were left...in a hurry.

A blue bedroom at the end of the hall still has books opened on the bed. The quilt is crumpled and a shattered glass adorns the bedside table. The window frame is half open, as if someone tried to climb out onto the stairs that cling to the side of the building.

A faded yellow room next door has stuffed animals strewn across the floor and a rainbow of pastel colored dresses slung about. The final room sports evidence of laser fire and a large rust colored bloodstain in the corner. The closet is stripped of all its contents. It's hard to tell if this was done by raiders or aliens, but the fact remains, there is nothing here to replace my torn shirt or shield me from the bitter cold.

I walk past the bathroom and give it a cursory glance. Wide rings of grime circle the inside of the porcelain tub. The ceiling tiles have fallen and crumbed over the toilet, revealing thin wooden slats above, warped by age and water leaks.

I move into the kitchen and step over a couple overturned chairs to dip low to look at a discolored family picture on the counter. I swallow down the longing I feel for my own parents as I stare at the smiling faces of a couple with two children.

The metal handles on the cabinets have corroded and the doors hang on their hinges. Faded purple lace curtains over the window have been yanked down and the window sports a jagged fringe of broken glass.

I head back toward the front room. By all appearances, the space is raider free but I can't tell for how long. The home is stripped of anything useful so hopefully no one will disturb me tonight.

My muscles ache as I sink onto the faded couch. A puff of dust rises in the air, I wave my hand to clear it. I half expect something to crawl out of the cushions but nothing appears. I beat the pillow with my hand then fluff it back up. Pulling my legs up onto the couch, I sink down onto the pillow, surprised by how far my head disappears into it.

I sigh as each muscle starts to relax. My fingers pass over the material of the couch, amazed by how deliciously comfortable it is. Never before have I laid on anything so forgiving. It curls to my side, cocooning me, giving support in ways a cave floor can't.

During the fall, I sometimes sneak out and make a bed of pine needles and lay staring up at the night sky. My best friend, Aminah, would sometimes join me and we would spend hours talking about boys. Of course, most of that time was spent discussing her budding love for Toren, the only guy she's ever cared for, and my complete lack of caring.

She always assumed that I would end up with Eamon. Truth be told, I did too, but only because he's my closest friend. Zahra loves to fawn over his golden tousled hair and wide, expressive hazel eyes, but I don't really see it. Not in the way a normal girl should. At least that's what Aminah always tells me.

Tears sting my eyes as I sink down off the couch and curl up on the hard floor. I tuck my hand beneath my head and reach behind me to remove one of my knives. I usually sleep with a weapon at home.

Home.

When I close my eyes, I can almost make myself believe that I'm home, safe and loved. I should never have left, especially on my birthday. Eamon will be disappointed. He hinted that he had something special he wanted to give me. Knowing him, he's whittled a new spear that's the perfect height and thickness for me.

I miss all of my friends, even Zahra a tiny bit. Why did I ever leave?

This place didn't exactly turn out the way I'd hoped. I came here thinking I could discover the truth behind the tremors and find a way to stop it. I know now that's impossible. The Diggers are already heading our way. How long will it take for them to find our caves?

The City is dangerous, exactly as my mother warned me it would be, but she was wrong about one thing…I found compassion here too.

My mind races with unanswered questions. Where is Bastien now? Did he make it back to his subway car? Is he waiting for me to return? I have no idea if I will be able to find the entrance again, but I vow to try. I have to know if he is ok.

My thoughts tumble into oblivion as sleep tugs me away. I go willingly, ready for a respite from my fears.

SIX

Even before I open my eyes, I can sense another presence in the room. It is subtle, like a tickling of your nose, but it's there. I control my breathing, keeping it steady as I listen.

There is a faint creak on the floorboard to my right. I curl my fingers ever so slightly around the hilt of my knife, muscles coiled and ready to spring.

I launch my knife through the air before I even open my eyes. I'm up and firmly planted in a fighting stance by the time the shadow rolls back to its feet and rushes away. I glare at the blade buried deep in the wood framing the kitchen doorway——a near miss, but still a miss.

The figure moves with stealth, shifting fluidly around the room. I reach behind me and grab my gun, flicking off the safety as I kick the end table toward my assailant. I leap forward in a dive and come up only four feet from the man, gun aimed at his heart. Emerald green light blinds me as I stare into a laser cannon.

I dive to the side and roll behind a cabinet. I stifle my heavy breathing, listening for footsteps in the apartment but hear none. I tilt my head back toward the door and try to hear anyone creaking on the floor in the hall or mounting the steps. All is silent.

"Who are you?"

The man shifts slightly. Why isn't he firing? The cabinet offers little protection from a cannon's blast.

"I don't want to hurt you," he calls.

I chamber a round. "Yeah, I've heard that one already tonight. Didn't work out so well for me last time."

"I'm not like Commander Drakon." The response is soft, barely above a whisper, but filled with a surprising hint of bitterness.

"Mutiny among the ranks. You really want to go with that story?" I scoff. "Boy, you all must think humans are *really* stupid."

"Not at all." He shifts closer to the window and I get a full view of his size. Although he stands nearly a head taller than me, his body is long and lithe. His lean form betrays the body of a skilled warrior, not a mindless brute like some of the soldiers back at the factory.

I need to be wary of this one. He's obviously not a stranger to hand-to-hand combat. "Are you planning to turn me in?"

I lean back against the cabinet, pointing my gun at the ceiling as I listen to his breathing. Although it is slightly elevated, he seems to be in control of his nerves, which isn't a good sign for me.

"Those are my orders…" The pause at the end of his words makes me peek out. The emerald light is gone, his laser completely powered down. Why didn't I notice the missing hum sooner?

"Something tells me you have another agenda." My fingers tighten around my gun. He might be foolish enough to power down his weapon, but I'm not about to give up my chance at the upper hand.

"I just want to talk."

My laugh comes out more like a bitter snort than a true laugh. I look around the edge of the cabinet and notice that he's nearly even with me. I'm quickly losing any form of protection this cabinet offers.

"Stay there!" He pauses in mid-step, slowly letting his foot drop back to the floor. "Don't come any closer."

To my complete surprise, he actually backs away. He bends at the waist, slowly and deliberately, and rests his darkened cannon against the wall and steps away. He holds his hands up in a gesture of surrender.

A dozen questions race through my mind at once. What is going on? Why is he surrendering his weapon? What could he possibly gain from speaking to me?

"I'm going to sit down now. Please don't shoot."

My lips press into a tight line as he skirts along the wall, his back pressed tightly to the peeling wallpaper as he inches toward the couch. I step out from behind the cabinet and lower my gun to follow him, my finger hovering just over the trigger in case I sense a trap.

As he turns to approach the couch, I see a flash of silver where his eyes should be. I blink, shocked to find that his eyes aren't a normal color at all, but appear more like the nickel my father gave me on my thirteenth birthday.

Even with the little experience that I have with the Caldonians, I know that his eyes are unique. He lowers his hands to shoulder height as he ducks under the wobbly fan that dangles from the ceiling by a few frayed wires. His gaze locks onto mine just before he turns his back on me and slowly sinks onto the couch.

For a moment, I just stand with my mouth gaped open. What the heck is he doing? One of the first things you learn in combat training is to never turn your back on your enemy.

Maybe that's what he's trying to prove. That I have nothing to fear from him.

The floorboards creak loudly as I inch forward, careful to remain well outside a normal diving range. The last thing I want to happen is for this guy to get his hands on me.

I slip past the edge of the couch and tuck myself into the kitchen doorway to my right. With my free hand, I tug my knife free of the doorframe and slide it back into my waist. From here, I can spin and race down the hall behind me to escape down the outdoor staircase if he decides to cause trouble.

I lower my arms, my left hand cupping my right as I keep the gun trained in his direction. "Who are you?"

"My name is Kyan, Son of Caul." The sound of his voice is almost musical, like wind chimes in a warm summer's breeze. I find the tone both alarmingly pleasant and worrisome. With a voice like that, anyone could be lulled into trusting him.

"Why did you follow me?"

"I didn't, not in the way you think, at least."

I cock my head to the side and tuck my lower lip behind my teeth. I didn't expect that answer. "Then how did you find me?"

"I could feel you."

"Feel me? What's that supposed to mean?"

He turns his head, zeroing in on me with his shiny gaze. "I can always sense one of my own kind."

I feel the blood drain from my face, pooling at my feet. I'm sure I look as pale as a spectral ghost in the dim light. "What did you just say?"

He smiles kindly. "I said that you are one of us, Illyria."

I whip my gun up and aim directly at his right eye. I know from this distance I won't miss. "How do you know my name?"

I know more than you think. Although his lips remain stationary, I can hear his voice as clearly as if he'd spoken the words aloud.

My mouth drops open as I take a step back. The gun shakes imperceptibly in my hands. "How can I hear you?"

"Telepathy. I can read your mind and you can read mine."

I shake my head emphatically. "No, I can't."

He presses his lips into a thin line. *It is in your blood, Illyria. In the very DNA that makes you who you are.*

"Stop it!" I cry, covering my ear with my free hand. "Get out of my head!"

"As you wish."

I'm not sure how, but I feel him withdraw from my mind. The complete absence leaves me feeling woefully empty inside, as if his feathery touch was natural. "So you can read my mind…that doesn't prove I'm one of you."

He cocks his head to the side. "You've developed abilities, yes?"

Apprehension trickles down my spine. "I don't know what you're talking about."

There is a sharp edge to Kyan's laugh. "Surely you know that it's impossible for a mere human to toss a metal staircase with their mind."

I blanch as small sparks of heat flicker in my fingertips. "It was an accident. I didn't mean to-"

"Oh yes, you did." He leans forward, locking me in place with his direct gaze. "Your mind allowed you to do exactly what your heart desired. You were angry, you wanted to save your friend and you did. Quite well I might add."

"How do you know about Bastien?" I demand.

Although he doesn't actually roll his eyes, his clipped words imply the action. "I can read minds, Illyria. It's not that hard to shuffle through your thoughts to see you're worried about him."

I lower my gun slightly. "Do you know if he's ok?"

Kyan shakes his head. "No."

"Are you lying?"

He smirks, pointing to his head. "Why don't you take a peek and find out?"

The idea is absurd but oddly appealing at the same point. *What if I really can read his mind? What would I find?*

I shake off my curiosity and rise to my feet. "Well this chat has been...insightful, but I think we're done here."

Kyan's smile falters into a mask of distress. He holds out his hands. "You can't go yet. There is so much that I need to tell you."

"Sorry but I'm not really in the talking mood tonight."

I edge past the couch and back toward the door, never letting Kyan out of my sight. I pause with my hand on the doorknob. Kyan twists all the way around to face me. "Please, don't leave. You don't know how dangerous it is for you."

"I can handle myself."

His silver gaze seems to brighten with urgency. "If you don't learn how to control your abilities, they *will* destroy you."

I hesitate a second longer. I think over his words and then narrow my eyes.

"You're trying to trick me into staying. Why? Do you have reinforcements coming? How long are you supposed to delay me until they arrive?"

"No, it's not like that," he protests, starting to rise.

I shoot off a warning shot. Fluff explodes from the arm of the couch. Kyan throws up his hands in surrender. He never once shifts to look at his laser cannon against the wall. I calculate it would take him a split second to leap over the couch to retrieve it but at least five to power it up. That would get me out the door and nearly to the staircase if I'm lucky, but he never makes a move.

"If you try to come after me, I will kill you."

His lips press into a tight line, but he nods in understanding. "You can't outrun your destiny forever, Illyria."

"Watch me." I shoot off one final round, severing the wire that holds the ceiling fan aloft and sprint for the hall.

I peer into the pre-dawn light, searching for any sign of movement. Fresh streaks of charred stone line the battered industrial street, evidence of the battle I fled only a few short hours ago. Has it really only been one night since I entered the City? It feels like a lifetime.

The street is void of life, but still I hesitate. Commander Drakon most likely posted a guard at the factory, just in case I'm foolish enough to return.

Nothing like being predictable.

To be fair, predictability has nothing to do with why I'm posted two blocks away from the factory. It has everything to do with desperation. After leaving Kyan to untangle himself from the ceiling fan, I ran as far and as hard as I could straight back toward the City lights. Even though my instincts screamed at me that I was heading straight into danger, I knew I had to go back to find Bastien.

I have to know if he's still alive.

Inching my head out around the corner, my gaze flits over the abandoned factory, searching each window for any sign of movement. Dawn is rapidly approaching.

The sky is painted with lavender and the stars and moon have receded, hiding until the night beckons them forth again.

"It's now or never," I mutter, bracing myself to run.

Deciding my nerves need a good three count, I lean into my stance, rise onto the balls of my feet and sprint the instant I hit one. I don't look around as I barrel straight for the rusted subway door, refusing to look anywhere but my goal.

The two block sprint is harder than I imagined. I begin to wind down half a block from the door. A stitch needles at my side, but I push through the pain. My limbs feel heavy with sleep deprivation, and I can't even remember the last time I ate anything. I know my body's energy reserves are dangerously low right now.

I yank open the door and spill into complete darkness. *I made it.*

Gasping for breath, I lean over, my hands on my knees and head hanging low. The stale air is a salve to my enflamed lungs. Rising up, I clutch my chest but wince at the raw flesh around my heart. I rub the tender skin, wishing there were enough light to examine it. I don't remember getting burned there.

I let my hand drop to cradle the stich in my side until the cramp fades. Once I've got my breathing under control, I press my ear against the cold metal door and listen. I can't hear any shouts or pounding footsteps following after me. Instead, an eerie silence greets me and I can't stop the shiver that races down my spine.

Maybe they've already found Bastien's camp. Maybe they're waiting for me in the tunnel below.

Leaning back against the grimy subway wall, I whisper a prayer for protection into the darkness. I don't really know who I'm speaking to or even if there is anyone out there still left to listen. My mother used to tell me that there were many religions before the Caldonians came. Some believed in one God, others believed in many. I don't really know what to think. My mother never shared her belief on the matter, but I have a sneaking suspicion that she only believed in one so that's the one I'm going with.

The black void presses in around me and my thoughts turn toward finding the flashlight. I search close to the door, my fingers fluttering over the chipped tile floor. I hiss as something sharp slices through my finger and grit my teeth against the foul curses begging to inch past my lips, as my fingers curl around the cold barrel of the light.

Blinking into the bright beam, I'm dazed by its brilliance. I lower the light and begin a rapid descent down the flight of stairs that lead to the track line below.

My light picks up the dull sheen of the winding track and I feel my heart tap out an excited staccato. I'm getting closer.

A second thought brings me to a dead halt. *If Bastien is alive, why didn't he use the flashlight for himself?*

The metal light feels weighty and cold in the palm of my hand. I try to shake off morbid thoughts but it's hard to find hope down here, surrounded by the deepest shadows I have ever seen. I stumble ahead for several minutes. At first I try counting the track junctions, thinking that will help me to find my way, but I quickly realize they all look the same. The last time I was down here, I wasn't paying close attention. I was too annoyed with Bastien to focus on the route.

Seconds drag out into endless minutes and I can't help but wonder if I chose the wrong tunnel. Maybe I should've turned back by the rat's nest or at the third junction where a sludgy pool of water stood high enough to seep into my boots. I don't remember hitting that puddle before.

I'm about to sink down to the floor to wallow in self-pity when I catch a glimpse of white in the flickering beam of the flashlight. I whip the light up and rake my gaze over the distant color. "That must be it!"

I don't let myself consider how many other abandoned subways cars there must be along these tracks as I dash down the line, careful not to tumble over the curve of the metal rail. The instant my fingers curl around the door handle, I know I've found Bastien's home.

Tossing the light through the open doorway, I hike my leg up onto the door and shimmy myself inside. I cry out as the torn flesh along my side oozes fresh blood.

I snatch the light off the floor and whip around, searching for any sign of Bastien. Several of the bags are missing from the overhead space, and the underside of the benches has been cleared out as well. My heart sinks and I drop onto the plastic bench along the wall. Judging by the fallen bits of wrappers and cans kicked aside, it looks like someone rummaged through this half of the car with great urgency.

"Every man for himself, I see."

Wiping my hands on my grimy pants, I rise and head toward the front of the car. I struggle to understand why his abandonment feels so personal. It's not like I even really know the guy.

With my fingers wrapped around the door handle, I catch sight of a bag sitting to my right. I turn and shine the light over a burlap sack bulging with supplies. A shred of paper lies on top. I reach for it and hold it under the light.

If you find this note, that means you're alive. Obviously, I am too.

I want you to get your crap and head for the woods. Don't come back here again.

~ B

I turn the paper over in my hands, sure that there must be something more to the note, but there isn't. Each scribbled word is tiny enough just to fit on the small space. There's no room for anything more eloquent, even if that were Bastien's style.

I release a bitter laugh and sink down onto the bench. "What did I expect? A personal escort back to the woods?"

My words spurn an intense yearning for home. I gather the neck of the burlap sack and toss the bag over my shoulder. It would've been heavy on the best of days, and today has by far been my worst.

I leap down from the subway car and carefully shove the latch back into place. I don't know why I do it, but maybe it's because some part of me wants to show respect for the home of the boy who saved my life.

SEVEN

I sense the blade at my throat before I actually feel the pressure of it against my flesh. "Halt!"

A smile crosses my face a split second before I shove my elbow back into the hard abdomen of the guy behind me. He grunts and drops his blade. "Holy crap, Illyria. What'd you do that for?"

I spin and shove Eamon back onto the ground, laughing as he clutches his bruised stomach. "You started it."

He rolls onto his side, his threadbare jacket soaking up the thin layer of snow that fell on the mountain overnight. "You knew it was me?"

"Of course I did." Offering my hand to help him up, I wince as he pulls against my arm. I feel fresh blood spread along my side and work to keep the pain from my face. If Eamon discovers that I'm injured, he will tear down the entire City looking for the guy who hurt me.

Eamon brushes himself off before stepping back, his frown already deeply set in place. I drop my gaze. "I'd ask where you went but I'd be a fool not to know."

I peek up at him through locks of grimy hair. I stumbled a few times on my way up the mountain, adding a couple clumps of mud and decaying leaves to the gnarled mess. Normally I can hold my own against our leader, Toren, on the steep slopes, and that's saying a lot considering he's the fastest runner I know, but I'm bone weary today. "I was right."

Eamon's lips settle into a deep frown. "What do you mean?"

"I mean those tremors were being caused by the Caldonians. I found the source."

He jerks his head toward the City in the distance, nestled in the valley about a three hour hike below. "I assume by the looks of you that you had something to do with that light show last night."

I wince as his gaze falls over the shredded remains of my shirt. I can only imagine what he must be thinking right now. "Maybe."

A growl rises from his throat as he snatches my arm and pulls me against his chest in a bone-crushing hug. "Do you have any idea how worried I was? Toren ordered me to be restrained so I didn't go after you."

I'm used to Eamon's admonishments. He's always felt like he had to protect me, from other guys, from predators in the woods and from myself. "I had to know if I was right."

His breathing is heavy, weighted with an anger that amplifies his unique eyes. Eamon's eyes have always fascinated me. Although everyone considers his eye color to be hazel, it looks like splashes of gold to me. Sometimes, on a warm summer's night, I almost think I can see light reflected in them, but today I can't bear to see the hurt I know lies within.

"You should have told me. I would've gone with you, protected you."

"I didn't want to put you in danger," I whisper, struggling to look at him. Of course Eamon would've wanted to go with me but I don't regret my decision. One person sneaking into the City was hard enough. Two would have been dangerous.

His strong hands grip around my arms. "You know I would have been there for you."

He pulls my face to his chest, cradling me as if I were a child. I close my eyes and cling to him, indebted to him for his sacrificial love. It is a constant, something I can rely on, even when it's infuriatingly restrictive.

His lips press against the crown of my head. "I can't lose you."

"You won't." I step back out of his grasp. With the noonday light streaming down through his thick mop of curls, he almost looks like an angel, minus the allergen inducing feathered wings and golden halo.

A rebellious smirk tugs at my lips. "I've got something for you."

He holds his frown for a second longer before he succumbs to my charm. "Fine, change the subject, but I'm not letting this slide, missy."

"Yes, sir!" I offer a mock salute that dissolves his anger entirely. I crouch down and rifle through the sack Bastien left for me.

Upon earlier examination, I was confused by the various shaped boxes and canisters within the sack, but I quickly realized that Bastien shared his supplies with me. Inside are various medicines and bandages that we desperately need, two boxes of ammo that I'm sure will fit one of the sniper rifles Toren has hidden away, and food. Lots of food. Most of the food I can't pronounce but I can tell by the pictures that it's edible.

"What's that you have?" Eamon's brow rises with interest as I hold out a dull red can with a flip top.

"Just pull that tab and take a swig." I grin and lean back against a tree as Eamon fumbles with the tab.

"Oh bugger," he grumbles as the thin metal snaps off completely and brown foam spills over his hand. His eyes narrow at me as he searches for any obvious signs of mischief on my part, which are, of course written plainly on my face.

"Just drink it."

He shakes off the foam and downs a big gulp. He comes up spluttering, red in the face, as he gags on the bubbles. I laugh until my sides ache and I'm forced to taper off into a chuckle.

"Urgh," he groans, tossing the can out into the woods. "What is that stuff?"

"It's called soda. I've been told it's very good."

Eamon's gaze sharpens. "Who says?"

I wince and clamp down on my tongue.

"Illyria?" He steps toward me, his voice low and dangerous. I know this voice. It's the one he uses every time we're on a hunt and I get too close to a mountain lion or wolf. "What aren't you telling me?"

I sidestep him and gather the bag over my shoulder, but Eamon motions for me to hand it over. I agree although normally

I would protest, insisting that I'm just as strong as he is. His eyes narrow as I easily consent to his help, but he remains silent.

"I'll explain everything when we speak with Toren. Is he here?"

"Yeah. He's waiting for you." Every muscle in his body tenses as he stares out toward the City. It looks so innocent from this distance, a lifeless husk buried within a mass of broken glass and twisted metal, but I now know how deceiving this view can be. I know what lies within the depths of that place now. "Were you followed?"

"No," I shake my head, knowing I did everything I could to keep my exit from the city a secret. I doubled back three times just to make sure no one was on my trail, but I never sensed anyone, or heard evidence that I was followed. I was alone when I left. "But the Caldonians are coming. Soon."

I skim my fingers along the familiar damp stone of the cave entrance as I duck under Eamon's arm. Once I'm inside, he replaces the blackberry bush over the tunnel. Shafts of daylight filter through its numerous tangled branches, lighting the narrow space. During the summer, it offers better protective cover from peering eyes but, for now, it's the best we can manage with winter knocking at our back door.

There are miles of tunnels within this mountain. Most of them have been left to darkness due to lack of use or supplies for torches. We only light the tunnels that we use daily. The others we must learn by feel; this tunnel is one of those.

Although I know this trail well, Eamon leads the way. It weaves through the earth, carving a path past countless off shoots and dead ends. One wrong turn and we would be lost for hours, but Eamon and I push ahead with complete confidence.

Our destination is the Temple. Aminah thought it a fitting title because of the odd altar-like stone in the center of the cavernous room we use for daily activities. Although she was only four when she named the space, the term has stuck ever since. I think the adults relented to the change to allow us to make the cave our own. As odd as it sounds, I'm glad they let the title stand.

The Temple is our gathering place for meals, songs and lessons. Once you hit your teen years, you get the pleasure of joining into the courting session. I find them to be both awkward and unbearable, especially when done around so many nosy kids.

My friends, Aminah and Toren, were always so natural at courting, probably because they never had eyes for anyone else. I envy them for it. They never had to bumble through first kiss attempts that ended with a black eye for the guy and me sent to my bed without dinner.

But the Temple holds fond memories as well. It is where I learned to wield a knife and think like a predator. To be honest, I'm surprised any guy had the nerve to try to touch my backside after seeing me train from hours on end with my daggers.

The domed space has four exits, located pretty much even with the cardinal points on a map. Each leads to a series of smaller rooms——cave closets, as Zahra likes to call them. For a girl whose only goal in life is to capture the heart of a future mate, I can see why this would be her first thought. Although we maintain a small stock of clothing, somehow Zahra manages to look stunning even in the rattiest of clothes.

Another wing I avoid is the children's area. I have no desire to attend to small children, whose noses always run and stomachs are always empty. I don't have the patience for whining.

My mother was probably right when she said I will be a terrible mom someday.

I refuse to enter one other place——the compost collector. Some people may prefer to do *everything* within the safety of the cave, but there are some things I prefer leaving behind in the woods.

Makeshift torches are propped against the wall, leading us the final fifty feet into the Temple. My legs are weary and my side wounds sting. All I want is to veer off toward the Cascades for a refreshing bath and then head straight to bed, but Eamon reaches back for my hand and tugs me forward.

How does he always know when I want to run away? I grumble silently.

"We're home!" Eamon shouts as he steps into the well-lit room. I groan at his attempt to make the little kids smile but can't help love him even more for it. Although I have a serious aversion to small children, Eamon dotes on each of them as if they were his own. Someday he will be a wonderful father...if he lives that long.

Toren looks up from the map he's studying atop the altar-like table and waves us over. I can tell by the look on his face that my absence caused quite a stir last night. I hang my head low and follow Eamon's lead, knowing a stern reprimand is waiting for me.

Eamon's hand is tugged out of mine as a flash of golden blonde slips in between us and wiggles close to his side. Zahra grabs my sack from his shoulder and tosses it carelessly to the ground. "I'm so glad you're back, Eamon."

I roll my eyes and dip low to retrieve my supplies, grateful not to have to watch Zahra fawn over Eamon. She does it every night we return from a hunt. Most nights I can hardly stomach watching her paw over him.

When Eamon looks back down at me, I turn to the side and gag on my finger. He laughs as Zahra shoots an icy glare at me before turning her simpering smile back to him. "Think you can help me in the kitchen? I'm making your favorite-Roasted rabbit."

I nearly applaud at his hesitation. "I'll be there in a few minutes. I think Illyria brought back some supplies with her. Why don't you take those to the pantry for us?"

Her scowl would bother me if I had the slightest inclination to care, which I don't. I didn't lay claim on Eamon. It was the other way around.

Aminah waves at me from the far side of the room. Although I can tell she's happy to see me alive, I know by the droop in her slender shoulders that my absence hurt her. Her auburn curls hang over her face, but I can see the puffiness under her eyes, evidence of a long night spent crying.

I wince and turn my back on her, sure that I'm about to hear all about it from Toren.

"Have fun?" He asks, rounding the stone table. He crosses his arms over his chest, and although I know it's his most intimidating pose, he struggles to carry it off like Eamon does.

"I wouldn't call it fun," I grimace, cupping the dried blood on my right side. Toren's gaze flits down and hardens at the sight of my wounds, barely hidden behind the scraps of my shirt.

He sighs and runs his fingers through his wavy chestnut hair. He keeps it short so his curls don't take over, but it's been a while since he had a decent trim. "Are you hurt?"

"Not really." I absently rub my chest, trying not to think of how differently last night could have gone for me.

"Hey! What's that?"

I turn to find Eamon peering down at my chest. I bristle and realize just how low my torn collar really goes. "Well if you have to ask-"

He snorts and pulls the tattered collar of my shirt to the side, exposing a larger amount of my chest than I would like. His finger brushes over my flesh and I struggle to hide my shiver. No one has ever touched me like that before. Even though it's hardly risqué, I've always kept a pretty strict no touch policy with all of the guys in the commune.

"Where did you get this?" He whispers, tracing the raw flesh with his thumb.

I tuck my chin and try to see what he's looking at. Whatever it is, I can see his concern mirrored in Toren's eyes. They exchange a glance as I shove Eamon's hand away. "It's nothing. Just a burn I got last night."

"That's no burn," Zahra says, sounding thoroughly bored with the topic as she appears next to Eamon.

Toren ignores Zahra, staring hard at me. I flinch under his gaze. He normally doesn't try to lord his authority over me but I can tell he's about to question me. "Where did you get that mark?"

"What the heck are you talking about?" I cry.

Aminah's feet whisper across the Temple floor as she ushers a small group of children out of the room. Several of them pause at the doorway, peering curiously back at me. I bite my lower lip, scolding myself for my outburst. There's no sense upsetting them with trivial things like a burn.

When Aminah returns she pushes past Toren to stand before me. "You can't see it, can you?"

"See what?" I try to hide my frustration, but it's hard. I'm too tired to be polite right now.

She reaches out and peels back my shirt, her eyes narrowing with concern. Eamon peeks over her shoulder and I'm struck yet again with self-consciousness. He chuckles as Zahra smacks his arm. "What? I'm just concerned is all."

My cheeks burn with embarrassment as Toren leans in for closer inspection. "Really? Am I a sideshow act or something? This is a bit personal, ya know," I snap.

Toren blinks and looks to Aminah, who smiles kindly. "Sorry, he doesn't always think about girls like that."

"Well, he should," I reply, turning away from Eamon and Toren. Zahra rolls her eyes and steps between us as a shield. I have no doubt this gesture isn't done for my benefit.

Her bright green eyes lock onto mine. "I'll tell you what it is so everyone can stop gawking at your…chest."

Zahra sports a haughty smirk as she forces out the final word. I roll my eyes. I'm way past caring about her petty jokes. Yes, I'm aware of the fact that I didn't develop quite as much as she did, but at least I can fit my hips through the narrow passage leading to the waterfall without having to turn sideways.

"It looks like a throne bush, rooted right over your heart and vining out. Sort of like that tattoo Bran used to have."

I remember Bran. He died when I was about seven years old. Mom said his tattoos were from before the Assault, when people imbedded ink into their flesh…on purpose. I never could understand the desire to do that. I only saw Bran shirtless a couple times but I distinctly remember a vining, scroll-like tattoo that decorated his shoulder and ran down the center of his back. He had other markings but none so fierce or memorable. In its own way, I found the tattoo to be beautiful.

"How is that possible?" I ask, pulling my shirt down so far I'm sure if Zahra hadn't been standing there I would have given the guys a real eyeful.

Aminah watches me, her doe eyes far too insightful for my liking. "You have no idea how this happened?"

I can tell by the edge to her voice that she's suspicious. I know if I try to speak that she will see through my poorly veiled lie so I opt for a shrug. It pulls the wounded flesh taut but I refuse the urge to grimace.

Zahra steps back as I cover myself and tucks into Eamon's side, completing our dysfunctional circle.

"I think it's time to tell us what happened last night." All eyes are on me as Toren waits for my response to his request, but mine are firmly planted on the floor. I clear my throat, my thoughts scattered as I rush to create a highly edited version of events.

EIGHT

There is only silence when I finish. I shift, awkwardly rocking my weight from one foot to the other as I wait for the news to sink in. I managed to leave out my harrowing escape from Commander Drakon and my confrontation with Kyan while still revealing the Caldonians' plans. Mentioning spending much of the night with Bastien was enough to visibly raise Eamon's blood pressure through the roof.

I know I fumbled through my cover up though. I can tell Eamon's not buying it, nor is Aminah, and Zahra looks irritated that I'm getting so much attention. I wish she'd just head back to the kitchen to finish prepping lunch.

Toren clenches and unclenches his fists at his sides. When he finally speaks, he sounds as if something is strangling his voice. "So, you're saying the aliens are digging their way toward us?"

I nod, nibbling on the broken edge of my fingernail. "I can't tell how far they've reached, but judging by the increase in tremors I'd say it won't be long until they find us. I can rest up a bit tonight and head out tomorrow to take a closer look."

"No! No way!" Eamon instantly protests. "You barely made it out alive this time. There's no way I'm letting you go anywhere near that place again."

I can tell by the tilt of Zahra's head that she's contemplating siding with me on this one. I suppose a normal person would be thankful, but I'm not.

"Look, I know what I'm doing now. I can get in and out without being detected. Bastien showed me the subway and I can just follow that to the other side of the city. I won't even have to come up to the surface until I reach the dig site."

"What makes you think the aliens don't know about the tunnels?" Aminah asks, curling her finger around a small clump of hair. Her heart shaped face is pinched with worry, her rosy lips pursed tightly. She cuddles into Toren's side, naturally leaning into him.

Aminah is the most fragile member of our group. Her big heart and delicate emotions are endearing, but poorly suited for this life. Maybe that's why we're best friends. Maybe opposites really do attract.

"I say let her go. She thinks she can do it, so let her."

Eamon scowls at Zahra, pushing her away from his side. "Well don't hold back how you really feel, Zahra."

"What?" She raises her shoulders in an indifferent shrug. "She's the one with a death wish, not me."

"And you're happy to stay behind, all fat, dumb and happy." I snap at her, my patience having fled completely by this point.

Her eyes blaze with anger as she lunges toward me. Toren catches her around the waist and spins her away. "Your cat fighting really is getting old," he growls at both of us. I plant my hands on my hips but say nothing. We elected Toren as leader for a reason after our parents went missing. I'm not about to buck his authority over something this small.

"Tomorrow Eamon and Illyria will both scout out the area and report back before nightfall."

Toren's tone resonates with finality as he releases Zahra. She huffs, smoothing the wrinkles from her shirt. I'm not really sure where she came up with the idea for her ensemble—a patchwork of colorful fabrics sewn together to create an ankle length skirt and tan cotton shirt knotted at her hip to reduce the bagginess of it—but it's obvious she spent a lot of time pressing it with a hot rock. Judging by the way that she watches Eamon from the corner of her eye, her efforts were meant solely for him.

"Aminah, please see to the children and reassure them everything is ok. Zahra, you may return to the kitchen fires to finish preparing the meal. Illyria, why don't you go get cleaned up? We can't risk your wounds festering."

"What's Eamon supposed to do?" Zahra pouts.

His wicked grin forms immediately. "I'm going to help Illyria take a shower."

I laugh and shove him away. "If you come within a hundred feet of that waterfall, I won't think twice about tossing you over the side."

My nose twitches as I breathe in a tantalizing aroma. I open my eyes and find a piece of warm meat dangling over me. "Rise and shine." Eamon grins.

I bolt upright and snatch the meat from his grasp, sinking my teeth into the juicy animal flesh. Despite my aversion to the gamey taste of wolf meat, I devour the chunk in two large bites. Eamon leans back against the wall with a knowing smirk tugging at his lips.

"Oh, get over yourself. I'm hungry," I say, pushing back the tattered blanket to rise from the floor. A longing for the soft couch in the abandoned home flits through my mind as I twist the kinks from my back.

I lift my hands high overhead and stretch toward the ceiling, arching my back. My fingers just graze the rock as I groan and sink back to the flats of my feet. "So what's with breakfast in bed?"

"One of the scouts found something."

My fidgeting ceases as I stare hard at him. "Have they found a real supply line this time?"

I would give props to Eamon for his calm demeanor, but the glow in his eyes doesn't fool me. He's just as anxious behind that stony façade as I am. I poke him in the stomach and race off, ducking low for the last thirty feet of the tunnel before I slide into the Temple.

"I see you got the good news," Toren says as he snatches up a sniper rifle from the altar beside him and crosses the room toward us. "You might want to keep it down a bit though. The kids are still asleep."

"Really?" I frown. It's impossible to tell what time it is from this deep within the cave system.

"You slept like the dead last night. Snored so loud I thought the whole mountain would fall in on us," Eamon taunts as he ducks out of the tunnel. He stands upright, reminding me of how much height he's added over the past year. His face has lost the childhood baby fat I used to love to tease him over. The lines on his face betray his maturity. By all intents and purposes, he's a man now. How did I fail to notice that?

"Ha-ha." I stick out my tongue at him over my shoulder before turning back toward Toren. "So are you sending us on another wild goose chase? I thought we were going to track the tremors today."

Toren shakes his head. "That can wait a day. Right now, our top priority has to be food, clothes and ammo."

I frown. "What about all of those supplies I brought back with me?"

Eamon scoffs as he stops at my side. "Zahra can't figure out what half that stuff is. She certainly didn't seem too impressed with your soda."

I grin back at him. Images of Zahra covered in sticky foam will keep me occupied for quite some time. Toren hands Eamon the rifle and motions for me to follow him to the map he was staring at the night before. On it is a grid of red x's and check marks. I recognize many of them as locations our parents hit before they died. The others have been faulty guesses of where the Caldonians might run the next supply line. We've been wrong four times in the past six months.

After the Assault began, our parents fled into the mountains with a small group of survivors. Not long after the smoke lifted they discovered a Caldonian base set up less than five miles away, an alien hub for transporting enough firepower to control the Midwest. The rebellion was born out of duty and honor. Our small group tried to hold off the Caldonians in the forest, to give America a chance to get back on its feet.

That never happened.

When the last of our parents died, many of us wanted to make a mass exodus right out of this region and leave behind the painful memories, but Toren convinced us to stay behind and honor our parents' legacy. To keep fighting. That was the day I renewed my oath to the rebellion, knowing that my place was right here.

"Antone stumbled across a group of Caldonians last night while on patrol. Apparently, there's some discourse among the soldiers about changing the route at the last minute. I think many still fear our attacks." Toren says, running his finger along a red line that runs near the base of our mountain.

"We haven't attacked in six months," Eamon says, rubbing the light stubble along his chin. I can tell he's just as frustrated as I am about this fact.

"I don't like it." I chew on my lower lip as I point to the ravine just beyond Toren's finger. "There's plenty of tree cover to hide in on either side. Why risk an ambush this far from their base unless it's a trap?"

Toren nods, withdrawing his hand from the map as he straightens his shoulders. "That's what I'm thinking. It's too easy."

"But can we risk not going?" Eamon asks.

"No." Toren shakes his head. "I'm only sending you two. No one else knows about this and I expect it to remain that way."

Everything about this mission makes me nervous and very suspicious. "You know this can't be a coincidence."

Eamon's stares hard me. "You think this is because of your little adventure into the City?"

I refuse to be baited by him as I grip the edge of the stone. "Bastien and I saw stuff we weren't supposed to see. It only makes sense that this Drakon would come looking for us. Maybe they think we're stupid enough to lead them right up to our front door. He can't possibly know that Bastien and I are strangers."

Rubbing his temples, I can tell Eamon is beginning to suffer from yet another headache. He's been having those frequently over the past couple weeks. I joked that it was just birthday jitters, but he brushed me off.

I've often wondered why I'm the only one who seems amused by the fact that our birthdays are all within a week of each other. Aminah says I have too much time on my hands to think up crazy fantasies, but Eamon has always claimed his belief that it is fate, or something equally ludicrous.

"I want you both to observe for now. Do not engage the aliens or give them any reason to sense your presence. I want to know what they're planning before we make our move."

I stuff my hands into my pockets and bite down on the sharp remark that pops into my head. Toren's right, whether I want to admit that or not. My gut tells me Eamon and I are walking into a trap. Better to get in and out alive.

Toren is a great leader, a million times better than I could ever be, but I don't always agree with his decisions. He moves with caution where I tend to be more adventurous.

I lean over the map and tap the weathered paper with my index finger as I survey the terrain. "If they come down this gully then we can watch from above. Eamon and I can split up, stake claim to a couple of pine trees and watch the parade without the Caldonians being any the wiser."

"Eamon?"

"It's a good plan." He winks at me before stabbing his finger near one of the x's upon a small elevation. "We'll set up here and here. If we're not back by sundown…" he lets his words trail off.

No one leaves the cave to find you after dusk and risks the safety of the entire commune. That's the number one law and we live according to it.

Toren gives us a curt nod. "Go on then. Just make sure you're back in time."

Eamon turns and heads across the Temple toward our dwindling armory. Toren snags my arm as I step away. I pause and look back over my shoulder. "Aminah will never forgive me if something happens to you."

"I know." And I do. It has taken Aminah nearly six months to reach the point where she can say her parents' names without bursting into tears. "We'll be fine."

A smirk pulls at the corners of Toren's lips. "It's not Eamon that I'm worried about."

I grin. "I *can* follow orders, you know."

"Can and will are two completely different things."

My laugh echoes around the domed room. "Don't I know it!"

NINE

The scent of pine surrounds me as I clamber up a large evergreen. Thick, bushy, boughs obscure me from sight as I settle into a crook and wait. Eamon should be in position by now but I can't see any sign of him. North—that's the only guide I have for his direction.

I sink back against the tree trunk and blow out a breath. It hangs in the air like a wispy cloud before me. I swipe my hand to disperse it and tie a wide strip of cloth over my mouth and nose. I tuck my hands into my armpits for warmth and settle in for what I fear will be a very long day.

The days are getting shorter and the winds more brutal. Winter has officially shoved autumn out the back door and locked away the heat, leaving little time for the leaves to decay properly. More snow fell overnight and, judging by the low hanging gray clouds and the rising winds, the sky is ready to unleash round two right on top of us.

"Perfect." I huddle into my sweater, smirking over how furious Zahra will be to find me swaddled in one of Eamon's shirts when I return. "Three layers of clothes and I'm still gonna be a popsicle by tonight."

The morning hike was enough to keep me warm but, now that I've found my hiding spot, the cold has begun to seep in, nipping at any exposed skin. As the minutes drag out into hours, I struggle to keep my extremities from falling asleep. I can't help but wonder if all of this is a ruse to waste my time instead of capture me.

Surely, if this is a trap, it's been laid for me. I don't really think Commander Drakon will let me slip through his fingers that easily. From the moment Toren pointed out the location of this ridge, I knew I was the intended target.

When I bend to smack life back into my toes, pain in my side flares and I'm forced to bite down on my lip to stifle a cry.

Pulling up the frayed hem of Eamon's shirt I can just barely glimpse the red gash raked across my pale skin. I did my best to wash the wounds last night but I fear the heat radiating from my right side. An infection has begun to linger in the area and that can be deadly out here if not treated properly.

All thoughts of my wound vanish when a sudden jolt makes me grasp the tree for stability. The pine needles tremble as another vibration rises through the tree bark.

What the heck was that? An earthquake?

I shove the boughs out of my way and cast a quick glance up at the sun to calculate it's general location in the sky. My best estimate is that there's only about an hour until sundown. Considering we have an hour hike back up the mountain, we're running too close for comfort.

Eamon should have sent the signal by now. It's his job to watch the sun.

Fear worms its way into my stomach as I look to the north. The vibrations through the branches come faster and harder. As I rise up onto my toes, teetering precariously on the branch, I realize the Caldonians are coming, but they aren't alone.

A large group of Squaddies scours the ravine below. Just beyond them is a sight that makes my skin tingle with trepidation and my stomach drop to the ground.

Three large metal orbs crash through the forest, splintering hundred-year-old pines into kindling. Their hulls are oil slick black with a triple barrel laser cannon perched atop the bulbous body of the eight-legged monstrosities. I've had my fair share of nasty run-ins with spiders in these woods but these are by far the scariest I've ever seen.

I didn't know the Caldonians built those spiders. I've only seen the Sky Ships before. Maybe these are the Droners Bastien spoke about. I gulp back my terror as I realize this isn't a new supply route, it's an interstate.

I frantically descend from the tree; my only thought is to get to Eamon. He would never have missed the signal unless he was in trouble.

My legs tingle as my boots slam into the snow. I wince, pausing only a second to sling my rifle around to the front before I dash through the woods, weaving through the trees with far less grace than usual.

I hadn't realized how bitterly cold the air had grown while I sat in my insulated hiding spot. The winds whip my hair into a tangled frenzy about my face as the first drops of freezing rain begin to pelt down from the sky. I yank my hair back and stuff it into my shirt as visibility quickly narrows and my pace slows. Each step becomes precarious as the icy mixture creates a slick glaze over the sloping ground.

My finger is poised just over the trigger, ready to fire the instant my position is discovered. My ammo is limited; I have to make every shot count until I find Eamon and get us out of here.

I cry out as a wide laser beam slams into a tree less than ten feet away and blasts me backward. I shake my head, ears ringing loudly as I scramble to my feet. The tree just ahead creaks as it plummets to the ground.

The metallic groan of the giant spider alerts me to the Droner's position. I dive behind a tree and clutch my rifle to my chest, fighting back against my rising fear as I realize there's no way I can compete with that thing's firepower.

Black clad figures disappear behind trees faster than I can take aim. I know I'm being surrounded and there is nothing I can do about it.

Looking at the trees around me, I notice that most are tall and barren. A variety of evergreens dot the landscape but even those can't hide me forever.

"Get the girl!"

The shout echoes through the ravine and immediately I'm on my feet and dashing back the way I came. The Squaddies' pursuit is loud and cumbersome as they tussle with tangled bushes that seem to appear out of nowhere in the fading light. The grinding gears of a drone send me flailing to the south, away from Eamon and parallel with the mountain. I don't know this section of the forest well enough to know of any hiding spots so I run as far and as fast as I can.

The trees narrow around me, herding me through a briar patch. I ignore the stitch in my side as I sprint along the uneven terrain. Liquid fire smolders in my chest, stealing away each breath.

I bound down a small slope, leaving the aliens scrambling up the other side. The earth unsettles around me and I ride it like a wave to the bottom. Misjudging the distance, I face-plant into the ground, choking on a mixture of snow and dirt.

"Over here! She's hit the ravine!" A voice calls from the top of the hill.

"Crap," I grunt as I push to my feet and stumble through the woods. My heart thunders in my ears as I gasp for breath. I can't outrun them.

Glancing back over my shoulder, I watch as a handful of Squaddies spill over the hill, only a few seconds behind me. I sprint through a small clearing and halt by the tree line.

I spin, pull the rifle up to my eye and fire off a few rounds. The shots fly wide but I manage to send three aliens crashing to the ground as the bullets zing past. I inhale deeply, hold it for a couple seconds and then release a long, slow breath. I take aim, zeroing in on a tree branch hanging directly above the aliens.

The blast shoves my shoulder back, jarring it in its socket. The bullet slams into a branch, burrowing deep into the flesh but it remains firmly attached to the tree. I grit my teeth and take aim again, knowing my window of opportunity is rapidly narrowing. With a second jolt to my shoulder, the bullet sends it tumbling to the ground.

I hear shouts but don't wait around to see if I hit anyone. Slinging the gun back over my shoulder, I turn and sprint into the trees, leaping over raised tree roots and fallen logs. Shadows kiss the far horizon as I burrow into the eastern forest, heading in the opposite direction of my camp. If I run much further, I will risk hitting the outskirts of the City.

I collapse against a tree trunk, sucking in great gulps of air. The stich in my side flares into an agonizing spasm among my ribs. A chill seeps through my clothing as the temperature continues to plummet with the fading light. Trickles of freezing rain drip down my neck, snaking down my spine.

The forest only partially shields me from the elements. Gusts of wind whip through the tall trees with ferocious vengeance. I hunch my shoulders and brush wet strands out of my face. I glance around, listening for the sound of boots on the packed dirt floor.

I lean my head back and look up through the trees that tower high overhead like naked arrows pointing to the darkened sky. Only a squirrel can climb high enough to reach those branches. Climbing is definitely not an option.

Dropping my gaze to the ground, I survey the landscape around me. In the fading light, it's hard to make out much more than clumps of rotting leaves whipped around by the winds, snagging in the hovels of gnarled tree roots. I can see a few bramble bushes scattered among the trees but nothing useful for hiding.

I'm going to have to keep running. This thought leaves me weary before I even take my first step. I hunch over to fill my lungs, praying the cold air will restore some of my former energy.

A grim thought sinks in as I realize I can barely see my hands propped on my knees. Dusk has arrived. There will be no one sent to search for me. I'm on my own, in unfamiliar territory. This night can't possibly get any worse.

Resolved to begin my run, I stand up but immediately freeze. A lone soldier stands less than ten feet from me. A mask is pulled up over his face to hide his features. I have no idea how he snuck up on me. My senses may be slightly dull from exhaustion, but I am far from careless.

His laser gun hums, glowing a beautiful shade of emerald. *He must know who I am.*

"Don't try to run. If you do I will be forced to shoot." I tilt my head at the musical lilt to the alien's voice. It exudes peace and calm, a sore contradiction for the weapon he has targeted on my heart.

I can't help but stare into his eyes. In the dim light, they seem to glow from within. When he blinks, sparks appear to ignite around his pupils—beautiful and terrifying at the same time.

He reaches up and pulls his face covering away. I stifle a gasp as my gaze falls over the smooth planes of his face. Shoulder length hair, as white as a frozen lake in the depths of winter, flows over his broad shoulders.

His sheer beauty steals my breath away. My eyes narrow as my fingers ache to reach for my gun. "Get out of my way."

He shakes his head. "Afraid I can't do that. I've got orders."

"I'm sure you do." I take a step away from the tree and he mirrors my movements, not allowing me any advantage.

His gaze shifts down to my chest where the strap for my rifle crosses, lying against my breastbone. "Remove your weapon and toss it to the side."

"Not gonna happen."

"I'm not asking." His gun buzzes as he fingers the trigger. Sparks shoot out from the cannon, fizzling out a couple of feet from me.

I stare down the alien as I pull the shoulder strap over my head and toss the gun out in front of me. "Further."

It takes three steps to reach my gun. Only two more will put me nose to nose with the alien. He watches my foot as I loop it under the gun and toss it to the side. "No, don't-"

I drop and sweep my leg around to knock him off his feet. He lands on his tailbone as I roll to my knees, elbowing him in the chest. With a flash of silver, I whip out my dagger, slice through the laser strap that runs across his chest and scramble away.

I crumple to the ground as he yanks my foot. My forehead slams into the ground and a wad of dirt fills my mouth as he claws up my back for the laser. I buck under him, trying to resist, but I can feel the gun slip from my fingers.

I roll away and leap to my feet, far more unsteady this time. He doesn't give me a chance to recover before he tackles me back to the ground. I gasp for breath as I beat against his back, scratching at the exposed flesh of his neck.

Sparring with Eamon could never have prepared me for this. The alien's reflexes are lightning fast and well executed, unlike Eamon's more cautious attacks.

It's not until he has me pinned me to the ground that I realize he's not actually trying to hurt me. He's merely restraining me.

"Stop fighting. You can't win." His voice is low, non-threatening.

"Watch me," I growl, spitting up into his face.

The instant he breaks eye contact, I toss my weight to the side and elbow him in the ribs. I roll over him and scramble to my feet. He grunts and effortlessly leaps up onto his feet, blocking my escape.

"Either fight me or let me go," I demand.

He slowly circles around me, watching. I counter his actions, easily sinking into my training. "Kyan insisted you be brought to him."

I pause mid-step. "You know Kyan?"

He rises from his slightly crouched position, puffing out his chest with obvious pride. "He was my trainer."

"Why are you hunting me?" I ask, wiping sweat from my brow.

"He needs to speak with you."

"Nice way to send an invitation," I growl, as I cast a glance toward my rifle. It's too far out of reach but maybe I can get him to move a bit to the right so I can dive for it. "I'm not going with you."

He rises to his full height, planting his feet. "Kyan warned me you would say that."

I search his eyes for any sign of fear, even a trickle of apprehension, but all I see staring back at me is stark resolution. I have no doubt this man will beat me unconscious just to follow orders.

I dive for my gun and pray that if I miss, death will come quickly.

TEN

One second my fingers are around the barrel of my gun and the next I'm flat on my back, staring straight into the alien's glowing laser. The heat radiating from the core drives back the cold night air.

"How did you do that?" I gasp, clutching my ribs, which are no doubt already forming a bruise from that blow.

The alien stares down at me. "You ask a lot of questions."

I snort as I glare up at him. "At least I'm not the one who's too chicken to pull the trigger." He frowns and the gun whirs to life

Smooth, real smooth, I silently rant as I struggle to rise to my feet. I stare him down, unwilling to blink for fear of giving him another advantage. The gun rises with me, steady in his hand. A strange tingling ripples along my shoulders as I hold my ground, but I ignore it.

"So what now?" I challenge.

His uncertainty plays visibly across his face. I take a step forward but freeze as the laser core flares from emerald to scarlet. I raise my hands. Fair enough. I've pushed my limits.

"You're going to have to kill me, you know," I say with as much bravery as I can muster. "I refuse to go back."

He opens his mouth to speak but jerks his attention to the side as three Squaddies approach at a run. "There she is!"

Kyan's lapdog steps back, allowing room for his kinsmen to take over. I glare up at him as the aliens knock me to the ground. "Good work," one of them calls over his shoulder. My captor nods and steps further back.

Cold metallic clamps close around my wrists. "No!"

I strain against the lock until the restraints slice into my flesh. Anger splinters my thoughts as I feel a new thorn branch tattooed around my heart. I welcome the heat this time.

"What will you do with her?" Kyan's messenger asks.

A large burly soldier yanks me to my feet. His dirty hands cup my cheeks, rolling my head side to side to get a good look at me. "She's heading back to the City. I'm sure we can find *something* useful to occupy her time until Commander Drakon arrives."

My vision snaps back into crystal clarity at his words, and I spit into his face. His leer shifts into a snarl as he raises his hand. I notice three of his teeth are missing before I try to duck. His fist slams into my jaw and my world careens as I whip around and slam into a tree. I scream as he plunges his hands into my hair and slams my face into the tree trunk. Chunks of bark grind against my cheekbone, tearing my skin.

His fingers snag in my hair, ripping strands from my scalp. I stumble back, expecting to plummet to the ground, but instead land in someone's arms. I scream and thrash, fighting to be free.

Flames lick across my shoulders and shoot down my arms. Anger shifts into rage, easing the pain of the raw flesh around my heart. My thoughts darken as I cling to the knowledge that when I get out of this, I will make them pay.

"Easy." Kyan's friend tightens his arms around my stomach, stilling my fight. I try to resist his attempt to pacify me, but the irritation rolling off him silences my reservations as I realize it's not directed at me.

"You didn't have to do that," he growls up at the vicious alien.

The man's chest rises and falls as if he'd run a marathon instead of beating up a defenseless girl. He clenches his fists, popping each knuckle in turn. "Commander Drakon won't care if she's a little roughed up, Beus."

"Perhaps not, but I do. Stand down."

A bushy eyebrow rises as cracked lips peel back to reveal those three missing teeth. "You've got no authority over me, dog. Commander Drakon supersedes Kyan."

I hold my breath as the other two soldiers close in around us. Their guns are no longer leveled at my chest, but at the alien beside me. I watch as their guns charge, glowing crimson. The cores rotate rapidly, spiraling into a collage of red as they finger their triggers. I glance up at Beus and am surprised to find him staring at me instead of his attackers. "I am sorry," he whispers.

Energy erupts from my chest, flooding down the length of my body. It sizzles against my skin, warming every inch of my chilled body. The air crackles with electricity around me. Steam rises in tiny wisps as trails of freezing rain along my neck turn to vapor. From the corner of my vision, I see my hair beginning to lift from my shoulders.

An invisible force fills me with strength and the pain from my wounds fades as my nerve endings alight. I feel powerful.

I look up at the sound of three triggers clicking back. My vision illuminates red with the full force of the lasers. "No!"

The shackles around my wrists snap open as I throw out my hands and knock Beus backward onto the ground. I dive on top of him and bury my head in his neck. Heat scorches the tips of my hair as I shield him with my body. The sound of splintering wood echoes around me and my chest vibrates as a tree behind us slams to the ground.

I raise my head and stare deep into the face of my enemy. I was wrong about Beus' eyes. They aren't just amber, there are flecks of dark chocolate mixed in as well. He stares at me, wide-eyed with shock.

His chest rises and falls, lifting my weight with ease. I can feel his heart racing against mine and smell the scent of his adrenaline laced sweat.

He doesn't speak as he turns his head to the side. I feel the hitch in his breath and turn to follow his gaze. Three bodies lie crumpled among the remains of a large evergreen that fell just to the right of us. Blood seeps from their ears and noses. I can't tell if they are breathing.

"What happened?" I gasp, scrambling off him.

Beus sits up, staring at me with a mixture of fear and awe. "How did you do that?"

"I have no ide-" I flatten to the ground as a laser fireball screams overhead, setting the trees around us ablaze. Smoke rises into the air as I cup my hands over my mouth.

"Watch out!" Beus lands on top of me and rolls us behind a tree as a second laser scorches a line straight across the ground we just occupied. "We have to get out of here. It's not safe for you."

I rise, viewing the world in slow motion. I can see the fear on Beus' face, but I don't feel it myself. Energy courses through my veins, electrifying my senses. "No."

Instead of running further into the woods, I step out from behind the tree and plant my feet. The large bulbous head of a spider drone rotates as a triple barrel cannon locks onto me. It stands nearly fifteen feet high, its eight legs buried deep in the frozen earth. It's hard to make out the contours of its hull in the dark of night, but there is no mistaking the deadly laser aimed straight at me.

Logically I know I'm facing down death, but I can't explain why I'm unafraid. No, I am more than that. I am mysteriously confident.

The large cannon heats up, swirling with far more ferocity than the guns the Squaddies carry. The laser blows back my hair as I take another step forward, challenging the metal beast.

"No, don't!" I ignore Beus' warning.

Blinding light spirals down the barrel of the gun and torpedoes toward me. "Stop!" I shout, without flinching.

Like a bomb detonating, a shockwave bursts from my hands, creating snow tornados as it races out from me. The invisible force barrels through the forest, bowing limbs and uprooting buried tree roots as it goes.

Heat clusters around me as I hold the laser beam aloft with my mind. A trickle of sweat winds down from my brow, but I show no other signs of effort. Beus steps out from behind the tree, amazement deeply etched into his features. It's not the red orb hovering over my head that he stares at, but me. "It is true."

"What is?"

He steps closer, reaching out his hand, as if he wants to touch me, but pulls back instead. His lips purse as his gaze flits over my face. "You don't know who you are, do you?"

"Does it look like I do?" I grunt, feeling the laser drop an inch. The longer I hold it aloft, the heavier it begins to feel.

"Kyan was right," Beus mutters to himself. I can feel the weight of his gaze. "Just look at what you've done. I've never seen anyone with such control."

"What the heck is happening to me?" I shift my weight and the laser orb moves with me.

He drops to his knees. "You're becoming the Shadow Walker."

"You're telling me I really am one of you?" I dart a glance at him, vowing to launch this laser at him if he doesn't start giving me some answers.

"Yes," he begins to wring his hands. "Your birthright happened sooner than we expected. Kyan needs to speak to you before it's too late."

His eyes widen with fright as he stares up at the awestruck alien leaning over the console in the spider drone. I can see his hands holding some sort of device to his ear as his lips move rapidly.

It's only a matter of time until the entire City pours out into these woods. I'll have every alien on my trail.

"They can't be allowed to find you. Not like this. You have to leave." Beus' voice trembles.

I snort. "You think?"

"No, it's not just the machines you have to worry about. It's everyone. You can't trust any of my kind."

"News flash, dude, I don't trust *you*." I turn to face the spider, but keep Beus in the corner of my eye.

I feel something shift within me, a new presence in my mind that I've never felt before. Something dark and sinister slithers slowly through my thoughts. Whispers of revenge, of death, breathe in my ear.

"What will they do with me when they find me?" I ask.

"Drakon will unleash you. You will massacre hundreds, thousands of your kind. You have no idea how powerful you are." Beus pales. "You're the weapon Drakon has been searching for, the tool to wipe your race off the face of your planet for good."

Illyria. I blink as a male voice penetrates my thoughts. *Don't give in to the Shadows. They will destroy you.*

"How do you know my name?" I shout, glaring at Beus. "And why the heck can I hear you in my head?"

The corners of his lips twitch. "It's not me."

I frown. "What's going on?"

He shrugs. "Try talking back."

Who are you?

You already know the answer to that.

"Kyan," I hiss aloud.

Beus' eyebrows rise. "That's not possible. His reach isn't that great."

It is because your mind connected to my mind, Illyria. You have summoned me, not the other way around.

A chill settles over my limbs and I feel the weight of the laser for the first time. An ache begins in my shoulders, pressing down on me.

I can help you and your friends, Kyan whispers.

What do my friends have to do with this?

Everything.

I don't want your help. I just want to be left alone, I shout back at him.

You need me. I have the answers that you seek.

The chill continues to spread as the flames recede from my arms, slithering back to my shoulders. The pain in my heart increases and I gasp as I feel a new scrolled mark appear over my breastbone.

Like a short circuit, I can feel the unstableness of my grasp on the laser. The whispers in my mind fade, and along with it my anger.

What are you doing to me?

Nothing. This is your own doing. Your power is fueled by your anger, and this empowers the Shadows.

You're not making any sense. I grit my teeth, fighting hard to keep the laser aloft.

You've unleashed a power that you cannot comprehend or even begin to control. With a single thought, you can kill everyone around you, but you are still vulnerable.

What power? I don't understand. Why can't anyone just give me a straight answer?

You will, but you must go...now! Beus will cover your tracks.

The instant I feel him withdraw from my mind, the ground begins to quake. I glance beyond the drone and see three more breach the hill.

"Go!" Beus screams. I nod and throw out my hands. The fireball slams into the hull of the spider and explodes in a rain of sparks. The black metal bubbles, dripping to the ground as the laser burrows through to the inner core.

"Run!" Beus shoves me ahead as he dives behind a tree. I glance back over my shoulder and watch as the spider begins to shudder and jerk, flailing about. The legs on the right side snap off as the alien within drops to the ground and sprints away.

I shield my eyes as a brilliant white light fills the drone's control room and then implodes. The blast hits me before I can reach a safe distance. Pain radiates through my back as I slam to the ground. I can taste blood as I rise, wincing at the needles of pain winding up my arms and legs. Small slivers of metal burrow into my flesh, cauterizing the skin around the entry points.

Beus rises from the smoke, his pale face smudged. Small tendrils of gray rise from his hair. "Just run. I'll stall them."

I turn to retrieve my rifle, but find it trapped beneath a burning tree branch. I consider reaching for it but Beus shoves me away. "Go!"

I turn and obey, dodging fallen tree limbs. Everywhere I look, flames devour the forest. The crater left by the drone's explosion has left an imprint that oddly looks like a meteorite strike I saw once in a book.

Ducking my head, I run flat out, unsure of where to go. All that matters is that I get away.

ELEVEN

I weave through the woods, struggling to maintain any semblance of a jog. The dense, low hanging clouds allow only a fleeting glimpse of moonlight to penetrate. The shadows blend into a gloomy, blackened void, making it nearly impossible to see five feet in front of me. The freezing rain has shifted into small pellets of ice, bouncing off the ground around me.

I collapse against a fallen pine tree, panting. My fingers ache from the cold, from nail bed to my palms. A near constant shiver alerts me that I'm teetering on the verge of hypothermia. I need to build a fire, but I can't risk it.

It has been over an hour since I heard any shouts. The ground has remained still under my feet, but I worry what will happen if I draw attention to myself. I know they are out there, somewhere.

I bend over and beat feeling back into my toes, stomping away the needles that prick my calves. I can't keep going like this. Shelter has become a necessity I can no longer ignore.

I try to stand, sinking into the unsettled earth running the length of the log. The soil gives way and spills into a space beyond. Dropping to my knees, I wiggle my fingers through the small hole, listening as clumps of soil patter as it lands below.

Realizing there's a small opening on the other side of the fallen pine tree, I throw my leg over and lower myself into the hollow below. A layer of ice pellets blanket a small section of the space, but the thick pile of leaves and fallen pine needles covering the ground is too inviting to pass up.

I sink to my knees and brush away the snow, grateful for the evergreen canopy that covers some of the space, sheltering me from the bitter winds. I scoop big piles of the foliage over my feet and legs to provide insulation and camouflage should anyone stumble across me in the night. I cover my waist and much of my chest before stuffing my hands under my armpits and lean back against the dirt wall. My teeth chatter so hard my jaw aches. I clamp down as tight as I can and stare up through the boughs to the clouds above. I've never felt so alone before, so completely isolated from my friends and my home. I know I should be grateful to be alive, but I struggle to think beyond my fear for Eamon. Did he make it back to camp? Was he captured? I can't bear to think of the alternative.

Fear for his safety keeps my eyelids open as the moon begins its slow voyage across the sky, behind the ever-shifting veil of clouds.

My eyes pop open and the sluggishness of sleep flees. I can hear the whispers still speaking to me. They haunt my dreams and now my waking moments too.

The hairs on the back of my neck rise as footsteps crunch through the thin glaze of ice on the ground above. Adrenaline pumps through my veins, waking every nerve in my body as I crane my neck to see. Only darkness meets my gaze.

I sink back and hold my breath as more footsteps approach. It's hard to tell how many there are from within this small hovel but, judging by normal alien scouting parties there should be at least five, each armed with a laser gun.

I press my fingers to the ground, silently waiting for the tremor of a spider drone. When none comes, I release a breath. At least they're alone.

A light flares nearby and the Caldonians' voices drift toward me on the wind. I can hear dissent among the group, mostly bickering over who has to hunt for food. Apparently, I'm not the only one left weary because of the manhunt.

"You two go collect firewood, but don't go too far. I don't like the look of this area. It's too open for my liking." The authoritative voice is gruff, but I detect a hint of distress in his tone. Perhaps tales of my exploits have spread quickly through the ranks.

I grin, silently pumping my fists as the Squaddies set about creating a camp.

Two figures pass by my den and I freeze. Even with the scant moonlight from above, a straight glance in my direction would probably betray my location. I silently lift prayers heavenward as the men stoop low and collect small branches for kindling.

My heart thumps against my ribs as the aliens move on, lumbering loudly through the ankle high iced leaves that blanket the hillside. I slowly rise, wincing as the pine needles fall in a rustling cascade around me. I hold my breath, waiting for the hum of a laser gun pointed at me, but it never comes.

Numbness steals feeling from my toes but I can't risk stomping. I bend over and rub the tops of my boots, breathing out a slow sigh of relief as the stinging cold begins to fade and feeling returns.

I duck low as the two aliens return, arms overloaded with firewood and kindling. My gaze flits about the forest, searching for the others. None appear as the two begin to make a fire.

My stomach is attacked by nervous tension as I ponder my escape. I can't stay here and risk being discovered, but my only chance of escape is to run parallel to them and head for a lake I know not too far from here. On my way back from the City I noticed a small hut perched near the shore as I passed. Maybe I can huddle down there for a while until the aliens move on.

I wait ten agonizing minutes until three more aliens appear from the woods. Their arms are full and their gait hampered by the weight of whatever it is they carry. As the soldiers stoop to unload their kill, I scramble out of the hollow and swerve to the left, away from the flickering light of the fire. The worn soles of my shoes slip and slide on the icy leaves as I barrel through the woods. Moonlight falls over the forest in muffled gray tones, just enough to see and be seen.

My heart plummets to my stomach as I hear a shout from behind me. "That's the girl. Get her!"

"Crap," I growl as I urge my legs to move faster. I twist through the trees, gripping their trunks to throw myself around the next like a slalom skier. Up ahead I can see large patches of sparkling water appear as the clouds shift to allow beams of moonlight through. I don't know if I can make it. The aliens saw me too soon.

My lungs burn with each icy breath; I pump my arms and try to push through the pain. I don't dare look over my shoulder for fear of slowing. I can hear their footsteps with agonizing clarity, spreading out to surround me.

Nearly there, I chant as the water comes into full view. I nearly weep with relief as a small boathouse and dock come into view. I immediately shift course and run full out. My pursuers shout a warning as they fight to ensnare me in their narrowing trap.

Heat singes the ends of my damp strands of hair as a red beam blazes past. The scent of burnt hair trails behind me as I leap onto the dock and race for the small boat at the end. My boots pound the weathered boards, unsettling the rusted nails as I pass. It's a miracle that I don't spill over into the frigid waters as I leap over a hole and land on the last remaining rickety board.

I snatch the towrope from a post and leap into the fiberglass vessel. My arms pinwheel as I fight for balance, terrified of capsizing the small motor boat. The sky streaks with crimson laser fire as I wrestle with the starter cord of the engine. It sputters and smokes but fails to start, beginning to float away from the dock because of my momentum.

"Come on!" I scream, beating the dented motor. My heads whips around as the first pair of boots hits the dock behind me. I'm running out of time. I kick the motor and then pull the cord. "Start!"

Idiot! I silently berate myself. *Of course it's not going to start. The fuel is probably fifteen years old!*

A blast of heat rushes down my fingertips and into the motor. The metal glows red just before the engine turns over. I whip the motor around and steer the boat away from the dock.

The small craft rocks wildly as an alien leaps from the end of the dock and crashes to his knees in the bow as the boat passes. Two more follow his lead but miss their landing and thump onto the side of the boat. One cries out as his ribs crack and he slips down into the wake of the boat. The other clings to the side with clenched fingers and awkwardly flips his leg over the side.

I grit my teeth and race toward open water, desperately trying not to think of how bitterly cold the driving winds are. If I can get far enough away from the dock, I might stand a chance against two Squaddies. Any more than that and I'm in big trouble.

Several laser beams blast from the shoreline as I twist the throttle and speed toward the center of the lake. The alien on the side yanks himself into the boat, dropping like an anchor against the hull, while the other rises and plants his feet, shifting his weight to compensate with the bouncing boat. I stare at him, silently panicking as I note the murderous gleam in his eye. This man does not intend to take me back alive.

His eyes are deep red velvet and his pupils are outlined with coal black. His fiery gaze, coupled with his freakishly large frame, is enough to make my blood run cold. There is no way I can take this man out on my own, not without a weapon.

Red Eye dips low and helps the other to his feet. The second alien, tall and lanky, turns his honey-colored eyes on me, crouching to crawl forward over the two rows of metal benches. Each move is in perfect sync with the boat, despite my best attempts to rock them out.

"I'm gonna have fun gutting you, little girl," Red Eye taunts as he leers at me over his partner's shoulder.

"But Commander Drakon wants her alive." The soldier looks back at Red Eye.

"What the Commander doesn't know won't hurt him, now will it?" Red Eye crouches low in the boat, waiting for his turn.

My skin begins to tingle as the soldier tosses rotted life vests overboard, clearing a straight path to me. The hairs on my arms stand upright as I meet Red Eye's fierce gaze and shiver.

The air crackles with energy as the clouds overhead begin to swirl, coiling like a venomous snake. I can feel power coursing through my veins in rhythmic waves, but I have no control over it. The winds seem to have a mind of their own.

I release my hold on the motor and grip the edge of the boat as it rocks in the rising waves, careening out of control. The soldiers hesitate as they glance between me and the swirling vortex overhead.

"What's she doing?" The lanky alien cries.

"Playing with your head," Red Eye grunts and pushes his partner forward.

A blast of wind hits the honey-eyed alien with the force a battering ram. I can hear his ribs crunch as he flies out of the boat and smacks into the choppy waves nearly twenty feet away. He sinks fast and without a fight.

I stare down Red Eye. Instead of fear in his eyes, I see pure, unadulterated rage. My stomach begins to twist as violently as the clouds as a funnel dips to the water's surface. With an explosion of mist, a waterspout forms. The winds beat against the hull of the boat as I huddle down low.

Red Eye grunts as he's tossed off his feet by the rising waves. I swipe my water-drenched hair back from my face as I wrench the motor around to steer directly toward the tornado. The alien's head whips around and, for the first time, I detect fear in his dilated pupils. "You're insane!"

"Just figuring that out, huh?" I shout back, fighting to hold the boat steady. A stinging pain grows just above my heart and travels toward my shoulder. I grit my teeth and ignore the new tattoo carving its way into my flesh.

"You'll kill us both!"

I nod. "Probably, but then again, I've got a feeling you're not man enough to stick around and play chicken with a tornado."

With a menacing scowl, he swears and leaps over the side of the boat. He bounces twice, tossed like a ragdoll, and sinks beneath the waves. I watch for a second too long and scream out as the motor is ripped from my hands. The world careens around me as the boat slams into a wall of water and hurls me out.

Pain envelopes my body as I slam into the lake's surface. I gasp for breath, fighting the pull of the swirling water as the clouds retract, silencing the tornado. Everything hurts as I fight back to the surface. My arms feel heavy and intolerably weak.

I dig and pull against the water, fighting to remain above the choppy surface. Glancing at the shoreline, I realize I'm out too far. I don't have the strength to make it.

I pump my arms, spinning in a circle in search of the boat, but it's nowhere to be seen. It's probably sinking to the depths of the lake by now.

"Help!" I scream, choking as water laps over my face. I spit out the glacial water and scream again until my throat is raw.

I can barely feel my feet or my fingers. The weight of my clothes is too much for me. I embrace the exhaustion and feel sweet relief, knowing that my struggle is about to be all over.

TWELVE

Wet hair whips about my face, tangling in my eyelashes. I can feel lake water clinging to my skin as frigid winds nip at my face and bare legs. My arms and torso are concealed within a warm, soft material I can't quite place. If feels almost like a coat, but I know I didn't have one on. I sway, moving in rhythmic motions as strong arms hold me close.

I try to remember where I am and why I'm being carried. My thoughts are jumbled as my eyes flutter open. I stare up into the dense treetops and see that night hangs thick over the forest, the moon glowing dimly behind the clouds. I become aware of aches spreading the length of my body. My lungs feel like fire in my chest and I feel incredibly weak as well.

What happened to me?

"Easy," a deep voice soothes. "You're safe now."

I roll my head and look up into my savior's face, shrouded by dark shadow. It's hard to make out any definite details. His scent is strongly masculine, tinged with pine and smoke. His arms are strong, easily carrying my weight. I close my eyes, overwhelmed by the effort it takes to think.

"That was quite a spill you took back there."

I shiver, unsure if it's from the cold or from the resonance of his deep voice. "Thank…" I frown, forcing the chattering of my teeth to cease. "Thank you."

His teeth appear to glow in the darkness. I can barely make out the fullness of his lips as he smiles. "You're welcome."

I wish I could see more of his face, but he remains infuriatingly veiled as he shifts to focus on our path through the woods. I reach up and rub my head, feeling a rather large bump over my temple.

Time seems irrelevant as I pretend not to stare at him. I fight back against the exhaustion that weighs me down. My curiosity over my guardian angel is too much for me to let go.

Strong calloused hands grip the back of my knees as he clutches me to his chest. His powerful body propels us easily through the woods. He never slows and never seems to fatigue.

"Who are you?"

His head tilts down as a wide grin stretches across his face. "Wow, you must've hit your head pretty hard back there, Princess."

"You!" I weakly struggle to be free of his grasp. "Put me down, Bastien!"

"Not gonna happen."

I fight to pull my fragmented thoughts together as I arch my back to make it harder for him to contain me. "I'm warning you…"

A deep rumbling laughter vibrates in his chest as his arms clamp down on my legs. Too weak to resist, I buckle and collapse against his chest. "You're going to get yourself hurt. You nearly drowned a few minutes ago, so chill out!"

What had been an invigorating encounter has turned into a complete annoyance. "Please?"

I can feel each muscle in his abdomen constrict as he chuckles. "Still pathetic."

I cross my arms over my chest and fume silently. I refuse to let him see how much it hurts me to do so. The muscles in my arms scream with pain and my back is beyond agony. A sharp stabbing pain radiates through my skull making me wish I'd remained unconscious.

"You left me." Perhaps I should be thankful that he pulled me from death's grasp, but all I feel right now is the sting of his betrayal.

His fingers tense around my arms as his stride lengthens. "I knew you'd make it out. You're a fighter, you're resourceful, and judging by that little display back there at the lake, I'd say you're more than capable of taking care of yourself."

"Apparently not," I grumble as I wriggle in his arms. It's hard not to think about how solid he feels against my arm. His strength is surprisingly pleasant.

My legs twitch involuntarily as sleep begins to snatch me away. Bastien glances down at me as he moves in and out of the moonlight. "You should rest. There'll be plenty of time to hate me later."

"I'm not done with you yet," I yawn. My eyes grow heavy and I realize Bastien has added a bit more sway to his step, to rock me to sleep.

As my eyes flutter closed, I think I hear him whisper, "I sincerely hope not."

When I rouse again, I instantly notice the difference. The biting cold is gone, along with any sign of a wintry gale. Flickering firelight dances along a gray stone ceiling overhead, which melds seamlessly with stone and trails to the floor that I now rest upon.

I swivel my head to take in my surroundings but halt when I find Bastien lounging against the far wall. Self-consciously, I duck further into the oversized woolen sweater that envelopes me. I tuck my knees up inside it, to hide my bare legs. It's only now that I realize how little I'm actually wearing. "You undressed me?"

He shrugs, tapping his fingers against the wall at his sides. "You were freezing. I had to get you warm."

Simply said, but the implication of his mischievous smile burns in my cheeks. Butterflies dive bomb my stomach as I cast him a guarded look. "Where are my clothes?"

"Back at the lake. I plan to go back for them once I know you're alright."

"Did you look?" I demand.

He smirks. "Now wouldn't you like to know?"

My low growl only produces a wide grin, which infuriates me more. "I didn't really see anything."

"How could you not? I'm practically naked."

I'm surprised when he looks unsettled. There's something lurking in the depths of his eyes. Admiration? Perhaps, but if I were to bet my favorite dagger on it, I'd say that it's tortured longing that stares back at me.

I look away, worried that if I keep openly staring at him I might give him the wrong idea. Or the right idea. My waterlogged brain can't seem to sort through the stunning man standing before me with the grimy vagrant I met back in the City.

His hair is clean, a contrast to the grungy matted hair he had the first time we met. I can actually see the raven's wing color tint in his hair. His face still sports light stubble, but it looks well kept. His pants, although still wet from his dive in the lake, look free of stains. It's amazing what a proper bath can do for a guy.

"I thought you were just a dream," I mutter.

"Do you always dream of handsome guys rescuing you?"

"Hardly," I scoff, rolling my eyes. "Besides, I never said you were handsome."

He gives me a knowing wink. "You didn't have to."

I scowl and rub my cheek against the neckline of the sweater. It is soft against my wind burned cheek. I blink, finally registering that Bastien stands before me completely and utterly shirtless. I look up and instantly wish I hadn't.

My gaze roams over the hard planes of his chest. When I dip lower to take in his wet pants, I flush and stare fixedly at the floor.

"Like what you see?"

"I've seen better," I snap, purposefully meeting his direct gaze head on. It's true that Eamon is nice to look at, but he's got nothing on Bastien. I bite my tongue and silently berate myself for even noticing Bastien's looks. "Aren't you cold?"

His muscles shift as he shrugs, but I refuse to show any reaction. "You need the sweater more than I do."

I'm tempted to rip it off and prove to him that I can handle the cold just as well as he can, but the thought of being practically naked in front of him, while conscious, is more than my pride can bear. Instead, I tuck my hands under my arms and lean back against the wall. "So where are we?" I ask, looking around the small space. A bundle of twigs rests against the far wall. I spy two overstuffed burlap sacks lying near the back of the cave. My stomach growls at the thought that they might contain food.

I let one hand drop to my side and curl around the blanket I sit on. It is thin and patched, but provides a satisfactory barrier between the floor and my skin. A small cloth bag has been stuffed to create a makeshift pillow.

"You living here now?"

His mood darkens as he looks toward the cave entrance. "It's homier than the subway car."

The sharp edge to his voice betrays his emotions. Bastien has never lived in the woods before. I can only imagine how difficult this transition must be for him. "I'm sorry you had to leave."

"It was bound to happen sooner or later. I'd just hoped to make it until summer."

I drop my gaze and tuck my arms around my calves as I press my cheek to my knees. The silence is thick between us, but not uncomfortable. "Thank you for saving me, twice."

He clears his throat. "Yeah, it's no big deal."

I shift to give my tailbone a break from the unforgiving floor and wince as the wool sweater grazes my side. Bastien is on the move before a gasp fully crosses my lips. His kneels before me and reaches for my side.

His face hardens as I bat his hand away. "You're hurt. We have to clean your wound or it'll get infected. I would've done it earlier but I was more concerned with getting you warm."

"I'm fine," I insist through gritted teeth.

I hardly see the flash of his hand before he cups my side, squeezing. I cry out and tears sting my eyes. "Fine, huh?"

I gulp down my cries, fighting for a credible defiant glare. Bastien pulls his hand back and shakes his head. "You're the most stubborn person I've ever met."

A pained smile pinches the corners of my lips. "I've been accused of that a time or two."

I half expect him to start lecturing me like Eamon or Toren would in this situation, but instead his familiar smirk settles into place. "I like that."

"Really?" I blink, shocked. "Most people hate that about me."

"That's a shame," he says walking over to kneel beside one of the burlap sacks. He opens the neck of the bag and rummages through the contents. "I find it rather appealing when a girl's not afraid to speak her mind."

I blush through the entire palette of reds before he shifts his attention back to me. I drop my gaze as Bastien approaches with a small bottle and cloth in his hands. He sets them down beside me before disappearing through the cave entrance. He returns with a handful of snow.

"Oh no. No way! I'm not letting you play doctor on me!" I hold out my hands in protest.

"Are you stubborn enough to let me risk frostbite for you?"

I smirk at his challenge and am almost tempted to prolong it, but notice the slight shiver in his fingers. I drop the smirk and submit silently. "I'm really going to regret this," I grumble as I lay down on my side and raise the sweater over my hip, exposing far more of my body than I care to think about.

Holding his hands together, Bastien lowers them over my side and breathes onto the snow, letting the water droplets clean my wound. He places the remainder of the snow directly onto the wound and I nearly moan with relief as it numbs the burning.

Bastien works with steady hands and complete confidence. I wonder where he learned these skills but remember that he said his mother was a teacher. Surely, she had some medical training when she worked in a school with children.

Dirt and blood stain the scrap of tan cloth he uses to clean around the wound. I hiss and try to pull back, but his hand clamps down on my thigh, holding me firmly in place.

"I need you to hold still. I don't have much of this medicine left," he says, as several drops of a cold liquid patter against my side. I can feel it foaming, burning. I groan, gnawing on my lip until the pain subsides.

"There," he says, placing a new scrap of fabric over my side. "That wasn't so bad, was it?"

Yanking the sweater back down over my hip, I rise gingerly to a seated position. He stares openly at me, the slight sheen along his forehead unmistakable as his eyes follow my legs as I curl them back into my sweater. "Do you mind?"

"Not at all."

I curl my arms around my legs, careful to make sure none of my bare skin is showing. "Pervert."

He shifts back onto his knees and tosses the empty bottle into the darkened rear of the cave. "I've been called worse by girls far less appealing than you."

"Girls? What girls?"

His jaw clenches and for a moment, I think he might actually flee my question but he surprises me. "You're not the first person to wander into the City, Illyria. Just the most recent."

My mouth gapes open. "Where did they come from? Somewhere close by?"

He turns so that only his profile is accessible in the flickering firelight. "I don't want to talk about it."

I want to press harder for details, but Bastien clams up completely. I grit my teeth and shove aside my curiosity for now.

The stinging in my side subsides slowly and I realize I have yet to thank him. My pride would seek to stop me, but my mother didn't raise a heathen. "Thank you, for tending to my wound, I mean. I uh…I appreciate the gesture."

Bastien looks at me from the corner of his eye. "Well, that sounded rather painful for you."

I chuckle and drop my head. My drying hair falls over my face, hiding me. I don't know what it is about him that manages to confuse and infuriate me so easily. I realize I don't have the longest of tempers, but where Bastien is concerned, I'm locked and loaded. "I'm not all that good with people. In fact, I kinda suck at it."

"No kidding."

Grabbing the makeshift pillow, I launch it at him. I wince and draw back my arm to protect the new wound etched into my chest. He glances over at me. "That's quite a marking you have on your back."

My eyes narrow as I glare at him. "And my chest?"

A smirk tugs at his lips. "Actually, that one is far more interesting."

I gasp and search the space for something else to throw at him. Unfortunately, the pillow was my only ammo so I settle with glaring at him.

"Where'd you get those markings from?" He asks, daring to glance back at me.

My shoulders rise and fall with a halfhearted shrug. "No clue."

He laughs and turns to face me. "Something else you suck at? Lying."

"Only to you," I grumble, absently picking at a loose thread on Bastien's sweater.

"Hmm," he rubs his stubbled chin. "I wonder why that would be."

My thoughts disperse as he arches an eyebrow. He inches closer, seriously invading my personal space. I can't breathe, can't think. He leans back, watching me fumble for a comeback, but every sarcastic retort abandons me during my time of need.

"You're a very intriguing girl, Illyria," he whispers, brushing a strand of hair back from my temple before he rises and moves toward the back of the cave. His steps are purposeful, as if he's actually trying to restrain the urge to sprint away from me.

I bury my head in my knees as I hear him riffle through his bag. I groan, silently berating myself for failing miserably at our verbal sparring.

I've never met a guy before who challenged me at every step, sometimes actually besting me at my own game. I don't know what is wrong with me tonight.

"What are you doing?" I ask, searching for him in the darkened recesses of the cave.

"Getting dressed. You're welcome to watch if you like." I can sense his smug grin before I look up to see it firmly seated on his handsome face. He walks back toward me, his movement fluid, confident.

"Where did you get that shirt?" I hiss, staring wide-eyed at the three red moons emblazoned across Bastien's chest.

He glances down at the black shirt. "Stole it off one of those Squaddies back in the City the night we were attacked. I don't think he needed it as much as I did."

I stare at him, my suspicion not quite abated. "How'd you get free?"

"I pretended that I saw you down the street and yelled for you to run. One of them loosened his grip to yell into his radio. Felt good to knock him out." His lips pull into a satisfied smile.

"So that's how you got out of the City," I mutter, mentally filling in the rest of the blanks. "You snuck out with the enemy. Clever but very foolish."

"What can I say?" He grins, sinking down beside me. "I live for danger. I've been living with that scum my entire life. They may think they're smarter than me, but I never back down from a fight."

"Me either." I toss him a wry grin. "Sounds like we both have a hero complex."

His eyebrow rises. "A what?"

"It's what my friends always say I have." I drop my voice to mimic Toren's gruff tone. "A hero complex describes a person's insatiable need to seek out danger for the purpose of making themselves feel good about their efforts."

Bastien snorts and nods. "Yeah, that sounds about right. Guess we have more in common than you thought, huh?"

My smile falters as I watch him. I can't imagine what life would be like living day by day completely alone. I wonder how many nights Bastien risked discovery just to go to the factory rooftop to watch the Caldonians below. I don't think I could last long without having anyone to speak to.

I sigh and hold out my hand. He eyes me suspiciously. "Take it," I say.

His fingers wrap around mine and I pull him close, ignoring the pain in my side. "Out here, the only people we can trust are the ones closest to us. You saved my life, Bastien. I owe you my trust."

At first, he looks taken aback. I don't blame him, because I'm shocked myself, but then a slow smile spreads along his face as his fingers tighten. His grip tightens on my forearm and I can feel his unspoken gratitude. "Don't make me regret this," I warn as I release his arm and sit back.

He nods. "This probably isn't the best time to crack a joke then, huh?"

I snort, shaking my head. "I'd be offended if you didn't."

His eyes seem to glow blue, mirroring the flames nearby, as they search my face. "You look exhausted. Why don't you get some rest? I'll head to the lake to grab your clothes and be back before sunup."

I ease back onto the blanket and let him place the pillow beneath my head. "Will you be ok without me for a while?"

I'm confused by how this sarcastic rogue can turn into someone so compassionate, so completely unpredictable, in the blink of an eye. "I made a tornado tonight. I think I can take care of a few aliens."

I anticipate his smirk before it appears. As I nestle down into the blanket, I try not to ponder how I'm able to predict his smiles or lashing sarcasm. Maybe it's because I am too much like him.

"That you can," he says as my eyelids droop.

A heaviness falls over me like a weighted blanket, warm and secure. My ears prick at the sound of scraping and I open my eyes to see him beating the fire with his boots, snuffing out the glowing embers at the fire's edge. The cave falls into darkness.

His footsteps shift toward the cave opening and I see his figure silhouetted against the sky. "Hey!" He turns back. I hesitate, feeling foolish. "Be careful."

"Always," he says and disappears into the night.

THIRTEEN

Soft light rouses me from a restless dream. I groan, wishing I could cover my face and go back to sleep, but the aches and pains spanning the length of my body refuse to be ignored. I open my eyes and stare up at the ceiling. The dull gray appears brighter in the late morning light.

My gaze trails down the walls and I set about surveying the cave. It is bigger than I first thought. What I assumed to be the back of the cave is really a corner. The light from the entrance is dim, but it's enough to see that the space narrows into a passage.

"I wonder if this somehow connects up with our cavern system." I pace the floor for a few minutes, unnerved by the amount of time Bastien has been gone. Maybe he got lost trying to find my clothes, or maybe he ran into that patrol of guards. My stomach churns at the thought of him in trouble.

A draft near the opening of the cave reminds me of my need for clothing. As warm and cozy as this sweater is, I would kill for a pair of pants right about now.

I turn and zero in on Bastien's bags. I rationalize that it's not technically stealing since he obviously confiscated his clothes from the aliens. My need for decency outweighs my morals so I dash for the bag and peek inside.

What I find in the depth of the bag brings tears to my eyes. I carefully remove a small, ratty brown teddy bear and clutch it to my chest. Did this belong to a sister perhaps? Or maybe someone he knew from the City.

I run my fingers over the bear's black nose where the felt is nearly worn off. One eye is missing and the other is scratched and dirty. A small puffed heart dangles from its hand— broken like the rest of this messed up world.

Tears dampen my lashes, but I swallow my emotions and try to remain detached. Growing up in the rebellion has taught me one very important lesson—pain is good fuel for fighting.

Living in the commune has never been easy. The sense of community, of belonging, was never something I wanted. I like my space, my privacy.

I like to keep people at a distance. Apart from Aminah and Eamon, I'm pretty much a loner. I prefer the solitude of the woods over the hectic cave life. Out there I am free to be me. No judging, no editing my thoughts to make people feel comfortable, no emotions. It's just the way I like it.

I poke down through the middle of the bag and search for a pair of pants. Small boxes tinkle as they shift, but I don't stop to inspect them. I brush my fingers against soft material and pull it free.

Holding up the black pants, I examine the foreign material up close. It is soft to the touch but looks to be as durable as leather. It will do. I dig deeper and pull out a matching black shirt. It will drape my slender frame like a tent, but it's better than nothing.

I eagerly lift Bastien's sweater over my head and lay it across the blanket, the cold nipping at my bare skin as I reach for the shirt. Suddenly, I hear footsteps behind me and I turn in surprise.

"Bastien!" I scream as I scramble to cover my near nakedness.

His head whips up, eyes widening as he comes to an abrupt halt. I can see the indecision in his eyes as he takes a step back.

"Go!"

He turns and jogs back outside, tossing my clothes toward me over his shoulder. "Guess that one was kinda my fault," he calls from just outside.

I run my hands over my face and release a nervous laugh. "Just don't peek!"

I scramble along the cave floor and snatch up my clothes, wincing at the damp still clinging to the worn fibers. I look back toward the alien clothes and groan. If I'm going to be warm, I know I have to wear them.

I pull on the pants, amazed at how warm the thin material is. I snag a bit of rope from Bastien's bag, wind it around my waist, and tuck in the billowing shirt. I roll up the sleeves and pat myself down. "You sure know how to make a statement," I grumble as I head for the cave entrance.

Lifting my arm to shield my eyes from the noonday light, I discover that Bastien has fled from the cave. "Over here," he calls.

I squint, fighting to adjust my vision to the brilliant, cloud-free day. I reach out a hand to steady myself as I approach the large rock he's perched on. Instead of connecting with rock, my fingers grasp something firm and warm. Forgetting about the glare, my eyes pop open as I realize that my hand has fallen rather high on Bastien's thigh.

"Hi." He grins as heat stains my cheeks and I wrench my hand back.

"Hi yourself." I wipe my hand on my pants and hoist myself up beside him. "Where have you been?"

"Foraging," he replies, holding up a handful of winterberries. My stomach growls obnoxiously as I cup my hands.

The instant the last berry plops into my hand; I toss back my head, emptying the handful into my mouth. The soft flesh bursts with flavor as I chew, savoring the sweet taste. "Thanks."

He looks down at the remaining berries and offers them to me. "Go on. You need them more than I do."

I hesitate, torn between wanting to snatch them from his hand and remembering to be a decent human being. It's a tough struggle with my stomach growling so loudly. "Seriously?"

He grabs my hand and rolls the berries into it. "I insist."

I know I should feel guilty about taking his food, but I don't. Well, not really. There is a slight twinge, but I choose to ignore it the instant the berries pop in my mouth. "Thanks."

He smiles and leans back. I follow suit, wiping the berry juice onto the side of the rock. "Why are you out here?"

"Just needed some time to think." He stretches his arms out before tucking them behind his head.

"About?"

"You." He rolls his head to face me. I blink, shocked by his direct gaze. "What happened last night?"

I clasp my hands in my lap and dangle my feet over the edge. "I was ambushed not too far from our camp. We got word that the Caldonians were on the move and we wanted to see what they were up to."

"We?" His brow arches.

I nod and turn away. "My friend Eamon was with me. We got separated when the Squaddies attacked. I'm not sure what happened to him."

Bastien is silent as I take a deep breath and continue. "I wasn't familiar with the territory so I was forced to run. I thought I'd made it, but an alien found me."

His arms clench beside me. "Did he hurt you?"

"No," I say, staring up into the sky. My eyes have adjusted to the brightness and now I can see large puffy white clouds dotting the blue sky. The weather has been so unpredictable lately. I suppose I should enjoy it while I can because once winter hits, it'll be gloom for several months. "He tried to save me, actually, but then one of those spider things showed up and shot at me—"

Bastien jerks upright, turning to stare down at me. "You were hit by a laser?"

"No," I hedge, looking beyond his ear instead of meeting his gaze. "I sort of…caught it."

His mouth falls open. "Caught it?"

I sigh and sit up, curling my legs under. "Apparently I can do that now, too."

Running his hands through his hair, Bastien lets out a deep breath. "Did anything else happen? Other than the tornado?"

I shake my head. "No, I don't think—" I cut off and eye him suspiciously. He's not looking at me now. Something is off. "What are you digging for, Bastien?"

He scratches his stubbled chin and purses his lips. "I, uh…something happened to me last night."

I turn my entire body to face him, my knees pressing against his thigh. My stomach clenches with worry when he refuses to look me in the eye. "Tell me."

He stares out into the woods. From here, I can see the lake in a small valley below. The water ripples in the sunlight, stunningly peaceful, but I know appearances can be deceiving. "Something came through the woods last night. It was like a force field, invisible but very real. It knocked me out when I was hunting beside the lake."

I dig my fingernails into my palms as I fight the wave of nausea that rolls through my stomach. I have a bad feeling about this.

"When I woke up I felt…different."

"Different, how?" I press.

He shrugs. "I don't know. I can't really explain it. Just…stronger I guess."

"So you haven't noticed anything else?" I lean forward, trying to judge the expression on his face, but he remains infuriatingly blank.

"Well, there was one thing—"

I hold up my hand. "Did you hear that?"

"Hear what?" He tilts his head and searches the woods around us. I already know that the voice I heard didn't come from the woods. The birds are still singing in the trees. If we were about to be attacked, the birds would have fled to the skies.

"I don't know," I frown, chewing on my lower lip. I know if I tell him I thought I just heard a voice calling my name he's going to think I'm crazy. "Probably just the wind."

Bastien leans over and presses his hand to my forehead. I flinch back, but he holds me still. "No fever, but you need to regain your strength. You almost died last night."

I know that he's right. Although I do feel better, I'm certainly not in top form. "I don't have time to rest," I grunt as I slip down off the rocks. Pain reverberates up my legs as I start toward the cave.

"Wait!" he calls after me. I hear him land with a thud and then rush to catch up. "Where are you going?"

"Home. They will have search parties out looking for me now that the sun is up."

He grabs my arm and spins me around. "I can't let you wander through the forest on your own."

"Then come with me."

"That's the second time you've invited me home with you." He grins. His grip loosens on my arm, but I notice he doesn't let go. "A guy might start to think you're up to something."

I laugh. "You know, I almost like you like this."

"Like what?" He asks.

"Real."

"Ah," he sighs. "I have my moments."

"You should show them more often."

His gaze flickers toward me. "Maybe I would, if I had a reason to."

A blush betrays me before I have a chance to hide behind my veil of hair. I catch a fleeting glimpse of his smirk before I get my mind right again. "Look, you can't stay out here alone. You're a City guy, not a tree hugger. You really should come with me."

He rubs his neck, a signal I'm quickly discovering reveals his unease. "I've been alone for a long time. I like it that way. No rules. No one to care about. It's easier that way."

"I get it, you know?" I drop my gaze.

The wistful tone in my voice makes him pull my chin up to face him. "You do?"

"Sometimes I hate living in the commune. People are always watching me, waiting for me to run out on another one of my harebrained adventures. Most of them say I'm too reckless. The kids hate me, which I'm pretty much cool with, and my friends are great. Sometimes I don't think they understand me, but they're the only family I have."

I step up closer to him, steeling myself to be okay with him in my personal space. This is the first time I've ever done something like this. My fingers tremble as I reach out as if to touch him but draw back. "Come with me, Bastien. I don't want to leave you here alone."

He looks off into the woods, his sadness painfully evident. "I told you. I'm pretty good on my own."

"Maybe." I step even closer to him, his eyes widening as I approach. I have to will myself not to step back. His breath appears to catch as I stop only a couple inches from his side. "I still want you to come."

He tilts his head, staring hard at me. "If I didn't know better, I'd think you were hitting on me, Illyria."

"You wish." I snort and turn to head back toward the cave. I don't wait around to see if he's going to follow me. I know he will.

FOURTEEN

Illyria.

I hold out my hand to stop Bastien. His grip tightens around the neck of the sack slung over his shoulder, his piercing gaze searching the forest for any sign of danger. When he sees none, he gives me a quizzical look. I press my finger to my lips and wait.

Illyria? Can you hear me?

I whip around, searching the late afternoon woods for the source of the whisper. The voice sounds so familiar, but nothing stands out to me. "I heard it again."

"Heard what? We're not going to start this again, are we?" Bastien shifts his stance, adjusting the weight of his bag. With two pairs of clothing missing and the blanket lassoed around the middle of the pack, Bastien managed to combine his two bags together. I noticed the care he took to replace the brown teddy bear, but he said nothing about it, so neither did I. Whatever sentiment this bear holds for him, I'm not about to pry.

"That voice. It sounds like..." I trail off as I realize why it's familiar to me. "It's my friend, Aminah."

"Out here?" He glances back through the trees toward the lake we passed only a few moments ago. He squints into the winds that lash out at us from across the wide expanse. We haven't seen a living soul since we left the cave an hour ago.

"No." I shake my head. "I think she's in my head."

I ignore Bastien's obvious disbelief as I close my eyes and listen. *Illyria? Are you there?*

Aminah? I can barely hear you. How are you in my head? Chatting with Kyan with my mind was crazy enough, but doing the same with Aminah is beyond bizarre.

I'll explain when you get here. Where are you?

I move past Bastien and sweep my gaze along the lakeshore. Judging by the sun, we are heading northeast. Once we hit higher ground, we'll have to veer slightly, but it should be almost a dead shot straight home.

By the lake. We'll be there in less than two hours.

Bastien stares blankly at me as he moves to block my view. "What's going on?"

"Shh." I wave him off. "I'm talking to my friend."

He shakes his head. "I'm not even going to ask how you're doing that."

"Good, cause I really don't know." I wait in silence for Aminah's response. When none comes, I worry that I've somehow disrupted our connection by speaking out loud.

Is someone with you? She asks hesitantly.

A friend. I can feel the waves of tension my response creates. Naturally, bringing a stranger into our camp will be met with great opposition, but the fact that it's Bastien will be especially hard for Eamon. He didn't take our little night in the City so well before. I'm not sure how I'm going to be able to tell him about this.

Toren is coming for you.

Wait! What? I step forward when the connection suddenly severs. It's an odd feeling, like a door closing in my mind. I'm aware of the disconnect, but have no clue how to open the door again myself.

"So, what's up?" Bastien asks.

I step back toward him and frown. "She said Toren's coming."

"Another friend, I'm assuming." He glances at the sky, frowning at the sun's rapid descent. The Sky Ships will fly over soon. Memories of our adventure with the Caldonians two nights ago weigh heavily on both our minds.

"Wouldn't it make sense just to wait for us to arrive?"

I shrug. "I would think so. She sounded a bit off when she said it though."

Suddenly, a blast of wind whips my hair into my face. Bastien drops his bag and leaps in front of me.

"Whoa! I'm not looking for a fight. I'm just trying to find my friend."

I poke my head out around Bastien and my mouth drops open. "Toren?"

Bastien looks back at me over his shoulder. "That's your friend?"

"How did you get here so fast?" I round Bastien's side and gape at Toren. His short wavy hair is tangled into a windblown mess.

Before he answers me, he gives Bastien a hard once over. Toren's eyes come to rest on the blade held firmly in Bastien's hand.

"It's safe," I say, motioning for Bastien to lower his weapon.

His jaw clenches as he darts a glance between Toren and me. He nods and slowly eases out of his tense stance. Toren doesn't show any hint of relaxing. "Aminah told me you weren't alone."

I look over at Bastien and fight to control my anxiety. If Toren doesn't approve of him, there's no way Bastien's stepping foot anywhere near our cave. "This is Bastien. I told you how he saved my life in the City. He saved me last night from the aliens again."

I can tell Bastien noticed that I edited out the part where I nearly drowned because of the tornado I somehow created, but he lets it slide. Toren's eyebrows arch as he crosses his arms over his chest.

"Is that so?" Bastien shifts from one foot to the next. I can't help but notice that each time he does, he inches a bit closer to my side. "Seems rather attached to you," Toren mutters, staring him down.

"I made a promise to myself to protect her back in the City. I don't break my promises." Bastien replies with cool confidence.

I step between the guys and rise up on my tiptoes so I'm eye level with Toren. "You know I would never risk everyone's safety if I didn't think we could trust him."

Toren rubs his chin, thinking it over. A part of me fears this decision won't go in my favor. I look toward Bastien and feel torn as to what I would do if that happened. I can't stand the idea of him being out here all alone.

"Fine," Toren begrudgingly concedes. "We'll let the group decide when we get back. Eamon will be furious if I keep you any longer. He's beside himself with worry."

"He's back? Was he hurt?" My voice rises an octave as I cling to Toren's arm. "I tried to find him, but the aliens came at me so fast I couldn't go back."

"He made it out alive but he's blaming himself for the attack."

"Stubborn fool," I grumble. "There's no way he could have known."

"Everyone knows that, but he's not listening to reason right now. Maybe you can talk some sense into him." Toren holds out his hand to me. "Grab on and whatever you do, don't let go."

Bastien steps forward and grasps my hand. "Hang on a second. I'm not letting her go, just like that."

Toren's face darkens with anger. "You have no claim to her. I suggest you back off."

"No," I plead, feeling like a rope tugged in two directions. "Stop it, both of you."

I pull out of Toren's grasp and place a hand on Bastien's arm. I try not to let my thoughts drift toward the fact that this is the first time I've willingly touched him. "It's ok. He's my friend, Bastien. You don't have to worry."

He lifts a challenging gaze to Toren. "Oh sure, he's got warm fuzzies written all over him."

I laugh and nod. "He has his moments."

Stepping back from Bastien, I accept Toren's hand. "So are you gonna tell me how you got here so fast?"

"Nope," he offers a smile. "I'm gonna show you. Hold on tight."

I push the tangled mess of hair out of my eyes as we appear at the edge of the cave within only a few seconds of leaving Bastien at the lake. I pry my fingers from around Toren's shoulders, offering a sheepish grin as apology for the nail marks I've left behind.

"How do you feel?" he asks as he holds me upright.

"Like I left my stomach three miles back." My knees buckle and I slump against his side. "How are you able to run so fast?"

Toren's jaw clenches as he turns. I watch his profile glow in the fading light. "I'm not really sure. Something weird happened last night."

He turns back and offers a strained smile. "We can talk about that when I get you home."

"Oh no." I hold out my hand to push Toren back. "You have to get Bastien."

"It's probably better if he stays—"

A ripple of anger makes my nausea vanish. "You promised."

He sighs heavily, averting his gaze. "You know Eamon won't be happy."

"Tough. I'm not leaving Bastien out there by himself. I owe him, Toren."

Gritting his teeth, he nods and backs away. "Fine. Don't move. I'll be back in a minute."

Only a whirlwind of leaves reveals his path as he blurs out of sight. I shake my head and lean back against the cold stone.

I don't understand what is happening to us. Aminah can talk to my mind, Toren can run faster than a bullet and Bastien can... I frown, realizing Bastien never told me exactly what he could do. *Has everyone been affected by my blast?*

A chilly gust of wind funnels past me as Toren and Bastien grind to a halt a few feet away and instantly separate. The tension between them is nearly palpable, but I fail miserably to hide my smirk as they brush themselves off like young kids with cooties.

Bastien runs his hands through his hair. I try not to stare at the cascade of black hair that falls back into place. When Toren catches me watching, I clear my throat and head deeper into the cave where darkness can hide my telling blush.

I listen to the shuffling feet behind me and smile at the murmured curses coming from Bastien. "Oh yeah, watch your head. The ceiling dips down here."

"Could've told me that earlier," Bastien grumbles from the back of the line.

I grin and quicken my pace. I can tell by the way that the blackness turns to charcoal gray that we are getting close. Two more bends and it will be a straight shot to the Temple.

FIFTEEN

The air feels cold as I rush around the corner and sprint the final leg into the flickering light of the domed Temple. I skid to a halt and appraise the scene before me. Children mill around, some lying on their bellies playing Aeon's Rift—a game using dried tree bark, splintered sticks, scavenged acorns and no small amount of cheating. I've always been an excellent player, which is probably why none of the children challenge me anymore.

I look about me, scanning the crowd for Eamon. I expected to be yanked into a crushing bear hug by now, but he is nowhere to be found. This worries me.

The rustle of fabric alerts me to Aminah's approach before her ice-cold fingers wrap around my arm. "Where's Eamon?" I ask.

"He said he'd wait for you in the armory."

I frown. "Why isn't he here to greet me?"

Aminah sighs and motions for me to sit with her. Apprehension begins to worm through my belly. The pinched skin around her eyes worries me, but no more so than the slight waver in her voice. "He was beside himself last night when he returned without you. It was all Toren could do to talk him into resting before going back out at first light."

I look across the Temple to the tunnel leading to the blackberry path beyond. "Why does he feel guilty? It wasn't his fault we were ambushed."

"You know Eamon," Aminah whispers, leaning against my shoulder. "He's always been so protective of you. He feels like it's his fault the aliens found you."

I curl my knees up into my chest. The unfamiliar alien garb billows over my legs despite how tightly I've cinched it around my waist. "There's nothing he could have done."

Aminah nods. "He knows that, but knowing the truth and accepting it are two different things."

I run my hands through my hair, wincing at the mass of tangles Toren's run left behind. I look beyond Toren to Bastien, who hovers just on the edge of the shadows lining the tunnel. He watches me with obvious discomfort, but I can't tell if it's for my benefit or because the entire room has fallen into a stunned silence at his arrival.

"Eamon's gonna be furious when he finds out you've brought him here," Aminah warns, following my gaze.

"I didn't have a choice. I couldn't just leave Bastien out there."

"I understand that, but Eamon won't."

I grimace. "Guess I'd better get this over with."

I help Aminah to her feet and turn to Bastien. "You good here for a few minutes?"

He shrugs and leans back against the wall, feigning an air of indifference now. He may fool everyone else but I know he's about two seconds from turning and racing back to his own cave. I start toward him but Aminah's hand falls on my arm.

"My name's Aminah. The grumpy one is my boyfriend." She jerks her head toward Toren then smiles warmly at Bastien and steps forward to shake his hand. "I'm sure you'd like a quick tour to get a feel of our home."

Toren's reluctance doesn't go unnoticed by Bastien or me, but I let it slide. Obviously, I'm not done fighting for Bastien's right to be here. "I'll be back as soon as I can."

I pull Aminah up close. "Try to keep Zahra distracted until I return."

"Too late," Toren mutters and I turn to see Zahra weaving her way across the crowded Temple.

I inwardly groan as Bastien does a double take. Zahra shoves a teenage boy out of her way and flashes Bastien a smile that would curl any man's toes. I roll my eyes and snap my fingers in front of Bastien. He blinks and refocuses on me. "You might want to grab a cloth, big boy. You've got a bit of drool running down your chin."

His smirk is as automatic as it is predictable. "Do I detect an air of jealousy, Princess?"

"Not at all." I shoot him a wicked grin. "But you should know she's like a hyena in heat, and you're fresh meat."

Bastien rubs his chin, no doubt worried there may be some truth to my quip. "Interesting imagery."

Aminah yanks me away as Zahra swoops in. "Eamon, remember?"

I grit my teeth as Zahra offers her hand to Bastien, batting her lashes for all they're worth. My stomach rolls with disgust, so I force my attention away. "Right. I'll be back, but I expect a full rundown of what's happened since I left. Don't think I've forgotten your little mind chat, missy."

Aminah's smile wanes as she darts a glance at Toren. He passes an equally loaded glance back before nodding. "When you return."

Weaving my way quickly across the Temple, I try to ignore the high pitched giggling that echoes behind me. I hunch my shoulders and pound my boots harder than necessary.

It's a good thing he likes Zahra. Less complication for my life, I chant silently.

I reach the far end of the Temple and skirt along the outer rim of the room, politely nodding at my fellow hunters who rise up to welcome me home. I catch a glimpse of Zahra's hand pressed against Bastien's chest. When she pushes her lips out into a pout and begins winding her blond tresses around her finger, I turn away and force myself to ignore the unusual pangs of jealousy that stab at me.

"So much for not letting him get to me," I mutter as I slip into the far tunnel and hurry past the flickering torches. I'm not really sure if I'm running toward Eamon or away from Bastien.

Soon I have to pause to let my eyes adjust to the pitch darkness. My fingers trail over the damp stone, cold and achingly familiar. It's good to be home. I only wish home hadn't become a place of such emotional turmoil.

I count out my steps silently in my head and approach our pathetically under stocked armory. The air takes on a chill as I approach the offshoot toward the Cascades. I long to take a dip beneath the icy waters, to wash away my pain and uncertainty. The two offshoots to the right would lead me on a daylong journey into the depths of the cavern system and ultimately lead me to a dead end.

I step through the open doorway into the armory and spy Eamon sitting near the rear of the long room, his shoulders hunched over. I know he can hear my approach, but he makes no move to acknowledge me.

"Eamon?" My call reverberates through the nearly empty space. He leans his head back, disappearing into the shadows, but remains silent. "Aminah told me you would be here."

His exhales a heavy sigh as I sink down a foot away.

I wait for him to speak. My anxiety begins to swell into frustration as the impatient part of me wants to scream at him to get over whatever he's dealing with and just come clean.

The more sensitive side of me thankfully wins over.

I reach out my hand and gently let it rest on his forearm. The muscles under my palm clench violently, but I grip his arm to prevent him from pulling away.

"You have to talk to me at some point."

"Don't." Eamon growls and shoves my hand away. "Don't try to tell me none of this was my fault. I've heard it from Toren and Aminah. I know what happened out there."

"So do I." I scoot forward so that my knee brushes his leg. "We were ambushed, Eamon. That happens in war."

"I should've whistled for you sooner. I knew I was pushing our time limit to get home but I wanted to wait a few more minutes." He groans and presses his head back against the stone. "If I'd followed the plan, none of this would have happened."

"Hey," I whisper, rising onto my knees. I place my hands on his arms, waiting for him to look at me. "You did exactly what you should've done. What I would've done if I'd taken point. It's who we are, Eamon."

He shakes his head. "I put your life in danger."

"We're all in danger." My fingers tighten around his arm. "I'm not a child that needs protecting anymore, Eamon. I can take care of myself."

"I know." He sighs heavily. Judging by the way his shoulders sag, he really does know. "If something had happened to you…"

I reach out and pull his face closer to mine, drawing him from the shadow so I can see him. "I'm fine. See?"

He reaches out his hands, his fingers dancing across my face and down to my shoulder. He nods, closing his eyes. "I'm glad you're back."

"Me too." I smile. "I never thought I'd say this, but I actually missed this place."

"And me?" He drops his gaze.

I laugh and punch him in the arm. "Of course, you. You're my best friend!"

Eamon's brow furrows as he nods and stares at the floor. My laughter falters as his Adam's apple bobs. "Eamon? What's wrong?"

"Nothing. It's just—"

"Illyria?" I turn at Toren's call as he ducks into the armory. He comes up short when he sees us sitting close together in the dark. Clearing his throat, he turns and faces the wall instead. "Sorry. I just thought you might like to know dinner is ready. After the kids are in bed we will talk about what's going to happen with Bastien."

Eamon stiffens beside me. "That guy from the City?"

I wince and toss a murderous glare at Toren. "Thanks a lot," I mutter as he backs out.

"What's he talking about, Illyria?"

I sigh and rise to my feet. Eamon quickly follows suit. I start to speak but think better of it. Instead I just shake my head. "Might as well get this over with, too."

I watch Bastien from across the Temple as the argument rises to new heights. Although I knew Bastien's arrival would cause conflict, I had hoped Eamon would see why I had to bring him back with me. Apparently not.

Their introduction didn't go over smoothly, to say the least. After nearly thirty minutes of ranting on Eamon's part, Toren has jumped into the fray while I sit back and watch with a headache building just behind my right temple.

Aminah quickly rushed the children through their dinner as Bastien and Eamon glared at each other across the room. I suppose a part of me should be grateful Eamon held off until the children were tucked into bed, but my gut tells me his anger only had time to fester.

Bringing my bowl to my lips, I try to block out Eamon's vehement argument as the warm liquid spills down my throat. My stomach growls, begging for more of the rabbit stew, but I know there's hardly enough to go around. I wipe my mouth with a cloth and push the empty bowl aside.

"This is getting us nowhere," I say as I swing my leg over the aged wooden bench and push up from the table. "The aliens that attacked Eamon and me last night weren't part of any supply line. They were looking for me, for us, and now they know we aren't too far away. How long do you think it will take Commander Drakon to divert all of his Grounders on this mountain? We don't have time to sit around and bicker. Bastien knows the City. He can help us track down the Grounders and see how much time we have left."

"To go where?" Aminah asks. "We have elderly and little children. This is their home."

"I know." I look toward the darkened tunnel leading toward the sleeping closets. "We are responsible for more lives than our own. That's my point. If we wait to be blindsided, many of them might die. Are you willing to take that risk?"

"No one is arguing with you, Illyria," Toren says from his place on the other side of the altar. He leans over the map, scouring for information that he might have previously overlooked. "We have the emergency exits in place, but there is nowhere for us to go."

"Then find somewhere," I growl. "Commander Drakon will stop at nothing until he finds us."

"How can you be so sure of that?" Eamon asks.

"I…" I frown and cross my arms over my chest. "I just am. I saw Drakon with my own eyes when I was in the City. Bastien and I humiliated him when we escaped. He doesn't seem like the kind of guy to take that well."

I force myself not to look at Bastien as I smooth over my lie. I can feel his intense gaze fall on me, but he remains silent.

"So why do you have to be the one to go with him?" Zahra pipes up. "Why can't Eamon go? Or Toren?"

"Typical," I snort, rolling my eyes.

She turns and glares icily at me. "Excuse me?"

"Seems your allegiances have switched pretty fast, Zahra. How quick you are willing to throw Eamon to the wolves." I turn to face off with her, rolling my shoulders back to broaden my stance. "Eamon can hardly stand the sight of Bastien and Toren is needed here to lead. Are *you* willing to volunteer?"

Zahra's eyes flash with resentment. "Of course not! You know I'm not a fighter."

"Thought not," I grin as I shove past her into the inner circle of my friends.

From the corner of my eye, I note that Bastien has cleaned himself up. His hair is still damp from his dip in the Cascades. One of Toren's old shirts now accentuates his broad frame. The pair of tattered pants seems to be a decent fit, apart from being too short in the leg. I wince as I see a large red patch over his right thigh and realize Aminah has given Bastien one of Eamon's pants to wear.

I glance between Eamon and Toren. Both appear in firm mutual agreement that Bastien is not to be trusted. Zahra is too smitten with him to possibly vote against his admittance to the group. Aminah's nose is scrunched, her head tilted to the side as if she's trying to listen to something.

She blinks and looks in my direction. *I'm listening to more than their words, Illyria.*

I flinch, shocked to hear her voice in my head once more. *You never told me how you are able to do this.*

Now is not the right time. The guys need to get this over with.

On this, we agree. Eamon is getting far more heated than I've ever seen and Toren doesn't seem to be doing anything to slow him down. Bastien stands only a few feet away, hands firmly clenched at his side, displaying amazing self-control in light of the obvious threat.

Aminah shifts her gaze toward Bastien, her eyes widening with curiosity. *What did you hear?* I ask.

It's not what I heard but what I saw. She turns to stare at me fully. *You were the cause of the blast?*

I suck in a breath. *How do you know about that?*

I would think it should be obvious by now. Bastien tells you he can do extraordinary things after getting hit with some invisible blast and you didn't connect the dots to my ability to read minds or Toren's super speed? You're slipping, Illyria.

I rub my forehead, feeling a headache expanding to take in the entire right side of my head. *What about Eamon and Zahra? Any weird developments?*

Her eyes narrow. *Eamon didn't tell you?*

Guess it slipped his mind. Even I can hear the bitterness laced through my words.

Aminah reaches out and grasps my arm, her expression soft with sincerity. *He's hurting right now. Don't blame him for keeping his secrets.*

What about Zahra? What's her gift? Please tell me it's something stupid.

The twinkle in Aminah's eye gives me a chance to hope. *Zahra can speak to animals. You should've seen her this morning. She woke up all puffy eyed and swearing like a trooper about all the noise. Seems the bats were rather chatty throughout the night.*

If it weren't for the raging dispute going on around me I would've given into the impulse to pump my fists in triumph. Seems fate does have a sense of humor. There is no one more deserving of such a gift than Zahra, who has been fearful of animals from birth. It's part of the reason she remains in the cave as much as possible.

What about Bastien? Can you tell what his gift is?

Aminah offers only a shrug in response as Toren turns to address her. "What's your opinion on Bastien?"

"He's not really my type," she smiles.

I cough, fighting to cover over my laughter. Bastien smirks, crossing his arms over his chest, shifting to lounge back against the wall.

The vein running down Toren's forehead pulses as he offers Aminah a watered down glare. "Anything you can say that might be a bit more useful?"

"Oh," she tries to cover over her smile. "He appears to be harmless and he seems rather devoted to protecting Illyria, per his oath, as he told you earlier."

And he seems abnormally good at avoiding thinking of certain aspects of your time together. Any reason for that? She tosses my way.

Sweat clings to my palms as I offer what I hope to be an indifferent shrug. *No clue. Guess you'll have to ask him.*

She stares long and hard at me as I do my best to keep my poker face firmly in place. When I begin to feel it crack, I quickly distract her. *What about Eamon?*

Her frown deepens as Toren shifts to address Zahra. His questions fade into the background as Aminah answers. *I don't really know. He hasn't said a whole lot since he got back. It's hard to read his thoughts though. They're jumbled.*

Meaning? I press.

Meaning his thoughts fragment from time to time. It's almost as if random thoughts leap into his mind and disrupt everything. I don't know what to make of it.

Zahra's shrill voice pulls me back to the brewing storm around me. "How dare you insinuate I have an ulterior motive, Eamon!"

"Enough." I shove the map out of the way, hoist myself onto the altar stone in the center of the room, and swing my legs back and forth. "Bastien is staying. He saved my life and I owe him. Besides, we could use his help around here."

Eamon starts to protest but I hold up my hand. "Things have changed. The aliens are moving into our area with some serious firepower. We need food, weapons and a really good plan." I let my gaze soften as I linger on Eamon's face. "Toren is needed here, Aminah and Zahra aren't fit for combat and I'm not letting the two of you out of my sight. So, that means I'm going with Bastien to search out the Grounders. End of story."

Eamon's protest won't be stopped this time. "No way. We know nothing about this guy. Does anyone else think it's strange how he just magically appears when Illyria needs him the most?"

Bastien's jaw tightens but, after a sharp glance from me, he remains silent. "If he hadn't been there last night I would be dead. You should be thanking him, not accusing."

Toren holds up his hands as he moves between us. "I hate to admit it, but Illyria's right. Although," he turns to shoot a warning glance in my direction, "I don't like the idea of you and him going alone into the City. You need to take someone else with you."

"Who? Mathias?" I can imagine the bumbling teen following us around. He turned fifteen about a week ago and has yet to figure out how to compensate for his enormous feet. "If we're ambushed, he'll either get us killed or captured. We all know he's about a dense as a box of rocks. I mean the guy actually thinks Zahra's hot." I grin smugly over at her.

Zahra's cry of indignation sounds dangerously close to a pig snort. Toren waves her off and focuses on his girlfriend. "Aminah?"

She purses her lips as she becomes the center of attention, a place she usually avoids at all costs. "Bastien seems fine to me. I haven't found anything in his mind that makes me think he's a danger to Illyria."

Bastien clears his throat, shooting me a guarded glance that I interpret to be concern for me. Toren watches the interaction before shifting to look at Eamon. "What do you think?"

Eamon's fingers pop as they clench into fists at his side. "Illyria's right," he grinds out. "Mathias will endanger them."

"So you think she should go with Bastien?" Toren presses.

He won't meet my gaze as he reluctantly nods. "He's proven he can take care of himself. Let's just hope Illyria's right about him."

I wonder if I'm wrong to push for Bastien's inclusion to the group right now. For the first time in my life, I've knowingly hurt my best friend and shoved a wedge between us that I'm unsure I have the ability to remove.

Toren shakes his head. "Fine, I guess Bastien stays. You two need to rest up tonight and head out in the morning."

Zahra squeals and rushes to Bastien's side, fawning over him with nauseating excitement. I turn my back on them and meet Eamon's piercing gaze. I hold it for a moment before excusing myself from the room. I'm desperate for sleep, but more than that, I need time to think.

SIXTEEN

Icy water laps over my skin in waves. I shiver as I dip my shoulders beneath the frothy surface, clenching my jaw to keep my teeth from chattering. The Cascades are both numbing and invigorating this morning. I'm not sure which effect I was going for.

"Now *that* is a beautiful sight."

I whip around, instantly covering myself with my arms. "What are you doing here?" I scream. "Get out!"

"Aw, don't tell me you're a shy one. I didn't peg you for that." Bastien grins as he throws his leg over a rock and settles in for what appears to be an annoyingly lengthy time.

Using one arm, I swim as quickly as I can away from the center of the pool and head straight for the rocks. Bastien seems completely unfazed by my rising fury and he grins down at me. He does however reach out to retrieve my dagger from the pile of clothes he's perched beside.

"Have you no decency?" I growl through chattering teeth. The water has definitely tilted dangerously toward the numb side now. If I don't get out soon I'll risk hypothermia, but there's no way I'm going to give Bastien the satisfaction of seeing me naked.

Twirling the dagger in his hand, he appears to contemplate my question. I roll my eyes and cling precariously to the slippery rock face. The current of the crashing water jostles me as I fight to remain covered. I kick my legs, battling against the churning pool.

"I suppose this might seem a bit forward of me, but I thought you might like to know it's time to go."

"Fine. Message received. Leave now!"

He leans over the edge, peering down at me. "And miss all the fun? I think not."

I grind my teeth in frustration and press my skin against the icy rocks. "If you don't leave, I'm going to lose some fingers and a handful of toes while I'm at it."

He cocks his head to the side. "You'd really risk life and limb just to save your pride? I've already seen it, ya know."

"Don't remind me," I growl, readjusting my grip on the rock.

His smile is smooth and filled with sultry promise. "I like to remind myself quite often actually."

"J-j-just you wait until I get out of here..." My teeth chatter so hard I struggle to finish my words.

Bastien grins. "Yes, well on that note I suppose I should go pack some supplies."

He rises from the rock and starts to walk away. Turning back, he holds my dagger in the air. "I'm sure you won't mind if I hold onto this beauty for a bit, hmm?"

"Don't worry. I've got more where that came from."

With a throaty chuckle, Bastien waves and struts away. I wait until I can't bear the pain in my toes any longer before splashing to the edge of the pool. I struggle to pull myself from the icy water and my arms shake as I flop onto the damp stone. I gasp for breath, shivering from head to toe.

"Illyria!"

I glance up to see Aminah racing toward me with a large cloth, mostly like a sheet from her bed. "Oh, that boy is going to be the death of you!"

Helping me to my feet, she wraps me in the cloth and begins to rub me down. I'm not a prude, but even being seen naked by Aminah brings a flush to my cheeks.

Aminah seems to take no notice of my lack of dress, her concern solely focused on to getting me warm. Some days I take her mothering instincts for granted, but today is not one of them.

"Thanks," I say through chattering teeth.

She nods tightly, her curls bouncing about her head as she dips low to rub my legs. I close my eyes, nearly moaning with delight as warmth returns to my extremities.

"What was he thinking?"

I shrug. "Bastien has an odd sense of humor."

"He could have killed you."

"He was trying to prove a point."

Her hands pause against my calf. "And that was?"

"That he's more stubborn than I am."

Aminah rolls her eyes and finishes drying my feet. "Sounds like you two were made for each other. Both hard headed and crazy to boot!"

I suck in a breath. "Don't say that."

She rises to her feet, standing about three inches shorter than me. "What?"

"I could never stand to be with a guy like Bastien because he's so…"

"Infuriating, challenging, sarcastic, dangerous, gorgeous…yes, I can see how there's nothing to like."

Her smile irks me. It seems so knowing. "I don't like him."

"Um-hmm."

"Whatever." I hobble over to my clothes, my toes lifted high to avoid touching any more of the glacial water that puddles on the floor. "Should I ask how you knew where I was? I didn't exactly leave a note."

Aminah taps her temple before lifting the sheet to give me privacy. I quickly pull on my clothes, grateful for the familiar scratchy feeling against my skin.

"I guess for once I should be grateful that you've been rummaging around in my brain."

She shakes her head. "Not yours. His. He fascinates me."

I arch an eyebrow as I sink to put on my socks. I try not to think about how the bottoms are nearly worn completely through; my big toe poked through the tattered material last week. "I didn't take you for the nosy sort, Aminah."

"I'm not. Well, not really. It's just that his past is so different than ours. I've never even come close to seeing the City before. His thoughts seem to be consumed by it." Aminah twirls one of her curls tightly around her finger. "He's lonely, you know. I think that's part of the reason he's so defensive all the time. He's trying to hide it, but you seem to be able to bring the best out in him."

"Lucky me," I grumble, lacing up my boots.

"It's not a bad thing that he's here, you know. Toren will come around."

"And Eamon?" I rise and twist my damp hair into a bun at the back of my head. I shove a splintered stick through it, grateful I remembered to bring it with me earlier. I'm not in the mood to deal with my hair right now.

"Eamon's jealous. You know that. He's never really had to fight for your attention before."

"Why would he have to fight for it? We're best friends, Aminah. We're together every day."

Aminah rolls her eyes, tucking a wild curl behind her ear. "You know it's not the same. Eamon cares about you. He can see the way Bastien watches you. And the way you watch him back."

"It's nothing." I try to shrug off her insinuations but fear there may be some merit to them.

She gives a knowing look. "Keep telling yourself that. Won't make it the truth."

I thrust my dirty clothes into a burlap sack and toss it over my shoulder. Aminah falls into step beside me. Tucking the sheet under her arm, we head back to the Temple. Although I can tell she wants to say more, she remains silent for the journey. I'm grateful for the silence. I can only imagine how my trip to the City with Bastien will fare now.

I hold out a beat up 12-gauge shotgun to Bastien but keep it just out of his reach. "My dagger, please."

"Please? Wow, I didn't think you were capable of being so polite."

"Fine." I shove the shotgun into his gut and grab the dagger out of the waist of his pants. "That better?"

"Much," he grunts, rubbing his abs. "What's eating you? Don't tell me you're still sore about that whole waterfall incident?"

I roll my eyes scathingly at him. "Please. I'm hardly the type to hold a grudge."

"Right." He grabs a half-empty box of shells and loads the gun. "Is this all the ammo you've got?"

"Yep. You're welcome to scour the woods for more if you like." I tuck two serrated blades into my waistband and pull my shirt over to conceal them. I grab a .9mm pistol and eject the clip to reload. I barely have enough bullets for one magazine. That doesn't instill a great deal of confidence about this trip.

"You know, it would be much easier if we just started stealing the Caldonian's laser guns."

I lift my head, eyes widening with surprise. "You think?"

"Well don't look so surprised, Princess."

"No, I'm not. It's just that I've been trying to convince Toren of that for months now but he's reluctant. He's worried we won't be able to handle them safely."

Bastien scoffs. "Point and shoot. How hard can it be?"

A small smile tugs at my lips as I slam the magazine in place and chamber a round. "Aminah seems to think you are and I are alike. Perhaps she's not that far off."

Bastien leans back against the wall with a definitively smug smile. "Do I hear a compliment in there somewhere, Princess?"

"Hardly. I think she was just pointing out my faults." I shoot him a contemptuous glance, toss my pack over my shoulder and head toward the Temple. Although I can hear him behind me in the narrow tunnel, I don't look back.

"Illyria, over here." Toren calls.

I weave my way through a mound of children, each scrambling over the next for the last handful of blackberries. My stomach growls at the sight of the sweet fruit, knowing it will be another year before I can taste them again. The thought crosses my mind to swoop in and steal a couple, but I'm already on most of the kids' bad side. It would surely earn me the meanest person of the year award....three years running.

Aminah seems to read my mind, without actually digging through my devious thoughts, and loops her arm through mine to steer me toward Toren.

"Another ambush?" I eye Toren's bowed head, deep in conversation with Eamon.

"You know Toren means well."

The muffled snort behind me makes me grin. Apparently, Bastien doesn't think so highly of Toren's methods either.

When Bastien and I arrive, Toren pats Eamon on the shoulder and rises to meet our gaze. "Scouts reported back some activity last night off to the east."

"What kind of activity?" I ask, leaning over his map. The area is one that I'm vaguely familiar with, but haven't spent enough time exploring because it runs right up to the City.

"They've been moving some heavy machinery," Eamon answers.

"And you want us to take a look at it?" Bastien asks from over my shoulder.

Eamon bristles but Toren places a warning hand on his forearm. "That's the plan. It shouldn't be too far out of your way." He points to a location less than a mile from where Bastien and I plan to infiltrate the City.

"Could be dangerous," Bastien says, crossing his arms over his chest as he turns to look at me.

"I'm game if you are."

Bastien nods. "You know I'm in."

SEVENTEEN

I can hear Bastien panting heavily behind me as he leans into the steep incline that will lead us to ground level. I'm used to this blind trek, but today I find my pace a bit sluggish, my mind riddled with a whirlwind of thoughts.

"Are you always this intense when you leave home?"

"No," I call back over my shoulder as I lead us around a bend and lean forward to dig into the sharp slope. We're almost there. I can see the light up ahead. "I'm like this when I'm *in* the caves. I don't like tight spaces."

"Or bickering among friends?"

I readjust my pack, tugging on the straps so that they fall more evenly over my shoulders. "That too."

"Can I ask you a question?" His boots slap against the stone as he rushes to keep pace with me.

I grit my teeth and prepare myself for the worst. "Do I have a choice?"

"No, not really."

"Go on then." The instant I step into the sunlight I feel as if a heavy weight has lifted from my shoulders. I lift my face and breathe deep the familiar scent of the forest—decaying leaves, dirt and pine.

Bastien waits until I stop soaking in my daily dose of vitamin D before speaking. "What's with you and Eamon? You guys seem rather intense."

I snort and turn my face into the wind. The air has a bite to it this morning, but the temperature has already begun to rise above freezing. Patches of blue sky peek through sagging gray clouds overhead, but there is a menacing storm system on the horizon. "Looks like we might catch a brief break in the weather. We should try to cover as much ground as we can while it's nice."

I turn before Bastien can protest and pound my steps into the mountain slope with a ferocity that slowly eases the burden in my mind. He keeps pace with me, never complaining or asking for a break. I plunge deeper into the woods, annoyed that Bastien's watchful eye lands on me frequently over the next couple of hours. When he realizes that his stares aren't getting the expected response, he releases an obnoxiously loud sigh. Annoyed, I whip around and slam into his broad chest.

Pushing off him to give myself some much needed personal space, I cross my arms over my chest. "You might as well spill it. I know you've been dying to say something since we left the cave."

I slip my pack off my back and sink down onto a fallen tree. The dampness of the bark seeps through my pants and onto my skin. I dig into my bag and pull out a small leather pouch. Tugging it open with my teeth, I close my eyes as the refreshing water flows down my parched throat. We've been going hard for well over two hours. Maybe it was a good idea to pause for a moment.

"It's nothing."

"Oh, come on. You've been giving me that look all morning."

Bastien scratches his stubbled chin. "Just trying to figure you out is all."

I toss him the leather pouch and settle back into the crook of the tree branches that rise toward the sky, like fingers bent with age. It's not exactly comfortable but it will do for now. Comfort in the forest is relative.

I watch as Bastien drinks deep from the pouch. "I'm not that complicated, you know."

"No?" He leans over to hand me the canteen back. "Then why is it you act like you're running away from your friends?"

"It's not them." I drop my gaze and fumble with the edge of my frayed sweater. "It's me. I don't want them to find out that I'm the reason they've become freaks."

Bastien steps up to a tree, slides down the trunk and then throws out his legs before him. "We aren't freaks, Illyria, and it's not your fault."

I roll my eyes at him.

"Ok, well maybe you did have *something* to do with it, but it's not like you did it on purpose. You can't control this…whatever it is."

"Exactly." I rip off a chunk of bark and hurl it into the underbrush, wishing I had something far more substantial to throw. "I'm dangerous. We've already established that, but what if I've endangered my friends too? I can't bear the thought of them getting hurt."

I lean my head back and close my eyes. I can hear him shift by the rustling of leaves, but I don't open my eyes. It feels good to be consumed by darkness. "It's more than that, isn't it?"

A groan escapes from my lips and I dig my fists into my eyes, fighting to block out my thoughts. "Have you ever thought you were going crazy?"

His chuckle sends warmth flooding down to my toes. The emotions I feel when I'm around him are both foreign and surprisingly pleasing. "Can't say that I have. Why do you ask?"

Slowly, I lower my hands and focus on him. He rolls his shoulders, rubbing out his tired muscles. When he notices my direct gaze, he lets his hand fall free.

"I hear things," I say. "Whispers in my mind."

His brow furrows as he sinks back against the tree to watch me. "What do they say?"

A chill creeps down my spine. "Sometimes it's hard to tell. They are usually a jumble in my mind, but sometimes, late at night I can hear them when I'm trying to sleep."

"Any other time?"

I tuck my legs up into my chest and rest my cheek against my knee. "I hear them when I'm about to lose control. They cheer for me."

A slight tremble in my fingers betrays me and doesn't get past Bastien's watchful gaze. "You're scared, aren't you?"

I don't trust my voice so I nod. A single tear slips down my cheek and falls to the ground below. It's mortifying but I can't hold up a cool façade any more.

Bastien leaps to his feet and kneels beside me. I watch him as he wavers between reaching out to comfort me and holding back. I laugh and wipe my cheek. "I'm not going to bite."

"I have my doubts about that." His fingers twine through mine and gently pull me down off the log. I sink into his embrace, comforted as he wraps his arms firmly around my back and pulls my head down onto his chest. The steady thrumming of his heart is calming.

"How is it that you can be so thoughtful one minute and so completely infuriating the next?" I whisper, curling my fingers around the soft fabric of his borrowed shirt.

I feel his smile against the crown of my head. "It's a gift."

I close my eyes and focus on the feel of his hands as he runs his fingers over my hair, soothing me like a little child just woken from a terrible nightmare. "I don't normally cry like this."

"One tear hardly counts in my books."

"Are you keeping track?"

He is silent for a moment. My head rises and falls with his chest. "I kinda like it."

I lift my head to stare up into his eyes. They are darker than usual, no longer the flickering blue of a flame. "Like what?"

"Keeping track of you." His breath unsettles the flyaway strands of hair across my face. I blink, shocked by the tender caress of his words.

"Is that a joke?" I whisper.

His hands tighten around my back. "Afraid not, Princess."

I'm suddenly all too aware of how close he is, how full his lips are and how tight his embrace has become. I place my hand on his chest. "Your heart—"

He leans in and brushes his lips against mine, his touch light and gentle. He reaches up to cup my cheek, his eyes wide and searching as he pulls back. My lower lip tingles as I run my fingertip across it, pausing to process his first touch.

"Are you ok?"

I nod, although my head is swimming at his nearness. The scent of his skin turns my thoughts into chaos. Without stopping to consider the consequences, I wrap my hand around his neck and crush my lips against his. My lips muffle his cry of surprise as I curl my fingers around the soft hair that drapes down to his neck.

As his hands curve around my back, I raise up into him, locking my hands together around his neck. The heat of his body pressed against mine is exciting, the movement of his lips sinfully intoxicating.

My breath comes fast and hard as I lean in closer, my knees digging into the dirt beside his thighs. I let my head fall to the side and Bastien's lips trace a line down my jaw, his fingers digging into my sides. The irrational urge to laugh bubbles up within me as I realize I've never done anything so completely reckless before.

I've gone head-to-head with a wolf while hunting, dove off the Cascades to satisfy a teenage dare and entered the forbidden City alone, but I've never let a guy get this close. If I had known kissing would be this intense, I would have done it a lot sooner.

I lean into Bastien, pressing him back to the ground. He goes willingly, his eyes searching mine as I lean down, hovering less than an inch over his lips. His fingers pull at my waist, silently begging me, but I smile and shake my head. He groans, arching up to meet my lips and I give in to his need.

The soil under my hands begins to shift as small tremors ripple out from me. There are no barriers between us, no sarcastic cracks or awkward banter. I realize that I want this, him, more than I want air to breathe. I feel rooted in place, as if my very existence was meant to bring us here, to this very moment.

Bastien pushes me up and rolls me onto my back, placing himself beside me. The coolness of the ground eases the scorching heat bearing down on me from above. Each time his fingers caress my bare skin, I feel drawn into him.

His chiseled body presses against the length of mine while his arm cradles my head. His lips leave a slow, blazing trail down my neck. I lean my head back to allow him access to the hollow of my throat and a shiver of pleasure washes over me as his breath tickles my delicate skin.

I react to every touch, every breath, and every pounding heartbeat. The smallest touch is torture and yet more satisfying than I could have ever imagined. I open my eyes and watch the trees tremble overhead as I dig my fingers deep into the dirt.

I feel alive, connected not only with Bastien but the world around me——the trees, the soil, the earth. Energy courses through my body, making my skin tingle with overwhelming sensitivity.

Bastien chuckles when I gasp, his lips pressing against the tender flesh just behind my ear. A thousand tiny goosebumps spread along my skin as he shifts to caress just above my waistline, moving slowly around from my back to my stomach.

He dips his head, softly tugging on my bottom lip with his teeth before pulling back. He teases me, taunts me.

The trees groan as a perfect, circular crater forms around us, revealing the maze of roots that burrow deep into the ground. The fallen tree I occupied only a few moments before is caught up on the outside of the sinkhole and rolls into a nearby tree, startling me. Reality comes crashing back in with the thunderous boom.

I push against Bastien's chest, frantic to be free of his embrace. He rolls onto his side, his brow furrowed with confusion at my sudden panic. "What's wrong?"

"This...this is wrong!" I scramble out from under him, clawing my way to a tree a few feet away. I cling to it, waiting for my heart to stop racing as I try to slow my breathing. The taste and feel of Bastien lingers on my skin.

"Are you ok?" He asks.

Bastien makes no move to come closer and I'm grateful for it. My mind screams to run, to flee this utterly embarrassing debacle but another part, one that I fear might just be the stronger side, begs me to sink back into his embrace.

"I'm sorry," I whisper without turning. "I don't know what came over me."

I expect him to break out with some witty comment that will embarrass me further, but instead, he remains silent. His silence actually unnerves me more than sarcasm would have. I can't help but wonder if he is mad at me for stopping or for starting this in the first place.

I slowly turn, never dreaming to see such tenderness from him. His gaze is kind, his body relaxed and completely undemanding.

"Are you ok?" He asks again, softer this time. So soft that it makes my heart melt.

I tuck my legs into my chest and stare at him, unsure of how to answer. Although I may be physically ok, I am an emotional wreck. I don't know what I was thinking to kiss him like that.

"I'll be fine. I just…I think we should just keep this between us for now."

His nod of agreement is immediate. "Of course."

"I just…" I close my mouth and try to think of the right thing to say, but know I'm about to fail miserably. "I've never been good with guys. I'm not really sure what to say right now."

Bastien's hair blows across his forehead and I'm gripped by his sheer, rugged beauty. My gaze lingers on the scar that peeks out around his dark stubble and I feel a slight pinch in my gut.

I know nothing about him. Nothing, beyond the fact that he has been willing to risk his life for me twice. He gave unselfishly of his provisions to see to it that I could survive. He's shown compassion to a complete stranger when it wasn't in his best interest to do so.

He brushes his hair back out of his eyes and smiles. "You don't have to say anything, Princess. Besides, I kinda like you like this."

"Silent?"

He leans in close. "Speechless."

I watch him with growing curiosity. "Why aren't you afraid of me? You saw what I did to those Squaddies at the factory and it barely phased you. Now I tell you I'm hearing voices in my head and practically jump you and you don't even bat an eye."

Bastien shrugs and leans back, shifting his legs. "Maybe I like a little danger."

I laugh, slowly coming down from my high. I'm grateful that our conversation has veered into more neutral waters. "Well that's obvious, but I think it's more than that."

The slight narrowing of his eyes tells me I've hit a bit too close to home for comfort. "Contrary to what you might think about me, I am a gentleman. I always keep my word, but I'm also a believer in forces in this world that go beyond our understanding."

"Like God?"

His eyebrow rises. "Who told you about God?"

"My mother. She said there were many, or just one, depending on who you spoke to."

Bastien nods. "That's about right. But I'm not talking about an all-powerful being. I'm talking about fate, destiny, the forces that drive us to be who we are."

"And what drives you?"

"Adventure." He grins. "Always searching for the unknown."

"And you view me as a puzzle to solve?"

He shrugs. "You are a mystery to me, that's for sure, but what I'm searching for is the source. Where did your abilities come from? How did you create that pulse that changed our DNA?"

I crinkle my nose, thinking back through the years of boring lectures I was forced to endure in the Temple as a child. "That's what we are made of, right?"

"Yes," he affirms. "It's the very fibers of our being. Somehow, I'm guessing you altered us. I, for one, would love to know how you pulled that off."

I chew on my lip as my index finger carves a swirled path through the dirt. The soil is damp and cold to the touch. It won't be long before the land is encased in ice, dormant for another season.

"There's something I think I should tell you." I scrape at the dirt embedded under my fingernails as I tell Bastien about my brief conversation with Kyan the night we were attacked by Commander Drakon's men. I can't bring myself to look at him, to see his reaction.

He is silent when I finish. "I think we should try to find this guy."

"We aren't out here for a man hunt."

"No, of course not. We're still going to spy on the Grounders, but I don't think it would hurt to look around while we are there."

A gust of wind sends my hair into a tangle whirlwind about my face. I hold it back, fighting to restrain it, but it's a useless endeavor. Bastien offers me a stick he's been whittling down in his fingers, peeling the bark back from the flesh. "Thought you might need this."

"How observant." I can feel my defenses rising.

I pull back as much of my hair as I can in my fist and wind it into a haphazard bun, shoving the stick straight through the middle.

"I'm not saying we do anything reckless, Illyria. I'm just saying we take a look."

I blink, stunned. "Do you realize you just called me Illyria?"

Bastien strips a layer of damp bark from another stick, the same thickness and length as the one that's doing a pathetic job of holding my crazy hair in place. "Must have slipped."

His slip doesn't feel all that accidental though, not after the heated moment we shared. Is it a coincidence that he spoke my name for the first time right after he confessed he has feelings for me? I highly doubt it.

I accept the second stick and spear it through my drooping hair. I hesitantly thank him for his gift. "You ready to move out? Looks like that storm's moving in fast."

Raising my hand to shield my eyes from the sun, I realize with a start that, while we've been chatting, the dark wall of clouds has indeed gained ground on us. "We don't want to be caught out in the open when that thing decides to dump it's load."

Bastien offers me a hand up. I rise and brush moss and leaves from my backside. "Wouldn't want to give you another reason to stare at my butt." I joke.

"Who said I need a reason?" He snatches my pack off the ground and holds it out to me. "How far do you think we are from the outskirts of the City?"

I rise up onto my tiptoes and peer over the trees that spread out in the valley below, coming to an abrupt halt at the City perimeter. "Two hours, give or take. It's pretty rough terrain."

"Well then I guess you'd better try to keep up." He takes off at a slight jog.

The winds begin to bend the treetops less than fifteen minutes after we set off again. Each step becomes arduous as we burrow through the gale. I've never felt the effects of a hurricane before but I have read about them. About how the storm can topple small shelters and uproot hundred-year-old trees and the tidal surge that can flood an entire city. As the gust lashes against my face, I wonder if the swirling clouds above might not be a cousin to a hurricane.

"What's going on?" I shout to Bastien, who has moved alongside me, twining his fingers through mine to help me remain upright.

"I don't know. I've never seen clouds like that before."

The muscles in Bastien's arms pull taut as he yanks me behind a thick tree. He presses me against the trunk, sheltering me with his body as he searches the sky. "It doesn't make sense."

"What doesn't?" I shout to be overheard by the roar that's emanating from the valley below. The forest grows dark as the clouds consume the entire sky, blocking out the bright sunshine overhead.

"I think it's a—" he cuts off, his eyes widening with fright as the sound of splintering wood rises among the deafening roaring.

My stomach clenches with fear as I watch trees ripped from the earth and tossed into the air, spun round and round the exterior or a monstrous vortex. "A tornado!"

Bastien's hard gaze focuses on me. "Are you doing this?"

I am numb from head to foot with fear. "Not this time."

His jaw clenches and when he glances back over his shoulder, his face drains of color. The half-mile wide tornado is clearing a path through the forest, straight toward us. "Run!"

I don't have to be told twice. My thoughts become frenzied as we scramble back up the incline, digging our boots into the earth as we fight to resist the strength of the whirlwind. The sticks in my hair yank free, ripping strands of hair from my scalp, but I hardly notice the pain.

"Run faster!"

"I'm trying." I throw my weight forward to counteract the pull at my back.

The harder I try to run, the more my feet slip. Bastien's hands land on my backside and push me up the hill. Any other time I'd take his hands off at the wrists for touching me, but right now I'm grateful for the extra help.

I grab onto tree branches, dragging myself the last fifteen feet up the embankment. Loose soil shifts underfoot, threatening to spill me to my knees, but Bastien's solid strength refuses to let me fall.

The roar behind us grows, bellowing so loudly I can't hear Bastien's shout right next to my ear. I turn to look at him, watching as his lips frantically move but I hear nothing. He yanks on my arm, and I stumble after him, blinded by the swirling debris surrounding us. Leaves, sticks and brambles rise into the air, pelting us with brutal accuracy.

It's almost as if this storm has one focus—us.

You can't outrun it, a voice calls.

I pull upright, shocked by the sudden invasion of my mind. I know this voice, deep but colored with the music of wind chimes blowing in the breeze. *Kyan?*

You have to fight back, Illyria. It's your only chance.

"What's going on?" Bastien screams into my ear. I can see his terror as his gaze moves past my face to lock onto the swirling monster less than a mile away. I don't have to look to know that it has changed course, following our retreat.

How can I fight a tornado? It's a part of nature!

Is the sky green? Is there any hail to go along with it?

I look overhead and see dark clouds, a swirl of gray and obsidian, but no hint of green. There is no rain, no hail, no sign of lightning.

How is this possible? I ask silently.

Bastien shifts beside me, anxious to move as the whirlwind draws closer. The pressure of his fingers against my arm grows as I linger.

Just as you made the waterspout, someone else is controlling this tornado. It's a trap.

I suck in a breath. Bastien's gaze refocuses on me. "What?"

"It's a trap."

His eyes glaze over, confusion taking hold until he watches the tornado shift again, bearing straight down on us. His lips peel back with anger. "What do we do?"

I want to shrug, to express my own complete lack of certainty but instead I close my eyes. "I'm speaking with Kyan."

"Oh great! That makes me feel *much* better."

"Shh!"

Kyan? What do I do?

Fight!

EIGHTEEN

A near constant gust coils around me as I plant my feet and face off with the tornado. Bastien's hand falls away from my arm as he mirrors my stance. I can feel his fear and hear the rapid pulse in his neck.

Blinking, I realize I can hear more than his frantic heartbeat. I can hear the branches overhead clacking out a disjointed staccato. Hear the groaning of the pine trees as they release their needles to the might of the vortex. I can also sense the steady breathing of a man within the eye of the storm.

I have no idea how the man can actually be *within* the deadly vortex, but he is there. I can feel him, even if I can't see him.

Look at Bastien.

My gaze turns, as if in slow motion, to focus on the man beside me. I notice how pale his skin is, the way his neck cords as he struggles to swallow, and the rise and fall of his Adam's apple as he fights to control his panic. When his fear-darkened eyes swivel to meet mine, I feel it, like an explosion of fireworks within my belly. Heat boils over as it seeps into every fiber of my being.

Bastien's mouth gapes open. "Your eyes—"

"I know."

I turn to face the tornado, now less than a quarter mile away. All hint of fear has fled and been replaced by black fury. The whispers rise in my mind, drowning out everything around me as I take a step forward.

The winds break against me, like waves against a rocky shore. I hear Bastien call to me but I ignore him. I continue to advance, slowly descending, facing off with my enemy.

You have great power, Illyria, but do not let it control you, Kyan warns. *Harness your power, unleash it, but do not kill that man.*

Why not? I can hear the unnatural growl attached to my words. It sounds dark and guttural, altering my usual voice.

Killing changes a person.

I've already killed, back in the factory and in the woods.

There is silence from Kyan's end. His hesitation makes my confidence waver slightly. *Deal with this. I will help you learn control afterward.*

I feel him withdraw from my mind. His sudden departure leaves me feeling both alone and rebuked. As I plant my feet, nearly fifteen feet ahead of Bastien, I realize Kyan's disappointment actually bothers me, that he would think I *meant* to kill those Squaddies.

"Illyria, come back! You're going to get yourself killed!"

I shake my head, unsure if Bastien can even see the movement against the deluge of debris spiraling between us. I watch as a clump of trees at the bottom of the hill cleaves from the earth and flies into the air. The sky is full of saplings, shrubs and pencil straight trees.

The ground ruptures underfoot, the soil parting, shifting. As the tornado begins its ascent up the hill, I hold my ground, staring down the black clad figure I can scarcely glimpse through the vortex. The cyclone contorts, violently shuddering as it appears to thrust upward, expanding in breadth along the cloud base and narrowing along the ground until only a tight funnel remains around the man. Buttery eyes of the fair-haired man rise to meet mine.

"You are either very brave of very foolish," the man bellows.

"I bet you'd like to know which, huh?"

"Not many have the guts to face off with me. Certainly never a human, but then Commander Drakon doesn't think you *are* human, does he?"

"The jury is still out on that one." I shift, flexing my hands at my side. The heat in my fingertips is nearly unbearable. I begin to wonder if all I'll be left with are singed nubs when this is done.

The man watches me with great intensity. I breathe deeply, catching a hint of his fear on the air. "You have two choices. You can run back to Drakon with your tail between your legs or we can fight. You're choice, but personally, I'm aching for a fight."

The cocky grin that stretches across my face feels foreign and I realize that I am no longer in control of this situation. Something has assumed the reins as the whispers form a hushed mob in my mind, dispelling any hint of trepidation on my part.

The man's stance stiffens at my insulting challenge. A vein running the length of his forehead, from scalp to the bridge of his bulbous nose, pulsates madly. "You dare speak to me like that!"

"Are all Caldonians this pompous?" I roll my eyes and plant my fists on my hips with an air of exaggerated mockery. "Of course I dare!"

With the rush of a thousand winds, the tornado descends over the man and eats up the terrain separating us.

Well, I've done it now, I silently grumble as I raise my hands and prepare to fight.

Instinct drops me into a crouch. I honestly have no clue what to do, or how to begin fighting a force of nature, but I close my eyes and wait.

I can feel a presence in my mind, like snakes slithering over my skin. The feeling is both repulsive and enthralling at the same time. The whispers rise in my mind, cheering wildly, taunting me to seek revenge. Mentally I cower away for their calls for my enemy's demise.

Let me show you what I am capable of, a voice hisses.

Images fill my mind— a field of mangled, severed limbs, and lifeless eyes pooled with blood. I walk among the dead, my clothes drenched in Caldonian blood...but it's not only my enemy's blood. I can see piles of humans rising to the sky, broken and tortured but hanging on to a shred of life. They plead to me as the stench of their burning flesh rises from the burial pyres, as they're set alight. I walk past without any offer of aid or sympathy.

Kyan? What the heck is that?

The Shadow, he responds. *It is powerful but as long as you can focus, you will be able to control it.*

The brutality of the images sickens me and I try to look away, but the Shadow laughs at my weakness. *Release me and I will show you real power.*

"No!"

I thrust out my hands toward the tornado and cry out as energy ripples down my arms. The air shimmers with gold and obsidian, a coiling inferno to rival my enemy's. It rampages forward, charging with increasing speed to consume the heart of the Caldonian tornado. The man within releases a blood curdling scream as the vortex alights with brilliant flames, licking up higher and higher to consume the clouds. The forest illuminates with an intense explosion of light as the blackened clouds and tornado appear to implode and vanish from sight. Warm sunlight spills onto the valley once more.

I fall to my knees, weakened and gasping for breath. Bastien rushes to my side, wrapping his arms around my shoulders as he shifts in front of me, cupping my face. "Are you ok?"

"I...I don't know." My voice wavers as the whispers in my mind taper off. The presence retreats, but I can feel its approval. Slowly I regain control of my senses.

Bastien's thumb brushes along my cheek, his gaze staring fixedly into my eyes a slow smile tugs at his lips. "Your eyes are so beautiful."

I snort weakly, collapsing into his embrace. "Black becomes me, huh?"

"No. I'm a sucker for girls with violet eyes."

I laugh and lean my head against his chest, breathing deep. "Is it over?"

He cranes his neck to see over my head and nods. I glance up when I notice his entire body tensing. "Did I...did I kill him?"

I stare into his handsome face, silently pleading with fate to be kind to me just this once. Bastien smiles and shakes his head.

"I don't think so. He seems to be breathing, but I'm guessing he's gonna have a nasty headache when he comes to."

"That he will."

I whip around to see Kyan standing less than ten feet from us. Bastien instinctively reaches down my back toward my dagger, but I still his hand.

"How did you find us?" I ask, amazed by how perfectly composed he looks, not a hair out of place.

Kyan approaches slowly, cautiously, never blinking as he watches Bastien. "I've been here the entire time. Joce is one of the best trackers we have. I knew if anyone could find you, it would be him, so I kept my distance until I saw him power up. It's hard to miss him once he sets his eyes on his target."

"Who is this guy?"

"This is Kyan," I say.

A low growl rumbles in Bastien's chest. "You let her fight him, knowing she could've died?"

"No," Kyan shakes his head. "I let her fight him because, without her, you and I would both be dead right now."

Bastien glances at me. I can tell he's frustrated with this answer. "Welcome to my world," I mutter.

When Bastien helps me to my feet, I brush off layers of debris from my clothes and try to shake most of it out of my hair. "Why are you here, Kyan?"

"I told you I would find you." He glances beyond me to the blackened grass, singed by my tornado. "I'm sure by now you have a lot of questions. I need to give you the answers."

"Why should we trust you?" Bastien challenges.

I glance over at him. "Weren't you the one saying we should search the City for him to *get* answers?"

"Yeah," he nods, glaring at Kyan. "But he didn't have to know that."

Kyan smiles and drops his gaze. I can tell by the glint in his eyes that he's doing more than listening with his ears. I lean close to Bastien. "He can read minds, too."

"Now you tell me," Bastien mutters, crossing his arms over his chest.

Raising his hands in a show of surrender, Kyan closes the gap between us. "I'm not here to make enemies, Bastien. I only want to help Illyria lean how to control her abilities. You've seen what she is capable of. If she can't learn to harness the Shadow within, the devastation you see before you is what the entire earth could look like. She's getting stronger with each day. I fear what will happen the next time."

"What is this Shadow you refer to?" Bastien asks.

"I felt it," I whisper, curling my arms around my stomach as I stifle a shiver. "It was in my mind, showing me things."

"What things?" Bastien steps closer to me.

I shake my head. "I won't let that happen."

"It won't. Not if you let me help you," Kyan says.

"And you think *you* can help her?" Bastien scoffs.

I glare at him and he wipes the smirk from his face. I turn to face Kyan full on. "How do you propose to help me?"

"By training you to control your emotions and harness your will. It will take time and no small amount of effort on your part. I can't say it will be easy, because there's never been anyone like you before, but I'm willing to try if you are."

Bastien throws up his hands in the air with irritation. "That's just great. We've got a traitor Caldonian who's willing to 'train' you but doesn't have a clue what he's doing. This doesn't feel right, Illyria."

"I know." And I do. I rub my hands along my arms, willing the goosebumps to disappear. The memory of that presence in my mind terrifies me, as do the images burned into my thoughts. "Kyan is the best shot I have. You thought so yourself, didn't you?"

"Semantics." His face darkens with anger.

Kyan appears at my shoulder. I stiffen but don't back away for fear of the ensuing fight Bastien is sure to initiate. "I can help her, Bastien, but it's going to take trust."

"Trust," Bastien scoffs again, rolling his eyes. "Yeah, like she's going to trust scum like you."

"I'm not talking about Illyria." His pointed gaze makes Bastien stiffen.

"Me?"

"You are her protector, are you not?" I can hear the lilt of barely restrained laughter on his voice. Such show of chivalry must not be common among Kyan's people.

"I am." Bastien raises his chin in defiance.

"Then you are going to have to bring her to me each day for training and trust that no matter what I ask of her, I'm doing it for her benefit."

"I'm not sure I like the sound of that." Bastien's hesitation comes through loud and strong. I place a warning hand on his arm.

"I understand, but this is the way it must be. Commander Drakon is aching to get his hands on Illyria. That much is obvious by Joce's presence. He's getting desperate. We can't let Illyria be captured before she has learned control. The effects would be devastating."

"Not to mention it would totally ruin my day," I grumble, thinking about the greedy glint I saw in the commander's eyes the night he watched me take out his men. He's power hungry, that much is for sure.

"So what's your plan then?" Bastien asks.

"It's simple. There is a rock formation about an hour south of your cave. Do you know it, Illyria?"

I scrunch up my nose, thinking of the landscape. It's a densely populated area with gnarled brambles and overgrowth of trees. As such, we have avoided that area for the most part. I'm not a fan of digging thorns out of my legs for hours on end, but I know of the place he speaks. There is a small arena in the middle of the brambles, about half the size of the Temple, which is surrounded by tall rounded boulders that create a nearly perfect enclosed circle.

Eamon and I discovered it about a year ago when we were out hunting. A young doe managed to get herself trapped inside, her leg snapped in three places. I don't like killing young animals but, upon Eamon's assurance that the deer wouldn't last the night with the wolves moving into our area, I made the shot. My only condolence is that she didn't suffer.

"I know it."

"Meet me there when the sun is high each day. I will be waiting."

"I can't. Bastien and I are heading into the City."

"Why?" Kyan's question comes out like a bark.

"We're hunting the Diggers."

"You won't find them there." Kyan glances between us. "It's a waste of a trip and highly dangerous. It's best for you to head back to camp."

"I'm not taking orders from you," Bastien says as he steps between us.

"It's not an order. It's a suggestion." Kyan says. "You want to keep her safe, right?"

Bastien's jaw clamps down as he nods. "Of course I do."

"Good. Then take her back home and meet me tomorrow."

Kyan turns to leave but I call out. "How will you make it from the City each day? That's at least a four hour walk."

"Who said I live in the City?" He turns and winks.

Cocking his head to the side, Bastien scrutinizes the alien. "I've got one more question."

Kyan's eyes narrow at Bastien and I can't help but wonder if he already knows exactly what Bastien is going to ask. "Why do you care so much about Illyria?"

For the first time, Kyan drops his gaze. "I have my reasons."

Bastien cross his arms over his chest, creating a rather imposing figure. "I look forward to hearing them."

NINETEEN

I lead as we hike back toward the caves. I shove thick branches out of our way as Bastien lets out an exaggerated sigh. I've known he's been ready to blow for the last thirty minutes, but hoped he would simmer down before we made it back to the cave. Obviously, that's not going to happen.

I release a branch and let it swing back, slapping Bastien right across the chest. "Hey!" he shouts, rubbing his bruised flesh.

"Well, I had to do something to distract you from your grumpiness." I turn and face him, holding the strap of my bag tightly across my chest. I don't want him to see the tremor that continues to ripple through my fingers after our encounter with Kyan an hour ago.

"I'm not grumpy. I'm worried."

"About what?"

He rolls his eyes. "Don't you find it the least bit odd that Kyan just happened to be waiting to see how you handled yourself back there?"

I offer an indifferent shrug, but even a blind man wouldn't have been fooled by my pathetic attempt. "I don't know. Kyan is…mysterious."

"That's one word for it. I've got a few more if you'd like to hear them."

I laugh. "You've got some serious trust issues, don't you?"

"Of course I do. He seems too invested in you. Too…protective."

"Hmm," I scratch my chin, as if in deep thought. "I wonder if that might describe another near complete stranger that I've run across this week."

Bastien scowls. "That's not funny."

"Didn't intend for it to be." I close the gap between us and place my hand on his forearm. I try not to think of how wonderful it felt to be wrapped in his embrace. "I don't think Kyan means to hurt me."

"How could you possibly know that?"

"Simple." I release his arm and reattach my grip on my pack. "He's let me walk away twice now and I'm still alive."

I turn away and adopt a determined march. Bastien rushes to catch up to me. "So what do you think about this whole training thing?"

"I don't know. It could be good."

His grasps my shoulder and forces me to stop, turning me to face him. "I may still be sort of a stranger, but I know you Illyria. You're freaking out, but are too darn stubborn to admit it."

I look down at the ground, unable to meet his gaze. A ring of mud clings to the edge of my boots. "So what? Wouldn't you be scared if you were me?"

Bastien gently lifts my chin with his finger. "Of course I would be, but not for the reasons you think."

I purse my lips as he continues. "I think we've pretty much established that I'm not a fan of the Caldonians. You know that my parents were killed by the aliens a while back, which is why you found me sewer diving with the rats in those subway tunnels, but I never really told you *how* they died."

His face clouds over and he frowns. "My dad was weak, malnourished, at the end. Mom worried for weeks before they were captured that he was coming down with some sort of respiratory illness."

My forehead furrows with confusion. I've never heard that word before.

Bastien continues, staring blankly into the woods. "He started coughing first. Deep and kind of chunky sounding. Then the wheezing began. He couldn't catch his breath. Mom tried everything she could to ease his suffering, but he developed a fever and it burned right through him."

"Nighttime was the worst. He would cough until he was red in the face and then empty his stomach all over the floor. He couldn't keep anything down. On that last day, his lips were starting to turn blue and mom got real quiet. I knew something was wrong but was too afraid to ask."

"So what happened?" I ask in a whisper.

Bastien closes his eyes to the memory. "I went out in search of medicine. Mom warned me to be careful not to be seen. Guess I didn't do such a great job. The Squaddies waited for me to slip in the back door before they came in through the front. I never even made it to my bedroom before my mom started screaming at me to run."

"What did you do?"

He turns so I can only see his profile, but even that is enough to betray the pain etched on his face. "I ran."

My throat constricts at the sob that rises in his throat. "I just left her there, defenseless. I should have stayed. I could have fought."

"No," I argue softly, placing my hand on his shoulder. "You would have been taken too."

"I know," he whispers. He wipes his nose with the back of his sleeve before he turns to look at me. "I slipped through my window into the apartment next door. I used to hate how close together the buildings were, but for once, I was grateful. I snuck up to the roof and covered myself with a tarp so the Sky Ships wouldn't see me when they arrived."

"I saw them drag my father out into the street. He was so weak he could barely hold up his head." He scuffs his toe into the dirt, digging a crater as he fights the emotions released by his admission. "He tried to push them away, but they put their laser to his chest and pulled the trigger."

"He fell to the ground, a huge charred hole where his heart had been only seconds before. I can still hear my mother wailing as two men drug her behind a dumpster at the end of the street. I buried my head and tried to cover my ears, but I could still hear them laughing as they abused her over and over again."

"Oh god." I cup my hands over my mouth, horrified.

Bastien clears his throat and shoves his hands in his pocket. "When they were done they just left her there, on the ground, and I knew she was gone. I could see her hand sticking out from the dumpster. It never moved."

My fingers tremble as my hand falls from my mouth. "What did you do?"

I've never seen such anger in a man before. His beautiful eyes look as hard as ice. "I waited for them to leave before I stood up. When I did, I saw *him* on the rooftop across from me. He was alone, unmoving."

"Who?"

"Kyan," he grinds out the alien's name.

"But surely it was dark. You can't possibly know it was him," I protest.

"I know," he snaps. "I've seen my fair share of aliens over the past few years and never have I seen one with his eye color. He recognized me today. I know it. That's why he was mocking me about being your protector."

"No." I shake my head, struggling to wrap my head around it. "Even if it was him, why would he just let you go that night?"

"Honestly? I think he's been following me. Following us. I think he's known all along this would happen. My bet is he's been waiting for us to find him."

I fall silent and let his words sink in. Is it possible that he could be right? Kyan can read minds from long distances. Maybe he really did plan all of this.

"You have to tell your friends, Illyria. They have a right to know."

I sigh, knowing he is right and despising him all the more for it. "I'll tell them. I just need time."

Bastien grabs my hand to stop me as I try to turn away. "You're supposed to start meeting with Kyan tomorrow. There's no more time left."

To say that my friends took my coming out party well would be the understatement of the century. Zahra was predictable in her fierce protests about my continuing to live within the confines of the cave. For once, I think I might actually agree with her. I'm like a ticking time bomb buried under hundreds of feet of sediment and rock.

Aminah was quiet but her turmoil was evident on her face. I could tell she was trying to dig into my brain but, with each attempt, I threw up a block that only frustrated her more. I don't know how I managed to keep her out, maybe it was just instinct.

Toren was livid. His face went through more shades of red than a ripening tomato. He yelled a lot, but that was to be expected. By the end of his tirade, he hit me with the 'I'm really disappointed in you' speech and stormed off with Aminah tucked firmly under his arm. I can't blame him. I did technically place the entire commune in danger.

Eamon was the hardest to face. His pain staked me right through the heart. Even though I know he's not angry at me for my actions, I've wounded him by hiding the truth…and sharing it with Bastien.

That night I went to the Cascades, needing the solitude and continuity of the rushing water to ease my guilt. The cold spray of the water felt amazing against my skin.

I stayed for a long time after everyone else went to bed. Even Bastien knew I needed to be alone and gave me some time to myself.

When I wake, curled into a tiny damp ball with my back pressed against the low row of stone near the falls, I groan and stretch to ease the pain in my lower back. I welcome the pain as penance, but I know it's not enough. My friends feel betrayed and rightfully so.

"You should have told me," a deep voice calls from the shadows.

I narrow my eyes and try to peer through the haze of mist that hangs in the air around me. "Eamon? How long have you been there?"

"Most of the night. I figured I'd find you here. You always did like to come to this spot to think."

My laugh is forced. I suck in a breath and try to pass if off as a cough but the silence between us is ripe with discomfort. "You obviously have something on your mind."

He steps out of the shadows looking despondent and haggard. "Why did you keep this from me?"

"I…" I begin but my voice cracks unnaturally. Clearing my throat does little to help the lump in my throat. "I never wanted to."

"That's crap and you know it!" He stomps into the glow of the torchlight. "You were trying to save your own skin. That's what cowards do and you've never been one of those before. Did Bastien tell you to lie?"

"No!" I cry. "He has nothing to do with this!"

Eamon scoffs, rolling his eyes. "Please. I'm not a fool, Illyria."

"I'm serious. I can't help it that he was with me every time someone was trying to kill me. It just happened."

"I should have been with you! Me! Not him!" Eamon's face contorts with anger. "I'm the one who looks out for you."

"I know," I whisper, stepping closer to him. "You've always been there for me, Eamon. I'm sorry you weren't the one to help me, but if he hadn't been there I would have died. You can't fault him for that."

He swallows several times before running his hands through his unruly curls. "Why didn't you tell the others about the two men you killed in the factory?"

The sound of the rushing waterfall covers my gasp, but my shock is no less evident. "How do you know about that?"

Eamon averts his gaze, focusing on the swirling foam in the pool below. "I saw it."

"How?" I demand. "Not even Aminah can get through to my mind right now."

"I'm not a mind reader," he spits out, as if the mere idea disgusts him. "I can see the future and the past when I focus."

I blink, sure that I've heard him wrong. As his expression hardens, I realize he's not in a joking mood. "When did that develop?"

He lifts his gaze to pin me to the wall. "The night you released that psychic blast."

I sink to the floor, overcome with grief. "I'm so sorry. I had no idea…"

"That I would find out."

"No!" I cry out as a tear trickles down my face. "That's not what I meant."

He turns away. His entire body seems stiff, unwelcoming. Fear threatens to overtake me as I surge to my feet and latch onto him, spinning him to face me.

"I knew it was my fault that everyone changed. I wanted to tell you, but I couldn't bear the thought of seeing this look on your face."

His chin draws up and his jaw clenches. "When did you become such a coward?"

"When I became deadly." I hang my head, pressing it against Eamon's chest. He doesn't make any move to console me and that makes me tear up even more. "I don't know what's happening to me, Eamon. I was terrified of getting you involved, of you getting hurt because of me. I can't bear the thought of losing you."

"And you thought lying to me was the answer?" He growls.

"No!" I jerk upright, fighting to look at him through a disarray of hair. "I was going to tell you when I had the answers. When I knew I could trust myself around you. These outbursts seem to come when I get really emotional."

For the first time I see a slight chink in Eamon's armor. "And you thought you might be emotional around me?"

"Of course! You're the closest thing I have to family, Eamon. I was terrified of losing you." I reach up and slowly press my palm against his face. "I'm so sorry…about everything."

He leans into my touch, closing his eyes. A small sigh escapes his lips. "I know," he whispers, placing his hand over mine. His other hand encircles my waist and draws me to his chest. I lay my head over his heart and breathe in the familiar scent of leather and pine, the smell of a hunter.

Hugging him feels like coming home. It is familiar, safe. He leans back into the wall and supports my weight as I nestle into him.

I've lost count of how many nights we have fallen asleep like this, our hearts beating in perfect unity. I guess, if I were to be honest, I can see why everyone thinks Eamon and I will end up together. He is the perfect match for me. Maybe *that* is why I have resisted for so long. Perhaps he's too perfect for me.

We lean like this until the muscles in my calves begin to quiver. I push off his chest and offer him a sheepish grin. "Am I forgiven?"

He extends a wry smile back. "You know I can't stay mad at you for long."

"I do." I hold out my hand to him and wait for him to clasp it.

Eamon pulls me back as I start toward the arched stone doorway. "I told you I saw what you did, but I also saw your grief afterward. I know you didn't mean to kill those men."

My smile falters as tears sting my eyes. "No. I didn't."

He squeezes my hand. "You're not a killer, Illyria. That thing inside of you is. If this Kyan guy can help you then I'm willing to give him a chance, but I'll be watching him."

I grin, tugging on his arm. "Always my big brother, ready to leap in and fight for me." As I lead him into the tunnel, I can't but notice the frown that settles over his features before we dip back into the darkness.

TWENTY

I move toward the stone circle, wary and alert. The birds sing their mournful tune in the trees, bidding farewell to autumn. Squirrels scramble around before me, winding around trees with last minute nut rations to store before winter hits. The trees quiver in the strong gusty winds, shedding the last of their lonesome leaves, stretching their limbs one last time before succumbing to a long winter slumber.

I pause, listening for any sounds beyond the large stone boulder before me. Instinct tells me that I'm not alone, but I can't see or hear Kyan. This puts me at a grave disadvantage, one that I'm loathe to accept.

Leaping up to perch atop the rough stone, I pause only a second to compare its surface to that of the concrete streets of the City. The texture is similar but this feels different, less manufactured.

"You're right on time," a voice calls from below.

I look up to find Kyan standing in the center of the circle, his hands splayed open in welcome. The firm press of my dagger at my back is calming but I have no doubt Kyan is already well aware of its presence.

"Won't you join me?"

I dart furtive glances all around, checking any blind spots before I spring into a flip and land less than twenty feet from him. His grin broadens as he turns his face to the side, as if he's smelling the air.

"Why don't you invite your friends to join us? I'm sure they would like to hear what I have to say firsthand."

Toren rises first, appearing directly over Kyan's shoulder on the far rim. Aminah's bouncing curls appear less than five feet to his left. Zahra, Bastien and Eamon each rise from different sections of the boulders. Apart from Toren, whose scowl would send a young child running for their mother, the others appear curious.

"I told you it wouldn't work. You can't sneak up on him." It's hard to keep the smug grin off my face as Toren helps Aminah down. Not that I'm trying very hard. Despite my attempts to convince him otherwise, Toren was adamant that his plan would work. I guess he had to learn the hard way.

Each of my friends descends into the barren circle and come to rest by my side. Even knowing my friends were nearby the entire time, it does admittedly feel better to have them within arm's reach. Bastien pauses next to my left side while Eamon towers to my right.

I can't help but notice the contrast between the two guys. Although they are not all that different in height, they have remarkable physical and personality differences. Eamon is fair skinned, light haired while Bastien is dark, rugged and self-assured. They are like opposing forces, light versus dark, noble versus dangerous. It's infuriating that both seem to be calling me in different directions.

"Now that you're all here, I'd like to begin with a few answers." Kyan turns to look each person in the eye. "I can tell you have a wide range of questions for me, but I'd like to speak first, if that's ok with you."

Toren shifts uneasily beside Eamon but says nothing. I glance toward Bastien and notice Zahra has actually severed her symbiotic attachment to his hip. She's leaning slightly forward on her toes, lips parted as she stares wide-eyed at Kyan. I glance at Kyan and notice the tiniest hint of a flush along his collar. He seems to be working rather hard to not look in her direction.

Kyan's offers me a tight smile with no explanation to follow. "If you will all take a seat."

He motions to the ground behind us. Toren grumbles under his breath as he helps Aminah down before settling in next to her, wrapping his arm protectively around her shoulders. I'm actually really surprised he allowed her to leave the safety of the caves. He must be desperate to get a read on Kyan through her.

Kyan sits and tucks his hands into his lap, offering each of us a warm smile. Bastien tenses as Kyan's gaze falls on him but quickly returns to me.

"I'm sure you have often wondered who and what we Caldonians are. We look like you in many ways, we speak, eat, and sleep like you, and yet we are distinctly different. Earth used to spend a great deal of time focusing on the mysteries of the stars beyond your planet. They made moving pictures about killer aliens who invade the planet. Obviously my skin is not green, nor do I want to eat your brains."

"Thank god for that," Eamon mutters over my shoulder. I shift and smile back at him.

Kyan continues on. "My race may be alien to you, but not to this planet. In my past, and your not too distant future, there will be a great war among worlds, a war that will eradicate all human life, apart from those who manage to escape. I won't bore you with the details of how time and space travel works. All you need to know is that my people have returned to save yours."

"You've got a funny way of showing it," Bastien growls darkly.

"Indeed." Kyan nods, his expression no less fierce. "The original plans, as presented to our assembly several years ago, was that of a peace mission. One that would help your people prepare for the coming war. We were misled."

"By whom?" I ask. Each of us lean forward, our full attention on Kyan's tale.

"A man called Aloysius, self-proclaimed King on Calisted, my home world. When he first approached the assembly, he spoke great words of wisdom, promoting peaceful sovereignty. Many people fell prey to his poisonous words, but a few did not. Those who opposed his climb to power were silenced. Over time, the disappearances began to add up but, by then, it was too late. He had built himself an army that was unmatched by any of the outlying planets. He took control of our government by might. The blood of thousands stains his throne."

"And he sent you here? Why?" Eamon speaks up.

"Aloysius is fueled by greed, for power and revenge. He was among the survivors who managed to escape the war. His wife and child were not so lucky."

"He's trying to save his family," Aminah whispers. Tears sparkle along her lashes.

"Yes." Kyan nods. "And no. Time passes differently on Calisted than it does here. One Earth year equals twenty-five there. Aloysius has spent many years moving past his grief for his wife. His greed has now replaced his mourning."

"How old are you?" Zahra speaks up. I glance over at her, shocked by the soft tone in her voice.

Kyan's cheeks flush as he looks at her. "We also age differently. The first eighteen years we grow like you, at a normal pace. After that, time seems to slow for us as we reach our eighteenth birthright. On your world I look twenty years old, but on Calisted I'm 68."

"So you're an old man then?" Bastien laughs, winking at me.

"Not at all. Our oldest living founder is nearly 780 years old, but on your world would only look 60. It is all a matter of perspective. On Calisted, I am still considered to be a teenager."

Glancing at Zahra, it's obvious she's relieved to hear this. I roll my eyes and turn away, catching Eamon's conspiratorial grin from the corner of my eye.

"So if this Aloysius isn't here to save his family, he must be here because of the war."

Kyan smiles at Toren despite the fact that he refuses to do anything more than glare back. "A very astute deduction, Toren. Yes, he has come back, because of the war, but not to help your people. He wants to win this time."

"How is that possible?" Eamon asks. "Human's obviously didn't do so well the first time around, and your king has done a pretty good job wiping us out now, so what's he playing at?"

A vision unfolds in my mind with crystal clarity. The air is filled with huge, hulking ships setting the night sky alight with fire and shrapnel. Men scramble along the war torn ground, dressed in tattered rags. They are battling hand-to-hand with giant men, each nearly seven feet tall with skin that looks shockingly like the scales of a snake's back. Their noses are thin slits of skin that gape open as they suck in great breaths of air.

Each alien is broad chested, with a patchwork of red scars and gruesome self-inflicted tattoos running down their bare skulls and along their spines. I can only imagine it be to a tally of the number of people they have slain. The ground is a river of blood. Bodies lie everywhere, dotting the landscape with decay and disease, but still the battle rages.

"They're here to replace us." I whisper, blinking as the image fades from before my eyes.

Kyan watches me closely as the others react with various outbursts. "You saw it?"

I nod. Movement to my right catches my eye and I turn to see Eamon's haunted eyes staring blankly back at me. His skin is void of color, his hands shaking at his sides. "There's nothing we can do to stop it," he whispers. "We're all going to die."

"No," Kyan says emphatically, drawing back our attention. "That's not entirely true. What you have both seen is only a glimpse of what *may* happen."

Bastien watches me closely as I fight back against the panic rising within. I shake my head at him and wrap my arms around my knees. He turns his gaze back to Kyan. "Is this why you're here? Why you care so much about training Illyria? She is the key, isn't she?"

"Yes." Kyan nods solemnly. He clears his throat and for the first time drops his gaze completely. This piques my curiosity as I watch an array of emotions flit across his face before he speaks. "Illyria is the Shadow Walker, the only one known to my kind. Her birth was foretold by three prophets long before I was born. They claim that she alone can bring balance to our worlds."

Zahra snorts in disbelief, but I don't give her the satisfaction of acknowledging her outburst. "What about my friends? I changed them somehow."

"No." Kyan shakes his head. "You didn't change them, Illyria. You released them."

"Care to explain that one?" Toren asks. Although there is still a definite bite to his tone, it has dropped a notch in the last few minutes.

Kyan sits forward and steeples his fingers before him. "When I first met Illyria, I told her that I could sense her because she was one of us. I've sensed her from the moment I arrived on your planet, but she was not alone. I have sensed each of you as well. You are all among my kind."

A gurgling sound rises from Toren's throat as he staggers to his feet. "That's not possible. We are nothing like you!"

Aminah tugs for his hand but he refuses to be consoled as he begins to frantically pace behind us. Eamon sits back, blowing out a deep breath as he tangles his fingers through his curls. Zahra's mouth gapes open in shock. Only Bastien keeps his calm, but I can tell that he's wondering if *this* is the reason Kyan allowed him to run the night his parents died.

"How is this possible?" Aminah chokes out. "We knew our parents, were raised by them in the caverns."

"You were brought to Earth as very small babies. You would have no memory of your true parents so all that you know is your adopted parents. After we arrived, I'm sure many children were adopted by those who survived. Whole groups of adults were rounded up and slaughtered in the streets, leaving countless children left to fend for themselves. You were among them."

"My guess would be that the adults in your group divided each of you into specific families and never felt it necessary to tell you the truth. The parents you were originally selected to be with probably didn't survive the invasion."

"And me?" Bastien challenges.

"You are different. Your adoption remained intact. The parents you knew got you when you were only a few days old and kept you safe all those years. They had no idea who, or what you are, but I can promise you that your memories of them are quite genuine, Bastien."

The tenderness in Kyan's voice surprises me. I can hear sympathy mingled with pain for Bastien's loss. "How did we come here then?"

"Soulmates are created in a lab on Calisted and births are predicted to the exact day. They are planned and widely celebrated. Your births were no different, but you six were special. The Oracles knew you must be protected from Aloysius so you were sent here, along with Guardians."

"Guardians?" Toren questions, pausing in mid-step.

"Their sole purpose was to get you here safely and place you with loving families. After that, they were free to assimilate into the human race."

"What about their eyes? Weren't they noticed?" I ask.

"Of course some of them were. Aliens have always been a source of great interest on Earth. Your government seized those that failed to hide their identity well enough. No doubt when we arrived in your air space they were tortured and put to death."

"How horrible," Zahra whispers.

"It's no worse a fate than what this scum has done to our people over the years," Bastien growls, eliciting a glare from Zahra.

Toren gives him an approving glance before addressing Kyan once more. "So what is Illyria's role in all of this? Or ours for that matter?"

"Each of you has been given an ability, a gift if you will. On Calisted, each child is given a gift, but only the best and brightest are trained. Those that grow up able to make flowers bloom at will don't make the army's cut, but there are those whose gifts can be used for tactical purposes. Aloysius exploited that and created a strong army. You six are among those who would've been trained and, as such, pose a threat to Aloysius, but none pose a threat greater than Illyria."

His gaze softens when he glances at me. "Illyria is special, unique. She falls into uncharted territory and once Aloysius discovers she is alive, he will stop at nothing to get her."

"Like Drakon?" Bastien asks.

"Oh no. Commander Drakon is a kitten compared to Aloysius. Drakon wants Illyria because of what she can bring him…favor with the king."

"So he wants me for this Shadow thing within me?" I ask.

"Yes and no." Kyan clears his throat, looking very uncomfortable with this line of questioning. "There is another reason he will want you."

"I don't like the way that sounds," Eamon mutters, slipping his hand through mine. I squeeze his fingers, grateful for his support. I would never admit this to a living soul, but all this talk of the future is starting to creep me out. I just want to go back to spending my days hunting, when life was hard but normal. When I was in control.

"Your parents were forbidden to be together, Illyria. They broke Caldonian law when you were conceived. As such, your birth was uncontrolled and unsanctioned. The results were…unfortunate."

Bastien bristles next to me, but Kyan raises his hand. "Peace, Bastien. Let me explain."

He strokes his chin and his brow pinches as he fights for words. "Illyria's parents were the descendants of a specific lineage that was meant to be kept apart by those who fear the Oracle's prophecy. When you were born, you were given the DNA that matches Aloysius' previous wife."

"Hold on a second," Toren throws out his hands, interrupting Kyan's story. "So you're saying that Illyria is somehow related to your king's dead wife?"

Kyan winces. "In a way, yes. Illyria is her own person, but she is the spitting image of Aloysius' former wife."

Bastien blows out a deep breath. "So once he sees Illyria, she'll be a perfect match for the woman he lost plus she's powerful on top. That's messed up, but in a way sort of brilliant."

"What do you mean?" Eamon asks, his tone ripe with warning.

"I'm saying what Kyan is obviously not wanting to. Illyria is bait. That's why he's here. To train her so that when she's presented to the King, she will be able to take him out. 'Cause let's face it, her presence here has made some pretty big waves among the Caldonians." He glances back to Kyan. "Am I right?"

The instant Kyan's head dips in agreement, shouts of protest rise around me. Toren throws his hands up in the air as Aminah jumps to her feet. Zahra looks like a spitting viper at the thought of my lineage to the throne. Eamon's bellowing protests ricochet over the circular stone walls, but I sit in numb disbelief. Only Kyan and Bastien remain silent, both watching me with great intensity.

I slowly rise to my feet and silence falls all around. All eyes zero in on me as I fight back the panic rising within. Eamon tries to step toward me, but I hold up my hand. "No. I just…I need a minute."

"Take all the time you need," Bastien says, motioning for everyone to sit back down.

I turn and walk toward the stone wall that towers nearly three feet above my head. When I leaped into this pit, I didn't really stop to think about how I would get back out, but now I jump without thinking, easily spanning the top of the rock and landing ten feet on the other side.

"Guess we can add freakishly long jumps to her list of gifts," Zahra mutters from below.

I lean forward and run. I have no idea where I'm headed, all I know is that I need to get away. I eat up the ground with ease, running faster and faster. I sprint around downed trees and across icy steams, never slowing, not even when my heart feels as if it might burst in my chest.

I head east, straight past the edge of the lake. I pass Bastien's cave and leap down to the valley below, running full out, as if Drakon himself were chasing me.

Finally, spent of energy, I collapse to the ground. I don't recognize this part of the woods. The trees are taller, growing at odd angles, as if weaving a living quilt through the space before me. I can see smoke rising in the near distance and tangled heaps of metal dotting the landscape. I sink back onto my knees and gulp in air, realizing that I've run a distance equal to four hours of walking in only a matter of minutes.

"Guess I can add Toren's speed to the list, too," I mutter to the empty woods.

I pull my legs up to my chest, resting my chin along my right knee as I rock. My mother used to rock me as a child. With a sharp pang, I realize the woman I knew wasn't really my mother, not by blood at least. My mind wanders, wondering what my real mother might look like. Did she have wild blonde hair like me? Were her eyes violet too or do they resemble a true Caldonian's eye color? Did she share my laugh or the dimple that appears on my left cheek when I grin?

My heart clenches as tears begin to form. I swipe them angrily away. I won't cry. I can't.

Your mother loves you, Illyria. Never doubt that.

I look up, not the least bit surprised that Kyan can still reach out to me. *Do you know her?*

Yes. He offers nothing else.

Will you tell me about her?

Someday, I will take you to meet her.

TWENTY-ONE

As the sun begins to sink toward the western horizon, dipping low behind the mountain, I slow to a jog. The run back to the camp took longer than earlier. I approach the blackberry tunnel at a slow walk and collapse down onto the damp ground. I tuck my legs into my chest, trying to hold myself together.

I'd thought an afternoon alone in the woods would be enough to deal with the flood of emotions Kyan hit me with earlier, but the closer I get to camp, the more panicked I feel. I don't know what to say to my friends, or even how to begin to fathom Kyan's claims that we are all Caldonian. I feel human, look human, but then again, so does Kyan.

I never wanted to be singled out, to be labeled special. All I want is to be left alone.

What was Kyan thinking by hitting me with all of that destiny crap? He knows I'm most volatile when I'm emotional. He should have known better. I could've lost control, hurt someone.

The question 'why me' is set on an irritating loop in my mind as the long shadows of the towering trees begin to recede across the ground. The heat of the sun fades from the crown of my head and I can see my breath in a cloud before me. Evening is coming and I feel no better than I did a couple hours ago.

My eyes are swollen and red and my head aches, with the fierce pounding of metal against stone. I feel like I can almost hear it, a tangible hammering that echoes through my mind.

"You ok, Princess?" I whip around, searching for Bastien, but he is nowhere to be seen. "Up here."

I crane my head back to see him perched high in the tree above me. "How long have you been spying on me?"

Tucking his head, he dives head first off the limb. My breath catches as his body curls and he lands gracefully on his feet at the last second. "Show off," I grumble bitterly.

"What's eating you?"

"Nothing." I drop my head to my knees again and focus on the pounding in my head. It feels stronger now that Bastien is here.

When he drops down before me in a crouch, I refuse to acknowledge his presence. "Come on. Talk to me. I know you're freaked out by what Kyan said."

"Am not," I grumble, turning away.

"Fine," he says, wiping his hands. "Just so you know, I covered your chores for you this afternoon. Probably going to have blisters for an entire week now."

"I didn't ask you to do that," I snap, lifting my head to glare at him.

To his credit, he doesn't back down. Instead, his gaze narrows and I can feel him doing it, that weird seeing into my soul thing and I break eye contact first. "You didn't have to. I wanted to do it."

"Why are you helping me?" I glare at him.

He opens and closes his mouth, his expression shifting from surprise to frustration. "Because I care about you, ok?"

I snort and duck my head. "You care about me? How sweet."

"Hey!" He yanks on my arm, forcing me to look at him. "I don't care how hard you try to push me away, I'm not going anywhere, so deal with it."

"Why?" I croak as my throat clenches.

Looking down at the tight grip on my arm, he releases his hold and sinks down heavily beside me. "I've tried to tell myself that it's nothing, a stupid whim, but no matter how hard I try, I can't stop thinking about you. Trust me, I've tried to forget about you, but you're just as stubborn in my mind as you are in person!"

"Now *that's* a great pick up line." I laugh bitterly.

Bastien's brow furrows and his jaw clenches. "I came out here to see if you were ok because I was worried. If you don't want me here, fine. I'll leave. I'm not going to stick around and be your punching bag."

Leaping to his feet, he turns and marches away.

"Wait!" I call out before he reaches the path. He stops but doesn't turn. "I'm sorry. I'm just...it's been a really bad day for me, ok?"

His shoulders rise and fall as he fights to control his frustration. I can feel it pouring off him in nearly visible waves. Guilt stabs at me and I drop my head. Every time he gets too close, I shove him away, like it's a reflex.

I hear Bastien's approach and look up. His expression is guarded. "I'm worried about you, Illyria. Hearing that destiny stuff was hard to take, more so for you, I'm sure. I get that, but that doesn't mean I like having my head bit off."

"I know," I whisper. "I didn't mean to. It's just that I'm scar—"

A loud cracking noise sends birds scrambling to take flight overhead. The ground rumbles beneath us and my blood runs cold. It wasn't just a hammering in my head I was feeling. "The Grounders have found us!"

Bastien yanks me to my feet as the ground quakes again. I fall against him, struggling to remain upright as the earth pitches beneath me. "We have to get everyone out of the caves. Can you run?"

"I'm not sure." My legs are beyond spent from my earlier run. "You need to go. Warn the others!"

"I'm not leaving you." Bastien's grip tightens on my arm.

"I'll go through there," I point to the brambles. "It's a back entrance. I'll get there much faster than taking the long way around. Get back to the Temple and get everyone out. I'll be there as soon as I can."

Bastien lingers, distress pinching his handsome features.

"Go! I'll be fine!" I shove him away and dash for the brambles. The thorns tear deeply into my flesh but I ignore the pain and the pounding right below me. I look back over my shoulder and breathe a sigh of relief that Bastien has obeyed my orders.

My chest clenches at the fact that I might never see him again. If he had known my plans, he would never have left me here, alone, with the Caldonians' digging machine right below.

TWENTY-TWO

Racing down the dark corridor, heat begins to build in my fingertips as I veer off the main tunnel and head into a rarely traveled area, following the sounds of the pounding. It echoes all around me, deafening with its growing intensity. My best guess is that I only have a couple minutes before they breech the outer wall. After that, it's anyone's guess as to how long it will take for the aliens to start pouring through the hole.

Even with the numerous dead end offshoots that the Caldonians will encounter once they are inside the tunnels, the thought of any of them finding their way to the Temple keeps me driving through the pain in my legs. I have to give Bastien time to get the children out.

Once they get out through the escape tunnel, I have no idea where they will go. Maybe they will head deeper into the woods. I wish we'd had more time to plan. Now that Drakon knows we're here, though, I'm guessing he will burn down the entire forest to find us. If Kyan knows my friends and I are the fulfillment of the prophecy, surely Drakon has put two and two together as well.

The walls around me reverberate loud enough to shatter glass. The ground is a constant tremble that makes my stomach lurch with growing nausea.

I skid around sharp bends, weaving deeper into the earth. One side of my mind, the part that contains the logical half, screams at me to flee, but the heat building in my chest presses me forward.

My fingers grip the curve of the final bend in the tunnel just as the ground rocks underfoot and I'm thrown hard into the stone wall. My shoulder throbs with pain, but I ignore it as the floor ahead of me begins to crack open. The opening branches out, eating up the base of the walls and rising to the ceiling. I back away, shielding my eyes from the bright light that pierces through the cracks.

"Well, I guess I found the machine," I mutter. "Now what?"

"Illyria?"

The call is faint, barely audible over the pounding drill that spirals up through the stone. It sends me sprawling, my tailbone smacking hard into the unforgiving floor. A hand wraps around my arm and yanks me back as the drill makes contact with the tunnel roof, making a cave-in imminent.

"Are you insane?" Eamon roars, lifting me to my feet. "You're going to get yourself killed!"

"I had to do something to slow them down!"

"Always the hero," he grunts, snatching my hands and racing back down the tunnel. I can see our distorted shadows dancing on the walls as the light spills over my shoulder. The drill grinds through the stone and then the deafening sound lessens as the machine powers down.

"We have to stop them!" I scream as I hear metal cranking from within the burrow. It sounds like a door opening.

"They're coming in from all directions. The Sky Ships landed a couple minutes ago."

My heart rises into my throat. "Did everyone get out?"

"Almost."

Fear strangles my voice as I follow his lead, confident in his ability to know the twists and turns. I stumble after him, weak and numb from the day. I can't bear to ask who didn't make it. I fear if I know I might never make it out of this cave alive.

Eamon yanks me around a corner and we stop just short of hitting the main tunnel wall. Already I can hear the pounding of boots but it's impossible to tell which way the sounds travel from through this maze.

My heart thumps wildly in my chest. I gasp in small breaths, sure that at any moment I will begin to lose it. I can't die down here.

"Follow me!"

I have little choice as Eamon darts back toward the blackberry bush entrance, nearly yanking my shoulder out of its socket in the process. All I can focus on is keeping one foot in front of the next. If I let myself think of how many aliens are racing toward us I might really lose it.

I can see flickering light against the damp walls in the distance. We're going to meet up with those lights in less than a minute. "Eamon?"

"Turn, now!"

I dive on instinct, following him toward a narrow crevice in the wall. We explored this section of the cave when we were children and could easily fit through the slim passage. Now I have to shimmy sideways to pass through the first twenty feet of solid rock that presses tightly against my chest and back. I suck in my stomach and slip through to the space on the other side.

Eamon doubles over as soon as he squeezes through, letting his diaphragm expand to suck in a full breath. I struggled to get through the gap, so I know Eamon must have.

"They won't find us here," he wheezes, pounding on his chest.

I press back against the wall, well out of the light that filters down from the small natural vent that opens about a foot over Eamon's head. Shouting rises and falls as the aliens rush past, unaware of our hiding place. I release a sigh as silence falls over the cave once more.

"What happened?" I ask, working to slow my breath.

"Bastien arrived only a few minutes before the Caldonians landed. They must have known they were getting close and sent word to Drakon. By the looks of it, he sent a whole battalion of aliens down on top of us."

"Aminah and Zahra gathered the children and headed for the southern tunnels but a cave-in forced them to retreat back to the Temple. Toren and Bastien collected the weapons and prepared to make their stand, but Kyan arrived just ahead of the Caldonians."

"Kyan?"

"Yeah. He said his people have a camp nearby, somewhere we can hide the children. The girls went with Kyan."

"What about Toren and Bastien?" My throat constricts at the thought of just the two of them against the Caldonian army.

"Toren set off our last two blast charges. Took out the main entrance, hoping it would slow them down. When you didn't show, Bastien tried to come after you but Toren convinced him I'd find you faster. Should've known you'd be pulling some harebrained hero crap again!"

I scowl at him. "Did they get out?"

Eamon shrugs. "I don't know. They were supposed to follow the girls, but I didn't stick around to see what happened."

I lean my head back and stare up into the light high above. It is faint on the sunniest of days but, with night beginning to fall, it won't be long before we return to pitch darkness in this small tomb-like room.

"We need to climb," I say as an idea forms in my mind.

"Climb that? Are you insane? It's at least a hundred feet straight up. We'd never make it," Eamon protests. He cranes his head back to take a closer look.

"And the alternative is to wait here to die while our friends are fighting for their lives?" I snap. I take a steadying breath and remind myself that Eamon would never risk our friends' lives if he could help it. "Can you see what happens?"

"No," he says, scrunching up his brow. "I can't clear my mind."

"Ok," I say, pushing off the wall to my feet. Exhaustion weighs me down, but I force myself to shake it off. "You go up first. I'll follow."

I watch as Eamon sizes up the small space. Although wider than the crack we just pushed through, it's not going to give us a ton of breathing room. "Fine, but you'd better be right behind me."

"I will be."

Eamon places his hands on the entrance to the hole, cupping his finger into the small notches in the stone. His muscles ripple as he strains to lift himself. A vein pops out on his forehead and his face slickens with sweat. "Give me a lift, will you?"

I kneel down beside him, locking my knee as he hesitantly steps down onto my thigh. His touch is light, much too gentle for a good push. "You're not going to break me."

"If you say so." With a mighty push, he stomps down on my leg and leaps into the narrow shaft. I bite my lip to still my cry as tears sting my eyes. "Do you need a hand up?"

"I'm fine." I squat down low and leap into the shaft. My hands and legs spread out to grasp the stone. I falter, sliding several feet before I get a firm grip.

"You ok down there?" Eamon's blond curls are illuminated as he dips his head to see me around his torso.

"Yep. Just keep going." It's hard to hide the pain from my voice as I peel my back off the wall. A small trickle of warmth down my spine confirms my suspicion that I just scraped a couple layers of skin off during my downslide.

Our climbing is as treacherous as it is tedious. It feels like we gain only a few inches before we have to stop and reposition. As we rise to the halfway mark, my arms begin to quiver violently. My toes are numb from attempting to curl around notches in the stone through my boots. My fingers are bloody and I'm pretty sure I've lost some of my fingernails.

"You're doing good. Keep going," Eamon coaches from nearly twenty feet above me. His progress is steady, sure. Mine is pathetically slow and stunted.

The higher we rise the easier it is to hear the thrumming of the Sky Ships' engines. Distant booms echo down the shaft but I can't tell from which direction they come. From time to time, I hear boots pounding past the crevice below, no doubt in frantic search of me. Drakon won't take kindly to losing his prized possession.

The thought of wiping that smug grin from his face keeps me moving. I gain speed on Eamon and manage to get to within ten feet of him when he reaches the last few feet of the tunnel.

"Stay where you are. I'll go up and take a look around to make sure the coast is cl—"

"Eamon!" I scream as hands reach down through the opening and drag him out. He kicks wildly, shouting as his legs disappear over the ledge. I can hear sounds of a scuffle overhead and a grunt of pain.

No!

The sudden intrusion of Kyan's voice in my mind nearly makes me lose my grip. *Kyan? What's happening?*

Stay where you are. They've got Eamon.

I know. I'm right below him.

Crap! Ok, stay put. I'll see if I can free him.

A tremor works its way from my head to my feet as I wait. The sound of laser fire overhead makes my blood run cold.

I close my eyes and focus all of my energy on the fighting overhead. At first, all I see is the back of my eyelids, but as the heat begins to simmer in my chest, an image forms. I can see Kyan fighting hand-to-hand with a broad chested ogre of an alien. Kyan takes a low jab to his ribs and crumples at the alien's feet.

I can hear Eamon shouting, his cries rising to a guttural scream as a stout alien with pumpkin orange eyes stomps on his arm and twists it around so far I'm sure it will snap. I grasp my stomach, sure that I'm about to be sick when I see a blur of color. Within the image, I see Bastien leap onto the stout alien's back, punching his ear repeatedly until he releases Eamon.

The sound of a laser charging just behind me makes me twirl around. I stare into the unblinking, dead eyes of Commander Drakon. A triumphant leer contorts his gaunt face as he flips from green to red.

"No!" I scream as the laser lances straight through my mental self and slams into the middle of Bastien's back. Smoke rises from his shirt and he collapses to the ground, his open eyes staring lifelessly up into the sky.

I wrench back from the vision, trembling so violently I wonder if it's me or an earthquake rippling through the sediment.

Rage blackens my vision as I press against the stone, shrieking as it begins to shift away from me.

Illyria? What are you doing?

Bastien is gone! I scream back.

No, he...

A tremendous crack forms in the walls around me. My arms tremble and legs quake but I push with all my supernatural might. The walls shudder as the ground begins to break up. Rocks fall from above, pelting me.

As the shaft begins to cave in around me, I don't have to see my eyes to know they are black. I can feel the venomous Shadow coiling around my mind, hissing in my ear. For once, I'm grateful for the whispers that cheer me on.

TWENTY-THREE

Darkness surrounds me like an oppressive cocoon. It is everywhere. Instead of giving into the terror of being buried alive, I close my eyes to try to focus. No sound penetrates my space, no hint of the outside world. That is an unbelievably disturbing feeling. I try to conserve my breaths, telling myself that someone will find me, but one nagging thought keeps me perched on the edge of panic— what if there is no one left to search?

I have tried to reach out to Kyan several times but find myself too weak to maintain any semblance of a connection. My arms ache, cramped between my head and the rocks hovering only inches above.

The sensation of falling through the earth was not nearly as frightening as when it tumbled in upon me. I was sure I was dead. Considering I feel like I'm sucking in fire every time I take a breath, that still feels like a very real possibility.

After what seems like an eternity trapped within my rock tomb, I've long since stopped analyzing the impossibility of my predicament. I have no clue how I'm able to hold back the avalanche of rock that caved in when I parted the earth, but the longer I remain imprisoned here, the heavier the weight feels.

Sweat beads along my brow as I press upward with my hands, trying to shift some of the crushing weight off, but my arms wobble under the pressure.

I can't do this on my own. Kyan, please find me soon!

Tears slip from between my clamped eyes as a sense of hopelessness falls over me. My back arches, strained by the weight that seems to increase with every passing moment.

I sink lower, contorting into a small, disfigured ball. The sound of rocks shifting all around wrenches a cry from my throat. Growing up in the rebellion, I knew death was not just a possibility, it was a likelihood. I accepted the fact that someday I would fall to the hand of a Caldonian who bested me, but never would I have dreamed up a death such as this.

My body begins to tremble as my legs give out on me and I collapse to the floor, my cheek pressed to the cold stone. The rocks shift again, pressing down on me. I try to press back, but I have no strength left.

I can hear the plinking of rock as it falls, altering to fill the space I have unwillingly provided. The sound is quickly followed by a scraping. I open my eyes and try to crane my neck back. "Hello?"

The rocks to the right of me quiver as they unsettle, inch by inch, but they are definitely on the move. "Can you hear me?"

My screams ricochet off the stone, drowning out any response that may have tried to poke through the moving stone. Silence is my companion once more, as infuriating as it is terrifying. I know someone is out there.

At this point, I really don't care. The thought of being able to see sunlight and take a deep breath of fresh air is enough to make me weep. It doesn't matter who is trying to rescue me as long as they get here soon.

"Help me!" I scream until my voice is hoarse. "Please! I can't hold it much longer!"

Shouts rise on the other side of the rock wall and I can hear the stone tumbling faster. My neck cramps as I crane to see the progress just behind me. Someone must have found the crevice Eamon and I used. The thought of Drakon forcing information out of Eamon sends a burst of heat racing down my arms and into my fingertips.

Trembling so badly I can hardly keep my hand aloft, I stretch out my fingers toward the rock wall. An invisible pulse ripples through the large stones, disintegrating them to a fine dust.

I gasp, choking on the gritty powder and suck in the blast of fresh air that pours through the opening. A hand grasps my foot and yanks me through the hole. The instant the heat retracts from my fingertips, the rocks collapse behind me with a thunderous roar.

My ankle pops as I'm pulled into the small space Eamon and I occupied not long ago. Strong arms wrap about me as I'm lifted into someone's lap. I double over, hacking up the particles in my lungs.

"That was a bit over-dramatic don't ya think, Princess?"

I jerk upright, ignoring the stabbing pain in my side as I stare into Bastien's beautiful blue eyes. "You're alive?" I croak, trying to blink away the mirage.

"Last I checked."

My world careens out of control as Bastien holds me close, cradling me like a little child, safe and protected.

"You sure do know how to make a statement, little lady," a voice calls me from my slumber.

I groan, raising my hand to hold my forehead. "I feel like I dove head first into boulder."

"That's not too far off, actually," the masculine voice chuckles.

My eyes flutter open and I stare up at an unfamiliar ceiling. It is wood instead of stone, slatted with uneven, knotted boards. The texture is rough, riddled with splinters. I ease my head to the side and wait for the nausea to subside as I look about me. The walls and floor match the ceiling. A tall wooden door with a rope latch rests off to my right. A crude table and chair set, hewn from pine, rests in the middle of the room. Low wooden cots, adorned with jet-black blankets neatly tucked under, line the far wall.

Light drifts in through a window on the opposite wall. The small square space is lined with a thick opaque plastic, tacked down with rusted, bent nails.

"How are you feeling, besides your headache?"

I try to crane my neck back to see who is speaking to me, but the muscles in my neck spasm painfully and I sink back down. "I will live."

"Yes, it seems you're quite the fighter. Kyan will be pleased to hear of it."

"I can't see you," I whisper hoarsely. My throat is parched, almost as if it's been weeks since my last drop of water.

"My apologies. I was just trying to finish repairing your head wound. You roused much sooner than I thought you would. You're a stubborn little thing too, I'd wager."

I hear a clink of metal and a scrape of a chair. A man comes into view, beautiful but older than any Caldonian I've ever seen. His face is kind and weathered. Wrinkles line his forehead and the corners of his eyes. They are the color of warm butterscotch, dulled with age. "Who are you?"

"My name is Brym." His voice is gritty, reminding me of dirt rubbing against stone.

"And you are Kyan's friend?"

He nods with a tender smile. "I'm his custodian, his keeper I suppose you would say."

"I bet that's a fun job."

He grins. "It's often challenging. He always was a difficult child."

"You raised him?"

"Indeed. Not long before his dad went off to train with Commander Drakon's forces, his mother became pregnant with a second child. She didn't survive the birth. With Kyan's father away, I was charged with his care. Been with him ever since." He wipes his hands on a cloth and I can't help but notice they are stained with blood. My blood. I begin to feel weak and am thankful that I'm lying down.

"What was he like?"

"Not all that much different than he is now. Always a dreamer, that one. I've never seen a child with such love of the prophecies. Can't say I was surprised when he enlisted for this mission. Years away from home meant nothing to him. He had nothing to stick around for, but had every reason to leave."

"Why?"

Brym pats my hand with a rough, calloused palm. "Because of you, dear."

The reminder of the destiny that's been dumped on my shoulders makes me want to flee. I grip the edge of the cot and try to rise up. "I need to find my friends."

"Easy. It's too soon. You need to rest. Kyan will be along to see you shortly."

"Why?"

His eyes darken imperceptibly. "Did he not tell you?"

"I'm guessing you're about to give me another cryptic answer," I grumble, sinking down onto the cot. Even though every part of me wants to crawl out of bed and find my friends, I remain immobile. My head feels much better this way.

"Those aren't my specialty." He winks. "Kyan is a healer and a darn good one at that. I'm sure he can fix you up in no time."

"And my friends?"

"All safe and accounted for, even the wee ones who were injured during the escape. They're getting settled in here nicely."

"And where exactly is here?" I ask, glancing back at the unfamiliar room. Although the wood offers a warm, rustic feel it still feels foreign and cold to me. The forest may be my sanctuary, but it has never been my home.

"My camp," Kyan says as he pushes through the door. Brym rises and bustles out of the room without so much as a goodbye to either of us.

I survey Kyan as he approaches my bedside, detecting a faint limp when he steps. "Are you ok?"

"Oh yes." He smiles with obvious exhaustion. Dark circles lie beneath his lower eyelids. His face is pale, almost as if he hasn't seen the sun in months. "It's been a long few days."

"Few days?" I jerk upright and instantly regret it as pain explodes like a bombshell in completely random places along my body.

Kyan presses on my shoulders and forces me back onto the soft blanket that's been rolled under my head as a pillow. "I must insist that you rest. If you try to resist me, I will be forced to knock you out again."

"Again?"

He nods solemnly. "The first time you awoke you were so distraught I feared you would hurt yourself. I had no choice." Although his words sound sincere, I can't help feeling irate over his casual use of unconsciousness as a means of subduing me. "Will you behave this time?"

I nod, wincing at the jolt of pain that skewers my eyes to my skull. I groan and grasp my head, feeling another wave of nausea.

"I'm sure Brym has informed you that I am a healer as well as a mind reader. As you can tell from my less than perky state, I've been run ragged repairing the wounds your friends sustained in their flight from Commander Drakon. I'm afraid it is up to you to heal yourself."

My eyes pop open wide. "Are you serious? Is this some cruel test or something?"

He smiles. "Or something."

"Unbelievable!"

Kyan leans in close, the tips of his hair brushing along my bare arm. "What you did with that mountain should have killed you in more ways than one. The sheer fact that you can draw breath into your lungs tells me that I have greatly underestimated you, but I fear the implications of your actions. Commander Drakon will not be swayed. Your abilities do not make him fear you. They entice him. You are in far more danger than you were before."

I drop my gaze. "I saw Bastien die."

"No. You saw a glimpse of the future, one that had yet to take place. Your assumption that it was happening in present time nearly killed your friends, Illyria."

Feelings of guilt wiggle through my intestines and sit heavily in my abdomen, increasing my nausea. "I didn't know."

"Exactly. You are developing abilities far faster than I had anticipated. We must begin your training at once otherwise we are all in danger."

I scowl. "I don't want to be like this, you know. I never asked to be a…freak."

Kyan's gaze softens as he rests his hand upon my arm. It is warm and smooth, a stark contrast to Brym. "No one chooses their destiny, Illyria. It chooses you."

He falls silent and sits back, releasing me. "There is more that I should tell you. I wanted to, but feared overloading you."

"Oh no," I groan, struggling to roll onto my side to face him. "It can't possibly be any worse than having some old pervert hot for me, can it?"

When Kyan refuses to look at me, I know this can't be good. "Tell me," I say, steeling myself for whatever he might hit me with.

He clears his throat and wrings his hands before him. "Do you care for Bastien?"

I scrunch up my brow as I roll the words around on my tongue. "What do you mean by care?"

He leans in closer, locking his silver gaze on me. "We both know why you lost control back at the caves. You though Bastien was dead. Not Eamon or the rest of your friends. Even with your abilities, you should never have been strong enough to cave in that mountain. So I've been asking myself how you did it. The only conclusion I can come to is that you're falling for Bastien."

I snort, rolling my eyes. "Hardly. The guy is infuriating. He spends all his time challenging everything I say, he's rude, insensitive—"

"Is he?" Kyan asks, sitting back. "Can you honestly tell me that he hasn't shown you his true self?"

I roll onto my back and stare at the ceiling overhead. "Why are you asking me this? Why force me to label it as anything more?"

"Because the fate of both our worlds rests on how much you *care* for him, Illyria."

"What are you talking about? How can my liking or not liking a guy matter to anyone?" I snap. The pounding in my head increases tenfold as I massage my temples. Even if I were to consider courting Bastien, I don't see how that is anyone's business.

"Do you remember me telling you that soulmates are created on Calisted?" I nod. "Even though your birth was not sanctioned, your soulmate was."

"And I'm guessing this is the part where you tell me that Bastien isn't the one for me," I sneer, crossing my arms over my chest.

Kyan purses his lips. "No, but apparently, you've begun to fall for him despite that."

"I'm not in love with him, if that's what you're implying."

He raises his hands in surrender. "I never said that word, but even if you choose not to say it, I think you know something is going on between you."

I grit my teeth and struggle to push aside the thought of the kiss Bastien and I shared. His touch rocked me far more than I want to admit. "So who is my soulmate then?"

Kyan bows his head. "Eamon."

"No way!" I jerk upright and cry out as pain explodes through my head. A stabbing in my chest reminds me that several ribs are broken. I suck in deep breaths as the pain subsides and I sink back onto the bed. "That's not possible. I mean...he's my best friend!"

Kyan offers me a mug of water and I raise up just high enough to let the cool liquid quench my thirst. He sets the cup aside and crosses his leg over his knee as I stare back at him. "Love is not a word that I was raised to toss around, Kyan, but I do know the meaning of it. If what you say is true, then Eamon and I are one heck of a dysfunctional couple!"

He steeples his fingers in front of his lips. "The feelings that you have for Bastien, which I know you are desperate to deny, should not be possible."

"Tell me about it," I grumble, shoving my hair back from my face. "The guy's a real pain in my butt!"

He doesn't crack a smile so I fall into an uncomfortable silence. Kyan's breathing slows as he closes his eyes. I watch as he tilts his head from side to side, mumbling so low I can hardly hear him. When he finally opens his eyes, I'm taken back by the intensity of his gaze.

"This is a choice that only you can make, Illyria, but I warn you to choose wisely. Walking away from your destiny for Bastien will bring great suffering to your people."

"I don't want to choose anyone! I just want to be left alone."

Kyan sighs and hangs his head. "I'm afraid that's not possible. One way or another you will be forced to make this decision."

"And if I choose Eamon? What will that do to Bastien?"

Kyan looks away. "No matter who you choose, someone will be hurt. The question you have to ask yourself is what are *you* willing to live with."

"That is the biggest guilt trip in the history of the world."

"No," Kyan says, pressing his hands to my forehead. A blessed coolness rushes over my body and the pain begins to recede as darkness steals me away again. "That is the truth."

TWENTY-FOUR

Winter unleashes its full might on us less than two days after I wake up from Kyan's second round of unconsciousness.
Contrary to his insistence that I find a way to heal myself, I woke to find myself completely healed. Although I was grateful for my pain to be a thing of the past, I should have known Kyan would have ulterior motives.

For nearly a week straight, I have spent twelve hours days with Kyan, trapped within the confines of the medical cabin I first woke up in. Kyan claims it is for our privacy, but I have a sneaking suspicion he was worried that either Bastien or Eamon would put a stop to his methods of training if they knew how hard he worked me.

My first task was to learn levitation, the simple act of focusing all of my energy on one object long enough to let it bend to my will. The results have been dismal at best, leaving Kyan silently frustrated and me bruised from head to foot. All I seem to be able to do is toss objects into the air and hurl them around. My control is definitely lacking.

Exhaustion has become a way of life for me now.

We have not spoken again of my feelings for Bastien and for that, I am eternally grateful. I'm still unwilling to admit just how deep my feelings for Bastien go, but I know I'm in trouble. The harder I try not to think of him, the more he consumes my thoughts. I think Kyan suspects my inner turmoil is what is stunting my training.

After a particularly disheartening day of training, I sink onto my bench beside Eamon with a bowl of rabbit stew that would normally be savory enough to draw me from thoughts. Tonight, it is impossible.

Bastien watches me from across the room while I pretend to eat, slinking into the shadows as Eamon eagerly takes up his place by my side. The first moment he shot me a guarded glance

I suspected he'd spoken with Kyan. The goofy grin that followed immediately after confirmed my worst fears.

Although I am grateful for his presence, there is a definite air of awkwardness between us now that I hate. The closer Eamon draws me in, the further I sense Bastien retreating. I can feel his confusion and his pain, just as I can feel Kyan waiting for me to make a decision.

"Hey, are you ok?" Eamon asks, poking me in the side. "You're really quiet tonight."

"Yeah." I instantly plaster on a smile that should have alerted him to my misery, but it doesn't. It hurts that he can't see through my façade to the pain lying beneath or maybe he does but is too afraid to admit it. "It was a long day. Kyan is a slave driver."

Eamon chuckles. "You should try working with Brym. Now *that* guy is full on. I haven't ached like this since we were kids in target training."

I can't help but smirk at him. "Seriously? You're using your brain, not having wooden chairs fall on you when you can't levitate them! There is no comparison."

He scrunches up his face and tilts his head, weighing out the difference. "Ok, maybe you win this one, but don't knock the mental weariness I'm dealing with. It's torture."

Toren draws Eamon into a conversation about Kyan's unusual request for all of us to meet up in the woods after our weapons training the following day, and I'm grateful to be forgotten for the moment. The whole camp is buzzing about Kyan teaching us to use Caldonian weapons. Thirty men reside at the camp, each on varying schedules so as not to raise any suspicions from Commander Drakon. At least half of them view me with undeserved awe. The other half appear to be waiting, but I'm just not sure what exactly they are waiting for.

I lift my empty spoon to appear to take another mouthful of stew and pause, feeling Bastien's gaze upon me. I lower the spoon to the bowl and raise my eyes to meet his. An ache grows in my chest. It has been days since we spoke. He knows I am avoiding him, but has no clue why.

Over the past few days, I've tried to figure out what to say to him. I'm unsure of how to explain something to him that I can hardly wrap my own mind around. My emotions are constantly on edge, longing to be with him, to see if he truly feels something for me, but fearing what might happen if he does. I try to swear off him, go cold turkey, but that is easier said than done now that I've accepted the fact that Bastien has crashed through my barriers and taken me captive.

His pain radiates across the room to me as I lurch to my feet, spilling a nearly full bowl of soup across the table. Zahra screeches as she leaps back, her shirt soiled. Eamon whips around to stare up at me, but he is not the only one. The din of voices has faded as many turn to watch.

"Sorry. Not feeling well," I mutter as I head for the door. I fling it open wide and dash into the blistering cold. Fierce winds and gusts of snow whip through the camp, chafing my cheeks within seconds. I wrap my arms about myself, hurrying along the ice-glazed path toward the cabin my friends and I now share.

"Illyria, wait!" Bastien's boots pound the ground, punching through the thin layer of ice.

Of course it is Bastien that follows me. He is the only one that knows the true reason I fled. "Leave me be, Bastien. I want to be alone."

"No." His grips my arm, pulling me around to face him. "You can't keep avoiding me."

"I don't...I don't want to," I cry through chattering teeth.

Bastien peels off his black wool coat and slings it around my shoulders. "Let's get you inside."

Unwilling to take no for an answer, Bastien places his hand upon my lower back and leads me toward our cabin. The instant I'm inside, he leans his weight against the wooden door and throws the latch in place. I count my steps through the dark room, mentally visualizing the sparse layout of our cabin, identical to the medical cabin.

My fingers tremble as I try to light the candle. After three attempts, Bastien rescues me and the candle blazes to life. He reaches for my hands, rubbing them between his. "You're frozen straight through."

"I'm fine," I chatter.

He gives me a knowing glance and leads me toward my cot, lifting the covers for me to slip inside. I pull off my boots and throw them aside. Bastien waits for me to wiggle out of my coat before wrapping the comforter around my shoulders. He turns his attention to lighting the fire. Once it catches, a warmth slowly emanates from the grate, warming my nose and toes.

"You followed me."

He nods, rising from his low crouch before the fire. "You knew I would."

That's true. I did.

"I can't keep watching you suffer like this," he says, dropping down beside my bed. "I know something is bothering you. Why won't you talk to me?"

"I've been…busy," I finish lamely.

"I'm not an idiot, Illyria. I know when I'm being shoved aside. All I want to know is why."

I open my mouth to answer but no words come out. I can't tell him. Not yet. Not until I know how to make my decision.

"Is it the Shadow? Are you getting worse?"

I shake my head. "No. I mean, it's not any better but I'm dealing with it."

He rests his elbows on his knees and buries his head in his hands. "It's me, isn't it?"

"No!" I cry, pulling his hands away from his head. "No, it's not you. You haven't done anything wrong."

"Then why do I feel like I'm losing you?"

I blink, surprised at the pain in his voice. "Losing me?"

"Of course. Haven't you figured out by now that I'm crazy about you?"

I swallow roughly, fighting to still the rapid thumping of my heart. "You are?"

"God, you can do be dense sometimes!" He pulls me down onto the floor with him. My feet become tangled in the covers and I spill into his lap. I struggle to push myself upright but he grins and pulls me closer.

"Do you want to know how I feel about you?" He murmurs as his hands wrap around my back.

Without waiting for a response, Bastien leans in and gently cups my face. A jolt of energy lances through me, making the ends of my hair rise off my shoulders. His eyes darken and smolder as he stares at me.

"Please," he whispers.

My entire world grinds to a halt at that one desperate plea. I shove all thoughts of my destiny away and crush my lips against his, clawing at his back. His muscles ripple as I sink down squarely on his lap, deepening the kiss until we are forced to break for air.

We pant in unison as I feel heat crashing against my heart, like the waves of the ocean, but this time it is different. The Shadow is nowhere to be found within the recesses of my mind. I am the one in control. This is my power.

The floorboards begin to quake, rattling against the nails that hold them down. The outer door bangs against the frame, fighting to be released from its lock. The table and chairs in the center of the room stutter across the floor, threatening to topple the candle.

I open my eyes to find our shadows dancing in the flickering light. I watch my shadow as I arch back and let Bastien's kisses dip down from the hollow of my neck to the neckline of my shirt. My skin is alive, my mind humming.

I grip his shoulder and pull upright, staring deep into his eyes as I fight for breath. He grins and places his hands against my waist. "If you wanted to rearrange the room, all you had to do was ask."

I laugh and drop my head onto his shoulders, flushing as I realize how intimately close we are pressed together. Easing myself off him, I pull my covers around me and sink onto the floor a foot away from him.

The intensity of his stare makes me self-conscious as I burrow into the covers. "Why do you look at me like that?"

"Does it bother you?"

"A little," I admit.

He grabs onto my cot and pushes up to his feet. "You're leaving?"

He tosses a mischievous grin back over his shoulder. "I thought you'd probably like to be alone for a while. You know, to gather your wits about you."

"But I...do you have any idea what you just did to me?" I exclaim, feeling my heart stutter as he kneels before me.

"I do, but only because you did the same to me. That's never happened before," he whispers. I can feel warmth spreading through my belly and know that I'm about to fling myself into his arms again. "You felt it, didn't you?"

I nod, completely speechless.

"Good. Don't forget it."

"Are you insane? How could I possibly forget that?"

Bastien places a single finger across my lips to silence me. I nearly groan with desire. "You may be too blind to see it, but I'm not the only one here that's in love with you."

His statement lingers in the air as he rises and strides out through the door. I sit, staring blankly at the door. *Did he just say he loved me?*

That single slip has changed everything. I know that I can never just be friends with Bastien again. He has pushed me across a line that I never dreamed could exist with him and now there is no going back. I want more. Much more.

I climb back into bed and snuggle under my covers, knowing that sleep won't be coming any time soon. I roll onto my side and pretend to be asleep when my friends return. I listen to their banter, all the while waiting for Bastien to return.

Long after my friends settle in for the night, I hear the rope latch shift. The door opens and closes, sealing out the frigid winds. Eamon mutters in his sleep and turns over. Zahra's snoring falters for a moment and then picks up it's annoying rhythm.

I listen as Bastien prepares for bed, waiting for the creak of his cot as he sinks under the covers. Minutes pass into what feels like an hour before I let myself roll over to look at him across the room. My stomach rises into my throat when I realize he is staring back at me in the fading glow of the fire embers.

A shot of cold races in to steal away the warmth from my cotton nest. I groan and try to pull the covers back over my face without opening my eyes.

"Not gonna happen."

I groan and open my eyes to see Eamon grinning down at me. "Go away," I grumble and roll back over. "It can't be morning yet."

"Actually, it's lunch time."

I shoot upright in bed and blink against the blinding sunlight pouring through the window. I ruffle my hair, wincing at the tangles. "I can't believe you let me over sleep. What about weapons training? Kyan said it was mandatory."

"It was...for everyone who's not already a weapon." He winks.

"Oh gee, thanks!"

"I tried to wake you three times. You nearly gave me a black eye a few minutes ago. What's with you? You went to bed hours before everyone else. Think you're coming down with something?"

I shrug indifferently as I sniff the air. "Breakfast?"

"Well if you really want wolf stew for breakfast, then be my guest."

I wrinkle my nose with disgust. "I hate wolf."

"And you are the biggest whiner I know. Now get dressed and eat up. Kyan is waiting."

I frown as I untangle from my covers. "Why do you think he wants to meet us out in the woods? Why can't he say whatever he needs to say here?"

"Who knows? He obviously thinks it's for the best," he calls as I dip behind a small wooden screen to wriggle out of my clothes. I pull on a black top and cammo pants. A part of me still feels uncomfortable wearing Caldonian garb but, considering my clothes were left in tatters after the cave in, I don't have much of a choice.

I twist my hair into a messy bun and try not to think about Bastien when I shove two sticks through it to hold it in place. "So where is everyone?"

"They are in the woods waiting for us. Hence why you need to get out here and scarf down this wolf."

I hear the clatter of wood against metal and realize Eamon is stirring the wolf slop that I'm supposed to eat. "He's insane if he thinks I'm touching that crap." I pinch my cheeks for color, trying desperately to look more awake than I really am.

"I heard that!" he calls.

"You were supposed to," I say as he taps his fingers against the table. I suck in a shaky breath, willing myself to be silent as I slide down the wall. Tears slip past my closed eyes, streaming over the curve of my cheeks. As soon as I swipe them away, more spill free.

This feels too weird. Eamon is taking this whole "destined to be together" thing a bit too well. Breakfast with Eamon used to be fun, but this...this feels weird, almost like he's going out of his way to care for me now. The possession in these actions makes me bury my head in my hands.

I'm not sure I'm strong enough to walk away from Bastien, not without giving us a chance to see if we would be worth fighting for. And what about Eamon? I have no idea how to accept his advances without crushing Bastien, or myself, in the process.

I don't even know how to go about wanting to kiss the guy whom I've only ever seen as my best friend. It's just...weird.

Silently, I allow myself to grieve the relationship that I know I'll never be allowed to share with Bastien, if I choose Eamon. It's not fair that my life should collide with Bastien's, just to be thrown back out of orbit so quickly.

I pull myself to my feet and splash frigid water on my face. I hold onto the small wash table, willing my fingers to stop trembling. I look up into small mirror that leans against the wooden screen and notice the purplish tint under my eyes. My skin is paler than normal, making me look worn and exhausted. I plaster on a smile and study my profile, realizing that even if Eamon buys it, I can't do anything to hide the dullness in my eyes.

I guess it could be worse. At least I care for Eamon. My silent pep talk doesn't make my smile look any less forced. I give up and let my cheeks sag. *Whoever designed my life must really get a kick out of watching me suffer.*

I take a deep breath and smooth out the wrinkles in my shirt before stepping out from behind the blind.

"Wow, you sure clean up nice," Eamon whistles. I eye the spread he's created at the table and stuff down my sigh. I lift the spoon and watch as the thick soup plops back into the bowl.

"This looks really disgusting." I push the bowl aside and return Eamon's disapproving glare head on. "It's not going to happen, Eamon so don't argue with me. I'll just wait for dinner."

"Fine," he snaps, losing his cool.

"What is with you?"

"I'm just…I'm trying to make you happy, ok?"

I blink, stunned by the pain behind his words. "Eamon, I…"

He holds up his hands. "No, please don't. I know this isn't what you wanted. It never was, was it?"

I swallow, wracking my brain for an answer. My lengthy delay draws a heavy sigh from Eamon. "I see the way you look at him. You think I don't, but I see more than you know."

I want to tell him that he's wrong, but I can't bring myself to deny it. Not to him. He deserves the truth. I owe him that.

"I'm sorry," I whisper. My voice sounds strangled as I clear my throat. "I never meant for it to happen."

"I know." Eamon blows out a breath as he runs his hands through his curls. The gesture is so familiar it hurts. "So where do we go from here?"

"I have no clue," I laugh weakly. "I kinda feel like we're at that awkward courting phase that I love to hate."

"Yeah," he chuckles. "I was never too good with those either."

"I remember."

He looks up at me and smiles, the first real hint of my best friend I've seen in over a week. "Hey, this is us we're talking about. We're best friends. It's not like you have to hide your snoring or weird jokes from me."

I punch him on the arm. "I don't snore."

"Says you."

I smile and scoot closer to him on the bench. "I know this is really weird, but we can get through this, right?"

He twines his fingers with mine and tosses me a lopsided grin. "Yeah, we can do this. We've known each other since we were toddlers so this should come naturally."

"I need time, Eamon. This is all happening so fast for me."

He leans in and bumps my shoulder, dipping his head to smile at me. "I'll do my best not to push you."

"Thanks," I smile and shove him back. "Just because we're destined and all doesn't mean you're allowed to start groping me though."

"Noted." A hint of red touches Eamon's ears. "You know you have to talk to Bastien, right? He has a right to know what's going on."

All hint of playfulness vanishes. "He's not going to take it well."

Eamon pulls me close, resting his head atop mine. "You brought a mountain down on top of you because you thought he was dead, Illyria. I know you're going to be hurting too."

"I'll deal." I shrug.

He shakes his head and rises, leaving the full bowl of wolf stew forgotten in the center of the table. "Always the hero."

"Someone has to be," I mutter and follow his lead out the door.

TWENTY-FIVE

Ten minutes later, Eamon and I emerge from the dense woods and step into a small clearing not much larger than our camp. "What is this place?" I ask.

"One of our training grounds," Kyan answers. I look up to find everyone else assembled.

Bastien watches me, narrowing his eyes at Eamon's hand pressed intimately against the small of my back. I step to the side, just enough to break contact, but Eamon shifts to take my hand in his.

"Glad you could finally make it," Toren calls, rubbing his reddened fingers together for warmth. "We expected you nearly an hour ago."

"Sorry. Someone decided to sleep half the day away." Eamon looks fondly toward me and I glance away, only to find Bastien's unreadable face. A coldness in his eyes warns me of his mood. He is obviously less than thrilled about Eamon joking about waking me up.

Kyan clears his throat and commands each of our attention. "I called you all out here to discuss our plans. Each of you are doing well with your training. I'm very pleased with how well you have stretched your abilities. They will serve you well in the war to come."

I drop my head as guilt needles at me. I'm the only one not improving. Aminah's ability to speak to minds has now expanded to sending mental images to anyone within a five-mile radius. Eamon can grasp an image of the future and manipulate it to see all angles at will. Toren's speed has increased, Zahra can easily lead an animal rebellion and Bastien...he has been training outside of camp. I'm not even sure what his ability has grown into.

"Why are we discussing this now? Surely Drakon won't attack in the dead of winter."

"Perhaps not, Eamon, but we need to be planning. Weapons need to be stockpiled and more recruits need to be found. We can't hope to win this war if we don't have allies within the City boundaries. I will be heading back for duty soon, as well as many of the others, and we will begin to feel out our comrades."

"And Illyria?" Bastien asks, purposely avoiding my gaze.

"She is struggling, I'll admit that. I'm still trying to discover her trigger, but I'm positive we will sort it out. Until then, I need to know where all of you stand."

"You mean whether or not we will let Illyria follow through with this harebrained suicide mission, you mean," Eamon growls. "Well, I'm not going to let it happen."

He winds his arm around my waist and pulls me close to his side.

Toren and Aminah's voices rise to agree with Eamon. Zahra remains indifferent, but it's Bastien's silence that worries me the most.

Is there another way? I silently ask Kyan.

Not if you want to save your friends.

I suck in a deep breath and exhale slowly, preparing myself. *Then I have no choice.*

You always have a choice. Kyan turns to watch the heated argument surrounding him. *Your friends love you.*

They won't understand.

Kyan turns to face me, listening to every tormented thought I am unable to express. He hears my fears, the pain choosing Eamon will cause and my concern about Aloysius seizing control of my powers. *You will be ready to face anything Commander Drakon throws at you. I promise you that.*

"This is my decision," I say loudly. My friends instantly fall into a stunned silence. "I know the risks, but Kyan is right. We need to start planning."

"You can't be serious," Eamon exclaims. "There's no way I'm gonna let you near that man."

"That's not your decision." I can feel my anger rising as his possessive nature kicks in. This is what I feared most about accepting him as something more than just a friend. I will belong to him in a way that will be suffocating to me.

Eamon looks around the group. "Isn't anyone else with me? Toren? Aminah? You two are on my side, right?"

"Of course we are, Eamon," Aminah soothes, casting an apologetic glance my way.

"What about you?" He stares pointedly at Bastien.

"I will support her desire," he replies stiffly, unwilling to meet anyone's gaze.

"Coward!" Eamon shouts. "You're not even going to fight for her, are you?"

Bastien's neck pops as his head jerks upright. The raw ferocity of his gaze pins Eamon in place. "This is Illyria's decision to make. Not yours. Not mine."

"She'll make the wrong decision and you know it," Eamon spits back.

Bastien snarls and leaps from his place to slam Eamon back into a tree trunk. "Have you even stopped to think about what this will do to Illyria? The fear and pain she will endure?" He shoves Eamon as he steps back. "All you think about is yourself."

Eamon splutters, his face shifting through several shades of red.

"Do you even know what true love is?" Bastien says, breathing heavily as he fights to control his anger. "It's letting the one you love go, even when you know it will destroy you. Are you man enough to do that?"

Eamon's face drains of color, unable to break eye contact. Bastien doesn't back down. "I didn't think so."

He walks straight past me, without even the slightest hint that he knows I am there. I clasp my arms around my waist, curling in on myself at his rejection. *Is this the pain I will endure when I tell him the truth?*

"That means nothing," Eamon stammers. "I just think there's another way."

Bastien turns and looks upon him with pity. "If you think there is, then you're a fool."

Eamon bristles. "So you'll just let her waltz into that psycho's palace and marry him?"

"No." Bastien's eyes go dark as midnight. "I'll kill him before he ever has a chance to touch her."

My focus blurs, darkening around the edges as images flood my mind. My skin tingles and the hairs on my neck rise. The images come so fast I can barely grasp what I'm seeing. I see a palace, beautiful and gleaming with colors, so radiant I nearly have to squint. An older man approaches me, his head adorned with a crown. I catch a glimpse of myself in a floor length mirror, leaned against a wall. I hardly recognize myself.

My hair is piled atop my head, coiling down my bare back. A smaller but identical crown nestles on my own head. A delicate slip of silk drapes my slender frame, hardly covering anything at all.

Just over the King's shoulder, I spy Bastien slipping in through the window. The image blurs as the King turns and tosses a knife. I try to look away, try to wash the image of Bastien's blood spilling onto the floor from my mind, but I can't.

Kyan? My mental voice sounds terribly shaken. *What was that?*

The future.

Will it happen just the way I saw? I hold my breath, praying that he will assuage my fears.

Yes.

My heart sinks into the pit of my stomach. *No. I won't let that happen.*

Focus on today, Illyria. That future is still far off. We can deal with it later.

Kyan steps forward to silence everyone. "I'm here to train Illyria so that when the time comes she'll be able to protect herself. The war has already begun among our people. We need to start the Rising, a rebellion of Caldonian and human brothers fighting side by side."

He looks to me with undeserved pride. "She alone can restore peace to our people. That is worth fighting for, worth dying for."

Toren rubs his chin, turning to scrutinize me. "If Illyria were captured during this raid, before she is ready, what would happen? How powerful is she really?"

Kyan appears reluctant to answer. *Please*, I call to him. *I need to know.*

He sighs. "I'm not sure there is any good way of explaining this. Okay, imagine your powers are like a pie. Each of you have been given a small sliver from that pie to use. But Illyria..." he pauses to close his eyes. "She is the pie."

Eamon frowns. "I'm not following you."

"My apologies. Perhaps I'm not explaining it right." Kyan clears his throat, scrunching up his forehead as he thinks.

"No," Bastien says. "It makes sense. You're saying that Illyria is the source...of all power?"

"Yes." My mouth goes parched as Kyan smiles. "She is an anomaly that cannot be explained."

"So that means—" Eamon pauses to glance at me. "We are all part of Illyria?"

"Oh great," Zahra rolls her eyes.

"What does this mean exactly?" Toren asks, silencing Zahra.

"It means that she is capable of doing anything if she believes she can. Unlike us, she can adapt to any ability that she is presented with. You have already seen how she has mirrored Eamon's gift of sight, Toren's speed and she appears to have an usually strong connection with the weather. She's adapting, learning."

"Like a chameleon," Aminah says. "She blends in with her surroundings, adapting to survive."

"Exactly," Kyan grins, looking relieved. "With enough time, Illyria will be able to mirror each of your abilities, but there is no end to what she can adapt to."

"And if I can't control it? What am I capable of?" I ask, drilling my gaze into Kyan.

He stiffens, working hard to avoid my direct eye contact. "Everything in the universe is bound to good and evil. Action and reaction. God vs. Satan. You get the picture. With Illyria, her own good and evil are battling."

"And if the evil wins?" Eamon asks.

His frown deepens as he stares at the snow-covered ground. I wait, demanding an answer. When he finally meets my gaze, I can see the depth of his fear. "You could tear apart this entire planet if you lost control."

My thoughts shatter in a million directions. Judging by Kyan's pallid complexion, he isn't joking, and that scares the crap out of me.

"Note to self: don't tick off Illyria," Eamon says.

"That's a good point. How do we keep her under control?" Toren asks.

A growl rises in my throat as I glare at him. "I'm not a dog you can put a leash on, Toren."

He raises his hands in defense. "I know. I'm not implying that. It's just…there are a lot of people that live here, Illyria. Do you want to risk their safety?"

I grind my teeth as I shake my head. "No, of course not."

"I'm in agreement with Illyria," Kyan says, silencing the murmurs flitting around the group. "A cage will only fuel her anger. I think we need to let her be herself."

Toren wraps his scarf tighter around his neck as the wind whips through the trees, sending gusts of snow swirling among us. "It's nothing personal, Illyria. We just don't want anyone to get hurt."

"Yeah, I get it. Thanks for your vote of confidence," I grumble under my breath. It hurts, more than I want anyone to know. Eamon pulls my hand into his and twines his fingers with mine.

From across the clearing, I sense a storm brewing within Bastien. The hairs on my arms rise as I look up to see Kyan and Bastien locked into a silent staring contest. My breath catches as Aminah's face drains of color. She must be listening in.

What's going on, Kyan? I ask tersely as Eamon and Toren continue to debate the implications my presence may have on the camp.

His face remains expressionless when he finally answers. *It's nothing to worry about.*

Bastien's thunderous face betrays his words. *Tell me!*

Kyan breaks off his staring match with Bastien to look at me but I am drawn toward Bastien. I gasp, shocked by the anguish marring his face. *What did you tell him?*

The truth.

I stare at Bastien, knowing this pain is the same I will be forced to endure each day that I pick Eamon over him. I want to smile at him, to give him some small reason to hope, but I can't. My destiny forbids it.

Bastien's face darkens as he turns and melts into the forest.

I'm sorry, Kyan whispers to my mind. *He's not coming back.*

"No!"

Eamon's fingers stiffen around my hand. "Illyria? What's wrong?"

Rage mingles with disbelief. *Bastien is the only one that truly believes in me.*

Someone is shaking me but it's hard to think past the aching in my chest. I can't lose Bastien. I'm not strong enough right now to let him go.

"What's wrong?" Eamon shouts at me.

"He's gone," I whisper.

Eamon looks around, confused. "Will someone tell me what the heck is going on?"

"Bastien left," Kyan informs him flatly.

"What do you mean he left?" Toren steps into the center of group, searching the woods where Bastien stood.

"Why would he…" Toren trails off as he notices for the first time how intimately Eamon holds me.

The Shadow is coming and there is nothing I can do to stop it, even if I wanted to.

"Illyria?" Eamon calls. "Talk to me."

The whispers rise and fall in my mind and a sense of foreboding calm falls over me. I swivel my head to the side just before the Shadow takes over. "You need to run."

Eamon flinches back. "What? Why do I need to..." his face drains of color as the lavender in my eyes fades to obsidian.

"Good riddance, I say," Zahra snorts, examining the dirt under her nails. "I don't think I could stand another minute of Bastien's moping."

"Zahra, no!" Kyan's warning comes too late.

Eamon flies through the air as I shove him out of my way and turn on Zahra. Energy flows through my veins and my hair crackles as it rises from my shoulders. I grin and stretch out my arms, curling my fingers. Zahra gags, clawing at her neck. Her eyes begin to bulge as I lift her high into the air, laughing at the gurgling whimpers that spill from her lips.

"You will never speak his name again," I growl, slowly closing my fist.

"Illyria, no!" Kyan throws himself between us. Only the dilation of his pupils betrays his fear. "You don't want to do this!"

"No?" I cock my head to the side, my voice low and guttural. "I'm pretty sure I do."

"This isn't you. It's the Shadow controlling you. You must fight it," he pleads.

My lips peel back as I bare my teeth at him. "I don't *have* to do anything."

With a flick of my wrist, Zahra careens through the air and slams into a large pine tree. Her screams cut off as she tumbles down through the boughs and falls limply to the ground. She groans, but doesn't move.

Kyan takes a step toward her but I snatch him in my grasp. "I don't think so. It's not nice to spoil my fun."

"Can you even hear yourself? This isn't the Illyria I know." Kyan struggles against my hold as thick dark clouds spill over the mountain and encircle us. The gentle winds become gusts as clouds swirl overhead.

"What is happening?" Toren shouts, cradling Aminah in his arms. Eamon inches toward Zahra on his hands and knees. A large welt has begun to form over his right eye where he hit face first against the ground.

Electricity crackles in the air, forking through the clouds overhead in brilliant white streaks. Thunder rolls in near constant waves.

"Toren," Kyan cries over the winds, "get them out of here!"

My head swivels toward Toren and he shrinks back. "Oh god."

I raise my hand and Toren tackles Aminah to the ground, rolling her behind a tree. "Fool! Do you really think a mere tree can stop me?"

I toss Kyan aside as I focus on the tree, easily yanking the ancient roots from the ground. Dirt pelts the clearing as I raise the tree and hurl it directly at my friends. Aminah's shriek lances through my mind, but I ignore it, watching gleefully as Toren struggles to keep her out of harm's way.

I uproot a second tree and take aim as Toren and Aminah reappear at Kyan's side. "Get the girls out of here," Eamon screams as I'm tackled from behind.

The instant he touches my skin, a jolt of electricity floods through his body. He cries out, rolling off me. I grab a handful of his shirt and raise him into the air before me. "I told you to run. You should have listened."

With a mighty howl, I hurl Eamon into the forest. The sound of his bones snapping against a tree trunk is lost to the winds.

Kyan glances up as I bear down on them. "Toren, go! Now!"

Aminah wraps her arms around his neck and they blur out of sight. I roll my head as I release a growl of rage that makes the trees shudder. Birds take flight as I throw out my hand and carve a path straight through the woods in the direction of the camp. Trees fly into the air, crashing back to the ground.

"They're gone, Illyria." Kyan says.

I turn and glare at Kyan. "Your bravery will get you killed one of these days, Kyan. Perhaps today is that day."

He struggles to his feet, battered and bruised. His approach is slow and cautious. His gaze flickers over my shoulder, hardening at the sight of Eamon's broken body. Both legs lie at awkward angles, one arms appear to be dislocated and a deep gash across his forehead pours blood. "Let him go."

"Why should I?" I throw out my hand and send a gust of wind and snow slamming into Eamon, propelling him back into a tree. His nose spurts with blood as I release him and he crumples back to the ground.

Kyan takes another step, but I mentally shove him back fifteen feet. He slams to the ground, grunting as I hear some of his ribs crack. He struggles back to his feet, grimacing around the pain. "You love him, remember?"

Even through the torrent of whispers in my mind, I remember the truth of his words. "Yes."

"Then why are you hurting him?" Kyan asks, struggling to rise to his knees.

I grin. "Because it's fun."

"This isn't you!"

I swirl my hands overhead, gathering icicles from barren tree branches. Like a game of darts, I toss them at Kyan, savoring his pathetic dance with death. "You're wrong, Kyan! This is *exactly* who I am."

He cries out as an ice dagger penetrates his palm. Blood drips from his wound, staining the snow crimson. He rises slowly to his feet, clutching his hand to his chest, keeping it above his heart.

I lift my face to the sky, holding my hands aloft as the clouds darken, bringing night to the land. Lightning lashes out at the trees that surround the clearing. Blue flames race down the dampened trunks, searing the bark as it rapidly combusts.

"Take her!" Kyan shouts.

My head drops in time to see Toren rise with Zahra in his arms. He sends a pointed glare at me before disappearing again. Enraged, I sweep my hand and level an entire row of flaming trees. One slams into the ground only a few feet away from Eamon. Kyan lurches forward, hands outstretched toward him.

"Please stop," he begs. "You're going to kill him."

A buzzing fills my ears as I look toward Eamon. For the first time, the whispers diminish and I see the destruction I have caused. He looks broken, like a child's toy tossed aside. A tear slips down my cheek as flaming branches fall from the trees all around, spreading the flames to areas beyond the clearing.

"What have I done?" I whisper.

A loud splintering from above sends scorching debris raining down on Eamon. The top half of a tree rocks in the wind, groaning as it snaps free and plummets to the ground.

"No!" I wave my hand and redirect the winds to shelter Eamon. Kyan falls to his knees, stunned.

"Toren! Get them out of here!" I scream.

A blast of wind seconds later announces Toren's arrival. His glare is unforgiving and I choke back a sob. "I don't know how long I can hold the Shadow back. It's too strong. You need to save them. Get as far away as you can!"

With a curt nod, Toren turns his back on me and races to Eamon's side. My best friend's moans of agony shred my heart.

"I'll be back for you," Toren calls to Kyan before he vanishes.

Kyan looks up at me from his crouched position, wary but hopeful. "Are you in control?"

"Barely." I grit my teeth as the whispers rise again. "It's too strong…"

"Fight back," Kyan says, stepping closer. "You are stronger than you think you are."

I shake my head, feeling like I've just been sucked into a cyclone of my own making. "You're training isn't working. I'm still dangerous."

Another step forward. "It takes time, Illyria."

"I don't have time!" A gust slams into Kyan's chest, doubling him over as he gasps for breath. "See? I'm already losing control!"

"You do," Kyan chokes out. "This is your destiny."

A snarl rips from my throat. "You want me to destroy Bastien. How is that some noble destiny?"

I thrust out my hands and pin Kyan to a tree. He howls as flames rain down upon his arm, singeing his shirt and the skin below.

"Illyria, no!"

I turn to find Toren facing off with me. His condemning eyes burn with anger and resentment. "Are you happy? You're going to kill us all!"

Listen to him, Kyan weakly calls to me.

I bend over, screeching as I yank at my hair. Rasping laughter echoes through my mind as I'm mentally shoved aside. My lips curl into a snarl and I leer at Kyan. "Get out of my head!"

Toren dives for Kyan, rolling out of the way as sharp icicles hurl down at them from the sky, forcing them to retreat deeper into the burning forest. The icicles shatter upon impact.

With a great gust of wind, I thrust up into the air, hovering over the thawing ground. Lightning streaks across the darkened sky, darting from the clouds to set acres of forest on fire. Smoke burns my nostrils as I rise higher. Lifting my arms, I pull down rain from the heavens. Swirling my arms about me, I create a nearly invisible barrier, shielding me from the elements.

Toren and Kyan huddle behind a tree, drenched by the torrential downpour I unleash upon them.

"Come out, come out, wherever you are," I taunt, rising into the air to see them.

"What are we going to do?" I hear Toren ask, his teeth chattering from the frigid rain. "We have to stop her."

"We have to stop her," I giggle obnoxiously. "Kyan can't save you Toren. No one can."

I watch as Kyan's jaw tightens with resolve. He pushes off the tree with his one good arm and raises his hands in surrender. "You want me? Here I am."

"So you are both brave and stupid," I grin, hurling an ice spear at him. It pierces his shoulder. Kyan cries out, stumbling, but he rises up again despite Toren's desperate pleas. Trails of blood wash away from the wound in the deluge of water falling from the sky.

"You're afraid of me."

"Of course I am," Kyan says, yanking the spear from his shoulder. "You are far more powerful than I realized."

I sneer down at him, sinking to hover ten feet in front of him. The trees about me explode, sending wooden shards into the air, pelting against my protective shield, but I am unaffected by their impact. "You're no different than the rest of them. I know what you all think of me, what you say behind my back when you think I'm not listening."

He ignores the sting of my words. "Fight back, Illyria. You are stronger than the Shadow."

"No, she's not," a maniacal laugh erupts as I stretch my arms out to my sides. Rain patters off the shifting force field. It glows, pulsating with blinding white light. "No one can control me. No one can stop me."

"I can."

"Bastien?" I spin in mid-air, shocked to see him standing less than fifteen feet behind me. He doesn't shift his gaze toward Toren as he sneaks out from under the trees. "Let her go."

"No." I barely recognize the deep grating growl passing my lips.

He steps forward with confidence. His eyes pierce through the shadow, straight to my soul. The whispers shriek in my mind. "Fight back, Illyria."

"I can't," I weep as I can feel the Shadow's grasp pierce deep into my mind, anchoring down for a fight.

Bastien's steps are steady, untainted by fear. "You have always been strong enough. You just have to believe it."

Tears stream freely down my cheeks as I fight to hold onto a shred of my sanity. "You came back."

Bastien nods. "I came back for you."

His words pierce through me like a flaming arrow, scorching the Shadow as it flees. My body spasms as I wrench back control. The bubble around me dissipates and my eyes roll back into my head as I plummet to the ground, unconscious.

TWENTY-SIX

An eerie calm greets me when I begin to rouse. My head feels like a spear has been shoved right through my left eye so I remain motionless apart from breathing. It feels better that way.

I can no longer hear the whipping winds or crashing of trees. Warm sunlight beats down on me from above. Everything appears to be back to normal.

"Illyria," Bastien whispers in my ear. "Can you hear me?"

"Give him room, Bastien." Toren's voice is tense, edged with anger.

I feel Kyan's chilled hands press against my temples and warmth rushes through my body. My fingers and toes tingle and the headache recedes, but I keep the mental block firmly fixed in my mind so Kyan can't pry further should he so choose.

"She will be fine. Her mind appears to have gone into some sort of lockdown," Kyan replies. "I think I might be able to get around it."

Toren shifts beside me. "Are you sure you want to do that?"

Bastien whirls around. "Are you serious?"

"Yeah I am," Toren snaps back. "You weren't here for the whole show, Bastien. She completely lost it, no thanks to you."

"It wasn't her," Bastien insisted.

"Maybe not, but what happens the next time you decide to leave? Imagine what would've happened if she'd been at the camp," Toren said, waving his arms around at the destruction.

Bastien hangs his head and his voice drops to barely above a strained whisper. "I won't leave her again."

"Someday you will have to," Kyan reminds him.

"I won't leave unless she's ready to say goodbye," Bastien amends.

"And you think she will be?" Kyan asks, cocking his head to the side.

"Yes. I know Illyria. She'll do whatever it takes to save her friends, even if that means marrying that King."

"And will you let her go?"

Bastien gulps loudly before answering. "I wouldn't love her if she did anything else. She was destined to save our people. I don't have a choice. I have to let her go."

Kyan clasps Bastien on the arm. "You know what it means to truly love her," he says proudly. "I'm just sorry you both have to sacrifice so much."

"I'm doing it for her."

"She knows that," Kyan assures him.

"How do you know?"

"Because she's been listening to every word you said."

Bastien rears back, staring down at me in amazement as he notices my open eyes for the first time. "Oh, thank god!"

He pulls me into his arms, cradling me to his chest. I sink into his embrace, wishing this moment could last forever.

Kyan rises to his feet, tugging Toren back. "Let's give them some time. I need to patch Eamon up anyways."

A gust of wind buffets against Bastien and me but we hardly notice. I lay there, silently wrapped in his arms for a long time.

I sit up, wiping away my tears. "I'm sorry about what happened. I didn't…you know I'd never…"

"I know," he soothes, pulling my hands into his lap. "I shouldn't have left like that. I was hurting, angry. I needed to sort things out, but I didn't go far."

He rubs his hands along my arms, caressing me with a tenderness I still find completely unexpected from him. "How did you know to come back?"

Bastien points to sky above. "I don't remember thunderstorms being a part of today's weather forecast."

I laugh and shake my head. "Why is it you can always make me smile when I should be groveling for everyone's forgiveness?"

He leans in close. "Because I know you. The good within you will win out in the end."

"And until then?" I press.

He grins and tucks a strand of hair behind my ear. "Kyan might need to smuggle out some of those hard hats they use on the building site in the City."

His hand cups my face, his eyes captivating me. Never before have I known what it meant when my mother said the window to a person's soul is through their eyes, but now I do. Staring at Bastien, I can see nothing but love in its purest form. He doesn't want to change me.

"You are the Shadow Walker. It is a part of you, Illyria." He brushes his thumb along my cheek and I lean into his touch. "I could never truly love you unless I accepted every bit of you."

"But look what I did…"

He pulls my face back from the destruction. "I will be here to help you, no matter what."

I pull away, withdrawing into myself. "But you can't. You're not supposed to."

Bastien sighs and leans back. I bite my lip, already feeling him retreating. "No matter what happens between us, I will always be here if you need me."

His voice is thick with emotion. I tuck my legs into my chest and bury my head in my knees. "I don't know if I can do this. I can't walk away from you."

"Eamon will be with you," he whispers hoarsely.

"He's not you!" I cry out. "He could never take your place."

He smiles weakly. "I wish I didn't love to hear you say that."

A sob rises in my throat as I close the gap between us, clinging to him. "I think I've fallen in love with you, Bastien."

He sucks in a haggard breath and turns his face away. "Now you tell me."

"No," I pull his face back and wait until he looks at me. "You need to know that. I will never stop loving you. Not when I'm with Eamon, or Aloysius."

I place his hand over my heart. "You will always be here."

He swallows roughly. "But you love Eamon, too."

"It's not the same," I protest.

He pulls his hand away, curling it into his lap. "Someday it will be."

"Kyan may think I was created to be with Eamon, and maybe on his world I was, but I know what my heart tells me. I'm meant to be with you."

"That just makes this that much harder." His voice cracks.

I sink back onto my knees, knowing that this is the moment I will regret for the rest of my life. Fate is cruel to let me fall in love and then force us to go our separate ways.

Bastien grasps my arms and crushes me to his chest. He presses his lips to the top of my head, breathing in deeply. "I'll miss this."

"Me too," I sob, clinging to him. I close my eyes and try to burn this moment into my memory, something to hold on to when life seems bleak. "I don't want to let go."

Bastien sighs. "I wish you didn't have to."

I lean back, noticing his vacant gaze has shifted away from me to the charred woods. He has already begun to lock down on his emotions. He's good at that.

"Kiss me," I whisper. Bastien's eyes close as he shakes his head. "Please."

He growls and throws himself away from me. "I can't."

"I won't be able to let you go if you don't." I hate myself for asking, for being weak, but I don't care. I can't bear to leave him without one last kiss.

When he turns back toward me, I see his lips are trembling, pleading with me to understand. "And I won't let you go if I do. Please just go, before I stop you."

I rise unsteadily to my feet. His shattered heart is all I can see in his eyes now. His shoulders slump as he turns and walks away.

"No!" I cry, racing after him. Bastien pauses but doesn't turn. I rush around to face him, staring up at him through tear-filled eyes. Cupping his face in my hands, I lean up onto my tiptoes and kiss just to the side of his lips. I whimper as my tears curve down my cheeks. Without another word, I turn and run.

Bastien is gone.

TWENTY-SEVEN

Apologizing to my friends wasn't an easy task. I know Zahra will never accept my apology, so I didn't even bother. Aminah was the first to offer a warm smile, always the forgiving heart. She worked on Toren for several days and eventually he came around, but I have no doubt he will be keeping an eye on me for quite some time. Eamon, on the other hand, was a different story all together.

Although I never saw condemnation in his eyes, I did see fear and no small amount of pain. He was already healed by the time I came back to camp, but there was nothing Kyan could do to mend his troubled heart.

Bastien returned to camp as promised, but stayed to himself that night. By the time I woke up the next morning, his cot was stripped and his clothes were gone. I tried not to let my panic show, but Eamon saw right through me.

I knew this wasn't going to be an easy road but, to be honest, it's proving much harder than I thought.

The relocation was Bastien's first sign of withdrawal, but there were many more to come over the next few weeks. He changed his training location, which drove him out into a blizzard when no one else would dare leave the warmth of the fires. He worked harder and longer than any of us, but eventually he was forced to remain at camp.

All the while, Eamon watched us, waiting for one of us to slip. I won't lie and say I wasn't tempted. To see Bastien's sarcasm wane and his smile vanish completely is gut wrenching, but his complete refusal to acknowledge my presence has been the worst part. He walks past me as if I don't exist. He sits with the Caldonians, his back toward me.

He never looks at me. Never hints at a desire to. Each day, as his face becomes drawn and the life in his eyes dulls, a little part of me dies too.

You did the right thing, Kyan's voice breaks into my silent nightly musings. The fire crackles nearby and a hearty banter rises from Bastien's table. I try my best to ignore it, for both my sake and Eamon's. *Bastien knows that too.*

My head droops over my cooling soup. I haven't had much of an appetite over the past few weeks. Eamon has tried to coax me to eat and even braved the blizzard to find me a nice rabbit to stew. I ate half of it just for his efforts, but I can't stomach food now.

I'm too young for this, Kyan. How can I save the world when I'm only eighteen?

I know this is not the path you would have chosen for yourself, he thinks, glancing at me from the end of the table, *but we do not choose our destiny. It is chosen for us.*

Yeah, that's the part that sucks. I sink my chin into my palm.

Kyan's face betrays his sympathy. *We each have our role to play, Illyria.*

I turn and look toward the fire, praying Eamon won't see the tears pooling in my eyes. *I don't how much longer I can take this. Eamon is pulling from one side and Bastien the other. Both are as miserable as I am. How can this be my path, to hurt everyone I love?*

There is no answer that can ease your pain. I'm sorry. I wish there was.

I pull away from him, locking him out of my mind. I need to be alone with my thoughts.

Eamon bumps my shoulder. "You ok?"

"No." I have found that even though the truth hurts, he wants to know. Over the past few weeks, our relationship has been strained, but Eamon has made great efforts to be a shoulder to cry on, even when he's the last person I should turn to. He knows my pain is still raw, but he waits, with as much patience as he can muster.

He is silent for a moment. "Do you want to talk about it?"

I laugh, knowing he can hear the bitterness that tinges it. "No. I think you've been through enough of my dysfunctional issues."

I reach over and squeeze his hand. He smiles hesitantly as I scoot closer and allow him to pull my hand into his lap. It's a small breakthrough, but my heart feels a bit lighter because of it.

He loves you, Illyria. Just give it a chance.

Gee. Thanks, Dad. I call back to Kyan.

Glad to see your sarcasm has returned.

The temptation to stick out my tongue at him vanishes the instant Bastien rises with his bowl and turns to walk out. His gaze lifts off the floor just enough to see my hand tucked into Eamon's. Bastien's face darkens and his shoulders hunch over as he rushes to set down his bowl and escape.

Perfect.

As soon as the snows begin to melt, Kyan puts me back onto a rigid training schedule. Although I'm thankful to be enjoying the outdoors again, I can instantly tell I've grown accustomed to sitting for long periods of time. I've become weak and lazy, or so he tells me over and over again.

"Focus," he scolds, batting the back of my hand for the third time in a minute. "You are supposed to become invisible, not the box!"

I wipe the sweat from my brow, irritated and sore from an entire day of wasted practice time. Once we discovered that I was dismal at levitation and even more so when it came to healing, Kyan moved me on to invisibility. The idea of that even being a possibility is preposterous to me but Jardin, Kyan's friend is a pro at it. He made me watch him disappear and reappear all morning so I could learn.

"Again!"

I groan and sink down onto the ground. It is cold and moist from the newly melted snow, but I don't care. I lay flat out on my back, palms pressed against my eyes. "Just face it. I can't do it! I can't do any of this stuff!"

"Self-pity does not become you," Eamon calls as he steps out of our cabin. The collar of his jacket is turned up to keep the biting chill out. He buries his hands deep in his pockets and his breath hangs in the air before him as he leans against the cabin's front porch post.

"An audience isn't going to help me," I say.

Kyan crouches down beside me. I look up at him and scowl. "I suck at this."

"It's not your abilities that are backfiring, it's your brain. We need to find a way to tap into your emotions…" he trails off, scrunching up his face as he falls silent.

"Care to share with the rest of the class?" I ask, intrigued by his sudden change.

"What's going on?" Eamon calls as he hops down from the porch and approaches. He squeezes my hand before helping me up. Even after nearly a month, this is the full extent of our relationship. Holding hands is innocent, but still weighty enough to riddle my mind with guilt.

Kyan rubs his jaw as he rises from a crouch and paces. His feet trample a muddy path through the grass. "Illyria's training is, I hate to admit, far more delayed than I'd have hoped by this point. It's not her fault, we just need to find a way to bypass her brain. Try something drastic…"

"And you've got a plan?" Eamon asks, giving my hand another squeeze. This one for comfort.

Kyan nods. "I don't think you're going to like it, though."

Eamon waves off his concern. "If it will help then we need to try it."

The tiny hairs along the nape of my neck rise. Something isn't settling well with me. Kyan is trying too hard to avoid looking at me.

I try to focus on Eamon when he places his arm around my waist. "I know you've been scared to use your abilities since you lost control in the woods. Maybe it's time to try again."

"We will have to use a trigger that can get past Illyria's safety guards…" Kyan trails off.

I groan, instantly understanding Kyan's discomfort. "We can't ask that of him," I whisper, shivering at the thought.

"Who?" Eamon asks, perplexed.

Kyan shuffles his feet, his head ducked low. I sigh, hating Kyan for even considering it. "He wants me to work with Bastien."

Eamon sucks in a breath. "Why would you even suggest that? He makes her volatile. Who knows what could happen!"

"Exactly my point, Eamon." Kyan steps up to him, staring down his obvious defiance. "He is her trigger. It should have been obvious from the beginning. He is the only one that can help her."

"No! There must be another way," Eamon protests.

"What is more important," Kyan asks, "your pride or helping the girl you love?" Kyan's question is harsh and brutally direct.

Eamon's lip curls with disgust and his teeth grind together as he fights to control his anger. "Fine, but just for the record, I'm totally against this idea. It will only cause trouble."

I have to agree with him, but for very different reasons. It has been over a month since Bastien and I last spoke. I would rather not confront him or the pain I'm trying to hide.

"I don't even know if he would be willing, Kyan. We're not exactly speaking anymore."

Kyan steps between Eamon and me, taking my hands in his. His smile is warm and understanding. "No matter what has happened between you two, you know Bastien would want to help. You just need to ask."

"But you know what this will do to him and to me. It's not fair!" I plead with Kyan, praying for any other solution even though I know there isn't one. We have tried countless ways to tap into my abilities, but each time I lock myself out. Bastien is the only one who can bust through my walls and bring out the Shadow.

"It's your choice, but you know the consequences if you don't."

Kyan's words hang heavy in the air. I look to Eamon and know he's thinking the same thing I am...they are going to need me to help with the Rising. Without my abilities, we can't possibly hope to win against Drakon's army.

"As much as you know I hate to say this, I think you need to try. Kyan is right." Eamon sighs, slumping with regret. "If anyone can trigger your powers, it's him."

"Are you sure?"

"Go on," he nods. "I'll wait here."

I blow out a breath, shocked that I am even considering this. "Where is he?"

"In the clearing. It's where he goes every day," Kyan replies.

This revelation cuts me to the quick. Why does he go back there? Is it to reminisce over the destruction I caused when he ran or to try to forget?

I leave with shoulders hunched and a heavy weight in my chest. I wind through the forest, trying not to notice the lingering damage from my rampage, or think about why it happened in the first place.

As I enter the clearing, I spy Bastien just sitting in the middle. His head is bowed and his legs are crossed, almost like he is meditating. He stiffens when I step down on a twig. His eyes widen in shock but his expression quickly sinks into a grimace as I approach.

"Wait!" I call out. "Please, don't go."

Bastien's face is void of emotion as he watches me. "What do you want?"

My voice catches in my throat at the sound of his voice. It is dull and lifeless compared to how it used to sound.

"Kyan sent me."

His cold exterior melts into crazed enthusiasm. "Does he need me for another scouting run?" Bastien has volunteered to join every group that has left the camp over the past month. His desperation to flee my presence has morphed into a need to pick a fight with enemy Caldonians.

"No. Actually...I need your help." My throat constricts making it hard to breathe, let alone speak. I drop my gaze and shift uncomfortably.

"*You* need my help?" He glances in my direction but can't quite make eye contact.

"I'm not doing so well with my training..." my cheeks flush with embarrassment. Bastien has always believed in me. I don't want to disappoint him, even if he is no longer a part of my life.

He steps forward, the tension in his legs making him look like a wooden toy soldier. "What can I do?"

There is no hesitation to his offer of help. My heart clenches painfully at his continued promise to be there for me. "Kyan thinks you can trigger my powers..."

Bastien's eyebrow arches. "How?"

A blush reddens my cheeks as I twist my hands, unsure of how to explain without feeling like a complete fool. "My mind sabotages me every time I try to practice so Kyan thought you could...unsettle me."

I look away as my embarrassment rises to torturous levels.

Bastien's silence is unnerving. I peek up at him and watch a wide variety of emotions play across his face—fear, doubt, longing and then finishes with smug pride. "Kyan knows your emotions for me are stronger than for Eamon."

"Yes," I whisper.

My admission appears to crack through Bastien's cocky façade. His shoulders slump as his entire being seems to droop. "I understand if you don't want to...if you can't..." I gush, eager for him to refuse.

I want to run and hide from the wounds seeing him has inflicted, but I remain. I am here for Kyan, but I'd be a fool if I denied that a part of me didn't want to be here too.

Bastien approaches, stopping less than a foot away. My vision is filled with his broad chest, etched to perfection in his tight fighting black top. His hair has been cut. It no longer falls shaggily over his ears, but has been trimmed short.

Up close, he looks sexier than I remember. The stubble on his cheeks makes him look rugged, irresistible. I gulp, painfully aware of how his presence makes me weak in the knees. Even after all this time apart, it feels like only moments have passed since I was in his arms.

He reaches out his hand, but reconsiders and draws back. "Will this help you?"

I nod, not trusting my voice to withhold the tremor rippling through me as he searches my face. He appears to be memorizing, or at least re-familiarizing himself, with my face. His gaze is soft as it slides over the curve of my cheek and comes to rest on my lips. They part with longing as I force myself to remain rooted in place.

He steps closer, entering my personal space. He pauses less than two inches from my nose. I close my eyes as his breath washes over my face. I stifle a moan and I open my eyes to find him gauging my reaction.

I want to reach up and touch him, to feel his pulse against the palm of my hand as I cup his neck, pull him close and lean up into the kiss that I'm yearning for.

The spell is broken when he retreats a few steps. He shoves his hands in his pockets and looks away toward the woods. "If it'll help, then I'm in."

I shiver against the cold void left in his absence. "Thank you," I whisper as he turns and marches toward camp at a fast clip, almost as if he is running away from me. I don't blame him.

Kyan waves us over as Bastien breaks through the tree line first. I follow, but make no effort to catch up. Eamon's jaw locks down when he sees the flush that rises along my neck. I shrink into my jacket, scolding myself for not holding it together better.

"I think it might be easier for everyone if you sit this one out, Eamon," Kyan kindly suggests, tugging him in the opposite direction.

Eamon pulls away and faces off toe-to-toe with Bastien. "I'll be watching you."

He turns and envelops me in a bear hug, his arms clenched tightly around my neck as he buries his face in my hair. He kisses my forehead and then smirks at Bastien over my shoulder. Apart from the slight curl of his lip, Bastien betrays none of the rage I can sense simmering just under the surface.

I blow out a breath as Eamon stalks off. He heads for our cabin and slams the door behind him. "I'm not sure this a good idea, Kyan."

"You're committed now," he says, looking between Bastien and me. It's hard to tell if he's following my neurotic feelings, Bastien's tight lipped emotions or Eamon's explosive frustration.

"So what now?" Bastien asks.

"You stand there. Illyria will do the rest." Kyan pulls me a few feet away. "Close your eyes, control your breathing and focus on Bastien. Only him."

When I approach Bastien, I know I won't be able to concentrate with him peering down at me; I go around to his back and position myself to face the woods. Just knowing he is right behind me is enough to make my pulse pound in my ears. I close my eyes and try to push the world away.

Nothing happens.

"I knew it wouldn't work," I mutter under my breath.

"Try creating a picture of Bastien in your mind," Kyan suggests.

Chewing on my bottom lip, I think about him, but all I can conjure up are his purple-ringed eyes, sallow cheeks and the dull, haunted eyes that refuse to look at me.

"It's no use." I throw up my hands, angry that I've failed again.

"Don't worry. We can try again..." Kyan's voice fades away. I turn and watch as an intrigued smile parts his lips. "That's not a bad idea, but are you comfortable with that?"

"What's going on?" I ask warily. Neither look at me as they keep their conversation private. Bastien turns and locks his gaze on me. I stiffen as he approaches, easily pushing my boundaries for the second time today. "What are you doing?"

"Making you uncomfortable." I have to widen my stance as he places his foot in between mine. He leans in so close, I'm sure he can feel the trembling of my lips. "You feel it, don't you?"

"Please stop," I whisper, darting a glance at Kyan, who is trying his best to hide a grin. "It's embarrassing."

"No can do, Princess. This is why I'm here."

"Close your eyes and try again," Kyan commands. I shoot a poisonous glare at him before he turns away.

I grit my teeth and close my eyes before facing Bastien again. I know this is a waste of time. It's impossible to concentrate when I can practically feel his chest pressed against mine.

"You're trying too hard," Kyan calls from behind me.

"Maybe you should open your eyes," Bastien whispers.

I peek up at him and am hit by the full intensity of his nearness. It's not just his proximity, but the look in his eyes, his unrepentant need. I have always known he wanted me, but this is the first time he has allowed his lust to consume him.

He presses his thigh against mine, leaning in to let his breath wash over my neck. My skin tingles, betraying me. I waver, fighting for each breath as his hands encircle my waist, pulling me against the length of his body.

Sweat beads along my brow as I roll my neck, allowing him access to my delicate skin. He lifts his hands and pulls my hair back. The feel of his skin against mine makes me moan with desire. Kyan fades out completely. There is only us.

"Breathe, Illyria," Bastien whispers in my ear.

His sultry voice smashes through my flimsy resolve. Passion, raw and untamed, flows through my body as I wrap my leg around Bastien, pressing intimately against him. Bastien lowers his head and presses his lips to my neck, sending me into a tailspin of hormones. His lips trace a slow line toward my jaw, tender and achingly controlled.

I want him to let go, to break through the bond that restrains him. I long for it as I ache for his touch. My hands splay across his back, begging him to continue.

"Whoa!" Bastien cries out and backs away, staring down at my body.

I stumble, irritated with his sudden rejection. "Why are you looking at me like that?"

"Well...technically I'm not. Look down."

I suck in a breath at the stunning smile that chases away the dullness in his eyes. His pride pours off him and bowls me over. It's hard to break my stare as I catch a glimpse of the boy I fell in love with. When I look down, my vision spins as I try to comprehend the complete lack of me. No torso, arms or legs. "I'm invisible?"

I squeal with delight and leap into Bastien's arms. He stumbles back, trying to compensate for my sudden weight. His arms tighten around my legs and back, easily holding my weight. "Warn me next time, will ya?"

"Opps. Sorry about that." I wrap my arms around his neck as Kyan rushes up, pumping his fists in the air.

"I knew you could do it!" He crows proudly.

"Yeah, it's great but now that I'm all turned on...uh...crap," I groan, slapping my forehead. I'm thankful neither of them can see my flaming red face. "How do I turn it off?"

Bastien smirks and tugs me closer as Kyan frowns. "I'm not really sure. Try backing away from Bastien."

He lowers me to the ground and backs away, his gaze remaining steady on the place he thinks he left me. Once he is about ten feet away, I feel the tightness in my chest release. The sensitivity of my skin diminishes and the warmth recedes.

"Well done," Kyan grins as I reappear. He cocks his head and his smile fades. "I think that is enough for today. Eamon has had about all he can stand."

I turn to find Eamon storming across the clearing toward us. I rush to his side, looping my arm through his to prevent him from pummeling Bastien. He offers me a tight smile before turning on Kyan. "You proved your point. It worked. Now let's find a better solution." He casts a murderous glare at Bastien. "I'm sure Bastien has better things to do with his time."

Bastien shrugs, unconcerned by Eamon's anger. "I'm sure I can make time in my schedule to help out with *anything* Illyria needs."

Eamon lunges, yanking me off my feet, but Kyan leaps between the two guys. "That is enough. There will be no fighting here today, is that understood?"

Bastien grins and backs away, his hands held up in peaceful surrender, but I know it's not over. The hard glint in his eye is too evident. "Not my fault you didn't like what you saw."

"Of course I didn't!" Eamon's face contorts into a mask of rage. "But just remember one thing, Bastien…you might be the hero of her dreams, but I'm her destiny."

Bastien stumbles backward, his face ashen. The hollow man returns with a vengeance as he casts one horrified glance at me and then flees to the woods.

"Good riddance," Eamon growls, tugging me close into his side.

I shove him away, furious at him. "How could you do that to him?"

"I knew you'd take his side!"

"No," I shake my head. "I chose you, that's true, but you don't have to be cruel about it. Can't you see that I've hurt him enough already?"

Eamon is taken aback. Kyan turns away from the woods to glare at Eamon. "Helping Illyria cost Bastien a lot today. I would think you, of all people, would know what it is like to desire something you know is out of reach."

Gulping hard, Eamon nods and drops his head. "Yeah, I guess I do."

"Will he be ok?" I whisper

Kyan steps between us and wraps his arm around my shoulder, comforting me as tears sting my eyes. "He knew what he was getting himself into when he agreed to help you."

"I wish I'd never agreed to try." Tears slip silently down my cheeks.

Kyan squeezes my shoulder and then steps back. "I'll go check on him if you'd like."

I nod and watch as he slips into the woods, wishing more than anything it could be me that goes to comfort Bastien.

TWENTY-EIGHT

As December gives way to a bitterly cold January, I struggle to keep Bastien from my mind. His seclusion has become far more pronounced. Days go by and I hardly catch a glimpse of him. When I do, my guilt swells to suffocating proportions.

Since that fateful training session, my relationship with Eamon has been tense. I can't seem to put Bastien from my mind and that has carved a chasm between Eamon and me. After two months, I had hoped to be a better girlfriend to Eamon, but I am failing miserably. The hand holding has advanced to minor cuddling, but I have yet to allow him close enough to risk a first kiss. I can't bear the thought of disappointing him.

Training sessions with Kyan are more frustrating now than ever. We know my trigger, but are unable to access it again, for obvious reasons, so I am failing once again. Even though Kyan doesn't show his disappointment, I know it's there. It's in the tone of his voice and at the end of his clipped words.

He pushes me harder now as winter progresses and the risk of attack becomes imminent. All I can pray for is that, when the time comes, and my life is in danger once more, some of Kyan's training will help me to control the Shadow within.

Today's lesson was the hardest of all. I step into the dining cabin and smile at Eamon's loud call. Limping to his side, I gingerly sit down on the wooden bench beside him. "No offense, but you look terrible," he says.

"Gee, thanks," I groan as I lift my leg over the bench. Even without scanning the room, I know Bastien is gone. He hardly ever comes in to eat any more. Probably still out practicing in the clearing. "Kyan has me trying to deflect objects. It's not going so well."

Eamon frowns, brushing his finger lightly across the fading bruise along my cheek. "He's pushing you too hard. Every night you come in here looking like you wrestled with a bear. I think you need to take a break. Drakon isn't foolish enough to attack in the dead of winter."

"We don't know that."

"I agree," Toren speaks up, leaning forward to join our conversation. "The scouts are showing movement among Drakon's ranks. It is possible they are planning an attack."

"Or they are moving out of the region. We have no idea what their movement could mean," Eamon protests.

I place a hand on his arm. "Either way I trust that Kyan knows best. I'm fine with his rigid training schedule, but I would kill for a nice dip in the Cascades."

Eamon's frustration melts away as he wraps his arm around my waist. "Maybe someday we can go back."

"Perhaps." I look toward the platter in the center of the table, grab a chunk of meat off and tear into it. It is lukewarm but tasty enough. "Kyan wants to advance me up to deflecting stun lasers next week. I might need you to carry me in here each night, Eamon."

Toren's eyes widen with surprise. "You can do that?"

"Apparently. Kyan thinks someday I might be able to deflect the red ones, but I'm not ready to test that one anytime soon!"

"He's insane!" Eamon growls. "If he thinks I'm going to let you..."

"Kyan would never put Illyria's life in danger. You know that, Eamon." Zahra's voice is tight with reproach at Eamon's protest.

A pounding begins in the back of my head, slowly inching its way forward as I chew down several more bits of meat. I hardly taste it. A deep weariness sinks into my muscles as I slump against Eamon.

"Maybe you should turn in early tonight." He suggests. I lean my head back into his shoulder and close my eyes. "I could come tuck you in."

My stomach lurches at Zahra's snicker. I open my eyes to see a faint flush rising along Eamon's shirt collar and silently groan. Even if I weren't desperately exhausted I would have found some way to put him off. I know he is waiting…but I just can't.

"No, I don't want to take you away from your dinner," I say, leaning in closer to reassure him. "I'll be out in less than a minute anyways."

"Are you sure?" Eamon watches me as I turn and push up off the bench, feeling more like a crippled old woman than a teenager.

"Yeah." I smile at him, dipping low to brush my lips against his cheek before heading out the door. I hope that that will ease his hurt feelings.

I burrow into the heavy lining of my coat and hurry along the path. Our cabin isn't the closest, but it is only a few minutes' walk from the dining cabin, an eternity in artic temperatures.

As I approach the unlit cabin, a light in the distance catches my eyes. I frown, confused by the candle flickering from the partially opened door of the armory. Only a couple people have access to that room. Something is wrong.

My exhaustion is shoved aside by an adrenaline spike as I rush forward, careful to avoid the icy bits along the sunken portions of the ground. I drop into a fighting crouch, ignoring the biting pain in my right leg. I mull over the idea of calling for help, but Kyan is out on patrol and I don't want to worry Toren and Eamon needlessly. Besides, it's been too long since I had a proper fight.

As I inch toward the door, I can hear footsteps inside creaking back and forth on the boards. I crane my neck, trying to peer around the door in hopes of catching a glimpse of the intruder. Silence falls over the armory and I go completely still.

The door bursts open and a dark figure leaps at me, pinning me to the ground. The weight of him is crushing as strong hands seize control of my arms. I fight back, arching my back, bucking wildly as I attempt to knock him off me.

His legs clamp down around my waist, painfully immobilizing my lower half. He grunts as I head butt him.

Blood sprays my face as his nose shatters. His grasp on my wrists loosens and I'm able to rock him off.

Clawing at the dirt, I pull myself across the ground, fighting to free myself from his hold. I kick back with my boot and am rewarded with a thud followed by a string of expletives. I reach out, straining for any form of weapon I can use against him.

My fingers wrap around a small, knobby tree branch, and I roll onto my back and come up swinging. A thud reverberates down my arm as I connect with his arm. With a sickening groan, he collapses and his weight shifts away.

I shove him off, freeing my legs. One hard kick to his stomach has him gasping in the dark. I scramble to my knees and stagger to my feet. Shooting pains torpedo down my right leg, slowing me to an awkward hobble.

Only a couple feet from the moonlit path, he slams me from behind, knocking me to the ground. My face smashes against the rocks, slashing through several layers of skin. Stars float before my eyes as I fight to remain conscious.

The man's weight atop me is unbearable as I free my arms. His body spreads along mine, pinning me face first into the dirt. I reach back and claw his arms, raking my nails down his exposed skin. I fight to call on my powers, confused by the Shadow's lack of appearance.

An elbow slams into my side and I feel my ribs crack. My cries are muffled by the ground. My attacker stiffens, hesitating. His moment of indecision is all I need. I snap my head back and connect with his chin. He howls with pain as I toss him off balance and crawl toward the path.

Aminah! My scream reverberates through my entire body and I grimace as pain echoes from every extremity.

In seconds, Toren will arrive, but for the moment I am alone and very much in danger.

"Get back here," a deep voice snarls behind me.

I reach the path as the last blow falls. A shriek rips from my lips as a boot connects with my right leg, shattering everything below my knee. I collapse to the ground, my leg bent at a sickening angle. My body convulses as I roll onto my side, screaming, cradling my shattered leg. The moonlight overhead blurs out of focus as the pain consumes my thoughts.

"Illyria?" The man cries out, his voice filled with dismay. "Oh God! What have I done?"

The world spins as I'm swept away by a torrent of pain. Loud sounds rise around me but quickly fade into a garbled mess. I feel woozy and welcome the sweet call of oblivion as darkness consumes my vision. The last thing I see, emerging from the shadows, is Bastien's face riddled with shame and horror.

"Bastien," I call as my eyes flutter open. Pain radiates up from my leg and my stomach clenches painfully with wave after wave of nausea. "Where's Bastien?"

"Kyan!" Aminah's scream makes me wince as pain lances behind my eye.

Hurried footsteps crunch on the ice-glazed ground. Kyan kneels beside me, tucking his hand under my head to help ease me up. "How are you feeling?"

"How do you think I feel? My leg can touch my freaking hip!" I groan and clamp my eyes shut. Yelling was a bad idea.

"I'm sorry I haven't had a chance to heal you yet. I've been a bit…preoccupied."

The instant Kyan's eyes flicker away from mine I know there is trouble that far exceeds my own. "Tell me."

He grimaces and darts a wary glance at me. "I've been trying to keep Eamon from killing Bastien."

I feel a dark and visceral panic at his words. "Take me there."

"No way," Aminah shakes her head. "You can't be moved like this."

"Kyan," I growl, staring him down. "Either you take me or so help me I will crawl the entire way on my own."

Kyan blows out a heavy sigh. "Fine, but I want it noted that I think this is a very bad idea."

"I second that," Aminah mutters from over my shoulder.

"Eamon doesn't stand a chance against Bastien," I grunt as Kyan pulls me into his arms. I bite down on my lip as tears spill from my eyes. My vision wavers, but I manage to remain conscious.

"Kyan, stop this. Please!" Aminah pleads, following right behind. "She's going to pass out again."

"No. I won't." I grit my teeth and force my mind away from the pain.

Kyan walks with as much care as he can manage, but each step is excruciating. I clamp down on my jaw to keep from shrieking or biting off my tongue. He carries me around the edge of the armory and back toward the center of camp. A large bonfire is blazing and Caldonians hoot and holler at Eamon and Bastien, each circling the other in the center of the cheering crowd.

Toren turns as we approach. His face is grim, his stance tense. "I've tried everything to stop them, but your men aren't helping things, Kyan. They keep egging them on."

"I will handle my men just as soon as I get Illyria somewhere safe."

"Put me down," I command.

Kyan's head whips down toward me. "You can't stand on your own."

"Watch me."

The instant I'm forced to stand on my own foot I know I've made a grave mistake. The pain is unbearable as I grip onto Kyan. He watches me silently, but his eyes speak volumes. 'I told you so' rings through loud and clear.

"What if you lose control again?" Toren protests as I hop forward, using Kyan for support. "There are over a hundred people here, Illyria. We can't risk it!"

I glare at Toren. "I'm not asking permission. Leave if you want to, take Aminah, but don't get in my way. If I don't stop this fight, one of them will end up dead."

Toren grinds his teeth and grabs Aminah's arm, dragging her away. I don't know if they actually leave the camp. A part of me almost hopes that they do.

"Kyan?"

His gaze swivels away from the fight before us. "I want you to leave, too."

"You can barely stand on your own. You need me!"

"No. I need to get closer. That is all."

"But…"

"Do this for me," I cut off his protest. "I need to know you are safe. My friends need you."

He relents slowly and finally nods as we reach the edge of the crowd. "I will get you through the mob."

The sound of fists hitting flesh and grunts of pain brings a familiar warmth to the palms of my hands. My anger rises as I catch glimpses of the guys locked in battle, their shirts off, backs rippling with sweat despite the frigid temperatures.

The crowd parts for us. Some back away, realizing this fight is about to get uglier, but others fill in behind us, eager to see what I will do. It is no secret around camp that the tension between these two guys revolves around me. Many are curious about our relationship. I'm guessing those are the ones who stick around to see what happens.

"Eamon!" I yell.

Eamon and Bastien go still, the whites of their eyes glowing in the firelight. Bastien staggers forward. "Illyria, I am so sorry."

His eyes bulge as Eamon grabs his throat. "How dare you speak to her? Look at what you did! Look at her leg!"

He throws Bastien to the ground, rearing back his leg to kick Bastien in the ribs. Bastien grunts, curling in on himself, but he doesn't fight against Eamon's attack.

"Stop! You're hurting him!" I hop forward and nearly black out from the pain. Kyan and Brym grab hold of me from either side. I offer a pained smile of thanks.

"That's the point." Eamon's pointed kick lands on Bastien's ribs again. The splintering of bones echoes loudly in my ears. Bastien's howl makes me see red.

"Time to go, Kyan."

He hesitates, but instantly releases me when he sees the swirl of black in my eyes. "Everyone back!"

Bastien rolls to his feet, his gaze narrowed as his lips peel back over his teeth. He stalks forward, only showing the slightest hint of pain. I know this stance and the deadly gleam in his eye. Eamon is in trouble.

He dips low and flies across the small space, his shoulder ramming low into Eamon's gut. Eamon flies backward, his head bouncing off the ground. Eamon gasps for breath as Bastien leaps on him, slamming his elbow down onto Eamon's chest. When he coils for another attack, I throw out my arms.

"Enough!" Eamon and Bastien fly apart, hovering ten feet above the ground. Eamon flails about, struggling against my hold, but Bastien falls slack.

"I had no idea it was you," I hear him murmur.

"I know." I wave off his apology. "It was dark and you were trying to protect the camp. I don't blame you."

Eamon's nostrils flare with anger. "Typical! You're just going to forgive him like that? He's the one who broke your leg, remember?"

I sway dangerously at the intense effort it takes to remain standing. I grit my teeth against the rising pain. "Does it look like I've forgotten?"

Eamon pales dramatically as he stares at my twisted leg. Bastien cries out as I collapse. They drop to the ground, released from my anger. "This childish fight for dominance is pathetic. I'm not a plaything you can toss back and forth." I struggle to pull myself to a sitting position.

Eamon grimaces as he rises to his feet. When he refuses to look at me, I know the truth. "You started the fight, didn't you?"

"Of course. He hurt you!"

"So you thought if you beat on Bastien for a while that'd make it all better? You know he would never have laid a finger on me if he'd known it was me."

"So you're going to forgive him? Like that?" Eamon snarls, shooting loathing glances at Bastien.

"What do you want me to do, Eamon? Hate him? Would that make you happy?" I snap, fighting to remain lucid.

Eamon approaches slowly, dipping low when he reaches my side. "You know that's not what I meant."

"But it would make it easier for you, wouldn't it?"

Eamon reaches for me, pulling me into his arms. "No. This is my fault, not yours or his. You're right, I lost my cool, but when I saw you lying on the ground I snapped."

I can easily imagine what Eamon must have thought when he found me unconscious with Bastien kneeling over me. He'd had no way of knowing what really happened.

I stare up into his anguished eyes and crack a weak smile. "Only a fool would challenge Bastien to a fight. As stupid as it was, I guess in some way I should be flattered."

Eamon laughs weakly. "Does that mean I'm forgiven?"

I shake my head. "I wouldn't go that far. We still need to deal with…"

"Where did Bastien go?" Eamon searches the empty lot.

"He thought it best to give you two some time alone." Kyan explains as he steps out from the shadows. He shoots me a knowing smile. "I left, but you should have known I wouldn't go far."

For the second time, Bastien has disappeared. The first time I was distraught to the point of nearly killing my friends. This time I feel numb. "Will he come back?"

"Yes. He just needs time to deal with his guilt."

I slump against Eamon and rest my head against his chest, soothed by the steady beat of his heart. He presses his lips to the top of my head. "I'm sorry," he whispers against my hair.

The part of my heart that belongs to Bastien feels cold and lifeless, but Eamon has laid claim to a part too——an equal half, overflowing with compassion and steady, unconditional love.

Maybe it is possible to love two men at the same time.

"Come on, let's get you into bed. I'm sure you're ready for Kyan to heal up that leg of yours."

"You think?"

Eamon lifts me gently into his arms and carries me into our deserted cabin. I don't know where Zahra got off to during the fight, but I suspect Toren and Aminah will return soon once they realize I didn't tear apart the entire camp. Eamon helps me strip out of my torn clothes, his eyes averted like a gentleman as I slip into a clean top. There's nothing that can be done about my pants for now and I can't bother to care.

I close my eyes as Kyan's hands close around my shattered leg. His mouth falls slack as a golden light begins to glow around my knee. I can feel the bone fragments drawing back into their original place. I release a sigh of relief as the pain fades and healing warmth floods the rest of my body, mending my bruises and cuts. "Thank you," I whisper as Kyan stands and heads toward the door.

"She should sleep well tonight," he says to Eamon before he leaves. Eamon crosses the room and dips low to tuck me in. He presses his lips to my forehead and turns to leave. "Will you…will you stay with me?"

Eamon's eyebrow arches. "You sure?"

"I just…I want to be held."

"Sure." He disappears behind the screen and hurries through a quick wash. When he reappears, his hair is wet but clean of dirt and blood. He grabs a spare blanket and pillow from his bed and lies down beside me. The bed is small, much too narrow for both of us to share but he doesn't seem to mind. He wraps his arm around me and rests his head atop mine.

I begin to feel the pull of exhaustion as I snuggle into his embrace. It has been too long since we slept like this——no pretenses, no expectations, just drawing comfort from each other. I miss this.

My thoughts flit away as I teeter on the brink of sleep. I resurface only for a second when I hear Eamon speak one last time, his voice barely above a whisper. "Thank you for choosing me."

TWENTY-NINE

Sunlight warms my face through the window overhead. I raise my arms and stretch, blowing out a contented sigh. I feel warm and safe.

A soft snore by my ear startles me and I glance over, shocked to find Eamon sleeping peacefully beside me. Loose curls tumble over his forehead, glowing bright gold in the morning light. I watch, hypnotized by the rise and fall of his chest.

How did I miss his transformation from a boy into the stunning man lying next to me? A faint blush rises on my cheeks as I realize how attractive he really is.

"Like what you see?"

"Oh!" I smack Eamon on the arm as a grin stretches across his face. "You were faking!"

Rising up on his elbows, he smirks. "I think that's the first time you've ever fallen for that. Must have had a lot on your mind."

He wraps his arms around me and pulls me back down. My hair fans the pillow as he hovers over me, his gaze searching mine. "Are you mad?"

"Surprisingly no."

"Really?"

I laugh at his obvious shock. "Really. This is nice."

He smiles and tugs me closer. As I rest my head against his chest, I feel him breathe out a sigh of relief. "I like the sound of that."

I listen to the noises that come and go outside the cabin door, the usual morning hustle and bustle. The frigid cold must have broken for so many people to be out and about. "They let us sleep late."

He nods. "Kyan probably told everyone to give us some time alone."

"How long have you been up?" I crane my head back to look through the clear plastic covering the window. It's hard to tell where the sun is located. All I can tell is that it is probably overhead.

"Several hours," he admits sheepishly.

"Why didn't you wake me?" I look up at him to see a blush seeping into his cheeks.

His smile falters and he closes his eyes. "Honestly? I didn't want this to end. I was afraid when you woke you would leave."

I'm not sure what to say. Being this close to Eamon feels good, but I fear it will end badly. I have perfected the knack of keeping him at arm's length, protecting my heart, but the harder I try to preserve my love for Bastien the deeper I wound Eamon.

"I do like this," I admit truthfully. I trace a finger over Eamon's chest, marveling at the difference a few months has made. Eamon's skin quivers under my touch and I hesitate. His hands tighten around my waist and I feel his struggle for restraint.

"Maybe…" he pauses to clear his throat. "Maybe we could try this again sometime."

I sigh and lift up on my elbow to meet him eye-to-eye. "I don't know if that is such a good idea."

Eamon groans and falls back onto the cot, his arm thrown across his eyes. "You are driving me crazy! I've tried really hard to be patient, but this isn't working. You need to decide if you're going to be with me or not. I can't take this hot and cold thing anymore."

I look away, ashamed. He is right. None of this has been fair on him and he has been exceedingly patient with me. "I want to be with you," I whisper.

"Really? 'Cause you've got a real funny way of showing it!"

I blink back the tears that threaten to fall. "I don't know what you expect from me, Eamon. I'm trying."

"What I expect?" He repeats, his brow furrowing as his arms falls away. "I don't *expect* anything."

I shake my head, exasperated. "Of course you do. You're a guy!"

"Hey now," Eamon protests, pushing up into a seated position. The blanket falls away to reveal his bare chest and I find myself struggling to look away. "This is me we're talking about. I've never tried to come on to you or push you for anything and you know that."

I sit up and cradle my knees to my chest as he gently cups my face with work-hardened hands. "I have loved you since we were children. There was never anyone else and there never will be. You are the only one who can infuriate me and make me ache to kiss you in the same breath."

"It's not that I'm not attracted to you…it's not even that I don't love you…" I trail off as my gaze drops to his chest. I reach out and gently run a finger down the curve of his bicep, wrapping my fingers around his forearm. He flexes unconsciously at my touch.

Eamon seems pleased with my closer inspection. "You look at me like this is the first time you've seen me."

I nod absently, tracing the corded muscles down to his hand. He twines his fingers with mine. "I think it is."

He stares at me with such open yearning that I have to suck in a breath to remember to breathe. "I'm a wreck right now, Eamon. No matter what I do, I keep hurting you and that's the last thing that I want. You deserve better than this, better than me."

"Shh," he whispers, pulling me closer. "You've been through a lot. I know that and I don't blame you. I just need to know if there is a chance we can be together. If you say no, then I will walk away and let you be, but if there is a chance, even the slightest hint of a desire to be with me, then tell me."

"I…" I pause, swallowing hard. "I don't know how to talk to you anymore. It feels like there is a wedge between us that I can't get past."

Neither of us verbally acknowledges who that wedge is, but I know we are both thinking it.

"I'm still your best friend," he whispers, reaching up to brush my hair out of my eyes. "No matter what happens, that will never change."

"A part of me wants to be with you…"

"And the other part wants Bastien," he finishes.

I bury my head in my knees, ashamed and broken. After all this time, my pain is just as raw as the day Bastien first walked away from me. He remains in my thoughts, in my heart.

Eamon's touch is light as he lifts my head and leans in close. "I know you love him, Illyria. I've always known."

"But I love you too," I whisper, shifting toward him. I unfold my legs and press against his side, my shoulder against his chest, our lips mere inches apart.

Eamon leans in, his lips brushing past mine to my ear. "I need you to be with me, completely. I can't keep wondering if you're thinking of him when you're with me."

His breath washes over my neck and I close my eyes, forcing Bastien from my mind. Eamon deserves that much. "Please choose me," he whispers.

Memories of all the years we've spent together filter through my mind—the laughter, pranks and challenges during training. Every memory I have of Eamon, before Bastien arrived, is filled with happiness. I need to see past my longing for Bastien to remember who Eamon has always been to me.

I search deep within myself for a shred of the girl I was when Eamon fell in love so long ago. So much has changed. I have changed.

"Why do you love me?" I ask, pulling back to see his response.

"Because you are beautiful in every sense of the word. I love the way your hair drapes down your back, shimmering in the sunlight." He runs his fingers through my hair, releasing it just over my shoulder. "I love your smile, how soft your cheeks are against my chest, how they flush when you are embarrassed."

He grins, stroking my cheek as it flames on cue. "I love how graceful you are, yet strong and confident. I love watching you hunt, the way you move and sort through problems. I love that you're not afraid to face challenges."

"But you always scolded me for those things," I protest.

"Of course," he smiles, lowering his hands to hold mine. "I was worried I would lose you."

"And now? What about the Shadow? I know you're afraid of it."

He cups my hands in his and draws them up to his lips. "I know you won't let it take over."

"How do you know that?" I ask, arching an eyebrow.

"Because evil and love can't mix."

Maybe he is right. Maybe that is why Bastien can talk me down, because love is the only thing keeping the Shadow at bay.

"What if you get hurt again?" I ask, averting my gaze. I don't want him to see how terrifyingly real my fear is of that happening.

Eamon places his finger over my lips to silence me. "It's a risk I'm willing to take if it means I get to be with you."

"I don't think I could bear to harm you again."

"Then don't," he murmurs, inching forward. He pauses, inches from me, waiting for me to make the first move. I hesitate, wishing that this could be simple, that I wouldn't feel guilt over kissing him.

This is what Kyan says I must do…but I don't know if I can.

Eamon's shoulders droop as he begins to pull away. "I'm sorry. I know you need space."

Reaching out my hand, I wrap it around the back of his neck and lightly brush my lips against his. "I choose you."

I know there is no going back now and that scares me more than I hope Eamon can tell. He holds still, giving me complete control as I slowly trace my lips along his jawline and back toward his ear. "Illyria," he gasps, his hands tightening on my arms.

His breathing becomes haggard as I kiss the corner of his mouth. I wrap my hands around his neck as I shift, trying to maneuver around the tangled covers to get closer to him.

"You're going to be the death of me," he gasps.

"Is that such a bad thing?"

Eamon groans. "If you don't want this to happen, then pull back now before I lose control."

I lean in and press my lips firmly against his, squirming as his hands splay across my back, molding me to his chest. Eamon plunges his hands into my hair, tugging loose the tangled curls so that they fall in waves over my back. I dance my fingernails across his neck, sinking deeper into the kiss.

The door behind us creaks open and I flail backward, landing painfully on the wooden floor. Pain shoots up from my tailbone as I look up, ready to bark out my annoyance at the intruder, but I stop short.

Bastien stands in the doorway, his hands violently shaking as he tries to cover a gaping wound in his stomach. His gray shirt is dripping with blood.

"Bastien!" I shriek, scrambling across the floor toward him as his legs give out. "What happened?"

I slide to a halt beside him, lifting his head into my lap. His skin is pale, his breathing labored as he coughs up blood. His eyes squeeze shut as tears cascade down his cheeks.

My head jerks up as shouts rise from all corners of the camp. I gaze out through the open door as Caldonians scramble from their cabins, armed with charged laser guns. Terrified, I glance back down at Bastien and notice his blood has begun to pool on the floor.

His head lolls to the side and glossy eyes meet mine. "They're coming," he gurgles. Then Bastien's body falls limp in my arms.

THIRTY

Eamon is at my side within seconds of Bastien busting through the door. He stares down at Bastien, the emptiness in Eamon's eyes confirming my worst fears. There is no way Bastien can survive a wound this extensive. "You have to do something," I plead.

"I'll get Kyan. Stay here." He races out through the door, ducking as Brym unleashes a red laser through the courtyard at a group of black clad Caldonians breaching the far side.

Bodies lie face down across the camp, the melting snow dotted with bright crimson. I shove the door closed just before a laser slams into the doorframe mere inches from my face.

"Hold on, Bastien. Kyan is coming." I lift his shirt and gag at the sight of the torn flesh across his abdomen. This is not a laser wound...it looks like he has been hacked by a serrated blade.

His breathing becomes dangerously shallow, so I shake his shoulders and pat his face, praying to get a response. "What is taking Eamon so long?" I cry.

I rip off the bottom of my shirt and press it against Bastien's wound. I shudder at the squelching sound and the warmth of his blood as it rapidly soaks through the material. He won't last long at this rate.

Kyan! I need you!

The wooden cabin creaks as a violent vibration ripples through the ground. My blood runs cold. "Oh god! The machines!"

Kyan! My scream is met only with silence. I lay Bastien's head on the floor and race for the nearest cot, yanking a sheet and pillow off. I race back to his side, slip the pillow over his stomach, then lace the sheet under his back, and tie my makeshift tourniquet tightly in place. It won't last long but maybe it can help prolong his life until Kyan arrives.

"I've gotta get you out of here," I grunt as I wrap Bastien's arm over my shoulder and try to lift him. I half carry, half drag him to the door. As I reach for the latch, the door bursts inward and Toren and Aminah dive to the side to avoid hitting me.

"Eamon sent us," Aminah gasps, clutching her side. "Kyan has sounded a retreat. There are too many of them."

"Drakon?" I ask Toren. He nods, his face grim and streaked with blood.

"We have to fall back to the emergency camp," Toren explains, grabbing Bastien from my arms. "Do you remember how to get there?"

I nod. "He won't last long without Kyan. Just get him there, ok?"

Toren grips my shoulder. "I will do my best. Take care of Aminah till I get back."

With Bastien cradled across his arms, Toren blurs out the door and I breathe a sigh of relief. At least Bastien is out of harm's way. I slam the door and slide down the wall beside Aminah. "You ok?"

Her face is pallid, her delicate fingers twisting knots in her shirt. "I saw Zahra fighting with one of them. I didn't see…" she trails off into whimpering silence. Her chin quivers as tears stream down her face.

I pull her to me, resting my head atop hers. Precious, fragile Aminah doesn't belong here…but I do.

Aminah begins to hum, plugging her ears against the screams outside. I look toward the window, feeling trapped. I should be out there fighting.

I fling open the door at the sound of a cry just below our cabin steps. A tall, ginger haired alien falls to a red laser. Aminah begins to hyperventilate behind me as she peers past to see dozens of our new allies staring lifelessly at the sky.

I watch as Balan, one of Kyan's best warriors throws himself over a man and disappears from sight. I have never been so grateful for his teleportation gifts as I am right now. Within seconds, the two of them will reappear in the safe zone, more than ten miles from this battle. Knowing Jardin, he's out there in the fray, completely invisible to the naked eye.

"I need to fight." I turn and look to Aminah. Fear widens her eyes. "Our men are being slaughtered. Maybe I can give them time to retreat."

"You can't!"

She shrieks, covering her face as Toren bursts through the door, slamming it shut behind him. He instantly drops to Aminah's side, soothing her. "It's just me."

Lifting her into his arms, he waits for me to open the door. "I'll be back for you."

I shake my head. "This is where I belong. I can slow them down."

Toren hesitates, obviously concerned by what I might be capable of now that Bastien is lying on his death bed. He grinds his teeth but nods in agreement. "Give 'em hell!"

"You got it," I call as he disappears with Aminah in his arms. I poke my head around door, ducking low to get a lay of the land. Nothing looks the same. Smoke lingers in the air like a thick fog. Moaning rises from the smoke. The scent of burned skin and hair makes my stomach roil.

The ground is a near constant rumble now. Judging by the loud splintering of wood in the distance, the spider drones aren't too far behind the Squaddies.

"Watch out!"

I react instantly, throwing myself off the porch as a large fireball slams into the cabin, exploding in a rain of slivers. I shield my head, crying out as the splinters bury deep into my flesh.

I crouch, choking on the thick smoke enveloping me. Blinking does nothing to help the stinging in my eyes as I rise to my feet. My ribs hurt, along with my head, but I push the pain aside.

With a loud crash, the first metallic spider leg pierces through a cabin roof on the southern edge of camp. It's giant cannon swivels toward the cabin beside it. Anger simmers in my belly as I watch my home go up in flames, and hear the cries of the dying all around me.

Dark clouds roll in, bringing with them a downpour. The fires are instantly quenched, the smoke disperses and I am left with a gruesome view of Drakon's handy work. We lost more men than I thought.

A flash of blue streaks across the courtyard, snagging my attention. I duck and race after Zahra, sure that Kyan won't be too far behind. I leap over a red laser that burrows into the growing mud and slide to a halt at the foot of the dining hall. Eamon has Zahra's hand grasped in his, peeking around the far corner.

"Get down!" I tackle him to the ground as a red laser slams into the wall behind him. Zahra screams and clings to Eamon.

"Where's Kyan?" I shout, rolling off Eamon to let him sit up.

"Gone." Zahra's lips quiver. She looks like a drowned cat with her hair and clothes plastered to her body like a second skin. "They took him."

Thunder rumbles loudly overhead as I scream, slamming my fist against the wall. Kyan was Bastien's only shot. "I have to go after him."

"No!" Eamon pulls me back. "They teleported him out of here. Drakon's not going to let you within five miles of him. That's why he was here."

I turn slowly to stare at him. "Drakon is here? In person?"

"Was," he corrects, looking increasingly worried that he just made a big mistake in telling me that.

I grit my teeth, fight against the urge to race straight into the City, and retrieve Kyan myself. "Toren will be back soon. See to it that he gets you and Zahra out of here."

"I'm not leaving you."

"This isn't up for discussion, Eamon," I state emphatically, shoving his arm off.

"You're right." He glares right back. "It's not."

I stare him down, annoyed that he's pushing the issue, but I finally relent. "Fine. Then get her out of here and meet me at the armory. We're gonna need what weapons are left to bust Kyan out."

Three more machines pulverize the tree line at the base of camp, sending us sprawling to our bellies. The ground quakes as they smash through the outhouse and move on toward the far row of cabins, lasers blazing through the rain. Steam fills the air in their wake.

The center spider swivels and locks us in its target. *Run!* Kyan's booming command has me on my feet before the crimson laser even begins charging. I grab Zahra's arm and drag her out of the way, Eamon close on our heels.

The explosion slams us to the ground. My body sinks into the rising muck as razor sharp debris falls around us. A thick cloud of sawdust hangs in the air around us.

"Illyria!" Eamon rushes to my side, pulling charred boards off my back. "I've got you."

His words come out in a jumbled mess as I pound my ear to still the loud ringing. Eamon lifts me into his arms and races toward Zahra. She lies nearly comatose near the medical cabin, one of the few buildings still standing.

Eamon sets me down and shakes my shoulders. His hair is plastered to his forehead, dripping red tinted drops onto his nose. He is hurt. I can see the blood seeping up from the crown of his head.

"I'm fine." I struggle to rise to my feet. "Just a little shaken is all. I heard him, Eamon. I heard Kyan."

"That's not possible," Zahra gasps, coming out of her shocked state. "He's too far away by now."

"I know what I heard. He's still alive." For the first time in my life, I reach over and give Zahra's hand a squeeze. "He's gonna be fine."

She nods, surprised that I'd offer her comfort. "Thanks."

"What are you doing just sitting here?" Toren grinds to a halt just behind me, taking in our battered appearance.

"Take Zahra to the safe zone and then come back. We need to gather the weapons," I tell him, crawling up the wall to support myself. "Eamon and I will create a diversion until you get back."

"It'll take me longer in this rain," Toren states as he pulls Zahra into his arms. "Is this your doing?"

I shrug. "Wouldn't be surprised."

Grabbing Eamon's arm, I yank him down the side of the medical cabin and pause at the end, surveying the war torn yard before me. The aliens seem to be congregating off to our left. They have yet to reach the armory, but it's only a matter of time. If they do, all our planning is for nothing.

The overhang above gives us a brief respite from the driving rain. I'm pleased to see that even Drakon's men are slipping and sliding in the mud. Eamon presses against my back, peering over my head. "We'll never make it without them seeing us."

Two machines lie beyond the soldiers, trampling everything in their path. The hum of lasers sounds like a swarm of bees. "We need a distraction."

"No, no way! I'm not going to let you go out there."

I turn and place my hands on his chest. "You know I can do this. If we don't get those guns we can't save Kyan. You know I need his help."

Eamon's face crumples under the full weight of my words. He knows I'm right. I can handle this…without him. I lift up onto my tiptoes and place a kiss on his lips. "I'll be careful."

"Ha!" He snorts. "Why don't I believe you?"

I grin and race out through the driving rain and straight into the heart of my enemy.

"It's the girl!" a soldier shouts, raising the alarm. "She's to be taken alive!"

The alien's chest is emblazoned with the familiar crimson moons, but this one is encircled by three red stars. I'm guessing he is someone important.

"Where is Drakon?"

He stiffens at my condescending tone. "*Commander* Drakon is not here at the moment. He returned to interview the traitor.

Once he is done with your friend's mind, there won't be much left."

A low growl rumbles in my chest. I glare at the tall alien, staring openly at the deep red gashes across his face that disfigure him. "If Drakon wants me so badly, why didn't he stay to capture me himself? Instead he sent you."

I walk into the center of circle the aliens quickly form around me. They stand rigidly, their guns poised and ready.

The Caldonian's smile is lacquered with hate. "Obviously he didn't feel you were important enough for his personal attention."

I glare back, imagining several different forms of torture for him. "If Drakon touches one hair on Kyan's head—"

"You'll do what? Glare at me?" He openly mocks. Chuckles rise all around me.

I laugh and cross my arms over my chest. "He hasn't told you who I am, has he, Scar Face?"

The flesh around the man's wounds turns deep red with anger. "How dare you!"

"No!" I shout, planting my feet. "How dare you! You come into my home and attack my friends? Drakon left you all here to die."

Only the sound of the driving rain can be heard now. Apparently, I got their attention. "Strong words for a girl who is unarmed and all alone."

I smirk and toss my drenched hair over my shoulder. "Only a fool would think me unarmed."

"I see no gun, no knife, no weapon at all."

I lean forward slightly. "The Shadow Walker doesn't need physical weapons."

The murmurs of the men around me rise as many of them take a step back. I can feel their fear mounting.

"The Shadow Walker is a myth," Scar Face spits.

"I beg to differ." The men shift uneasily as I lift my hands out. Energy courses through my body and sparks flicker along my skin.

"Be careful, my dear. Electricity and water don't mix well." The man taunts.

"Not a problem," I sneer back. I wave my hands overhead and a nearly transparent dome forms overhead, sealing everyone inside. Rain pelts loudly from above, but not a drop slips through. Water gushes like a waterfall over the sides, cascading to the ground.

"Hold your ground!" Scar Face yells as his men scatter. "It's a parlor trick. She's trying to scare you."

The soldiers fall back into place as the hum of charged lasers doubles in volume. I grin and twirl around to look each man in the eye. "I think your men believe in the Shadow Walker now."

Scar Face casts a glance back over his shoulder as two spider drones approach the invisible barrier. When he turns back to me, his smirk reeks of confidence. "We can do this the easy way or the hard way." He raises his weapon to aim directly at my heart. "Personally I hope you choose the hard way."

"Then today is your lucky day." I stand my ground as he trains his sights on me. He stares down the barrel of his gun, unnerved by my lack of concern.

"Only a fool would stand off against Commander Drakon's army. He has never lost."

I shrug and plant my hands on my hips. "That's because he hasn't come up against me yet, but trust me, I *am* coming for him."

He fingers the trigger with gleeful anticipation. "I wouldn't do that if I were you," I advise. "I assure you, I am capable of much more than mere tricks."

Scar Face glowers at me. His soldiers brace for impact as a green light spirals out of the end of his weapon. I raise my hand and cast it aside with little thought. It slams into an alien's chest to my right, dropping him woodenly to the ground.

"How'd you do that?" The first hint of fear seeps into Scar Face's voice.

"She is the Shadow Walker." The murmur spreads like wildfire through the men. Many of them turn tail and run. The dome ripples as they flee into the woods.

"Seems they believe me now."

"Stop!" He bellows, waving his arms at his men. "I order you to stop!"

The Caldonians hardly acknowledge his shouts as they run full out, leaving their leader behind. "It's just you and me."

With a jerk of his hand, the spider drones lurch into action, bearing down on us. "I think not."

I glance over my shoulder at the armory and find the door closed. It's impossible to tell if Eamon is still inside or if he and Toren got away safely. I have no choice but to hold my ground. I eye the approaching monsters with feigned disinterest, although my pulse thumps madly against my neck. "Do you honestly think they will slow me down?"

Scar Face throws back his head and cackles. It sounds rough and gritty. "You've got guts, but you're a bit too cocky for your own good."

Two massive cannons swivel, locking me in their targets. Diverting a small laser is one thing, but diverting one of those is a whole other story. Everything within me shouts to run, but I can't risk them hitting the armory. I have to draw their fire. I open my stance and brace for a fight that I know I might not win.

Gut wrenching shrieks fill my mind, driving me to my knees. The world spins before me as pain blisters my mind. I claw at my head, wishing I could dig the pain out. My heart plummets as I recognize my name being called over and over again.

Kyan! Oh God, what are they doing to you?

Get out of my mind. He'll sense you! Kyan's howl is fierce, deafening.

I'm coming for you. I promise I will make Drakon pay!

No! Kyan screams. *You can't come here. You're not ready.*

I'm physically thrown back as Kyan shoves me out of his mind. I shake my head, fighting to still a shudder as the echoes of Kyan's screams reverberate through my thoughts. Rage burns in my chest and the whispers rise, sealing out everything else. I grasp hold of the power, embracing the Shadow's thirst for revenge.

I rise slowly to my feet, my hands and clothes matted with mud. My vision darkens as my pupils melt into liquid black. "Drakon just made a huge mistake," I growl.

"Attack!" The cry comes from behind the machines. Scar Face, with all of his blustery bravado, has fallen behind his safety net.

I slash my hands down to my sides and wide slits appear in the first machine. The metal groans as it is peeled back to reveal a soldier within. He scrambles out of his seat as I raise my hands again. With a crunching of bones, the alien lands in the mud, groaning as he cradles his broken ankle. I lift the machine into the air and toss it aside. It crashes through thirty feet of trees before coming to rest, lying on its side, the crimson core flickering out of existence. Only a cold shell remains.

A second machine takes it place. It's cannons boil over as I hold my hands out before me and close my fists, twisting my hands around. As the laser spirals down the cannon, the metal twists, sealing the flame within.

I duck as the machine explodes. White-hot metallic debris rains down around me. A small shield replaces the towering dome to protect me from the shards as they pelt the ground.

"Is that the best you can do?" I scream.

Scar Face turns and flees, sounding a retreat to any Caldonians that may be left. I sink to my knees as I pull away from the Shadow. It gives up control, but not without making its lingering presence known. It has left, but has not gone far.

I hang my head in the fading drizzle, breathing deep as exhaustion tugs me to the ground. I flop onto my back, gasping for breath.

"Illyria!"

Eamon rushes toward me, his feet splashing in the puddles as he dives for me. "Are you alright?"

I nod. "Tired."

He pulls me into his arms, patting my face as my eyes begin to fall closed. "Wake up, Illyria. I have to get you to Bastien."

"Bastien?" I rouse just enough to wince at the reminder of his wounds. "Is he…"

"No," Eamon shakes his head. "But it won't be long. You have to help him."

"I…I can't. I don't know how to heal him."

Eamon cups my face, forcing me to focus on him. "You have to try. If you can't heal him, he's going to die."

THIRTY-ONE

I can't wrap my mind around Eamon's words. Bastien can't die. It's not possible. How could he be in my vision of the future if he dies now?

"Toren says he's fading fast. He needs you, Illyria."

Panic lances through my exhaustion. "Take me to him."

"I can't," Eamon says. "They are ten miles away. We won't reach him in time."

Toren!

Seconds later, a gust of wind ruffles Eamon's hair. He turns, shocked to see Toren standing behind us. "How did you…never mind. Take Illyria to Bastien. I'll just hang out here until you get back."

"Take this," Toren says, handing Eamon a laser gun before picking me up into his arms. My head lolls against his arm. "Is she strong enough for this?"

Eamon shrugs. "She took out two drones on her own. I don't know how much she has left in her."

Toren places my arm over his shoulder and I weakly hold on. I catch one final glimpse of Eamon standing in the middle of our camp's ruins before my vision blurs brown. Seconds later, Toren slows to a walk. Shouts rise all around as we approach.

"Where is he?" I croak.

"Over here," Aminah calls. As Toren carries me through the milling crowd, I estimate that roughly forty people remain. Most have burns on their bodies. Some limp on twisted knees or sport cloth bandages over their faces where wood impaled their flesh.

Gently placing me beside Aminah, Toren rises and tells her he's going back for Eamon. The scent of blood draws me to Bastien's side. I feel his neck, barely detecting a pulse. His cheeks are sallow. His limbs have grown cold and his chest barely rises and falls.

"I did everything I could to stop the blood flow, but I'm not a healer. I don't really know what I'm doing," Aminah says. "Can you help him?"

"I have to try." I rest my head atop his chest, no longer able to hold it up on my own.

"He's lost so much blood. I don't know how he's hung on this long," Aminah mutters, mopping Bastien's brow. Her trembling fingers betray her fear.

The blood on his shirt has dried to a faded maroon. I stare at the wide stain, remembering how his life literally drained out on the floor of my cabin.

"I need you to hold me up, Aminah." I lock my gaze on her. "Promise me, no matter what happens you will make sure that I don't let go."

"But if you can't..." she begins to protest.

I cut her off. "Promise!"

"I swear." She grips my waist and places my hand on Bastien's arm. Closing my eyes I struggle to focus, unsure of how to even begin to heal him.

Bastien? Can you hear me?

Silence. My head droops onto Aminah's shoulder. "He can't hear me."

"Don't give up hope."

Illyria?

I feel a rush of strength at the sound of his weakened voice. *I'm here. I'm going to save you.*

I tighten my grip on his stiff hand. *I'm cold,* he whispers to my mind.

Just hang on a couple more minutes.

This time there is no response. *Bastien?*

Fear makes me claw at the veil that has fallen over my mind. I direct my waning power into my hand, the way Kyan taught me, willing healing fires to pass on to Bastien. Through my closed eyes, I can sense a glow and feel heat burning in the palm of my hand.

"You're doing it!" Aminah cheers.

"It's not enough," I gasp, scrunching up my forehead to try and increase the flow of warmth radiating down my arm from my heart. I can only manage a small spark instead of the bonfire I need.

"Help me," I cry, latching onto Aminah's arm. My head rises slightly off her shoulder as I draw power from her, and her strength mingles with mine. There is an explosion of heat within my chest, radiating outward.

Like lava flowing out of an active volcano, my life force seeps down my arm, singeing the hairs on my forearm as it goes. It reaches my fingertips and then makes the small leap over to Bastien's limp hand. I begin to tremble violently but I clamp down, refusing to let go.

In my mind, I can see Bastien's body enveloped by golden light. I watch as the torn flesh slowly knits itself back together, sealing the wound with newly formed skin. Blood cells rapidly multiply, replacing all that has been lost. Bastien's breathing steadies and his pulse regains its former strength.

"You did it!" Aminah cries, releasing my hand as she leans over Bastien.

The instant she releases my hand the glow goes out, snuffed from existence like a candle blown in the wind. I slump over Bastien's body, my mind shutting down just before everything begins to darken.

"Illyria!" Aminah screams. The alarm in her voice doesn't faze me as shadows fall across my eyes. I feel my energy burn out, like an ember smoldering into ash, completely used up. I sink into the void…gladly embracing the chance to rest.

"How could you let her do it? She could've died," an angry voice rises nearby.

"Let her? I couldn't have stopped her even if I'd been here," another voice spits back.

"Someone should've knocked her out!"

"It was her choice," a resigned voice responds. "You would have done the same for her."

A tense silence surrounds me. I can hear feet shuffling on the ground. "You're right, but what she did was stupid and reckless!"

"Of course it was. This is Illyria we're talking about. She does stupid things...especially for you." I recognize the bitterness of this voice and realize Eamon and Bastien are at it again.

A hand cups my face as I struggle to open my eyes. The pain in my head is blinding. All I want to do is escape to the void once more. "I think she's coming around," Aminah calls.

I wince at the volume of her voice. Heavy footsteps rush toward me. I feel, rather than see, the crowd tighten around me. I moan, feeling weak and oddly disconnected, but alive.

"Can you speak?" Aminah asks, softer this time.

"I'm fine."

Strong arms pull me into a sitting position. I blink and smile at Toren, thankful a neutral friend chose to help. I'm not sure I can bear to hear Bastien and Eamon bicker any more. I take a steadying breath before searching for Bastien. He hangs back in the crowd, his head hung low.

"You look better," I call weakly.

He runs his hand gently along his closed wound. A scar trails across his stomach, the only evidence of his dance with death. "Yeah, but you look terrible."

"Didn't look so hot yourself a few minutes ago," I remind him.

"You shouldn't have done that," he insists, his face stern with reproach.

"I lived," I say, shrugging feebly.

Ignoring everyone around us, Bastien dips down before me. "But you could have died. You've never done that before. It could have..." he trails off as his face pinches with anguish over what could have been.

"It was worth the risk," I whisper, low enough that only he can hear. He leans back as he strangles off a groan between gritted teeth. He lurches to his feet and takes off before anyone can see the pain in his eyes.

Eamon rushes in to take his place as Toren and Aminah control the crowd to give us some privacy. Eamon cups my face and kisses my forehead. "I thought I'd lost you."

"I'm sorry I worried you. I didn't know how else to save his life."

"I know," he whispers, pressing my hands together and kissing each of them in turn. "If I weren't so mad at you, I'd be really impressed."

I smile. "It's no big deal."

"Says you." He brushes his thumb along my cheek. "Are you really okay? Bastien was right, you do look awful."

"Yeah, I'm just a bit off at the moment. I can't really figure out what's causing it. Probably just need to rest."

"Of course. Lie back and I'll get you something to eat. Toren's called a meeting of the survivors soon so that should give you about an hour or two to sleep." He turns and points to a crowded clearing just over a row of low bushes. "I'll be right over there if you need me."

"I'll be fine. Go on, get!"

He grins and places a kiss on my lips before hurrying off. I sink down to the ground and curl my arm under my head. I don't actually mean to fall asleep, but the next time my eyes open, the moon is well on its way toward the western sky. I sit up and stretch, surprised to find Eamon lying behind me, his soft snores rising and falling.

I untangle myself without disturbing him and head toward the dwindling campfire. Several men surrounded the space, some snoring while others appear restless. Only one person remains beside the fire.

"Bastien?"

He raises his head but doesn't turn. "I was wondering when you would wake."

I move around to the side of him and drop down onto one of the log seats, holding out my hands to the fire for warmth. "I thought someone would wake me."

"Eamon thought it best that you get some rest. He's worried about you," he says stiffly.

"I'm fine," I hedge.

For the first time, he breaks his gaze with the fire to stare at me. "I know you're not. I saw it in your face earlier. You looked panicked. What aren't you telling us?"

I sigh, running my hands through my hair. "My powers are gone."

"Gone? As in forever, gone?"

I shrug. "I don't know. I overdid it today. If I hadn't been able to draw from Aminah's powers, you would be dead right now."

"That's why you passed out," he whispers, watching me very closely. "How do you feel?"

I turn to look at him. "Empty. Like there's a huge part of me that is missing."

His jaw clenches as he turns back to the fire. "Maybe it's for the best then."

"What is?"

"Eamon has talked the others into leaving you behind when we attack tomorrow."

"Tomorrow?" I gasp. "Do we have enough guns? Enough men?"

"You don't remember anything, do you?" I blink, confused. "You had a vision while you were passed out. Aminah read your thoughts and deciphered Kyan's location. He's in the heart of the City, right in front of the Shard. That's where he will be at noon tomorrow."

"Why?"

Bastien closes his eyes. "He's bait…for you."

"Me?" I lean back, shocked but at the same time not the least bit surprised Drakon would stoop this low. "We have to save him."

"We will."

I stare at him, zeroing in on the inflection in his voice. "Why do I get the feeling I'm not included in these plans?"

"Because you're not. I'm sorry." He tosses a branch onto the fire and watches as the sparks rise into the air. "I was overruled."

"But that's not fair! Kyan needs me. I can't just leave him there."

Bastien glances over at me. "You said it yourself, your powers are gone. Who knows if it's temporary or permanent. Eamon will never let you go." He rises from his log, pausing beside me. "I truly am sorry. I know this a fight with your name written all over it."

I kick at the edge of the fire, wishing I had something more substantial to hit. "Take me with you."

"What?" He turns back.

"I don't have to fight. I just…I need to be there."

Bastien hesitates just outside the ring of firelight. I can tell he's mulling it over. "Goodnight, Illyria."

He disappears into the dark, leaving me alone. I sit and stare at the dwindling fire, embracing the cold that seeps through my clothes and surrounds my heart, filling the empty recesses of my mind. It reminds me that I'm still alive.

When the sun begins to rise on the eastern horizon, I rise and return to Eamon's side. I stand over him, watching as he stirs. His hand searches the ground for me. He jerks upright, blinking against the blinding orange sunlight until he focuses on me.

"Illyria? Are you alright?"

"That depends." I let my arms unfold and sink down onto a small stump. "I heard about how your decision to leave my behind was nearly unanimous."

"Now hold on," he begins, tucking his legs under. "You know that I'm doing this for your own good."

"I do and that is what infuriates me, Eamon. Since when have I ever been able to sit out of a fight?"

He shifts uncomfortably. "I'm a hunter. I always have been. With or without my abilities I can still fight. You know I will take out any Caldonian that crosses my path."

"And Drakon? What will you do when he captures you, because that is obviously the reason for this ruse."

I look down, unable to meet his fiery glare. "I don't know, but I have to get Kyan back. He's the only one holding me together right now. If I lose him…"

"Exactly." He shifts onto his knees and walks toward me, placing his hands on either side of me. "This isn't a normal fight anymore, Illyria. The stakes are too high. Never before have you been in such grave danger."

He reaches up and runs his fingers along my cheek, slowly, tenderly. "You know I couldn't live with myself if something happened to you."

I close my eyes and release a heavy sigh. "So what am I supposed to do, sit around here and wait to hear if you're still alive? What about Aminah and Toren?" I make sure to leave off Bastien.

His hand moves around to cup the back of my neck, pulling me close as he rests his forehead against mine. "I know this is a terrible thing to ask of you, but it's for the best. I have to know that you are safe."

Eamon's gaze searches mine as he lowers his head, hesitating before kissing me. I want to pull back, to let him see the full brunt of my frustration, but I can't do that, knowing this might be the last time I see him.

I lean into his kiss and close my eyes so he doesn't see what this moment costs me. He envelops me in his arms and I give in, praying I don't go to whatever hell my mother believed in because of this betrayal.

He pulls back and smiles down at me. "Thank you for understanding."

"Of course," I smile, feeling a part of my heart shatter. As much as I love Eamon, I know that whatever the future holds for us, he will never truly stop trying to change me. I suppose a part of me should be grateful that he cares enough to want to protect me, but I'm not. A warrior never wants to be treated like a child.

Eamon kisses my nose and releases me, standing upright. "I need to see Toren about our plans. Will you be ok for a bit?"

"Sure," I shrug. "It's not like I'm going anywhere."

As he disappears toward the makeshift camp, I pull my knees to my chest and rest my cheek against them. A myriad of emotions spiral through me, most of them potent enough to create any number of natural disasters. Perhaps it is a good thing my abilities are lost to me.

I stare out into the woods, watching brilliant shades of red splash across the sky, chasing the shadows from the woods. The forest is quiet today, as if even the animals know an epic battle is about to begin without me.

Illyria...

My spine jerks straight. *Kyan?*

I don't have much time. He will know I've spoken to you.

Then don't! I cry back, remembering his torture from the day before.

I must. You need to know... his voice trails off.

Kyan?

A scream pierces through my mind, sending me tumbling off the log. *Kyan!*

Not gone. Powers... his words are broke, cut off by a blood-curdling cry and then only silence resounds in my mind. The silence is a million times more terrifying than his shrieks. Is he still alive or have I just heard Kyan's death?

I roll to the side as I lose the contents of my stomach into the low brush. I have no idea how one man can endure such terrible torture.

I call repeatedly, but never feel the touch of his mind. Terrified for my friend, I stumble into camp in search of Bastien. He is the only one who might still be able to help me.

THIRTY-TWO

People scurry past, each one prepping to dismantle camp and head toward the City. I watch the flurry of activity from the sidelines, desperately searching for any sign of Bastien but he appears to have vanished.

Zahra offers me a half-hearted farewell before heading to join the men. Toren gives me an awkward hug before stepping back to allow Aminah a turn. She wipes tears from her eyes as she clutches me in a hug. "Please don't do anything rash while we are gone."

"You know me. I love being a babysitter." I try to smile, but it falls flat. Anyone else would be better at looking after the kids than I would be. Even Tomen, the eldest among the group despite only being eleven years old.

She pulls me to her again, squeezing me with more strength than I knew she possessed. Maybe she isn't as frail as everyone thinks. "He's not here," she whispers into my ear. "Toren sent him away early this morning to scout ahead."

My shoulders droop with disappointment and something more, something visceral. "I understand."

She pulls back and gives me a knowing smile. "He's the best fighter we have. Bastien will be fine."

I nod and step away. "Take care of everyone," I call to Toren.

He nods with grim determination. "I will do my best."

"I know."

Toren pulls Aminah away as Eamon approaches. He has changed into new clothes to match the other Caldonians. Unlike Zahra and Aminah, Eamon is on the front lines and must look the part. Fear clutches my heart thinking of the numerous ways this could go wrong for him. What if he is mistaken for being on the wrong side? What if our own men shoot him by accident?

"Hey," he says, stepping up to wrap me in his arms. This time I allow my tears to fall unashamedly. "It's going to be ok."

I try to nod but he's squeezing me so tight to him I can barely move. "I know."

My feet lift off the ground as he whirls me around like a little girl. When he sets me down, he grins as he kisses my cheek. "I'll be careful. I promise. You can't get rid of me that easily."

His goodbye kiss is brief, but filled with loving promise. I wish I could fully return the sentiment but he slips from my hands, waving a farewell as he disappears into the trees.

I read doubt and no small amount of fear on each of the faces that pass by. They are gravely outnumbered and their best weapon is being forced to stay behind, a broken tool that is no longer useful.

It doesn't take long for the noise of their passing to fade. Their hike to the City will take a couple hours from here. Toren will help to lead them at a quick pace, slowing only at the end to help conserve their energy for the fight.

From my crazed ranting, while I was unconscious, they deduced that Kyan's execution is set for noon. They know a location and a time, but are unsure of the means. All they know is that it will be public.

Time slows, inching ahead at a snail's pace. As the sun begins to climb the morning sky, I sink to the ground, fully prepared to wallow in self-pity for the remainder of the morning.

"I hate this!" I scream, launching a rock at a tree. I feel only a small amount of pleasure as it carves a small notch out of the bark.

"Still got your temper, I see," a voice calls from behind.

Startled, I spin around and come face to face with Bastien, who leans lazily against a tree. "But I thought…"

"You thought I left without saying goodbye." He walks directly up to me. I nod, speechless by his sudden appearance. "To be honest, I did consider that. I spent most of the night fighting with myself. In the end, I convinced myself that I could go through with it. Apparently, I was wrong."

I look away, desperate for him to not see how glad I am by his weakness for me. "You're not supposed to be here. Toren needs you."

"I did my job and once I'm done here I'll catch back up." His smile captures my heart all over again, just like the night he pulled me from the lake.

Through the weeks of separation from him, I have learned one thing—love can survive anything. It is invincible. Nothing can stop it.

I know, within the very fibers of my being, that I am meant to be with Bastien. I have never doubted it, but what I want most in life doesn't seem to matter.

"Why are you here?" I ask.

"You didn't think I was going to let them leave you here, did you?" I suck in a breath as he grins down at me, offering me his hand.

"Are you serious?" I curl my fingers around his hand and he pulls me upright. I try not to focus on the warmth of his body when I stumble against him, as pins and needles prick my calves from sitting in one position for too long. He wraps his arm around my back, steadying me until I regain control.

"You're a fighter, Illyria, and fighters tend to do stupid things when they are left behind. Eamon might not realize that but I do, so I'm taking you with me. I'll leave you on a rooftop on the outskirts of downtown. You'll be safe there as long as you keep your head low."

I grin, instantly falling in love with his plan and him all over again. "Thank you…for understanding."

He reaches out and gently runs his finger along my jaw. He opens his mouth to speak, but thinks better of it. Clearing his throat, he turns and looks to the sun. It is almost noon. "The battle starts in less than an hour. We will have to hurry."

"But the City is miles from here. I won't be able to keep up with you now that my abilities are gone." *Not gone…*Kyan's words echo through my mind.

"Not a problem," he grins, lifting my arms to twine around his neck. "We're going to fly."

"Fly?" My mouth gapes open with shock. "So *that's* what you being doing in the woods all this time!"

His grin widens. "I had a lot of free time on my hands so when Kyan said that was the natural progression of my abilities, I decided to perfect it."

"And did you?"

"I guess we'll find out." He wraps his arm tightly around my back. His flame-blue eyes darken to deep sapphire as I mold my body around his. His jaw tenses as I close my eyes to the desire rising within. To be this close and not be able to really touch him is unbearable.

"What about the kids?" I ask.

"I've already got that sorted. Stop worrying!"

I feel my feet lift from the ground. When I open my eyes, he clears his throat and cracks a smile that doesn't quite quench the fires I can see burning in his eyes. "I know this will be nearly impossible for you, but I must insist on a no groping policy during the flight."

I laugh. "Nice to see the old you peeking through."

His smile falters. I could kick myself for bringing up the past. "Sorry," I mutter.

"No, it's fine." I brace myself as he crouches low and shoots straight into the sky. His take off is smooth and effortless. "Show off."

Bastien looks pleased, but quickly turns away. I close my eyes against the biting winds, imagining how wonderful this would feel on a warm spring day.

"Open your eyes," he whispers.

When I do, I gasp, realizing we are soaring only a couple feet over the treetops. If I were to stretch my fingers out I would be able to touch them. "This is amazing!"

Bastien grins. His cheeks are flushed from the thrill of being in the air. "I know. I never get used to it."

"Shouldn't you be looking where you're going?" I tease as he returns his focus to the tree line. "I'm not sure it's safe to fly with you."

Rumbling laughter vibrates through his chest into mine. "I thought you liked danger."

"You know I do!" I spread out my arms and soar like a bird, arching my back so the tips of my hair slap against the treetops. It is exhilaratingly freeing. I wish this would never end.

We dip with the curve of the mountain, following a straight line toward the far horizon where I can just spy the tip of the Shard tower. "What happened to you the other night?" I ask.

He grimaces. "I'm sorry. I needed time to think…"

"Not that." I pull my arms back in and focus on Bastien's profile. His hair whips around his face, no longer in long strands. I find that I actually miss the rugged style. "Who attacked you with a knife?"

The skin around his eyes pinch as the fresh memories of pain washes over him. "You don't miss anything do you?"

"Not when it comes to you," I whisper.

His voice sounds strangled when he speaks. "After the fight with Eamon, I took off. I couldn't stick around and watch…" he trails off. "Anyways, I landed somewhere halfway between here and the City. I paced all night, trying to figure out how to apologize to you."

"But you didn't have to." I place a hand on his chest and he breathes out a heavy sigh.

"I should never have let him bait me. It was my fault you were hurt. I should have just let him hit me."

"No," I shake my head, spluttering as great clumps of hair are blown into my mouth. I pull them free. "I don't blame you, Bastien. I never did."

He nods but stares straight ahead. "I was on my way back when I was jumped in the woods. I didn't even see it coming."

"But Drakon's men use lasers, not knives."

Bastien nods. "Apparently he has some new recruits."

"So he's rounding up mercenaries too now?" I mutter.

"There were only five of them. They wore tattered clothes with a three moons emblem cloth tied around their arms. The one holding the knife bested me before I even knew he was there."

"I didn't think that was possible." I frown.

Bastien winces. "I should've been more careful. I knew Drakon's men were on the move. I shouldn't have left."

I squeeze his arm. "You did what you had to do. No one would fault you for that."

"The families of the men lost at the camp back there might," he mutters.

"They would have found us eventually. This wasn't your fault."

"I wish you'd stop saying that," he growls. He dips low, sweeping down into the final canyon before the straight shot into the City. From this height, I can spy the glistening waters of the lake where he saved me.

"Why? Do you want me to blame you?"

"Maybe," he admits.

"Tough luck. I don't and these things just happen."

Bastien falls into a tense silence as he sails so low the tips of the trees snap against my shirt. I cling to him, unafraid but worried about the landing. At the edge of the forest, Bastien dips to hover only a few feet over the ground, under the radar of the Sky Ships that circle the inner blocks of the city.

"There's so many of them," I whisper.

He nods. "Looks like Drakon has called everyone in for the fun." He grinds his back teeth as he flies down several blocks.

I count the small circular manholes as we pass over. When I reach twenty, Bastien veers straight up and levels off at the top of an abandoned building. It is higher than many of the others in this area. The brick along the building face is scorched but the street is clean. Drakon's army has been working overtime to clean up this section of the City.

"You should be safe here," Bastien says as his feet touch the ground and he releases me. I step back, slightly wobbly at first, but surprisingly thankful to be on solid ground.

Bastien moves toward the low roof edge, his hand pointed toward the Shard building only five blocks away. "We know Drakon is holding Kyan there. That is where we will concentrate our attack. Keep your head down and, if for any reason the fighting comes your way, I want you to run and don't look back."

"But—"

"No," Bastien snaps, rounding on me. "For once you are going to listen to me. If you can't promise not to get involved, I swear I will fly you out into the woods again and leave you."

My mouth gapes open at the ferocity of his demand. The urge to fight back rises up within me, but I squelch it back down. "Fine."

He turns his back on me. "When the battle is over, I want you to leave if I don't come back for you. Head straight back to the emergency camp and wait."

Without looking at me, he steps up onto the ledge. "So that's it? You're just going to leave me like this?"

I don't know what I was expecting once we arrived, but this cold sendoff wasn't it. "I have no other choice, Illyria." His voice lacks the emotion I know he is feeling.

"You always have a choice."

"Do I?" He turns and faces me, leaping down from the ledge. "You took that choice away from me a couple months back, remember? What I want, what you want, doesn't matter anymore. This is the chosen path. You can't deviate from it."

His fists clench tightly against his legs. His shoulders are taut as he approaches. "What do you want from me, Illyria. You drew a line and I've done my best to respect it."

"I know," I whisper, dropping my head in shame. I've tried to stop loving him, to try to forget but it's hopeless.

"This isn't fair," he growls.

I hide behind my hair, wishing I had been strong enough not to call out to him. "I'm sorry…for everything."

Bastien growls, gripping my arms and shaking me. I lift watery eyes to meet him. His anger falters and he pushes aside my damp hair with a finger, curling it gently behind my ear. "What do you want from me?" He asks gently this time.

Staring into his eyes, I know he will be my undoing. That's not going to ever change. "I want you."

His breath catches. "Don't do this," he pleads. His grip on my arms tightens. "You can't ask that of me. Not now."

I sob and try to pull away from him. "I'm weak without you. I don't…I don't know how to live up to Kyan's destiny if that means sacrificing my heart."

Instead of releasing me, Bastien crushes me against his chest. He lifts my chin and stares down at me with liquid fire in his eyes. His lower lip quivers as his breathing becomes haggard, fighting with his resolve. Mine is completely shattered.

Without closing his eyes, he lowers and brushes his lips against mine. I forget how to breathe as the earth stands still. Every kiss is slow and controlled, but I can feel the passion within him begging to be released. I sink into his embrace, desperately wishing I never had to let go, that time would move on without us and allow me this one small gift.

Bastien lifts me into his arms and lowers me to the ground, covering my body with his. My skin trembles beneath the trail of his lips along my collarbone. His hands roam down my arms, grasping my slender waist as he pulls me up into him. I can't get close enough to him. My heart aches for more.

I wrap my legs around his waist and part his lips with my tongue. He groans against my lips, as the fires burn deep within my soul, rejuvenating me. I plunge my hands into his hair, begging him.

His hand slips under my shirt, splaying across my abdomen as I press up into him "Bastien," I moan against his lips, feeling as if my heart has just woken from a long hibernation.

He pulls back as the fire in his gaze dies out. He gasps for breath, shaking his head to clear his mind. "We can't do this."

Bastien scrambles away, wiping his lips as if I've burned him. "I'm sorry. That shouldn't have happened."

"Bastien…" I beg.

"No," he waves his hand at me. "That is exactly why we can't be together. I want you too bad to ever be able to let you go again."

His face crumples with despair. I don't have the heart to beg him to stay, to force my weakness upon him.

"I have to go." He backs away. When he reaches the rooftop ledge, he steps up and pauses before leaping. "Goodbye, Illyria."

THIRTY-THREE

From my high vantage point, I strain to watch as Bastien leaps from rooftop to rooftop. His dismissal stings far more than I would like to admit. It's my fault though. I was a fool to beg him to take me back when I had no right to ask for such a thing. Nothing has changed. My destiny remains, as does my vow to be with Eamon.

Even as the pain of Bastien's rejection floods into my heart, I know that if given the chance to do it all again, I wouldn't change a thing. I'm not strong enough to live without Bastien. I know that now. The question is…how long will he be able to hold out?

And what of Eamon? Can I really crush him yet again? I close my eyes and fight back the guilt that crashes over me. I never meant to hurt him. I wish there was another way.

I duck low as the hum of Sky Ships rises into the air, echoing down the long streets that lead to the heart of the city. Moving into position, I peer over the rooftop ledge to see spider drones patrolling the streets. Fear settles into my stomach as I search for my friends among the mass of aliens.

There is no way we can win this war…not without my powers.

The sun beats down on me, warming the black roof so I hardly notice the chill in the air. An eerie silence falls over the City, a calm before the storm.

In the distance, a building explodes in a cloud of brick dust. Black clad soldiers race down the street, chasing after a figure that blurs out of sight as soon as he hits the main street. *Toren.*

My fingers dig into the metal ledge as I watch flashes of red light up the streets before me. Brym leads a small group of soldiers down a side street, pausing to slap small devices onto the walls before racing away. Seconds pass and a ripple of explosions rocks the eastern quadrant.

To the south, a black cloud approaches at an impossible speed. I blink, shielding my eyes to see that it is not a cloud, but an enormous flock of birds. Once they reach the Shard, they circle overhead, cawing loudly before dive-bombing on the aliens below. The Squaddie's screams rise over the birds' cries as red laser beams shoot wildly through the air. Wolves, coyotes and mountain lions attack from the north, barreling past my building to tear down anyone in their path.

Beus and Brym lead a sneak attack on the Shard's courtyard but are held back until the birds finish their battle. To the west of the Shard, I spy Bastien leaping from building to building, drawing fire away from where Zahra and Aminah huddle. Toren blurs into sight and disappears with Aminah in his arms. I search for him until I see him reappear a few blocks over. He deposits Aminah with Eamon and races back for Zahra.

He never makes it.

A spider drone blasts through a building one block between them. I watch in horror as Toren tries to slow as the building tumbles down upon him, but he slams into the debris with enough force to knock the air out of him.

"No!" I shout. I slam my palm against the railing in frustration.

Anger bores into my chest as I watch my friends struggling to survive. They won't last long outnumbered like this.

I rise and pace the rooftop, desperate to join in the fight. My steps falter as Aminah's shriek pierces through my mind. *Illyria! Help us!*

I race back to the ledge, searching for any sign of my friend. I cry out when I see that a Squaddie has Aminah slung over his shoulder and two others drag an unconscious Eamon through the double doors of the Shard.

A gust of wind blows my hair over my face and I turn to find a battered Toren limping my way. "Toren!"

His knees give out on him as he falls to the roof. I rush to his side, pulling his head into my lap. A deep gash oozes over his eye, the blood blurring his vision. "Oh God! You're hurt!"

"They knew our plans. Drakon must have pulled them out of Kyan." He grunts, cradling his ribs. "We can't win."

"I know. I've been watching. Where is everyone else?"

"I don't know." His face pinches with pain. "I haven't seen Bastien or Eamon. Zahra was gone when I finally got around the debris. I think she's going after Kyan.

"Eamon?" My brow furrows with confusion. "You don't know?"

He rises up onto his elbow. "What?"

I glance away, toward the Shard. Aminah's screams linger in my mind. "Aminah and Eamon were captured."

Toren jerks upright, wincing at the pain in his side but determined to go after her. I push him back. "You can't help her. Not like this."

He opens his mouth to protest but nods. "Then she needs your help."

"You know I can't. I don't have my powers."

"Then find them!" He roars. "For all we know, Drakon is torturing Aminah just like he did Kyan. I can't..." he gulps. "You have to stop him."

I lean back from him as my doubt swells. "What if I can't?"

Toren's expression is grim as he turns to look at me. "Then we are all going to die."

"No pressure then," I mutter as I push up to my feet and begin pacing. I have no idea how to tap into my powers. I never have. How does one flip a switch when there is none to be found?

"Bastien."

I turn back. "What did you say?"

"He's your trigger," Toren grunts as he tries to rise to his feet. Sweat glistens on his forehead as he wavers, but remains upright. "You have to think of him."

"It's not that easy. Just thinking of him isn't enough. I have to see..." I trail off as I spin to search the rooftops. The City is vast, spanning numerous miles. It would be nearly impossible to find him on a normal day, but his acrobatics have created quite a stir among the Sky Ships.

I squint, raising my hands to block the sun as I watch a tiny figure in the distance leap from a rooftop and slap the underside of a Sky Ship. Red lasers charge as he coils in midair and shoots off. I hear the boom of the blast seconds after the ship erupts into a fiery ball, plummeting to the earth.

"Watch out!" I scream uselessly as the shockwave catches up to Bastien, slamming him to the rooftop of a lower building. I rise up onto my tiptoes, searching for any movement through the cloud of smoke, but I see none.

I watch, praying that he will shoot out of the smoke to go play chicken with another Sky Ship, but he never appears.

The trembling begins in my fingers, radiating swiftly up my forearms and into my shoulders. Like an uncontained explosion, rage spills into every cell within my body as three Sky Ships converge on Bastien.

Images suddenly invade my mind, driving me to my knees as Aminah calls out to me. *Drakon has Eamon!*

I can see Eamon lying unconscious on the floor. His hair is bloody and matted to his forehead. His left cheek is swollen and a bruise has begun to form on his jaw. His breathing is labored as his back contorts, his face pinched with agony.

He's been like that since Drakon started digging around in his mind. He's still breathing, but he's in bad shape, Illyria. He needs your help.

I curl my fingers around the metal railing. It groans under the pressure as it molds to my fingers. "Whoa!" Toren cries, pulling my hands away to inspect the damage. "How did you do that?"

I ignore him, focusing on the surge of energy coursing through my body. My hands shake as they rise up beside me and the air crackles with energy. Rage crashes against me in unrelenting waves, each time building in intensity.

My body quakes and my teeth chatter as I rise up onto my tiptoes. I gasp for breath as my skin begins to burn. Power swells in my chest. "It's too much," I cry as currents of agony flood my body. "I can't control it!"

Toren backs away until his spine presses against the roof access door. His fingers curl around the door handle, ready to run.

Calm down. You can handle this.

"Kyan?" I scream aloud.

Close your eyes and focus on your breathing. Let the Shadow come.

I'm scared! It's too strong this time. I don't know if I can—

You can. You were born for this moment. His voice is strong, confident.

I close my eyes and try to think past the pain. The whispers have risen to riotous jeering in my mind. The Shadow waits just on the edge, waiting, watching.

Command it to come to you.

How?

You will know.

I sink within my mind, imaging myself on a beach. The water is crystal blue, the skies cloudless and the sound of palm trees swaying lazily in the air soothes my mind. I look to the distance and see thunderous, rolling black clouds rampaging toward me. I dig my feet in and hold my ground as it approaches.

The Shadow blocks out the light and I plummet into complete darkness. Only the forks of white lighting that hit the churning water light my vision. Fear cripples me.

I raise my hands overhead and throw my head back, staring the Shadow head on. *You are not in control of me!*

My face brightens with brilliant white as a streak of lightning slams into me. My chest burns and my lungs collapse in on themselves as I'm consumed with pain. I cry out as the fire sears my flesh. Tears cascade from my eyes as I struggle to remember to breathe, to think.

Fight for Bastien, Kyan calls through my rising screams.

I bring my hands to my chest and draw the lightning away, balling it into my hands. The clouds overhead roar as thunder crashes all around. I close my hand over the lightning, sealing out all light as I absorb the energy. I clamp down on my jaw as violent tremors send me crashing to the ground.

"Illyria!"

Opening my eyes, I look up to see Toren kneeling above me. He reaches out for me, but jerks his hand back as an arch of energy zaps him. "What happened to you?"

I rise slowly, holding my head in my hands. "I think I just joined myself with the Shadow."

"Is that a good thing?" he asks hesitantly.

"I guess we will find out." I place my hands on the ground and flip up to my feet. The movement is effortless.

Well done, Kyan calls weakly. *Believe that you are invincible and you will be.*

"Uh, Illyria…?"

I turn to look at Toren. "What?"

"Your hair…it's black."

I lift my hair off my shoulder, filtering the obsidian stands through my fingers. I let the strands slip through my fingers.

"Don't get me wrong, it's not a bad look it's just…freaky," Toren says, averting his gaze. His eyes widen with fright as he raises a finger to point directly behind me.

My hair whips around my face as I turn to see a Sky Ship bearing down on us. Toren grabs my arm and yanks me toward the door. "Run!"

"No," I shake him off. I walk toward the ledge and wait for the ship to approach. It's laser core swirls as the cannons charge. "I'm not running anymore."

Energy ripples along my skin. I feel alive and deadly. I grin as the crimson laser slams into my chest. It knocks me back a step as it spreads along the length of my body, curling around me with blistering heat. I lean my head back and breathe deeply as the heat sinks into my flesh, completely absorbed. My mind is abuzz with the added energy.

I lower my head and grin. "I guess Kyan was right."

"How did you do that?" Toren calls from the open rooftop door.

"I'm invincible." I stretch out my hands, curling my fingers inward like claws. The ship shreds down the middle, spiraling to the ground in a rain of sparks and molten metal. The explosion rocks the building.

Toren limps quickly to my side. "I'm not even going to ask."

"Come here," I command, holding out my hand. He stops beside me, eyes open in wonder as I press my hands to his chest. Healing warmth glows instantly from my fingers. He gasps as the cracks in his ribs mend.

The glow fades and I pull back my hands. "Better?"

"Yeah, but didn't that weaken you?"

I grin. "Not this time."

Toren looks past me toward the building where Bastien fell. "You need to go after him. I'll go after Aminah."

"You won't be able to get through," I warn.

He offers me a sad smile. "I have to try. Get to Bastien and then help Zahra with Kyan. I'll hold the fort until you arrive."

"I'll get there as soon as I can." I clasp Toren on the back. "You want a lift?"

"Nah, I'm good. Just go."

I turn and race for the edge, ignoring Toren's cry of alarm as I leap into the sky. The air whips around me as I dive off the building and fly down the main street. I stay low to remain under the Sky Ship's radar until I reach Bastien.

The broken buildings blur past as I tear down the streets. Below me, soldiers whip their guns up to shoot at me, but their laser beams fall far behind. I throw out my arms and veer down two blocks before shooting straight toward the four-story brick apartment building where Bastien fell.

Three Sky Ships hover over the building, but their lasers remain dark. This worries me. If Bastien is alive, he won't still be on that rooftop. A flash of red to my right sends me spiraling through the open window of an apartment and straight through the opposite side. I curl around the edge of the building and come up on the backside of a spider drone. It's laser cannon scans the skies for me.

Dipping low, I grab hold of one of its back legs and yank it into the sky. My mind screams that this should be impossible, but I hardly feel the weight of the machine. As I clear the top of the roofline, I spy Bastien's crumpled shape in the middle of a Caldonian circle. The soldiers are approaching cautiously.

I grit my teeth and launch the drone straight at the nearest Sky Ship's starboard engines. The Caldonians on the rooftop scatter as the ship collides in mid-air with another. In a cloud of fire and smoke, the drone plummets to the ground.

The third ship is forced to retreat half a block and is quickly engaged by a ground force I can't see. Perhaps Brym and Beus have made it to this section of the city.

I land on the roof beside Bastien in a crouch. I slowly rise, spreading my feet wide to face off with the recovering Caldonians.

"Get the girl!"

I turn at the vicious snarl that rises from my left. "You!"

Scar Face struggles to maintain an air of authority as his men retreat, leaving him alone to face off with me. "You got lucky the first time, girl."

"My friend convinced me not to chase after you. Unfortunately for you, he's not here right now." With a flick of my wrist, I slam Scar Face into the railing and press him back so that he's dangling head first toward the ground. "Where is Kyan?"

"I'm not telling you anything," he grunts.

I drop him a foot and grin at his pathetic scream. "I'm only going to ask one more time. After that, I will give your men the same opportunity. I'm sure one of them will be more than happy to help."

"You kill me and Drakon will take pleasure in shredding your mind!"

"I do like a challenge," I call over my shoulder as I release my hold on him. His screams ricochet between the brick buildings before abruptly cutting off as he hits the ground.

I turn and face the remaining seven men. Only three of them are daring enough to raise their lasers at me. "I need to know where my friend is being kept. If you tell me, I will let you live."

A young boy steps forward. "I will help you, and so will these men." He points to three other soldiers who have their lasers lowered to the ground. "We are a part of Kyan's Rising."

I narrow my eyes at the boy. Although he looks to be only a year or two younger than me, I see great wisdom in his young eyes. "What's your name?"

"Carleon, Son of Drabis."

"Why have I never seen you before, Carleon?"

He drops his gaze. "Kyan felt it best for me to remain behind."

"Why?"

"I'm too young," he mutters.

My gaze flickers toward the three men who hold lasers pointed at me in their trembling hands. I reach out and mentally snatch their weapons from their hands. I squeeze my hand into a fist and the guns crumple inward. "Go. Leave the City and I will let you live."

The men scramble for the door, slamming it behind them. I turn toward Carleon and his men, each laying their weapons on the ground in submission as I approach. I reach out and touch Carleon on the shoulder. "War does not care what age you are, and neither do I. Can you fight?"

"Yes," he nods. I look beyond him at the other three soldiers who nod enthusiastically. "Then you're going to need your weapons."

They grin and pick them back up, their lasers humming to life. "Switch to stun. There has been enough death here today."

I turn and look back toward Bastien. "Where is Kyan being held?"

"In the courtyard of the Shard, but you can't get there from here," Carleon says.

I drop down beside Bastien, grateful to see the steady rise and fall of his chest. He's alive. "Can I trust you with this man's safety?"

Carleon puffs up his chest as the men form a half circle around me. "With our lives."

Tears slip down my cheeks as I stare down at Bastien, smoothing the hair away from his face. He is covered with bruises and his legs are broken in several places. Lifting his shirt, I wince at the sight of blood pooling in his belly, just below his skin.

I let my eyes fall shut and summon the healing fires. They come fast and bright and the golden glow spreads along Bastien's body. The cuts and bruises begin to fade and his abdomen returns to flesh color. I sink back onto my knees, breathing hard.

"You're a healer?" Carleon gasps. "And you can fly?"

I push up to my feet, feeling slightly weakened by the second healing. "I can do far more than that."

Rising up onto the rooftop ledge, I turn back. "Get him somewhere safe and don't let him leave. I will come back for him once I'm done with Drakon."

"Be careful," Carleon warns. "Commander Drakon is a Mind Bender. He has been trained, as Aloysius' second in command. Don't underestimate him." I nod, casting one last glance down at Bastien before I leap from the rooftop.

THIRTY-FOUR

I land one block back from the courtyard that leads to the front doors of the Shard. The grass has long since died out, leaving behind a desolate space. A large fountain occupies the center of the courtyard, chipped and cracked from the battle that rages all around. Piles of bricks dot the space. Blood splatters everything in sight.

Caldonian soldiers form a circle around a tall wooden platform. I peer around the edge of a building and frown. Kyan stands in the center of the platform, his legs and wrists bound. He is leaned back against tall branches piled into a large pyre. Flickering torches reside on either side of the platform.

"Barbarians!" I swear softly.

Zahra is nowhere to be seen, but my guess is she's biding her time. The cawing of birds is gone, as are the howls of the wolves.

I raise my gaze toward the towering building overhead and know that Drakon is up there. I wonder if Toren managed to find a way to free them or if he too has become a prisoner.

Anger simmers in my belly as I step out into the open. Kyan lifts his head and I have to fight back my revulsion. There is hardly any patch of skin that has not been blistered or cut. One eye is completely swollen shut, the other partially. His lips are split and blood drips from both ears.

My anger turns to burning wrath as his one decent eye locks onto mine. *Eamon won't last much longer. You have to leave me.*

"No!"

The cry sends soldiers into a frenzy as they face off with me, lasers aimed directly at my heart. *I don't know if you can absorb all of their shots. Don't risk it.*

Don't worry. They won't get the chance to shoot!

Dark clouds swirl overhead as winds whip into strong gales. My hair lashes against my face, obscuring the veil of black that falls over my eyes. I stretch out my hands and yank ice shards from the sky, keeping a protective bubble around Kyan.

The aliens scream and dash for cover as large splinters of ice pierce their flesh. They shield their heads as blood dots the ground. The ground ripples underfoot as great chasms tear through the earth, sealing the aliens within.

Don't kill them. They are only following orders, Kyan calls to me.

I look to Kyan and sever the bonds holding him to the pyre with my mind. He falls to the ground.

"Kyan!" Zahra races out from the lower level of the Shard. I raise my hands and wave off the ice storm as she leaps onto the platform and pulls him into her arms.

I turn toward the wounded aliens. "Surrender and your lives will be spared. Lay one finger on my friends and I promise you a painful end."

Racing toward the platform, I reach Zahra's side. Tears stream down her cheeks as she looks at me. "Thank you. I didn't know how to save him."

I nod and focus on Kyan. "Let me heal you."

"No!" He croaks. "You have to get to Eamon. Drakon thinks he's the one you will fight for."

I grit my teeth, hearing the unspoken truth behind his words. Drakon will use Eamon's sanity as leverage against me. I stretch out my hand and levitate a laser gun to Zahra's side. "Stay with him. If any of the Caldonians attack, I want you to use this."

"Count on it," she growls, clutching it in her free hand.

"They won't..." Kyan coughs, holding his sides. "We will be safe."

"I hope you're right." I pat him on the shoulder and sprint for the Shard. It is time to finish this.

The interior of the Shard is rather surprising. Plush couches line the lower floor while potted plants and other unique trinkets dot the sitting area. My shoes whisper against the plush white carpet, leaving bloody boot prints in my wake.

Despite the battle waging outside, the Shard is ominously quiet. No screaming, no whimpering, no humming lasers. A shiver ripples along my spine as I ascend the stairs.

I imagine the Shard used to be a very impressive building, rising high above all the others. The glass-panned tower must have stretched up to the clouds. Now it is but a shell of its former glory.

Pictures hang on the walls, images of a life I have never known—children playing in parks of lush greens and autumn leaves, men tossing fishing lines into water, spending a leisurely day at the lake. Each image captures my attention as I pass, but I force myself to search for the top floor.

When I reach the opening at the top of the final stairway, I can feel Drakon, like a tiny portion of the Shadow is calling to me from the end of the hall. Fear worms its way into my mind as I approach. I haven't seen any sign of Toren yet.

The hallway widens to reveal a large sitting area. Cracked leather chairs form a quaint semicircle around a darkened screen. The carpet is slightly worn here, evidence of a great amount of traffic.

Blood droplets draw my attention toward the closed double doors. I take a deep breath before opening them but I walk into the room with an air of confidence.

"Ah, Illyria," Drakon grins as he turns to face me. "I was wondering when you might show up."

"I got a little preoccupied with your army outside. Sorry about those Sky Ships. I hope they weren't too important."

A vein running down his forehead pulsates as he grits his teeth. "All is fair in love and war."

His black uniform is pristine, creased to perfection. His hair is shorter than I remember. His left breast is proudly emblazoned with his many medals of honor. "You didn't have to primp just for me," I jeer as I step further into the large space.

The room is circular in design, lined with curved windows to give a panoramic view of the City. I can imagine Drakon sitting behind the large mahogany wood desk, staring out at his empire like one of those Roman Caesars my father told me about, never satisfied with the world they command.

Aminah rests against a tall wooden cabinet off to my right. Her eyes are wide with fear, and her skin is frightfully pale. A growl rumbles in my chest at the sight of her broken leg and fingers pushed so far out of joint it make me nauseous.

Her eyes flicker to the side and I follow her gaze to a pair of legs sticking out from behind a large black leather couch. The pants are darkened with blood. *Toren!*

"I see you've noticed the state of your friends." Drakon tsks, shaking his head as he clasps his hands behind his back. "It's a pity you didn't come sooner. You might have been able to save them some of their pain."

My teeth grind as I glare at him, where he remains perched on the edge of his desk. "Where is Eamon?"

"Oh, I should have known you would come for the boy. Silly me," he gloats, sweeping his hand behind him.

My chest clenches at the sight of Eamon curled into a ball of agony just beyond Drakon. Aminah was right. This man is no fool. He has kept his most prized leverage well out of reach.

"What do you want?" I ask, stepping into the center of the room.

From this point, I can reach Aminah in three steps and Toren in five. Even if I did manage to get them out of here, Eamon is sure to suffer the consequences.

"What I have always wanted, my dear. To help you fulfill your destiny. Although," he taps his fingers on his lips, "I do think I preferred you as a blonde. The black is so…dramatic."

"Sorry to disappoint," I grin, flexing my fingers against my side.

He notices every twitch I make. A grin stretches across his thin lips as I feel him touch my mind for the first time. It comes like the swift jab of a sword, invading and deadly accurate. I can feel my skin pulsate as I allow the Shadow to drape over my mind.

Drakon is thrown off his feet as I mentally shove him aside. Hairline cracks appear in the glass window behind his back as he slides to the floor. He rises, his beady black eyes livid as he wipes a drop of blood from his ear.

"I see the true Shadow Walker standing before me now. Impressive." His anger fades as a glint of greed makes him giddy with desire. "Perhaps we can come to some sort of an agreement."

I don't let a smile form this time. I want him to think that I would consider making a deal with him even though I've just proven he has no power over me. "Go on."

"I will let your friends go if you agree to join me. I can teach you how to unleash your powers. I can offer you riches beyond your wildest dreams."

"And my friends?"

"Will be allowed to return to their hovel you called a home in the woods. They will be free to rebuild."

"And they will be safe?" I press.

His eyes narrow. "Safe enough. I can't promise that *all* of my men will obey my commands."

I approach, making each calculated step count. I can sense his nervousness. "No deal."

"It is a fair offer," he protests, shrinking back slightly. Drakon glances toward Eamon, producing terrifyingly horrific screams. "I wouldn't do anything rash, my dear. Poor Eamon's mind is hanging in the balance. One wrong move and you will be feeding him with a spoon for the rest of your life."

Anger rips through my mind as I restrain the urge to squeeze the life from him. "You seem to—"

The window behind Drakon explodes inward, sending glass splinters shooting through the air. Aminah shrieks and ducks as the shards rain over her. I wave my hand and create a protective barrier over her head and the glass patters harmlessly against the wooden floor.

Drakon rises to his feet, his face a minefield of bloody gashes. "Who dares disrupt me?"

A figure rises from behind the sofa in a whirlwind of papers caused by the gusting winds funneling through the broken window. "I dare," Bastien growls.

I throw out my hand and shove Drakon's desk directly at him as I leap to Bastien's side. I close my eyes and focus. He cries out as I pummel him to the floor, disappearing completely.

"What are you doing?" He growls in my ear.

"Saving your life."

From the other side of the room, Drakon lunges for the laser concealed under the desk and takes aim in our direction. His eyes roam the empty space. "That's a clever trick," he growls stepping around his desk.

He lowers his laser and I roll Bastien to the side only a second before the laser slams into the wood where we were laying. "Don't let go of me," I whisper in his ear as I pull him to his knees.

Drakon shoots off random shots, growling as each one fails to hit us. "I'm not in the mood for games today, girl. Come out now or I will fry your friend."

Aminah whimpers as Drakon approaches.

I lean up into Bastien's ear. "When I let go you will be visible again. Get Aminah and Toren out of here. I will take care of Eamon."

I can feel him shaking his head beside me. "No. I came for you, not them."

"I'm waiting," Drakon calls.

I roll Bastien until we are behind an overturned chair. My fingers move across his face until I find his chin. With a whimper, I crush my lips onto his and then dive away from him. I roll to my feet behind Drakon, completely visible.

He turns, gun aimed at Aminah's chest. "Sorry. Your time was up."

I scream as he fingers the trigger. Bastien tackles Aminah out of the way, as the laser hits the floor. He leaps to his feet with her in his arms and dives through the open window.

"No!" Drakon growls, leaping to the side of the couch to get a clear shot at Toren. "He can't save your friend this time."

I stretch out my hand and yank the couch toward me, sending Drakon tumbling end over end. He crumples to the floor, his laser spiraling out of his hand. I bend over and grab Toren, lifting him into my arms as I race for the window.

Bastien! Catch!

I toss Toren out of the window and watch as Bastien speeds up to meet him, slowing at the last second to match Toren's speed so he doesn't break his back. Toren's head flops as he lands in Bastien's arms.

"I'm coming back for you!" Bastien shouts before he races to place Toren on the ground.

Heat explodes along my spine and I collapse against the window frame. I can see the red glow of the laser fire flickering against the window beside me. A sneer curls my lip as I rise to my feet and turn to face Drakon.

His face drains of color. "That's impossible!"

I roll my neck as heat radiates up my spine and curls around my heart. Drakon backs away, tripping over the mess of papers that line the floor, fallen from his overturned desk. He stretches out his hand and Eamon's back arches, his neck tensing as he screams.

"Not too close, Illyria. I still have your precious Eamon."

No matter how I look at this situation, I can't find a way out without risking Eamon's life. Although I seem completely capable of breaking Drakon's attempts to latch onto my mind, I am unable to break his connection with Eamon's.

"Fine," I throw up my hands. "You win. Release Eamon and I will go with you."

Drakon's eyebrow arches. "How can I trust you? As soon as Eamon is gone you can toss me straight out that window."

"Let my friends come for him. Once they are through the door I will release full control to you."

He cocks his head to the side. "A tempting offer."

I nod. "One I know you can't pass up. Not if you want to win favor with Aloysius."

He blinks. "You know of him?"

"I know what my destiny requires." I reply flatly.

"And yet you would still go with me."

I nod.

"Fair enough." He retracts his hand slightly and Eamon's back sinks to the floor. Exhaustion mars his face but the excruciating pain has faded. "Call your friends."

Kyan?

I'm here.

Are you well enough to join me?

I'm healed. Bastien and I are on our way.

I stifle the cry rising in my throat at the deal I have just made with the devil. I know what I risk, the complete loss of my own mind, but the risk is worth it.

Drakon has agreed to release Eamon to you and allow you a pardon. The war is over.

Kyan is silent for a moment. *At what price?*

Me.

No! You're not ready! Kyan's protests make me close my eyes against my tears.

It's already done.

I sever the connection and wait. "They are on their way."

Drakon's grin turns my stomach. "Excellent."

"Let me see him," I say, stepping toward Eamon. Drakon hesitates, but relents with another reminder of the hold he has over Eamon's mind. I dip down low beside Eamon, gently pressing my lips against his bruised temple. "Please forgive me."

Drakon cackles behind me. "How touching."

"Kyan already told you everything you needed to know. You didn't have to hurt him."

"True," he nods. "But I do so enjoy my job."

I turn and glare up at him over my shoulder. "Be thankful you have a hold on him. If not, I promise you I would find a much slower way for you to die than tossing you out a window."

The skin around his eyes pinch, but he grins down at me. "Aloysius is going to have so much fun breaking you, girl."

I turn at the sound of Bastien and Kyan busting through the door. I frown, confused as to why Bastien didn't just fly Kyan up through the window, but then I notice the strain lining his face. Bastien is near exhaustion.

"Take Eamon and leave the City," I say aloud as Kyan dips down beside me. When he is near enough to whisper, I lean in. "Don't stay in the mountains. Drakon will not keep his word."

Kyan nods in silent agreement as he rises with Eamon's arm thrown over his shoulder. Eamon's dead weight is a struggle for Kyan, but he manages. I look to Bastien as Kyan stumbles past.

"I'm not leaving without you." His voice is low, heavy with emotion.

Pain crashes through my thin veil of confidence and I feel my grip on the Shadow weaken. Drakon's face lights up. "Ah…so he's the one!"

Bastien's stance tenses as I face off with Drakon. "Try to hurt him and I swear you will regret it," I threaten darkly. Electricity sparks in the air around me, but Drakon only shrugs.

Kyan lugs Eamon out into the hall. He pauses and turns back for Bastien. "Bastien?"

He shakes his head. "I can't make myself leave."

"You have to. It's the only way to protect you." I plead with him, begging him to see the truth of my words.

Bastien shakes his head, planting his feet on the floor. "Not without saying goodbye."

"Not gonna happen, pretty boy. You fooled me once, but I don't fall for the same trick twice."

I whip around, unleashing the full extent of my anger on Drakon. He watches the swirl of shadow in my eyes. "Either I get to say goodbye to him or our deal is off."

He splutters, going red in the face as his vein becomes more pronounced. He eyes Bastien and then me. "We have a ship to catch. Make it fast."

Bastien leaps forward, taking me in his arms. I cling to him, desperate to glean strength from him, as his tormented soul is laid bare before me. I can see love, unfathomable in its depth. "Please don't do this. Come with me," he begs.

"I can't," I whisper. "He can still destroy Eamon's mind."

A sob rises in Bastien's throat as he crushes his lips against mine. His hands tighten around my arms, pressing me against the length of his body. I want to mold myself around him, to savor this one last kiss, but Drakon shoves us apart.

"That's enough. Get a move on, boy."

"I love you," I cry out as he shoves Bastien toward the door.

Tears dampen Bastien's cheeks. "I will find you. I promise!"

"I think I might throw up," Drakon mocks from behind me.

"Have you no decency?" I hear a rustle of fabric and turn to see him rising with a laser gun in his hand.

"I guess not." He raises his gun and fires straight at Bastien's heart.

THIRTY-FIVE

Rage fragments my thoughts as I watch the scarlet laser shoot toward Bastien. A guttural snarl rips from my throat as I throw out my hand and shove Bastien out of the way. He tumbles end over end as the beam slams into the wall behind him, leaving behind a scorched divot.

My control over the Shadow shatters as I bear down on Drakon. He fires off three shots at me, but instead of absorbing them, they deflect off me like light on a prism. Drakon ducks as the lasers careen away.

Lightning forks in the sky as the dark clouds begin to swirl overhead, forming a perimeter around the City edge. Three tornadoes descend to the earth, tearing apart the City outskirts as they converge toward the Shard.

The building quakes as the ground rolls underfoot. Drakon cries out as the metal frame of the building rocks, spilling him off his feet. From the windows beyond, I can see deep crevices carving in the earth. Spider drones spill into the holes as Caldonians dangle from the crumbling ground. Entire blocks of buildings tumble into the sinkholes.

Apple sized hail is hurled from the sky and forks of lightning strike at the land, charring everything in its path. Fires rampage through the broken city, sealing off the aliens' exit.

Drakon's laser gun rises into the air, crumpling as I clench my fist. Sky Ships implode in midair, careening to the ground, rocking the city with their explosions. Shrapnel and ice fill the air as I pin Drakon to the wall.

In the distance, I watch as the Caldonians' homes are leveled, leaving nowhere for them to hide. The tornadoes collect glass and rubble from the ground, sending deadly debris whipping through the air.

Drakon watches in disbelief at the annihilation of his beloved city. "You can have Eamon back. I promise to release him to you if you will spare my life."

"You are in no position to make deals." I curl my fingers, slowly crushing his windpipe. His eyes bulge as he claws at his throat. Gurgling cries spill from his lips.

The desk and chairs whip into a cyclone about me, sucking up papers and shattered picture frames off the floor. "Help me," he gurgles, glancing down at Bastien.

"No!" Bastien cries as he races toward me. "Don't do this. He isn't worth it."

He is buffeted by the winds, ducking out of the way, as the couch breaks into three pieces and lifts into the air.

I rise into the air, the center of the deadly vortex. Bastien shields his eyes as a golden light emits from my chest. I raise my hands above my head and a ball of energy spirals in my hands.

Bastien's hair stands on end as he pushes his way toward me. "Don't let the Shadow consume you!" He screams over the roar of the swirling winds. "If you kill him, I will lose you!"

I shake my head, trying to push out his words. The whispers rise in a symphony within my mind. Bastien cries out in pain as he clasps onto my hand. He sinks to the floor, jerking as if he's just been electrocuted.

"Bastien!"

I throw out my hand and envelop Bastien in healing light. His convulsions cease, but his face remains contorted.

"See what you made me do!" I scream at Drakon.

"Remember who you are," Bastien pleads weakly.

I scream, yanking at my hair. The rage is too strong. I'm losing control.

Bastien rises unsteadily to his feet. "Do you love me?"

"Yes," I whisper hoarsely. "More than anything."

"Is your love for me stronger than the Shadow?" He asks, rising to his feet. He inches toward me, buffeted by the winds. As the electricity fades around me, he reaches out and cups my cheek in his hand.

"Yes." Flashes of violet return to my eyes and the Shadow begins to lift.

"Then fight back!"

My body slams against the ceiling, consumed with rippling energy. My back arches as I scream. Light shoots from my chest, glowing with pure, blinding luminescence. Bastien shields his eyes from the light, unable to handle the sight of my raw power. The light blinks out of existence and I collapse to the floor.

Papers, desks and books fall from the air. The clouds break apart, letting sunlight stream through once more. The tornadoes spin themselves out and the ground ceases to quake. People, all over the City, crawl out from their hiding places.

As the Shard ceases rocking, Bastien throws himself to my side, rolling me over as he cradles me against him. His lips find mine and tears leak down my face as I wrap my arms around him. Drakon slumps to the ground, unconscious.

Kyan races into the room, stopping in the doorway to survey the damage. Laser scorch marks line nearly every wall. Everything has been turned upside down and Bastien and I embrace in the middle of it all.

He clears his throat. "Um…sorry to interrupt, but I was wondering if you were done tearing apart the City."

I flush furiously as Bastien releases me. I squeeze his hand and nod. "Sorry about that."

Kyan grins. "The war is over, thanks to you." He turns and looks to Drakon. "You didn't kill him."

Bastien wraps his arm around my shoulder and pulls me in close. "I told you she was stronger than the Shadow."

"So you did," Kyan nods, dipping down beside Drakon to check his pulse. "I think it's only fitting that we send Drakon back to Aloysius to tell him the good news of our victory here today, don't you?"

I laugh and accept Bastien's hand up. "I wish I could be there to watch."

I tug Bastien toward the door, but he pulls back. "I'm gonna hang out here for a few minutes. Why don't you head down and check on everyone? I'm sure Aminah is dying to see you."

Bastien's earlier warmth has begun to recede, leaving a cold dread in his wake. I force a smile and pause in the doorway. "You'll come find me, right?"

He hesitates before nodding. I slip out of the room and wrap my arms around myself as I start the long trek down the stairs.

Aminah dashes across the courtyard when she sees me emerge from the Shard. A brilliant smile greets me just before she throws her arms around me. "Thank you for saving Toren!"

"And you," I chuckle as she steps back. "Glad to see you on two legs again."

She nods, her flattened curls thick with blood and tiny bits of debris. "Your friend healed me. I think he said his name is Carleon."

I grin and look up to see the younger boy eagerly waving at me. I wave back and squeeze Aminah's hand. "Is everyone ok?"

A knowing smile makes her eyes twinkle as she looks over my shoulder. "Why don't you ask him yourself?"

I spin around and find myself scooped up into Eamon's arms. He lifts me off the ground, twirling us around. He glows with happiness as he kisses me. "So, I hear I have you to thank for saving me. I think I make a pretty hot damsel in distress."

Aminah shifts away, returning to Toren's side, but I hardly notice. It feels too good to be in Eamon's arms. "I was so worried about you! How did you survive Drakon?"

He slides his hands down my arms and twines his fingers through mine. "I just kept thinking about you."

I blush furiously as he cups my cheek, brushing his thumb across my skin. "I never get tired of making you blush."

His fingers shift to lift a thick clump of hair from my shoulder. "Love the new look," he grins mischievously. "I think I could really get used to the new you."

I flush and run my fingers through my hair. "It's different, that's for sure."

"I like it," he grins, wrapping his arms about my waist. "It's sexy."

My blush deepens under his adoring gaze. I clear my throat and let my head rest against his chest so I don't have to hide my discomfort. "How many did we lose?"

"More than we would have liked. Most of the men have burns and bruises. Nothing that can't be mended."

I look at the courtyard filled with people milling about. Many are bloody, bandaged with whatever clean fabric can be plucked from the rubble. Entire blocks have been leveled by my devastation.

"Many of them are already joining our forces. Kyan was right, most of these men didn't want this war. They were just following orders. Once we get them cleaned up and rebuild part of the City, I think we'll be ready to start planning the next battle."

I groan. "Oh, please let me recover from this one first!"

Eamon laughs, tucking me under his arm. "I still can't believe you did all of this."

"A woman scorned," I mutter under my breath.

He pulls back to look at me. "Something must have really ticked you off."

I avoid his gaze, knowing that he will figure it out easily enough on his own. I shelter my face from him with a veil of raven hair. It is cowardly to hide but, even still, I do.

Eamon sighs. "It was him, wasn't it?"

"Do you hate me?" I whisper.

"Never," he says into my ear and then pulls me around to kiss my forehead. His lips pause against my skin before he pulls back. "I think someone wants you."

I look up, surprised to see Bastien standing close to the Shard, waiting for me. I look to Eamon, unsure if I should leave him. He shoots me a weak smile. "Go on."

The walk to Bastien is slow and painful, filled with conflicting emotions. As I approach, he turns and disappears around the corner of the building. He waits for me halfway down the block with his back turned toward me.

I wait in tortured silence for him to speak, shifting from foot to foot with unease.

"Now that Drakon's army has fallen, we will begin assimilating many of the soldiers into our ranks. Kyan intends to keep the momentum going, to strike while Aloysius is weakened."

"That makes sense," I respond, confused as to why this matters to me.

When Bastien turns, I can see that his face is drawn with exhaustion. "Kyan needs someone to lead the army while he remains behind to continue your training."

"And he chose you?" I suck in a breath, reaching out to grab his hand, but pull back when he bristles and steps away. My stomach clinches painfully.

He shakes his head, staring fixedly on the ground. "I volunteered."

"No!" I cry, stepping closer, ignoring his obvious discomfort. "Why would you do that?"

"I can't stay here anymore. You're with Eamon now. If I stayed I'd be in the way and I...I don't know how much more I can take," he whispers, his voice cracking pitifully. "It's best for everyone."

"But you kissed me...on the roof...in Drakon's room..."

Bastien's face crumples in shame. "I know. I'm so sorry. I was weak..."

"Weak?" I whisper. "That's why you..." Bastien nods, refusing to meet my gaze. "No. I don't believe you!" I cry, rushing forward. "Look at me!"

Emotionless eyes rise to meet mine. I reel back, shocked by the hollow man standing before me.

"You're really leaving?" The clear blue sky disappears as dark thunderous storm clouds brew directly overhead. Thunder rumbles and lightning flashes, but I barely notice. Bastien lifts his face as the first drops of rain fall from the sky. He closes his eyes as the rain patters against his face.

The downpour drenches us within seconds. Bastien's dark hair plasters to his scalp and his chest rises and falls as he struggles to gain control over his emotions. When he opens his eyes, I see only deep sadness. His hope is gone.

"This is why I can't stay," he points to the churning skies above. "You're too emotional when you're around me. Your powers are growing quickly and you can't control them when I'm nearby. I can't stay and take the chance of someone getting hurt."

"But if you go, I will be hurt!" I plead, knowing that I'm not fighting fairly.

"I'm sorry. I can't keep denying myself if I stay so the only thing I can do to help you is leave."

I shake my head, backing away. "No. We can find another way."

"There is no other way."

"We could try," I whisper.

"Why? So we can torture each other some more? So we can keep living a lie, hoping that things will work out in the end? It won't, Illyria, and you know it."

"Don't you love me?"

Bastien closes the gap between us, placing his hands on my arms. "More than life itself. That's why I have to go."

"It's not fair!"

"No," he shakes his head, "but it's the right thing to do."

In all the time we've been apart, I have never wanted to run away from my destiny so badly as I do in this moment. All I want in life is to have Bastien by my side, but fate has dealt me a different hand.

"I will miss you," Bastien says.

I wrap my arms about myself as I sob, knowing there is nothing I can do to change this. He pulls me into his arms, resting his head atop mine. I can feel his pain churning within him just before he steps back.

"It's time for the rain to stop, don't you think?"

I nod and close my eyes, pushing back the clouds. The last few raindrops mingle with my tears as they fall from the sky. "I wish things could be different," I whisper as I dry my eyes.

Bastien swallows roughly. "I know."

"Will I see you again?" I drop my head, trying desperately not to think of what my life will be like without him. As hard at it was to see him every day, knowing that I couldn't have him, never seeing him will be far worse.

"I'll drop in from time to time." His lie is so obvious that a fresh rain of tears floods from my eyes. He is leaving…for good.

"Please don't do anything reckless while you're gone," I plead.

"Nothing more than usual," he forces a laugh. "Same goes for you."

I nod and wipe my nose with the back of my sleeve. "When do you leave?"

"Now." He looks beyond me and I turn to see Kyan waiting. "We're transporting Drakon to another location nearby. There's a ship waiting to send him on to Calisted with our message."

"I have to go." His brave façade falters as he walks past me. The sag in his shoulders tears at my heart. I can't just stand here and let him leave. Not like this.

"Wait!" I race around him and throw myself into his arms. I pull his face to mine before he can protest. Crushing my lips against his, I try to express every ounce of my love with one final kiss. It isn't enough. How can it be? But it's all I have left to give.

With a whimper, I pull back. "Please come back."

Bastien fights hard to clear the emotion from his face. He finally manages something close to expressionless, but he can't hide the burning agony darkening his eyes. He clenches his jaw and steps around me. "Goodbye, Illyria."

He straightens his shoulders and marches away. He doesn't stop, doesn't look back. He leaves me, standing alone, in the war-ravaged street with my heart utterly shattered.

I sink to my knees and feel a chasm widen in my chest. I have no idea if I will ever see him again. It is too painful to be near each other, but unbearable to be forced apart. I weep for the love I have been wrongfully denied.

Strong arms envelop me. I look up into Eamon's face, full of understanding and forgiveness. I cling to him, desperate for him to make the pain disappear. I sob until my sides ache and his shirt drips with my bitter tears, and still he says nothing. He just holds me.

My tears dry up slowly and I pull back to look at Eamon. His gaze is sympathetic. "I'm sorry that he left you," he murmurs against my hair. "He'll be fine. He's the best fighter we have."

"What about us?" I whisper.

Eamon smiles against my head. "That's entirely up to you."

My mouth falls open as I lean back to look at him. "You mean you still want me, after all of this?"

"Always," he presses his lips to mine. "Nothing can ever change that."

I smile. Maybe there is still hope. Maybe, just maybe, I can be happy with Eamon. My heart will forever long for Bastien, but I know I'm lucky to have Eamon by my side. He will never take Bastien's place in my heart, but maybe I can make a new place for him.

As Eamon leads me back to the courtyard, love and pride swells in my chest, driving back my sorrow. My friends and family are here, willing to stand by my side as we strive to change the fate of our world. This battle may be over, but the war has only just begun.

The Rising was a success. We fought hard and won our first victory, but there is much work to be done. The days ahead will be long, filled with danger and uncertainty, but I am ready to embrace my destiny, no matter what the future holds for me.

NOTE FROM THE AUTHOR

Thank you for taking this journey with me into Bastien, Illyria and Eamon's lives. I hope that you have enjoyed Book I of the Rising Triloy. Your reviews are greatly appreciated!

All books in this series are available now on all ebook platforms and paperback.

RELINQUISH

The rising is over, but the war continues to rage. King Aloysius knows Illyria exists and will stop at nothing to possess her. Jealousy drives a wedge between Illyria and Eamon. When Bastien reveals himself as her guide into enemy territory, an ambush lands them in captivity. Illyria is faced with the truth that she is not ready to face her destiny…or let Bastien go again.

ABOUT THE AUTHOR

Author Amy Miles has always been a bit of a dreamer. Growing up as an only child, and a military brat to boot, she spent countless hours escaping into the pages of a book, only to spend the following days creating a new idea of how to twist up the story to make it unique.

Since becoming a mother, Amy has slowly nourished her love of the written word while snatching writing time in the midst of soiled diapers, tumbling over Legos and peering around mounds of laundry and dishes that never seem to go away. Once her only son started school, Amy was free to let her fingers dive into dark mythology, tales of betrayal and love, and explore human nature in its rawest form. Her love of seeing the world from a different angle bloomed.

Amy is the author of several novels, including her popular young adult immortal books, The Arotas Series, which are an Amazon and iBooks bestselling series. Unwilling to be defined by any one genre, she proceeded to flip over to a science fiction/fantasy based idea with her Rising Trilogy. She then dove into contemporary romance with her novel, Captivate and explored the depths of her own faith with In Your Embrace.

She is currently working on completing her Immortal Rose trilogy, a prequel to her Arotas novels. She has also embarked on two new journeys this year, one in the form of a co-written banshee trilogy, The Hallowed Realms, which is currently represented by GH Literary and she breached another genre with her upcoming adult horror novel, Wither.

CONNECT

Sign up to receive Amy's Newsletter:http://bit.ly/1jkG1Hn
Join her at www.AmyMilesBooks.com
Follow on Twitter: @AmyMilesBooks
Instagram: Amy Miles Books
Facebook: www.facebook.com/AmyMiles.Author

Printed in Great Britain
by Amazon.co.uk, Ltd.,
Marston Gate.